Garfield

BY JIM DAVIS

VOLUME 5

ROSS RICHIE CEO & Founder • MARK SMYLIE Founder of Archaia • MATT GAGNON Editor-in-Chief • STEPHEN CHRISTY President of Development • FILIP SABLIK VP of Publishing & Marketing
LANCE KREITER VP of Licensing & Merchandising • PHIL BARBARO VP of Finance • BRYCE CARLSON Managing Editor • MEL CAYLO Marketing Manager • SCOTT NEWMAN Production Design Manager
IRENE BRADISH Operations Manager • CHRISTINE DINH Brand Communications Manager • DAFNA PLEBAN Editor • SHANNON WATTERS Editor • ERIC HARBURN Editor • REBECCA TAYLOR Editor
IAN BRILL Editor • CHRIS ROSA Assistant Editor • ALEX GALER Assistant Editor • WHITNEY LEOPARD Assistant Editor • JASMINE AMIRI Assistant Editor • CAMERON CHITTOCK Assistant Editor
KELSEY DIETERICH Production Designer • EMI YONEMURA BROWN Production Designer • DEVIN FUNCHES E-Commerce & Inventory Coordinator • ANDY LIEGL Event Coordinator • BRIANNA HART Administrative Coordinator
AARON FERRARA Operations Assistant • JOSÉ MEZA Sales Assistant • MICHELLE ANKLEY Sales Assistant • ELIZABETH LOUGHRIDGE Accounting Assistant • STEPHANIE HOCUTT PR Assistant

CHAPTER ONE

"TIME AND TIME AGAIN"
WRITTEN BY
MARK EVANIER
ART BY
ANDY HIRSCH
COLORS BY
LISA MOORE

"CURSE OF THE CALZONE CREATURE"
WRITTEN BY
SCOTT NICKEL
ART BY
DAVID DeGRAND
COLORS BY
LISA MOORE

CHAPTER TWO

"THE MONSTER UNDER THE BED!!!"
WRITTEN BY
MARK EVANIER
ART BY
ANDY HIRSCH
COLORS BY
LISA MOORE

"GARFIELD TO THE RESCUE"
WRITTEN BY
SCOTT NICKEL
ART BY
GENEVIEVE FT

CHAPTER THREE

"BEAUTIFUL BALLOONS"
WRITTEN BY
MARK EVANIER
ART BY
ANDY HIRSCH
COLORS BY
LISA MOORE

"REVENGE OF THE ZOMBIE MEATBALLS"
WRITTEN BY
SCOTT NICKEL
ART BY
DAVID DeGRAND
COLORS BY
LISA MOORE

CHAPTER FOUR

"GARFIELD GOES TO (DIS) OBEDIENCE SCHOOL"
WRITTEN BY
SCOTT NICKEL
ART BY
ANDY HIRSCH
COLORS BY
LISA MOORE

"PET FORCE: THE FEARSOME FOUR STRIKES BACK!"
WRITTEN BY
SCOTT NICKEL
ART BY
GARY BARKER
INKS BY
MARK & STEPHANIE HEIKE
COLORS BY
LISA MOORE

LETTERS BY
STEVE WANDS

COVER BY
GARY BARKER & DAN DAVIS
COLORS BY LISA MOORE

TRADE DESIGNER
JILLIAN CRAB

ASSISTANT EDITOR
CHRIS ROSA

EDITOR
SHANNON WATTERS

GARFIELD CREATED BY
JIM DAVIS

SPECIAL THANKS TO SCOTT NICKEL, DAVID REDDICK, AND THE ENTIRE PAWS, INC. TEAM.

CHAPTER 1

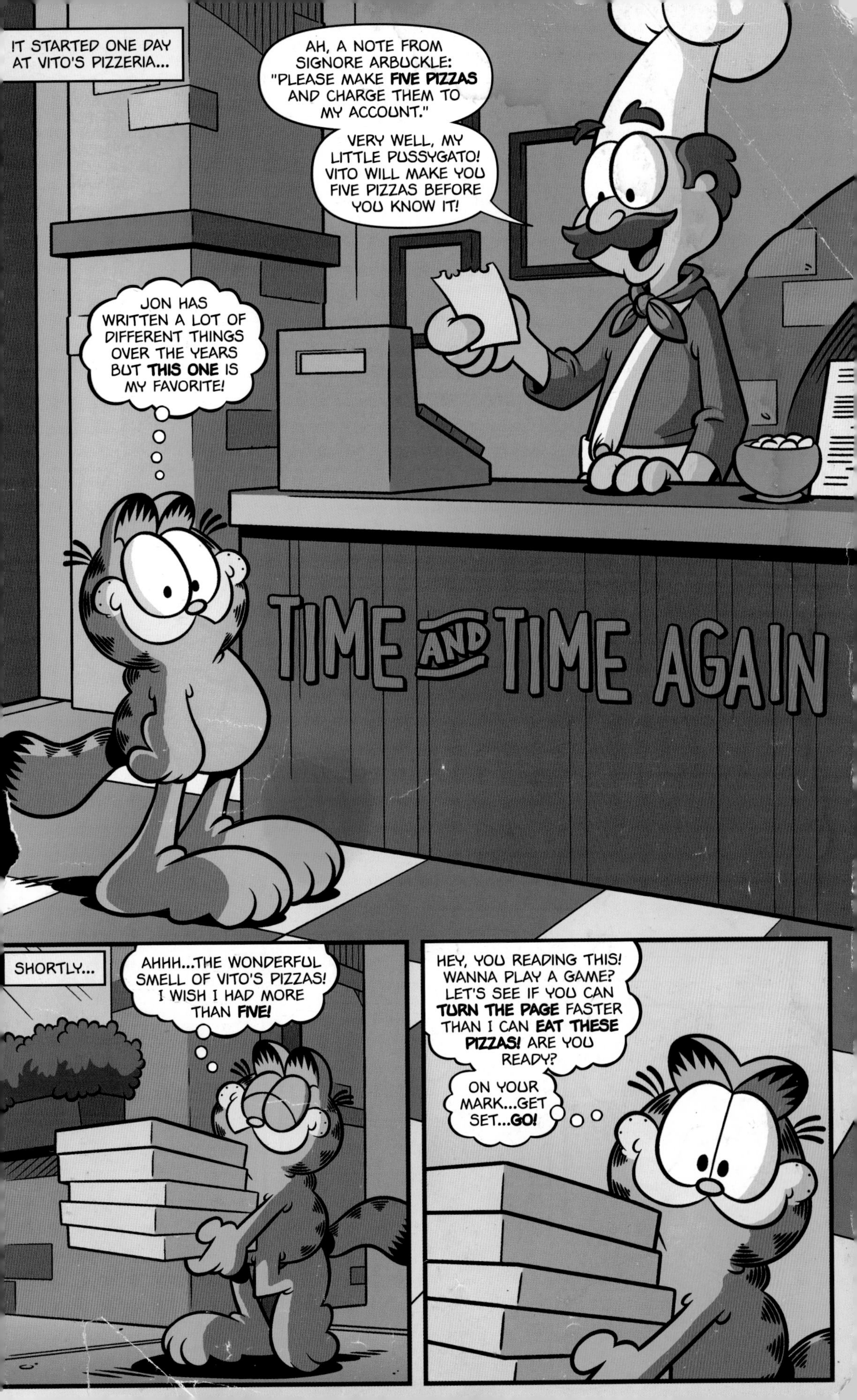

IT STARTED ONE DAY AT VITO'S PIZZERIA...
AH, A NOTE FROM SIGNORE ARBUCKLE: "PLEASE MAKE **FIVE PIZZAS** AND CHARGE THEM TO MY ACCOUNT."
VERY WELL, MY LITTLE PUSSYGATO! VITO WILL MAKE YOU FIVE PIZZAS BEFORE YOU KNOW IT!
JON HAS WRITTEN A LOT OF DIFFERENT THINGS OVER THE YEARS BUT **THIS ONE** IS MY FAVORITE!
TIME AND TIME AGAIN
SHORTLY...
AHHH...THE WONDERFUL SMELL OF VITO'S PIZZAS! I WISH I HAD MORE THAN **FIVE!**
HEY, YOU READING THIS! WANNA PLAY A GAME? LET'S SEE IF YOU CAN **TURN THE PAGE** FASTER THAN I CAN **EAT THESE PIZZAS!** ARE YOU READY?
ON YOUR MARK...GET SET...**GO!**

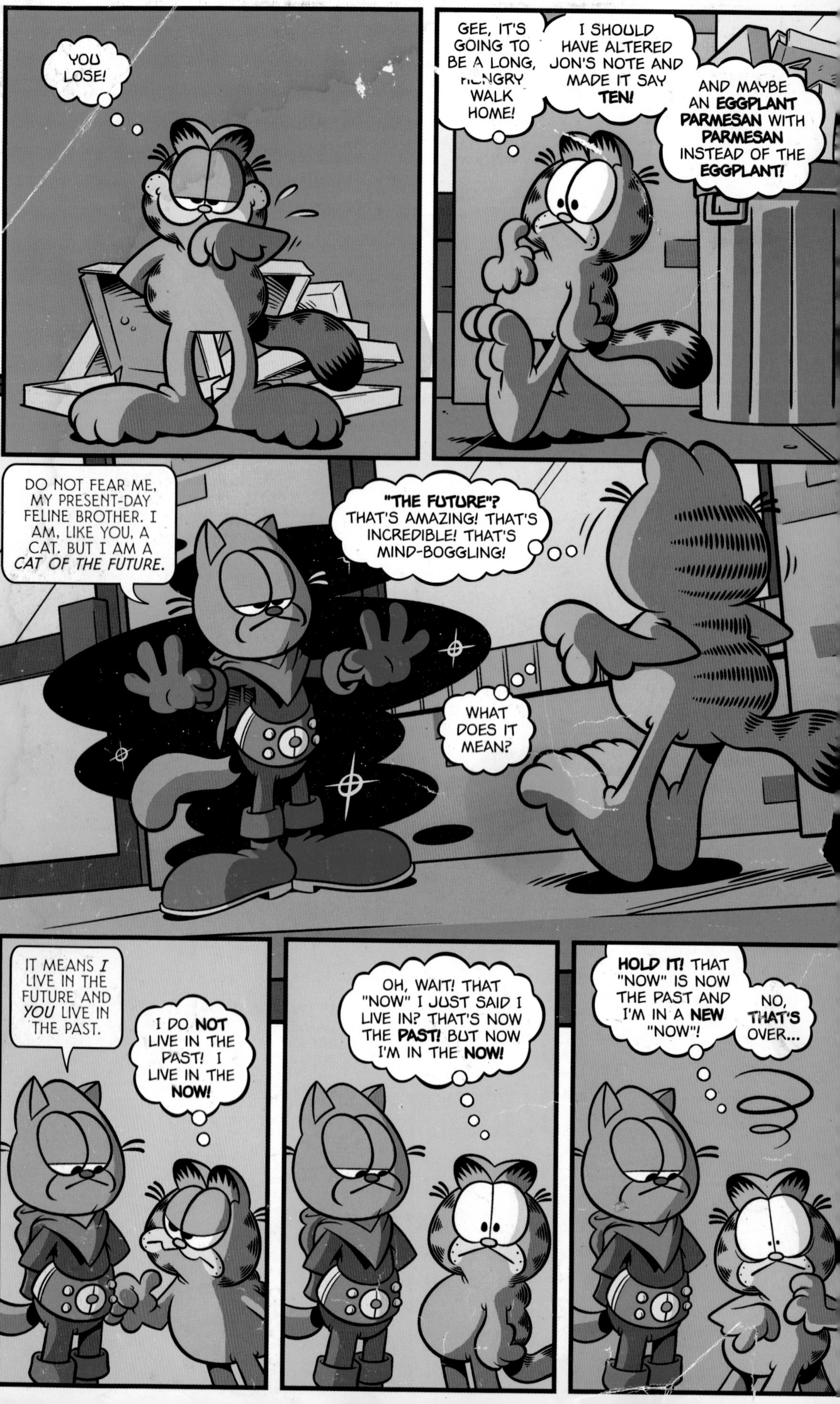
YOU LOSE!
GEE, IT'S GOING TO BE A LONG, HUNGRY WALK HOME!
I SHOULD HAVE ALTERED JON'S NOTE AND MADE IT SAY **TEN!**
AND MAYBE AN **EGGPLANT PARMESAN** WITH **PARMESAN** INSTEAD OF THE **EGGPLANT!**
DO NOT FEAR ME, MY PRESENT-DAY FELINE BROTHER. I AM, LIKE YOU, A CAT. BUT I AM A *CAT OF THE FUTURE.*
"THE FUTURE"? THAT'S AMAZING! THAT'S INCREDIBLE! THAT'S MIND-BOGGLING!
WHAT DOES IT MEAN?
IT MEANS *I* LIVE IN THE FUTURE AND *YOU* LIVE IN THE PAST.
I DO **NOT** LIVE IN THE PAST! I LIVE IN THE **NOW!**
OH, WAIT! THAT "NOW" I JUST SAID I LIVE IN? THAT'S NOW THE **PAST!** BUT NOW I'M IN THE **NOW!**
HOLD IT! THAT "NOW" IS NOW THE PAST AND I'M IN A **NEW** "NOW"!
NO, **THAT'S** OVER...

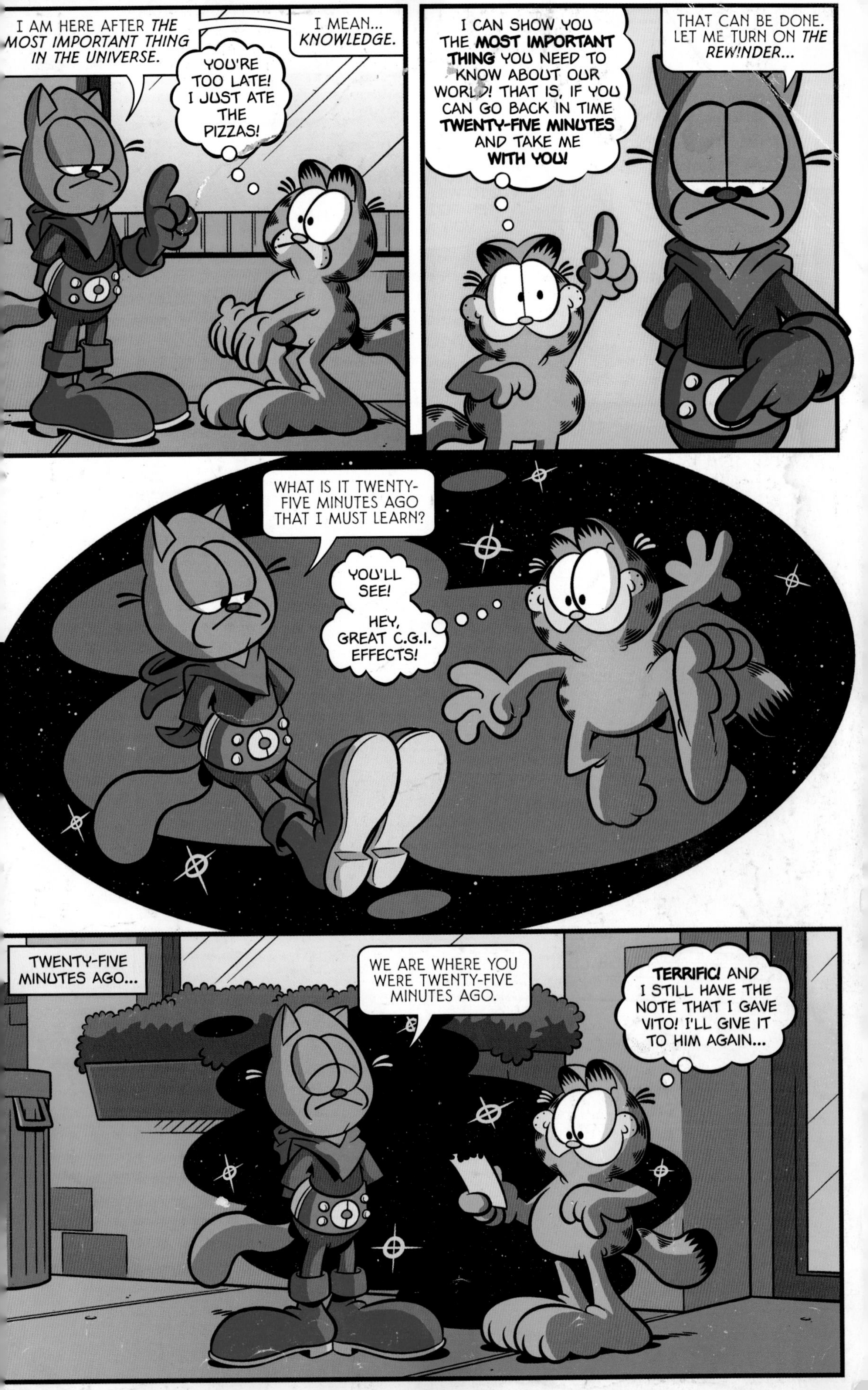
I AM HERE AFTER THE MOST IMPORTANT THING IN THE UNIVERSE.
I MEAN... KNOWLEDGE.
YOU'RE TOO LATE! I JUST ATE THE PIZZAS!
I CAN SHOW YOU THE MOST IMPORTANT THING YOU NEED TO KNOW ABOUT OUR WORLD! THAT IS, IF YOU CAN GO BACK IN TIME TWENTY-FIVE MINUTES AND TAKE ME WITH YOU!
THAT CAN BE DONE. LET ME TURN ON THE REWINDER...
WHAT IS IT TWENTY-FIVE MINUTES AGO THAT I MUST LEARN?
YOU'LL SEE!
HEY, GREAT C.G.I. EFFECTS!
TWENTY-FIVE MINUTES AGO...
WE ARE WHERE YOU WERE TWENTY-FIVE MINUTES AGO.
TERRIFIC! AND I STILL HAVE THE NOTE THAT I GAVE VITO! I'LL GIVE IT TO HIM AGAIN...

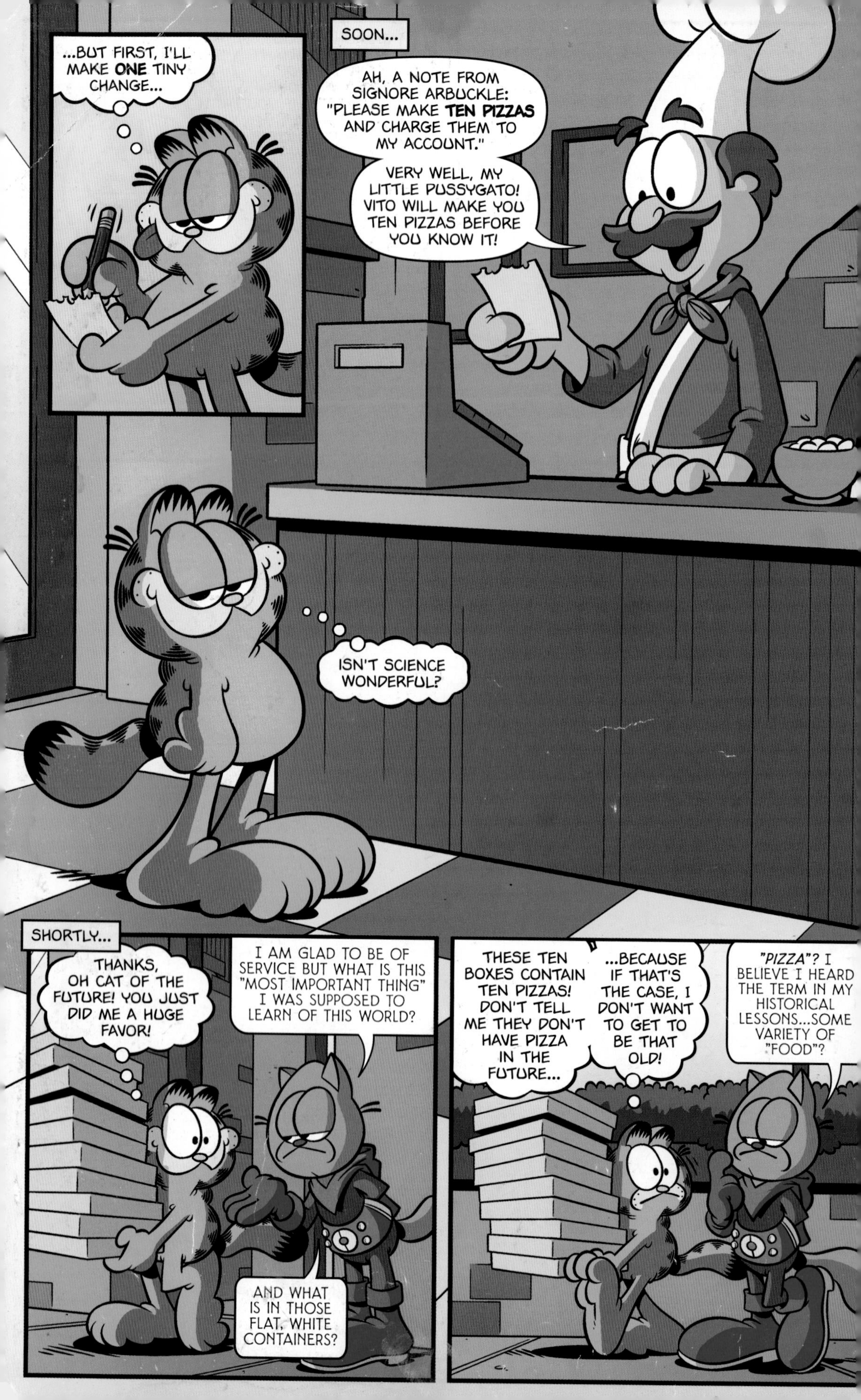
...BUT FIRST, I'LL MAKE ONE TINY CHANGE...
SOON...
AH, A NOTE FROM SIGNORE ARBUCKLE: "PLEASE MAKE TEN PIZZAS AND CHARGE THEM TO MY ACCOUNT."
VERY WELL, MY LITTLE PUSSYGATO! VITO WILL MAKE YOU TEN PIZZAS BEFORE YOU KNOW IT!
ISN'T SCIENCE WONDERFUL?
SHORTLY...
THANKS, OH CAT OF THE FUTURE! YOU JUST DID ME A HUGE FAVOR!
I AM GLAD TO BE OF SERVICE BUT WHAT IS THIS "MOST IMPORTANT THING" I WAS SUPPOSED TO LEARN OF THIS WORLD?
AND WHAT IS IN THOSE FLAT, WHITE CONTAINERS?
THESE TEN BOXES CONTAIN TEN PIZZAS! DON'T TELL ME THEY DON'T HAVE PIZZA IN THE FUTURE...
...BECAUSE IF THAT'S THE CASE, I DON'T WANT TO GET TO BE THAT OLD!
"PIZZA"? I BELIEVE I HEARD THE TERM IN MY HISTORICAL LESSONS...SOME VARIETY OF "FOOD"?

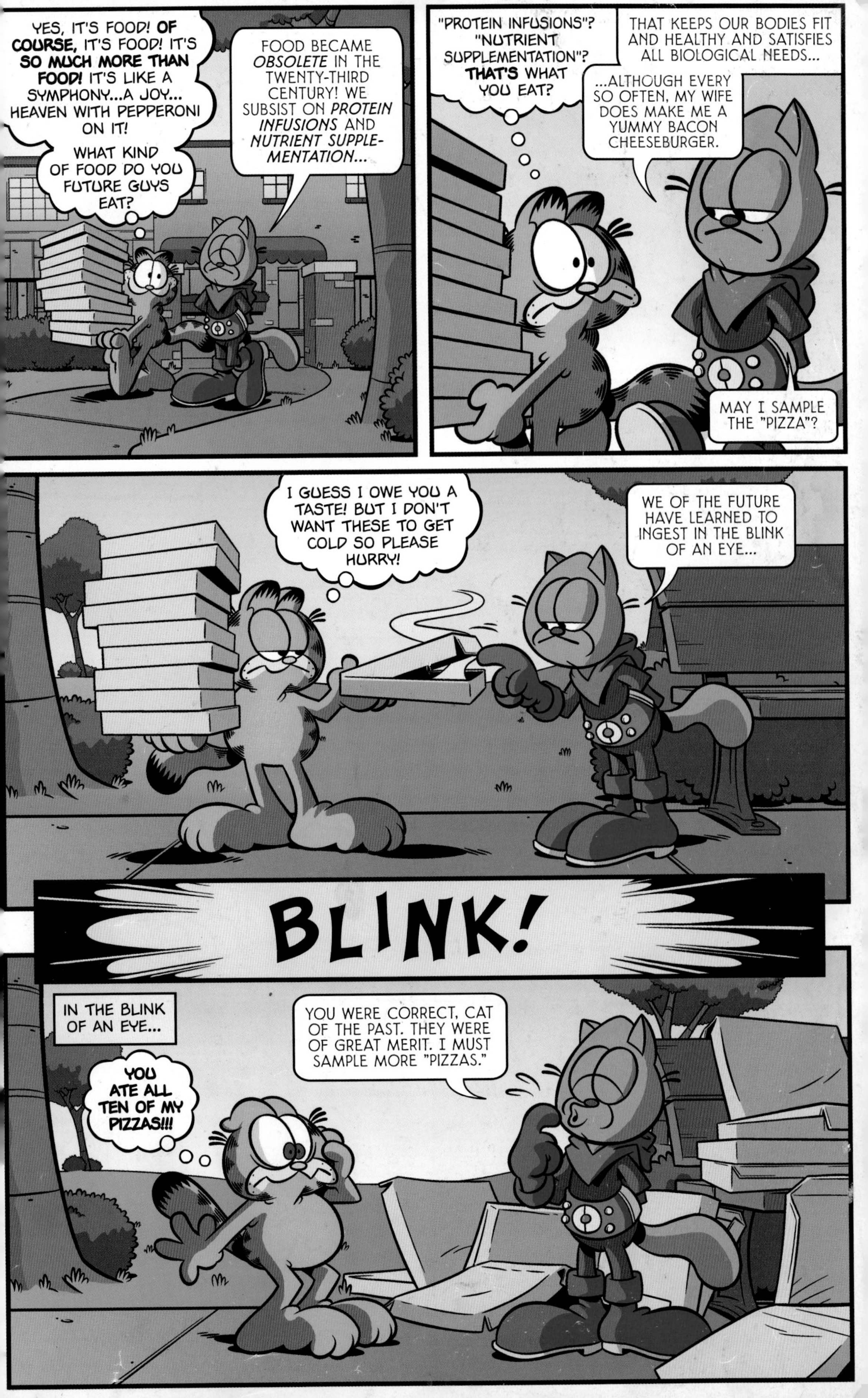

YES, IT'S FOOD! OF COURSE, IT'S FOOD! IT'S SO MUCH MORE THAN FOOD! IT'S LIKE A SYMPHONY...A JOY... HEAVEN WITH PEPPERONI ON IT!
WHAT KIND OF FOOD DO YOU FUTURE GUYS EAT?
FOOD BECAME OBSOLETE IN THE TWENTY-THIRD CENTURY! WE SUBSIST ON PROTEIN INFUSIONS AND NUTRIENT SUPPLEMENTATION...
"PROTEIN INFUSIONS"? "NUTRIENT SUPPLEMENTATION"? THAT'S WHAT YOU EAT?
THAT KEEPS OUR BODIES FIT AND HEALTHY AND SATISFIES ALL BIOLOGICAL NEEDS...
...ALTHOUGH EVERY SO OFTEN, MY WIFE DOES MAKE ME A YUMMY BACON CHEESEBURGER.
MAY I SAMPLE THE "PIZZA"?
I GUESS I OWE YOU A TASTE! BUT I DON'T WANT THESE TO GET COLD SO PLEASE HURRY!
WE OF THE FUTURE HAVE LEARNED TO INGEST IN THE BLINK OF AN EYE...
BLINK!
IN THE BLINK OF AN EYE...
YOU ATE ALL TEN OF MY PIZZAS!!!
YOU WERE CORRECT, CAT OF THE PAST. THEY WERE OF GREAT MERIT. I MUST SAMPLE MORE "PIZZAS."

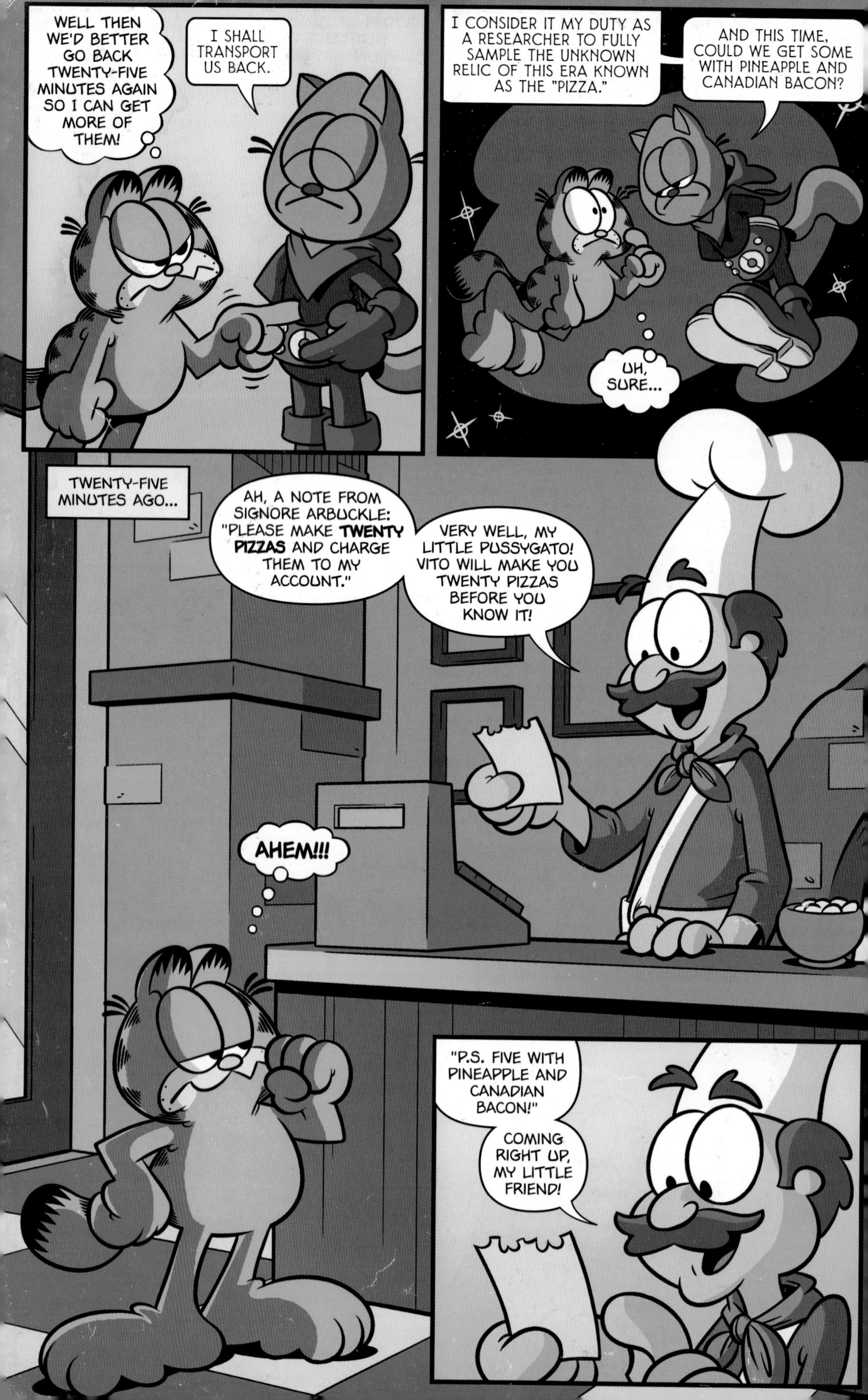
WELL THEN WE'D BETTER GO BACK TWENTY-FIVE MINUTES AGAIN SO I CAN GET MORE OF THEM!
I SHALL TRANSPORT US BACK.
I CONSIDER IT MY DUTY AS A RESEARCHER TO FULLY SAMPLE THE UNKNOWN RELIC OF THIS ERA KNOWN AS THE "PIZZA."
AND THIS TIME, COULD WE GET SOME WITH PINEAPPLE AND CANADIAN BACON?
UH, SURE...
TWENTY-FIVE MINUTES AGO...
AH, A NOTE FROM SIGNORE ARBUCKLE: "PLEASE MAKE **TWENTY PIZZAS** AND CHARGE THEM TO MY ACCOUNT."
VERY WELL, MY LITTLE PUSSYGATO! VITO WILL MAKE YOU TWENTY PIZZAS BEFORE YOU KNOW IT!
AHEM!!!
"P.S. FIVE WITH PINEAPPLE AND CANADIAN BACON!"
COMING RIGHT UP, MY LITTLE FRIEND!

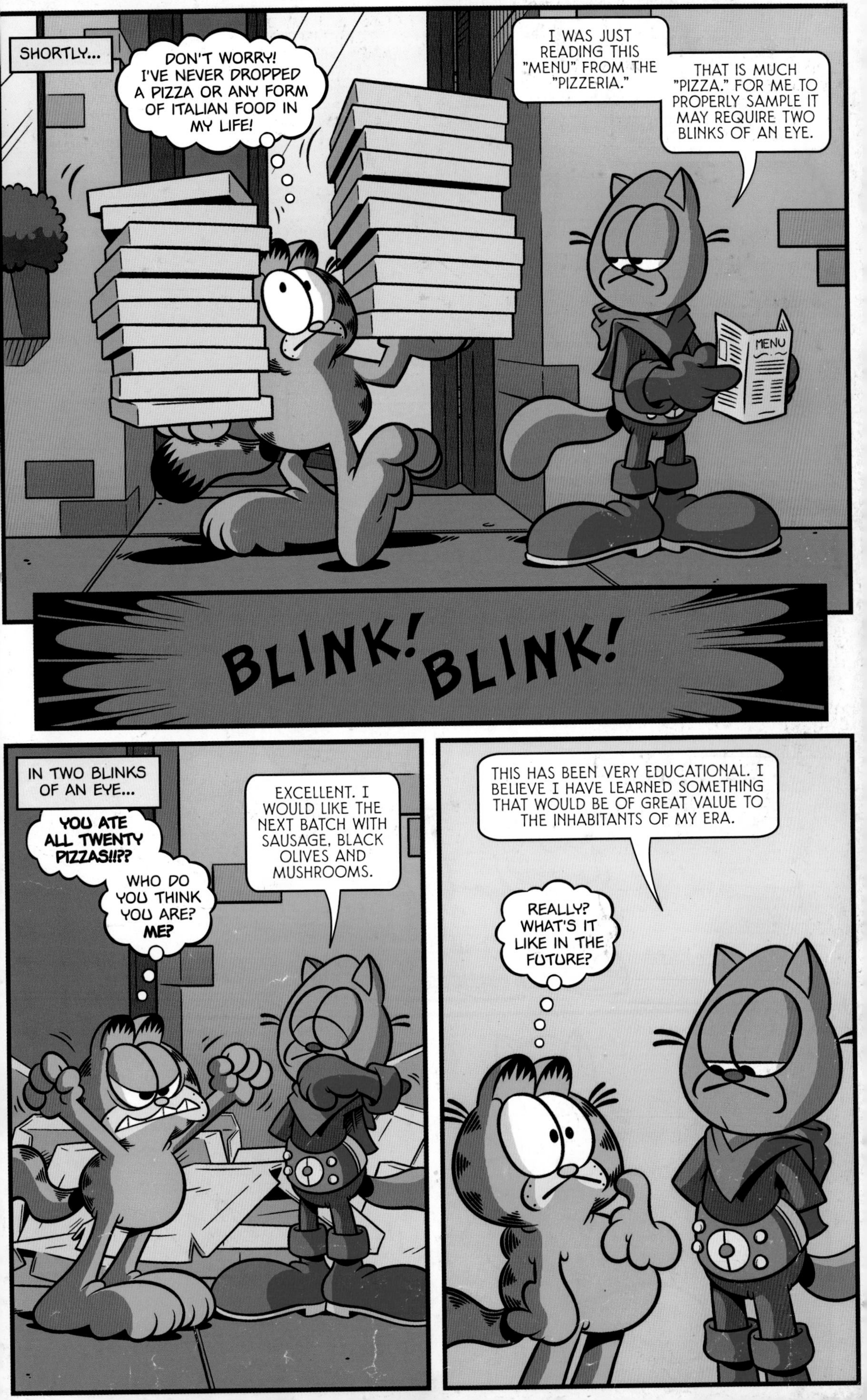
SHORTLY...
DON'T WORRY! I'VE NEVER DROPPED A PIZZA OR ANY FORM OF ITALIAN FOOD IN MY LIFE!
I WAS JUST READING THIS "MENU" FROM THE "PIZZERIA."
THAT IS MUCH "PIZZA." FOR ME TO PROPERLY SAMPLE IT MAY REQUIRE TWO BLINKS OF AN EYE.
MENU
BLINK! BLINK!
IN TWO BLINKS OF AN EYE...
YOU ATE ALL TWENTY PIZZAS!!??
WHO DO YOU THINK YOU ARE? ME?
EXCELLENT. I WOULD LIKE THE NEXT BATCH WITH SAUSAGE, BLACK OLIVES AND MUSHROOMS.
THIS HAS BEEN VERY EDUCATIONAL. I BELIEVE I HAVE LEARNED SOMETHING THAT WOULD BE OF GREAT VALUE TO THE INHABITANTS OF MY ERA.
REALLY? WHAT'S IT LIKE IN THE FUTURE?

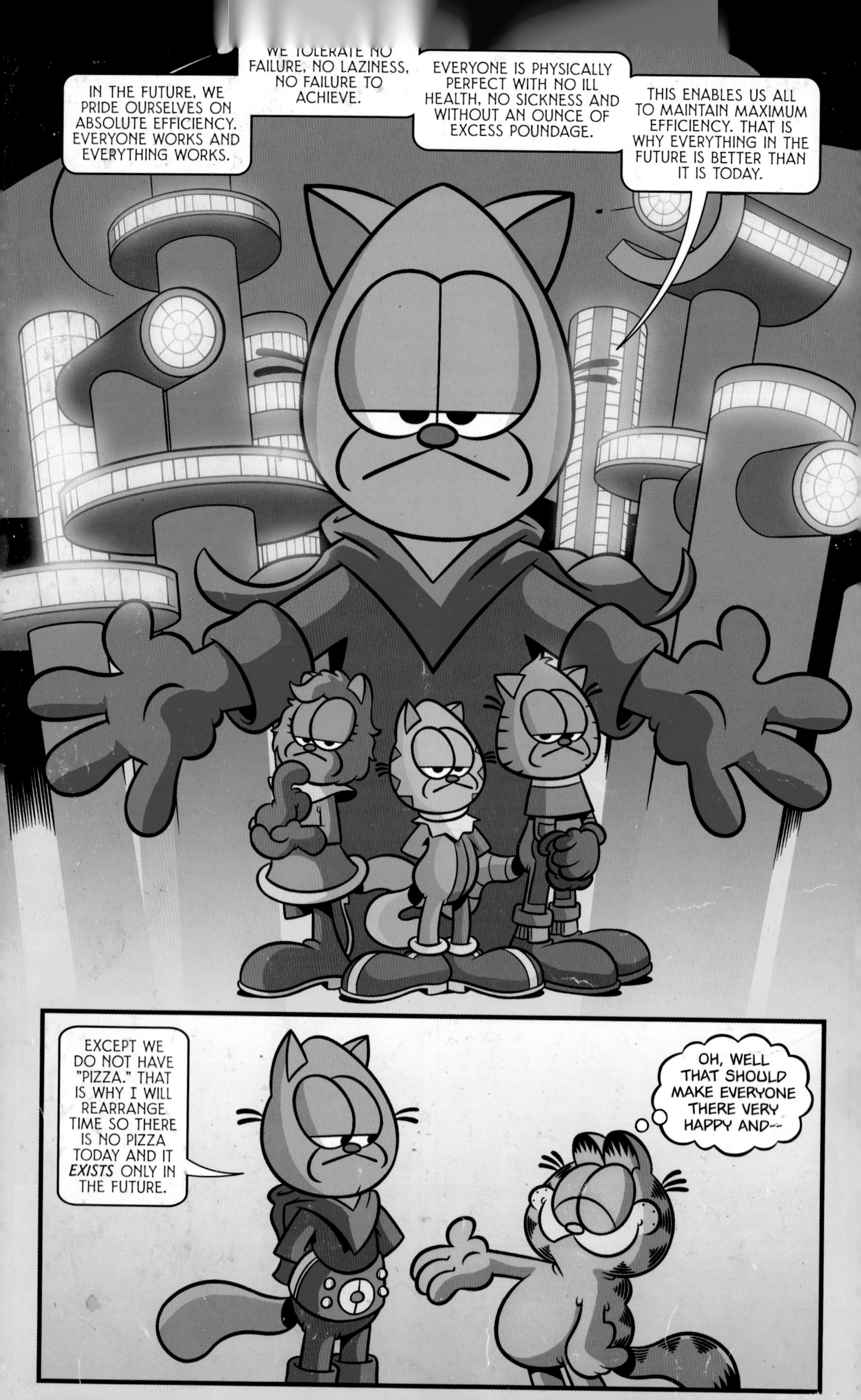
IN THE FUTURE, WE PRIDE OURSELVES ON ABSOLUTE EFFICIENCY. EVERYONE WORKS AND EVERYTHING WORKS.
WE TOLERATE NO FAILURE, NO LAZINESS, NO FAILURE TO ACHIEVE.
EVERYONE IS PHYSICALLY PERFECT WITH NO ILL HEALTH, NO SICKNESS AND WITHOUT AN OUNCE OF EXCESS POUNDAGE.
THIS ENABLES US ALL TO MAINTAIN MAXIMUM EFFICIENCY. THAT IS WHY EVERYTHING IN THE FUTURE IS BETTER THAN IT IS TODAY.
EXCEPT WE DO NOT HAVE "PIZZA." THAT IS WHY I WILL REARRANGE TIME SO THERE IS NO PIZZA TODAY AND IT *EXISTS* ONLY IN THE FUTURE.
OH, WELL THAT SHOULD MAKE EVERYONE THERE VERY HAPPY AND--

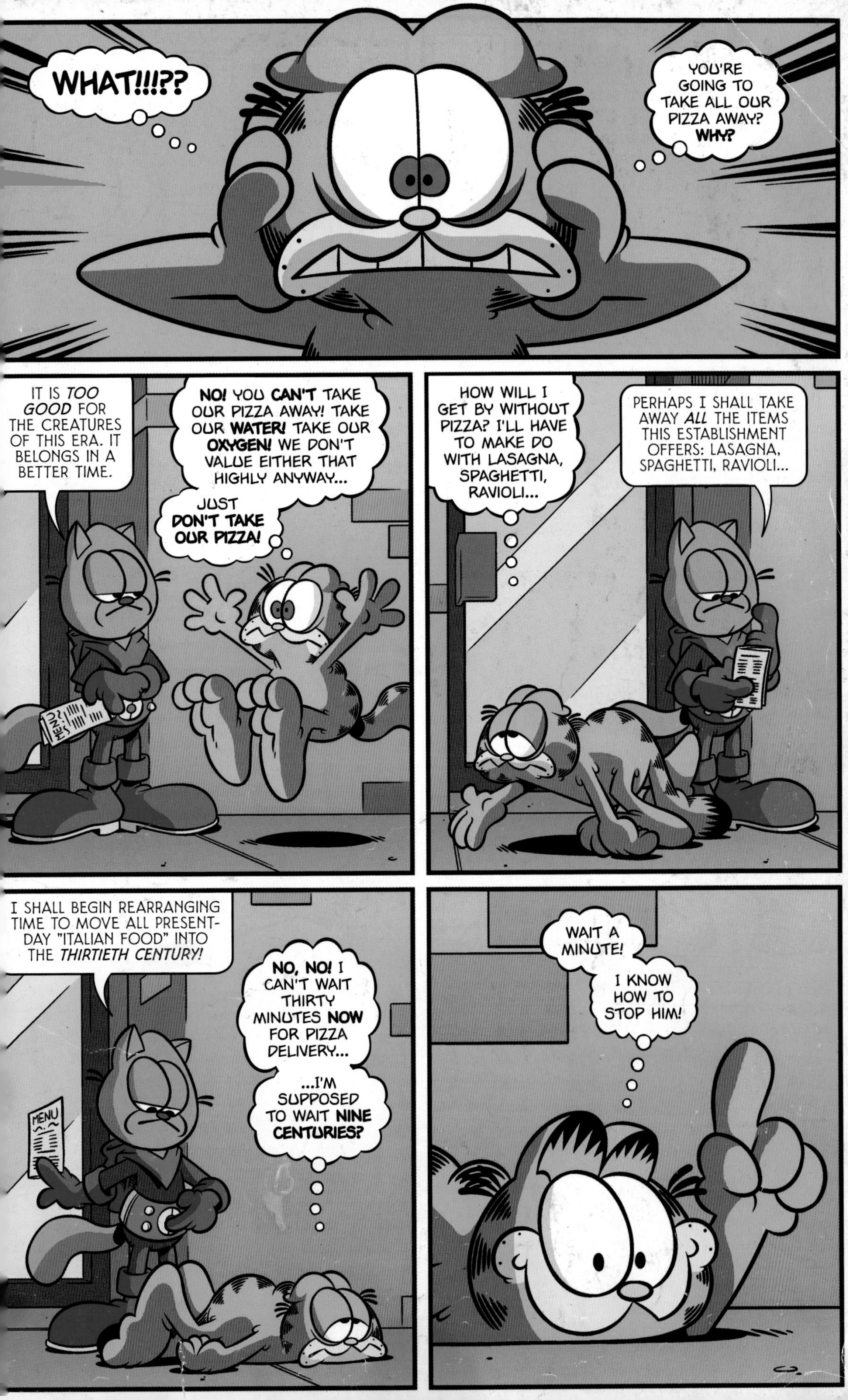
WHAT!!!??
YOU'RE GOING TO TAKE ALL OUR PIZZA AWAY? WHY?
IT IS TOO GOOD FOR THE CREATURES OF THIS ERA. IT BELONGS IN A BETTER TIME.
NO! YOU CAN'T TAKE OUR PIZZA AWAY! TAKE OUR WATER! TAKE OUR OXYGEN! WE DON'T VALUE EITHER THAT HIGHLY ANYWAY...
JUST DON'T TAKE OUR PIZZA!
MENU
HOW WILL I GET BY WITHOUT PIZZA? I'LL HAVE TO MAKE DO WITH LASAGNA, SPAGHETTI, RAVIOLI...
PERHAPS I SHALL TAKE AWAY ALL THE ITEMS THIS ESTABLISHMENT OFFERS: LASAGNA, SPAGHETTI, RAVIOLI...
I SHALL BEGIN REARRANGING TIME TO MOVE ALL PRESENT-DAY "ITALIAN FOOD" INTO THE THIRTIETH CENTURY!
NO, NO! I CAN'T WAIT THIRTY MINUTES NOW FOR PIZZA DELIVERY...
...I'M SUPPOSED TO WAIT NINE CENTURIES?
MENU
WAIT A MINUTE!
I KNOW HOW TO STOP HIM!

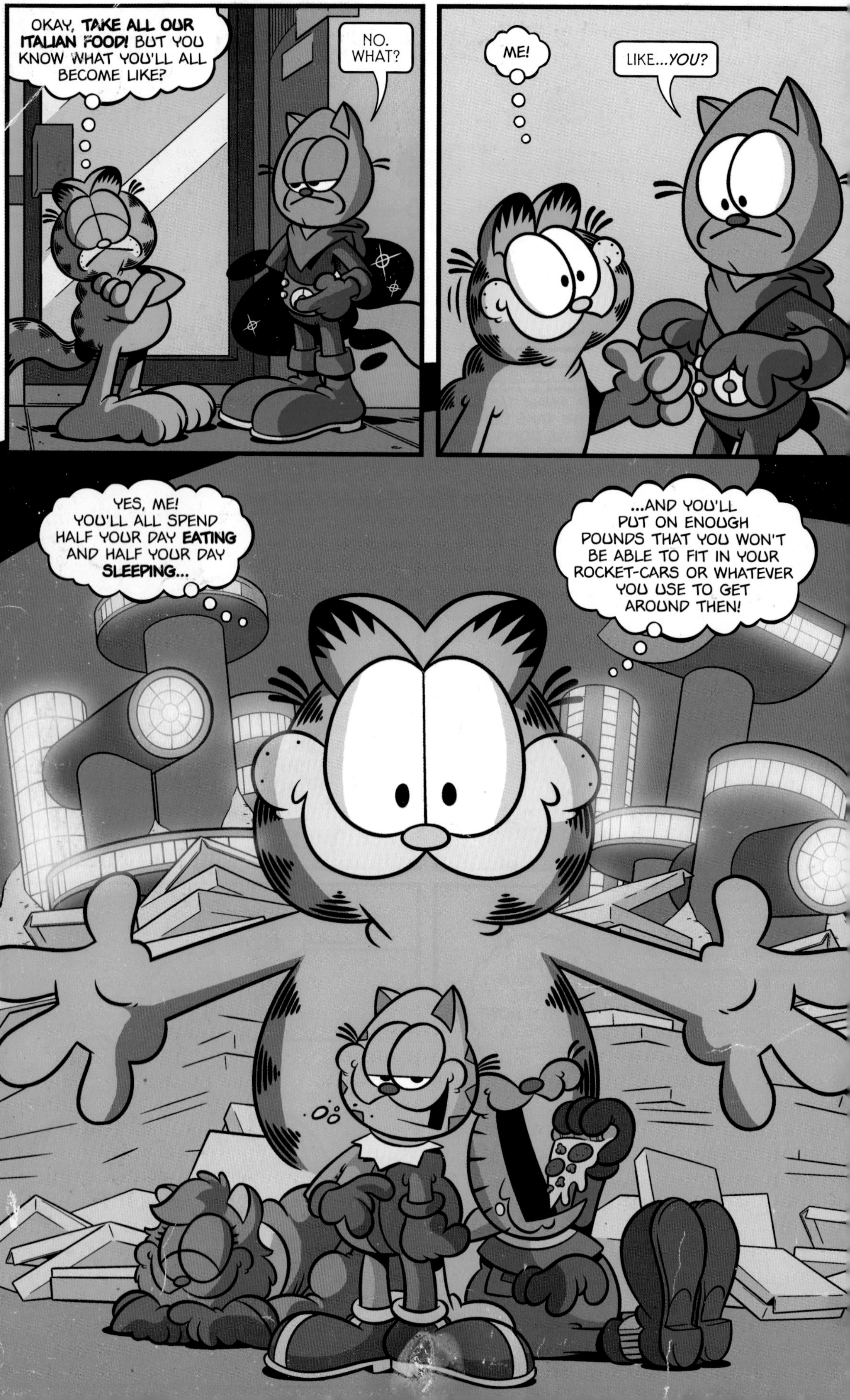
OKAY, TAKE ALL OUR ITALIAN FOOD! BUT YOU KNOW WHAT YOU'LL ALL BECOME LIKE?
NO. WHAT?
ME!
LIKE...YOU?
YES, ME! YOU'LL ALL SPEND HALF YOUR DAY EATING AND HALF YOUR DAY SLEEPING...
...AND YOU'LL PUT ON ENOUGH POUNDS THAT YOU WON'T BE ABLE TO FIT IN YOUR ROCKET-CARS OR WHATEVER YOU USE TO GET AROUND THEN!

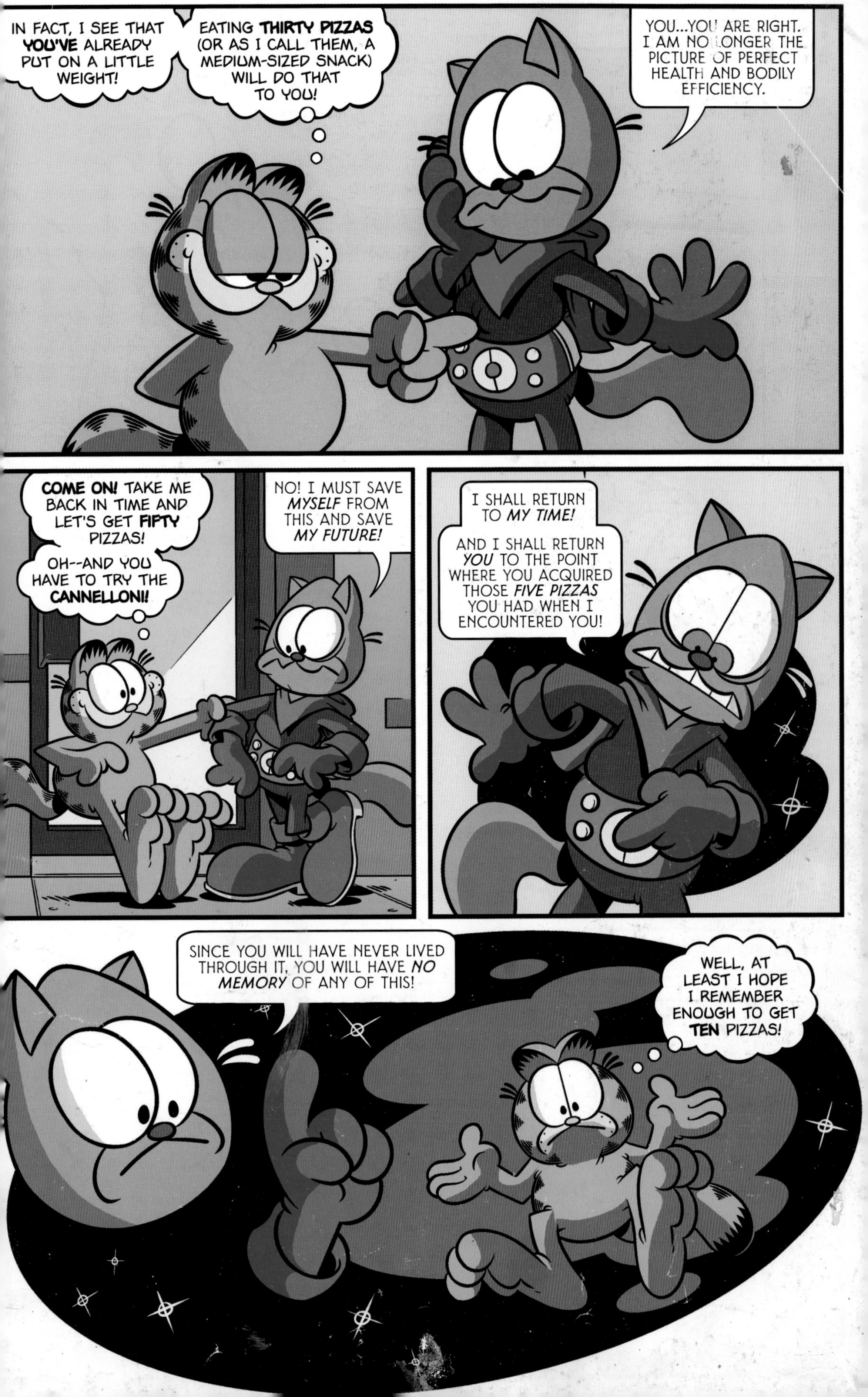
IN FACT, I SEE THAT **YOU'VE** ALREADY PUT ON A LITTLE WEIGHT!
EATING **THIRTY PIZZAS** (OR AS I CALL THEM, A MEDIUM-SIZED SNACK) WILL DO THAT TO YOU!
YOU...YOU ARE RIGHT. I AM NO LONGER THE PICTURE OF PERFECT HEALTH AND BODILY EFFICIENCY.
COME ON! TAKE ME BACK IN TIME AND LET'S GET **FIFTY** PIZZAS!
OH--AND YOU HAVE TO TRY THE **CANNELLONI!**
NO! I MUST SAVE *MYSELF* FROM THIS AND SAVE *MY FUTURE!*
I SHALL RETURN TO *MY TIME!*
AND I SHALL RETURN *YOU* TO THE POINT WHERE YOU ACQUIRED THOSE *FIVE PIZZAS* YOU HAD WHEN I ENCOUNTERED YOU!
SINCE YOU WILL HAVE NEVER LIVED THROUGH IT, YOU WILL HAVE *NO MEMORY* OF ANY OF THIS!
WELL, AT LEAST I HOPE I REMEMBER ENOUGH TO GET **TEN** PIZZAS!

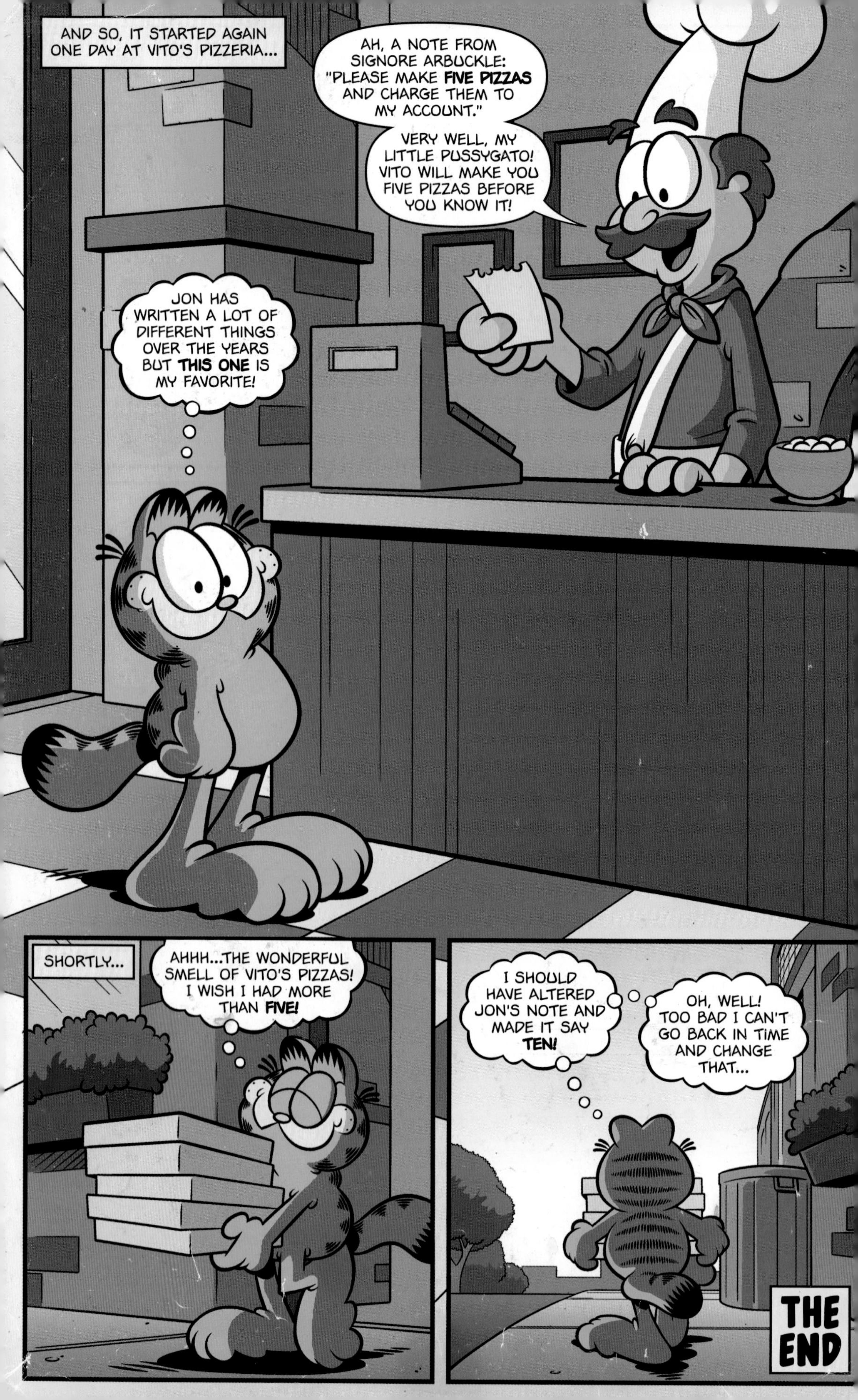
AND SO, IT STARTED AGAIN ONE DAY AT VITO'S PIZZERIA...
AH, A NOTE FROM SIGNORE ARBUCKLE: "PLEASE MAKE **FIVE PIZZAS** AND CHARGE THEM TO MY ACCOUNT."
VERY WELL, MY LITTLE PUSSYGATO! VITO WILL MAKE YOU FIVE PIZZAS BEFORE YOU KNOW IT!
JON HAS WRITTEN A LOT OF DIFFERENT THINGS OVER THE YEARS BUT **THIS ONE** IS MY FAVORITE!
SHORTLY...
AHHH...THE WONDERFUL SMELL OF VITO'S PIZZAS! I WISH I HAD MORE THAN **FIVE!**
I SHOULD HAVE ALTERED JON'S NOTE AND MADE IT SAY **TEN!**
OH, WELL! TOO BAD I CAN'T GO BACK IN TIME AND CHANGE THAT...
THE END

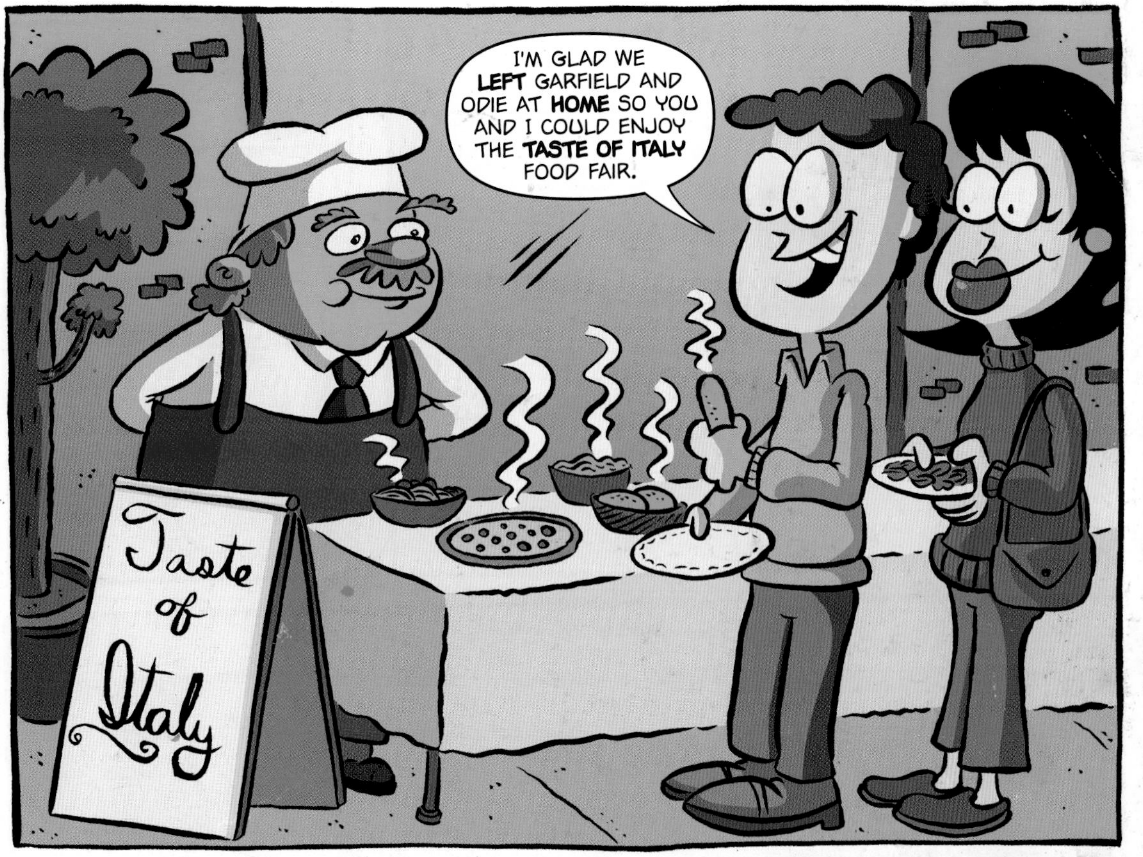

I'M GLAD WE LEFT GARFIELD AND ODIE AT HOME SO YOU AND I COULD ENJOY THE TASTE OF ITALY FOOD FAIR.
Taste of Italy

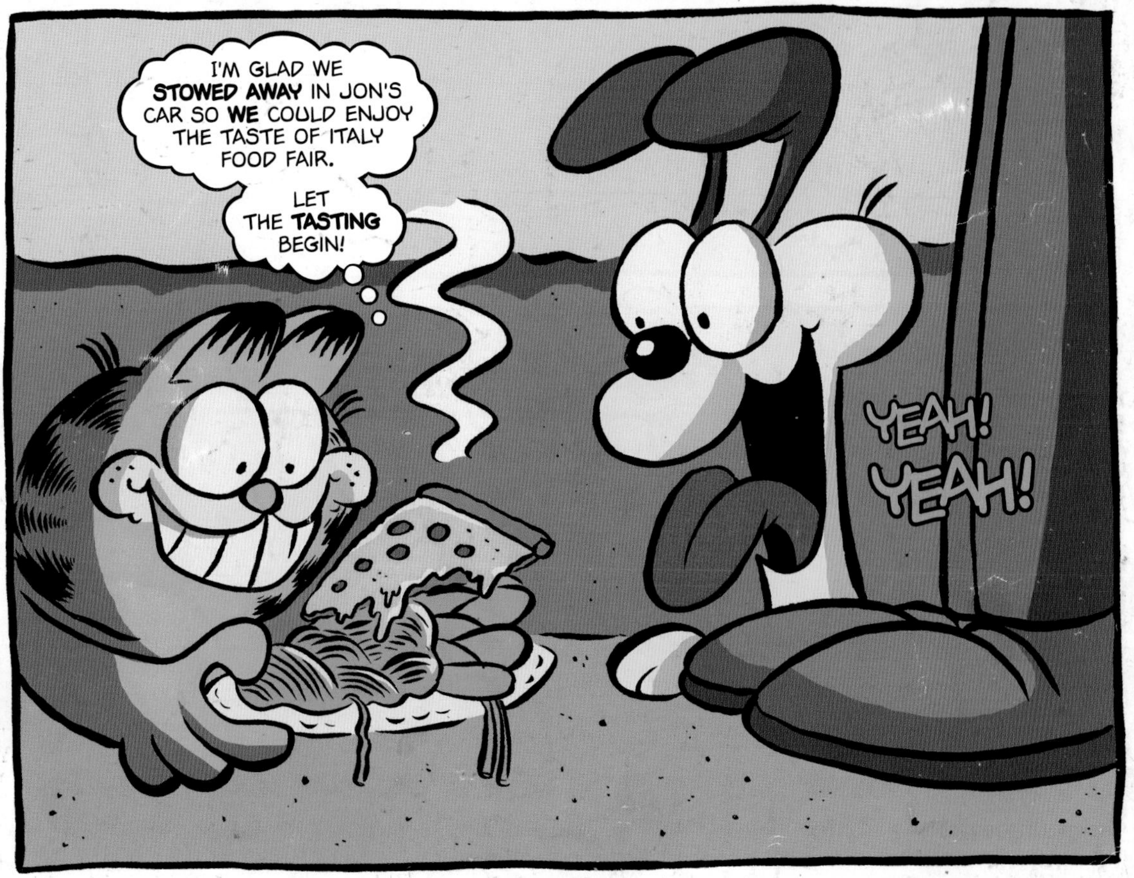

I'M GLAD WE STOWED AWAY IN JON'S CAR SO WE COULD ENJOY THE TASTE OF ITALY FOOD FAIR.
LET THE TASTING BEGIN!
YEAH! YEAH!

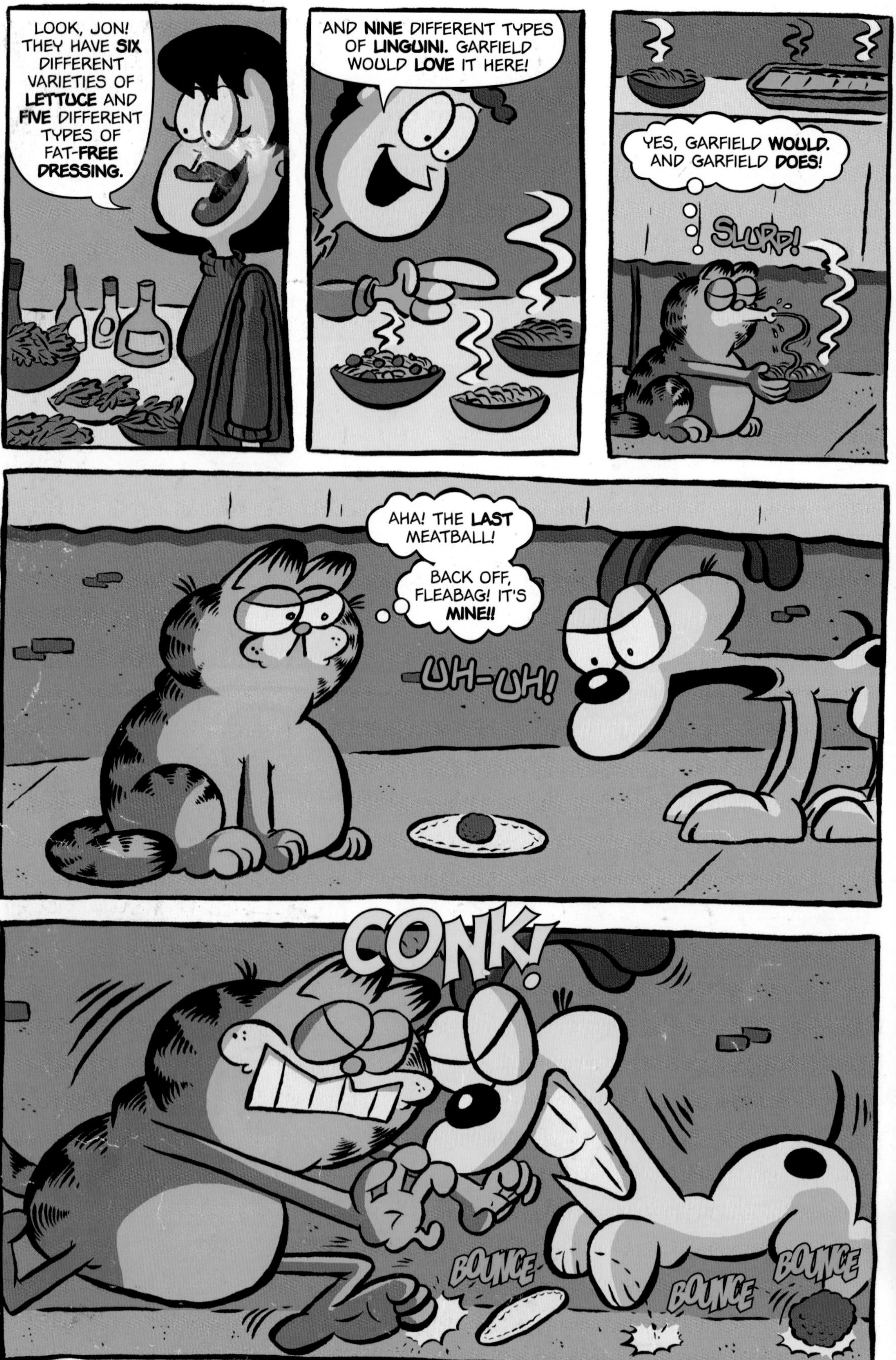

LOOK, JON! THEY HAVE SIX DIFFERENT VARIETIES OF LETTUCE AND FIVE DIFFERENT TYPES OF FAT-FREE DRESSING.
AND NINE DIFFERENT TYPES OF LINGUINI. GARFIELD WOULD LOVE IT HERE!
YES, GARFIELD WOULD. AND GARFIELD DOES!
SLURP!
AHA! THE LAST MEATBALL!
BACK OFF, FLEABAG! IT'S MINE!!
UH-UH!
CONK!
BOUNCE
BOUNCE
BOUNCE

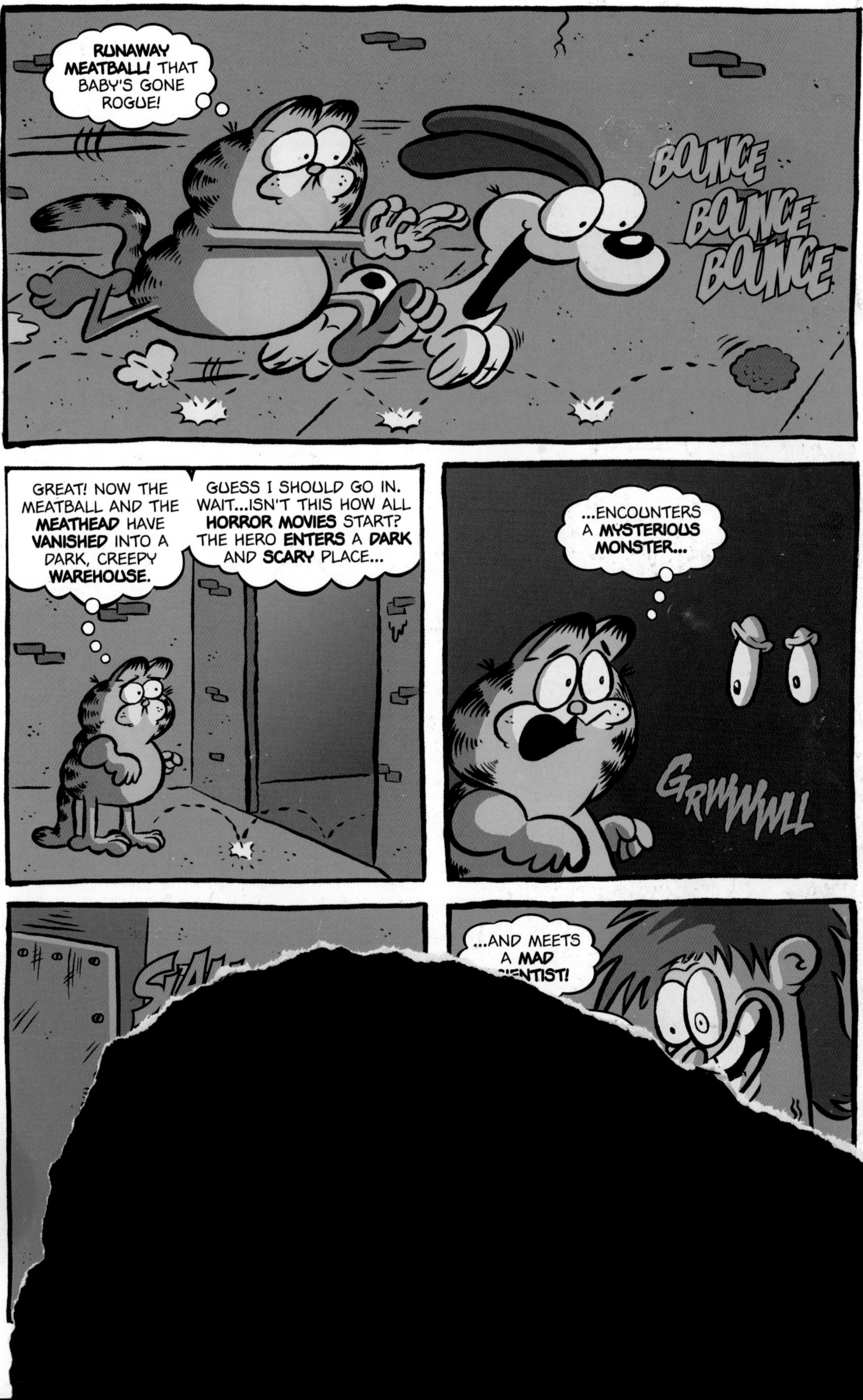
RUNAWAY MEATBALL! THAT BABY'S GONE ROGUE!
BOUNCE
BOUNCE
BOUNCE
GREAT! NOW THE MEATBALL AND THE MEATHEAD HAVE VANISHED INTO A DARK, CREEPY WAREHOUSE.
GUESS I SHOULD GO IN. WAIT...ISN'T THIS HOW ALL HORROR MOVIES START? THE HERO ENTERS A DARK AND SCARY PLACE...
...ENCOUNTERS A MYSTERIOUS MONSTER...
GRWWWLL
...AND MEETS A MAD

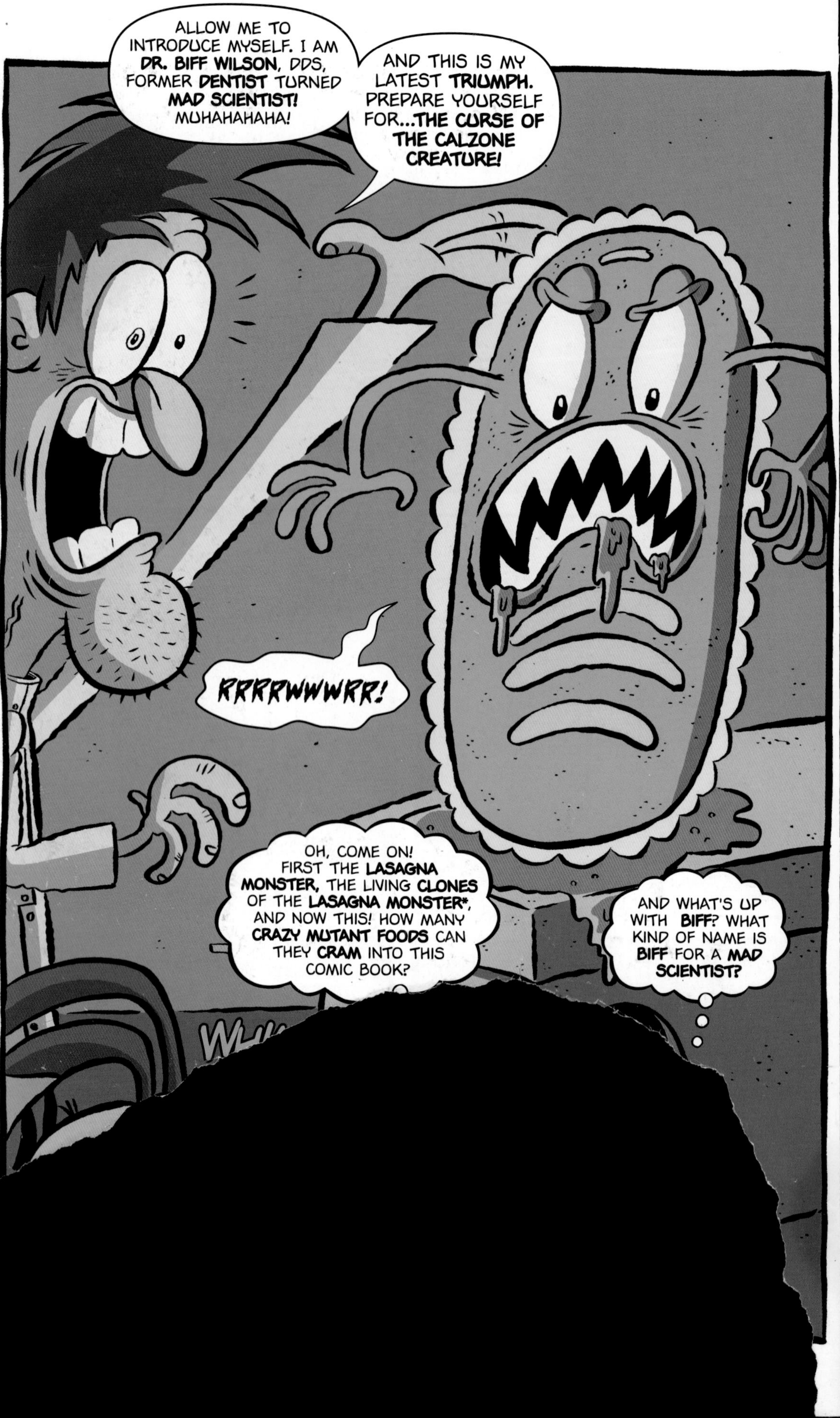
ALLOW ME TO INTRODUCE MYSELF. I AM DR. BIFF WILSON, DDS, FORMER DENTIST TURNED MAD SCIENTIST! MUHAHAHAHA!
AND THIS IS MY LATEST TRIUMPH. PREPARE YOURSELF FOR...THE CURSE OF THE CALZONE CREATURE!
RRRRWWWRR!
OH, COME ON! FIRST THE LASAGNA MONSTER, THE LIVING CLONES OF THE LASAGNA MONSTER*, AND NOW THIS! HOW MANY CRAZY MUTANT FOODS CAN THEY CRAM INTO THIS COMIC BOOK?
AND WHAT'S UP WITH BIFF? WHAT KIND OF NAME IS BIFF FOR A MAD SCIENTIST?

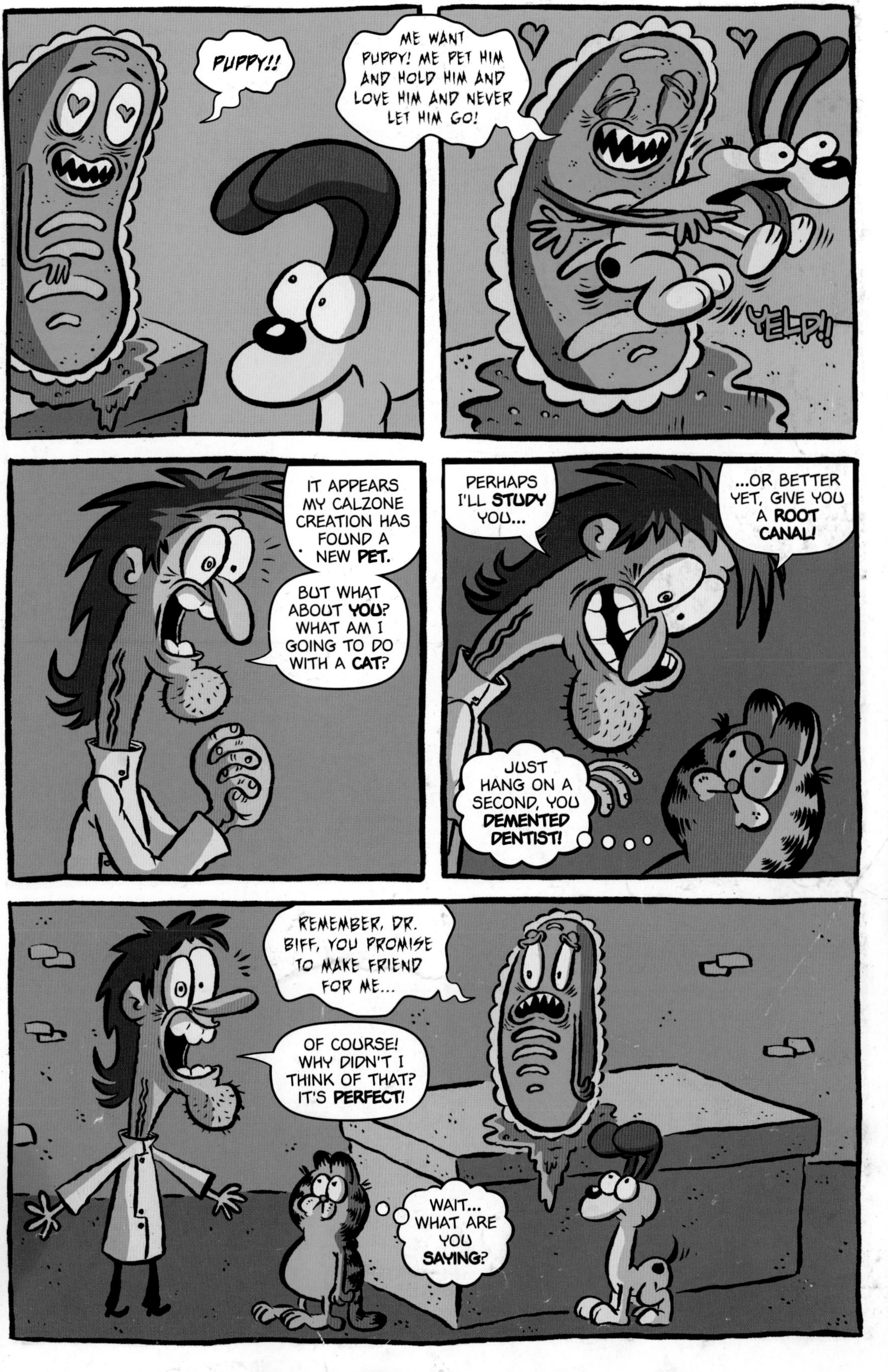
PUPPY!!
ME WANT PUPPY! ME PET HIM AND HOLD HIM AND LOVE HIM AND NEVER LET HIM GO!
YELP!!
IT APPEARS MY CALZONE CREATION HAS FOUND A NEW PET.
BUT WHAT ABOUT YOU? WHAT AM I GOING TO DO WITH A CAT?
PERHAPS I'LL STUDY YOU...
...OR BETTER YET, GIVE YOU A ROOT CANAL!
JUST HANG ON A SECOND, YOU DEMENTED DENTIST!
REMEMBER, DR. BIFF, YOU PROMISE TO MAKE FRIEND FOR ME...
OF COURSE! WHY DIDN'T I THINK OF THAT? IT'S PERFECT!
WAIT... WHAT ARE YOU SAYING?

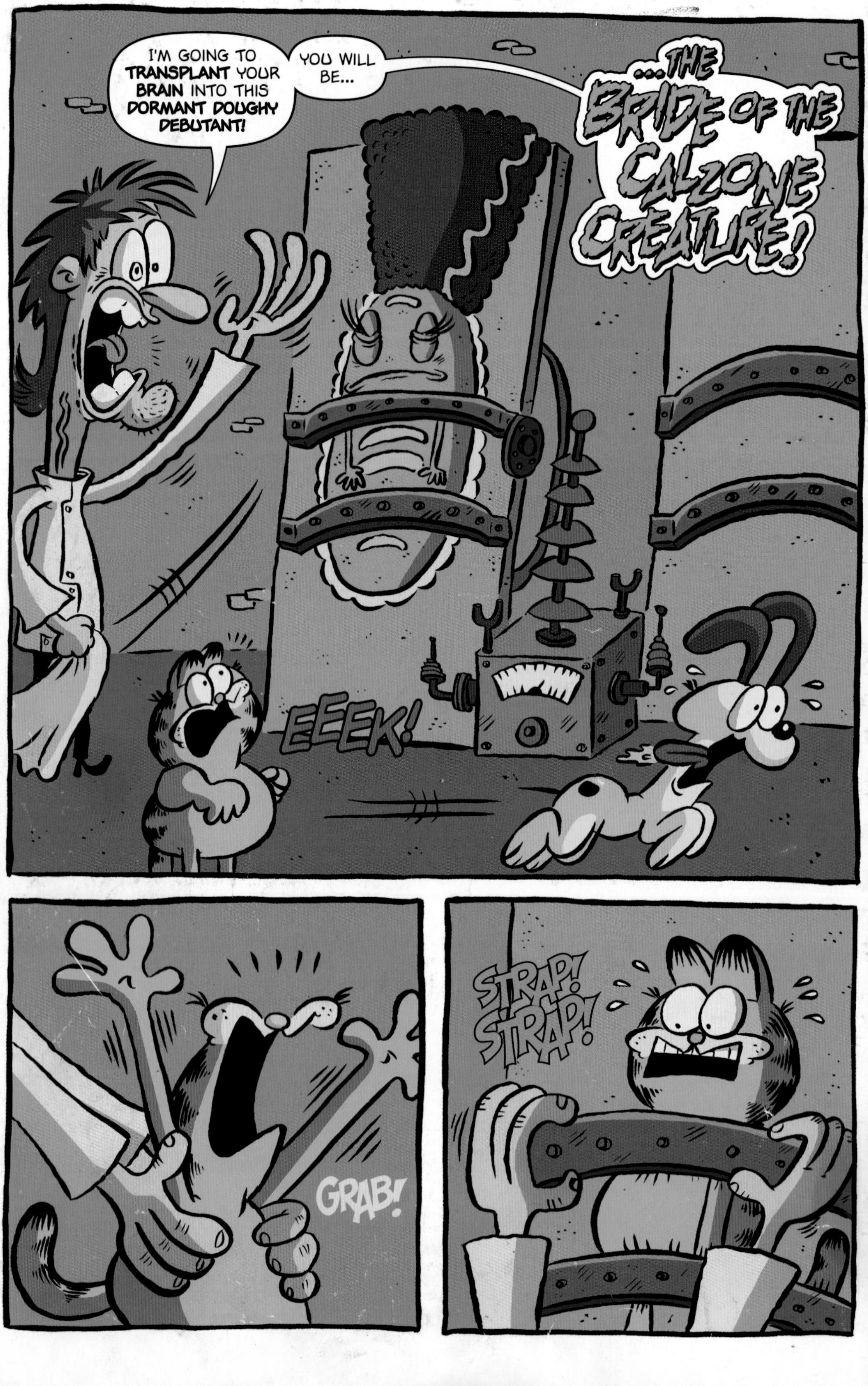
I'M GOING TO TRANSPLANT YOUR BRAIN INTO THIS DORMANT DOUGHY DEBUTANT!
YOU WILL BE...
...THE BRIDE OF THE CALZONE CREATURE!
EEEK!
GRAB!
STRAP! STRAP!

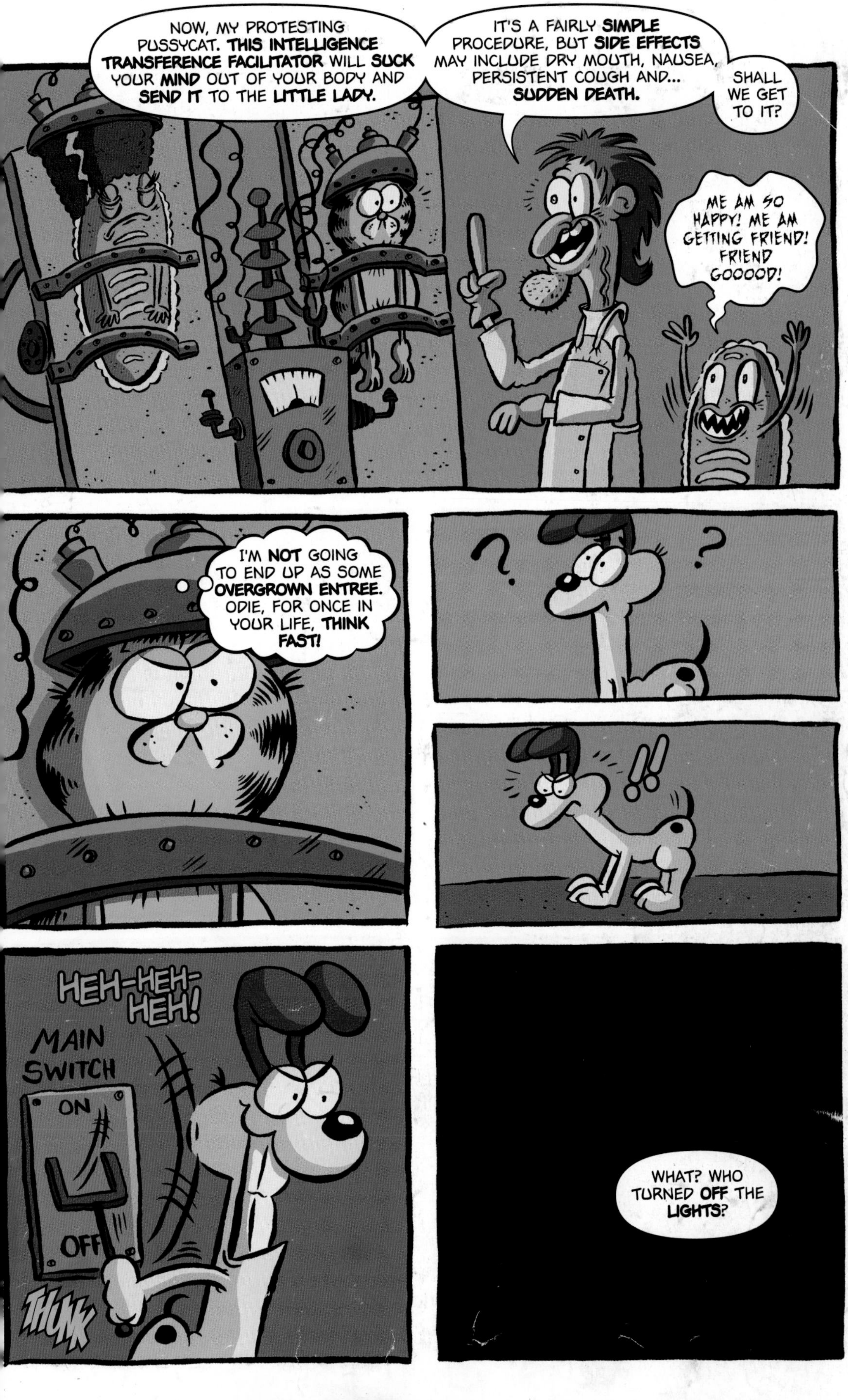
NOW, MY PROTESTING PUSSYCAT. THIS INTELLIGENCE TRANSFERENCE FACILITATOR WILL SUCK YOUR MIND OUT OF YOUR BODY AND SEND IT TO THE LITTLE LADY.
IT'S A FAIRLY SIMPLE PROCEDURE, BUT SIDE EFFECTS MAY INCLUDE DRY MOUTH, NAUSEA, PERSISTENT COUGH AND... SUDDEN DEATH.
SHALL WE GET TO IT?
ME AM SO HAPPY! ME AM GETTING FRIEND! FRIEND GOOOOD!
I'M NOT GOING TO END UP AS SOME OVERGROWN ENTREE. ODIE, FOR ONCE IN YOUR LIFE, THINK FAST!
?
?
!!
HEH-HEH-HEH!
MAIN SWITCH
ON
OFF
THUNK
WHAT? WHO TURNED OFF THE LIGHTS?

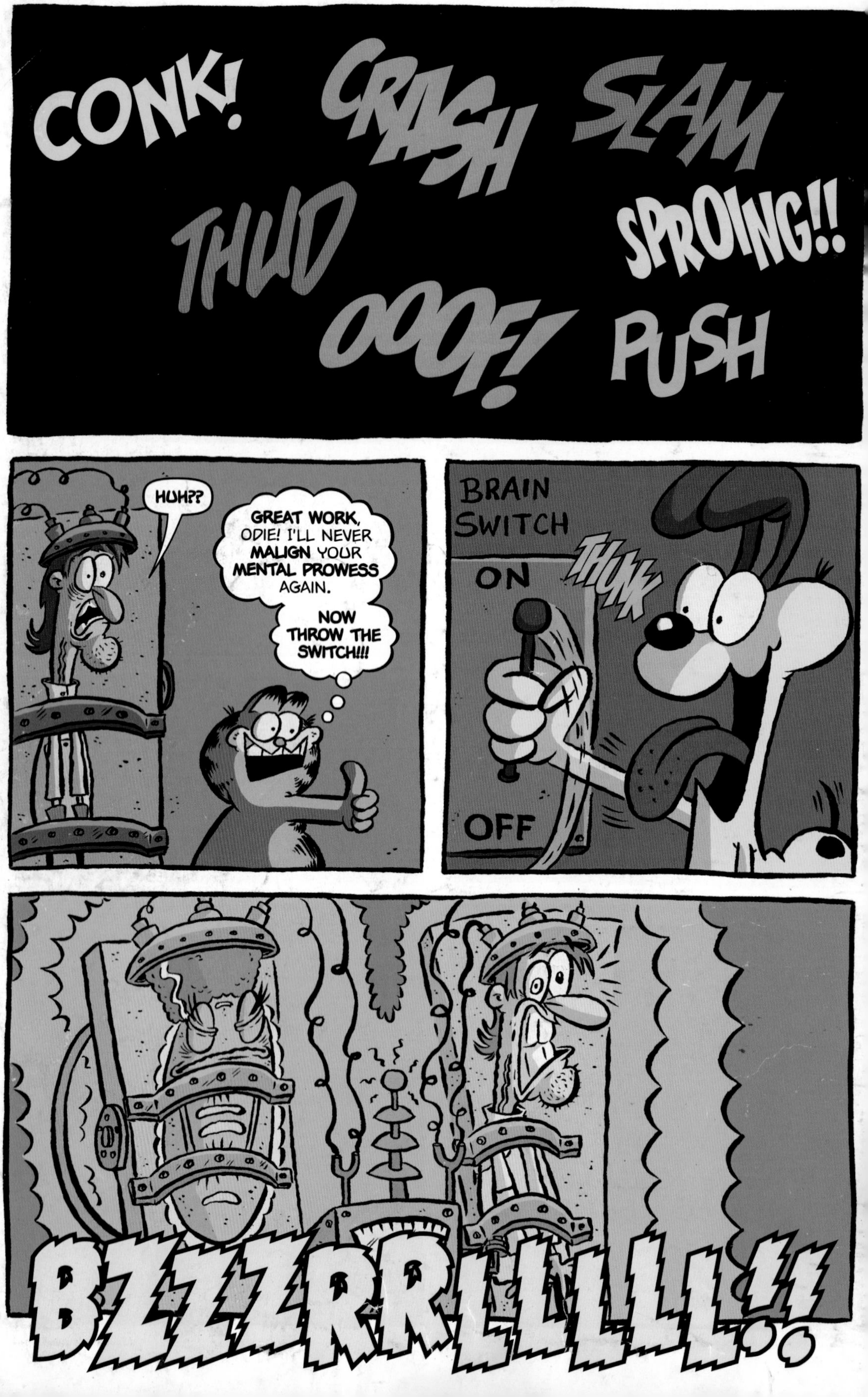
CONK!
CRASH
SLAM
THUD
SPROING!!
OOOF!
PUSH
HUH??
GREAT WORK, ODIE! I'LL NEVER MALIGN YOUR MENTAL PROWESS AGAIN.
NOW THROW THE SWITCH!!!
BRAIN SWITCH
ON
OFF
THUNK
BZZZRRLLLLL!!

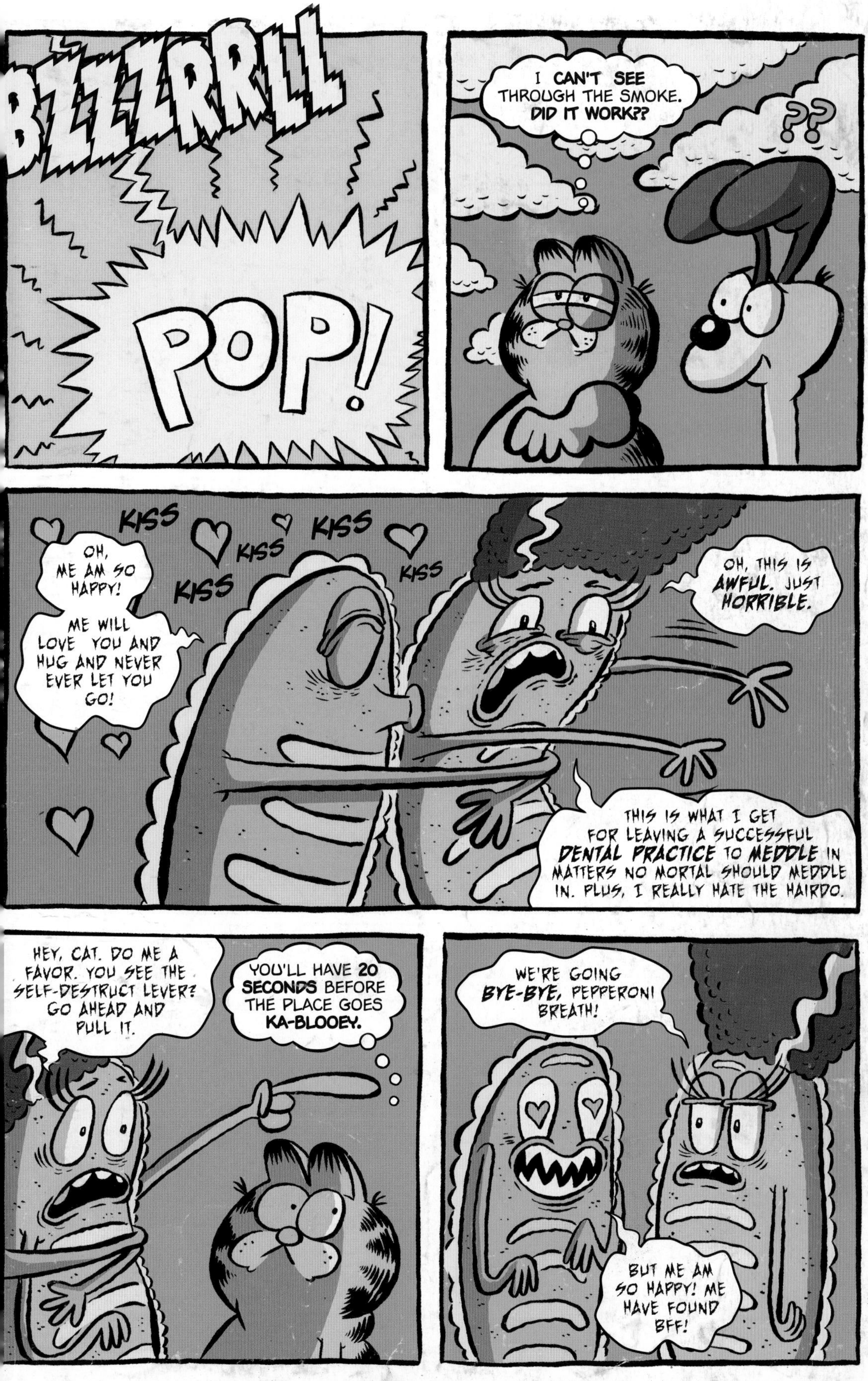
BZZZZRRLL
POP!
I CAN'T SEE THROUGH THE SMOKE. DID IT WORK??
??
KISS
KISS
KISS
KISS
KISS
OH, ME AM SO HAPPY!
ME WILL LOVE YOU AND HUG AND NEVER EVER LET YOU GO!
OH, THIS IS AWFUL. JUST HORRIBLE.
THIS IS WHAT I GET FOR LEAVING A SUCCESSFUL DENTAL PRACTICE TO MEDDLE IN MATTERS NO MORTAL SHOULD MEDDLE IN. PLUS, I REALLY HATE THE HAIRDO.
HEY, CAT. DO ME A FAVOR. YOU SEE THE SELF-DESTRUCT LEVER? GO AHEAD AND PULL IT.
YOU'LL HAVE 20 SECONDS BEFORE THE PLACE GOES KA-BLOOEY.
WE'RE GOING BYE-BYE, PEPPERONI BREATH!
BUT ME AM SO HAPPY! ME HAVE FOUND BFF!

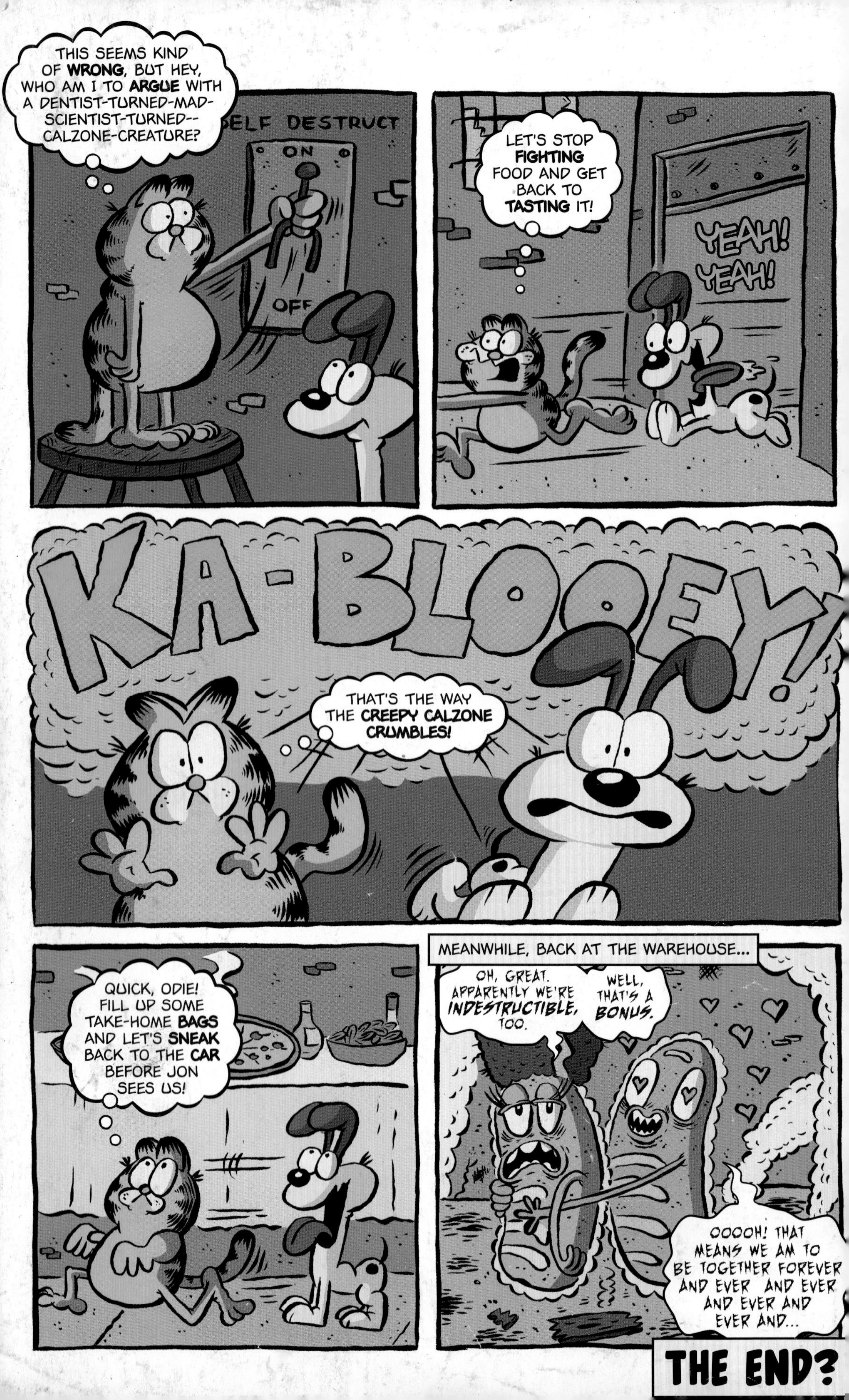
THIS SEEMS KIND OF WRONG, BUT HEY, WHO AM I TO ARGUE WITH A DENTIST-TURNED-MAD-SCIENTIST-TURNED--CALZONE-CREATURE?
SELF DESTRUCT
ON
OFF
LET'S STOP FIGHTING FOOD AND GET BACK TO TASTING IT!
YEAH! YEAH!
KA-BLOOEY!!
THAT'S THE WAY THE CREEPY CALZONE CRUMBLES!
QUICK, ODIE! FILL UP SOME TAKE-HOME BAGS AND LET'S SNEAK BACK TO THE CAR BEFORE JON SEES US!
MEANWHILE, BACK AT THE WAREHOUSE...
OH, GREAT. APPARENTLY WE'RE INDESTRUCTIBLE, TOO.
WELL, THAT'S A BONUS.
OOOOH! THAT MEANS WE AM TO BE TOGETHER FOREVER AND EVER AND EVER AND EVER AND EVER AND...
THE END?

CHAPTER 2

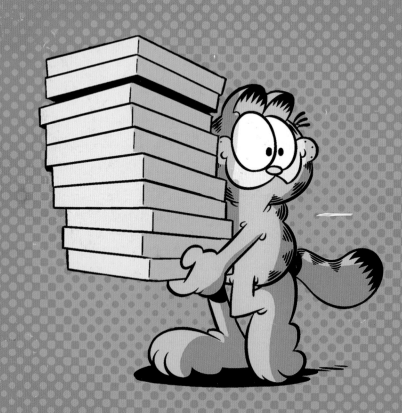

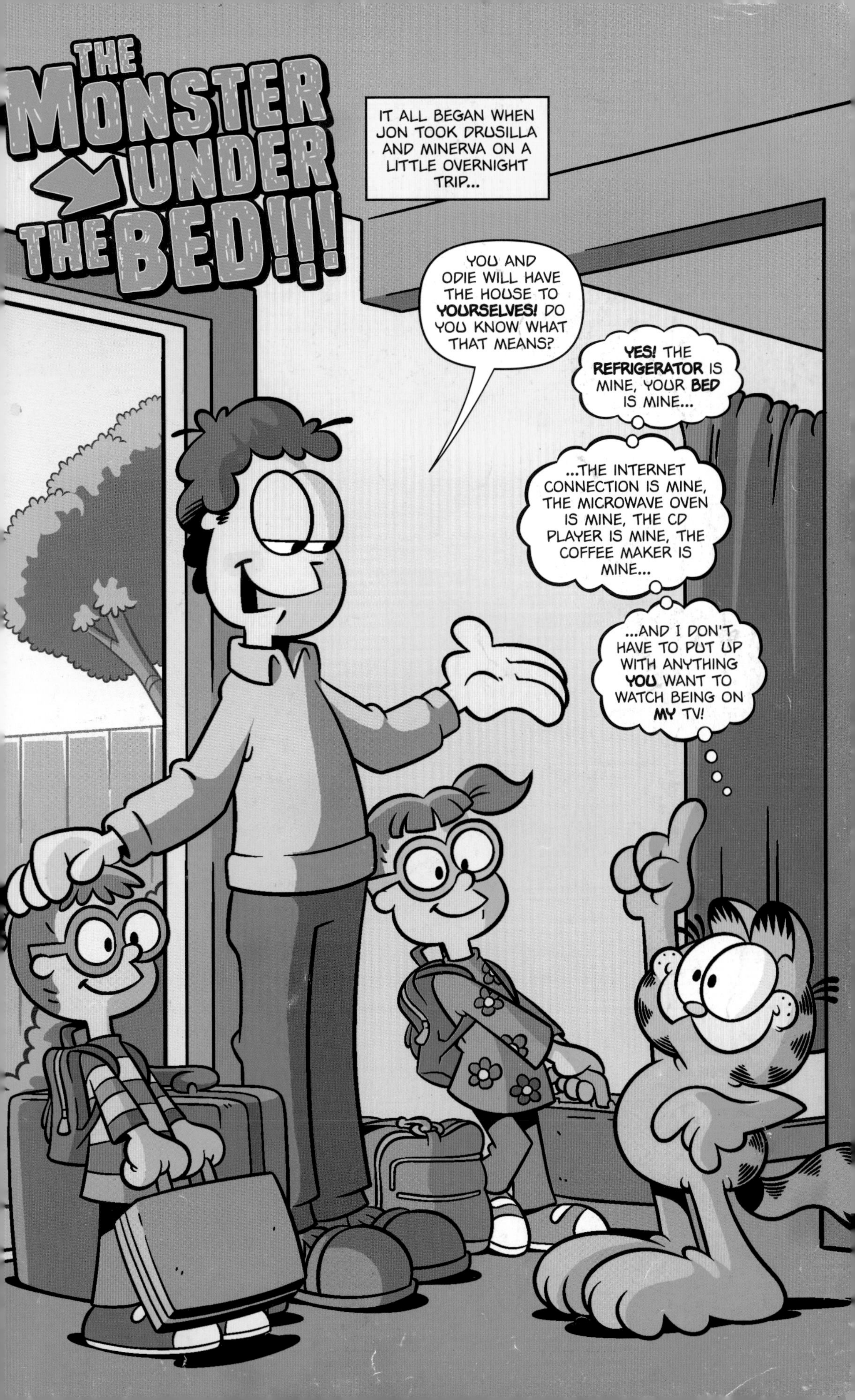
THE MONSTER UNDER THE BED!!!
IT ALL BEGAN WHEN JON TOOK DRUSILLA AND MINERVA ON A LITTLE OVERNIGHT TRIP...
YOU AND ODIE WILL HAVE THE HOUSE TO YOURSELVES! DO YOU KNOW WHAT THAT MEANS?
YES! THE REFRIGERATOR IS MINE, YOUR BED IS MINE...
...THE INTERNET CONNECTION IS MINE, THE MICROWAVE OVEN IS MINE, THE CD PLAYER IS MINE, THE COFFEE MAKER IS MINE...
...AND I DON'T HAVE TO PUT UP WITH ANYTHING YOU WANT TO WATCH BEING ON MY TV!

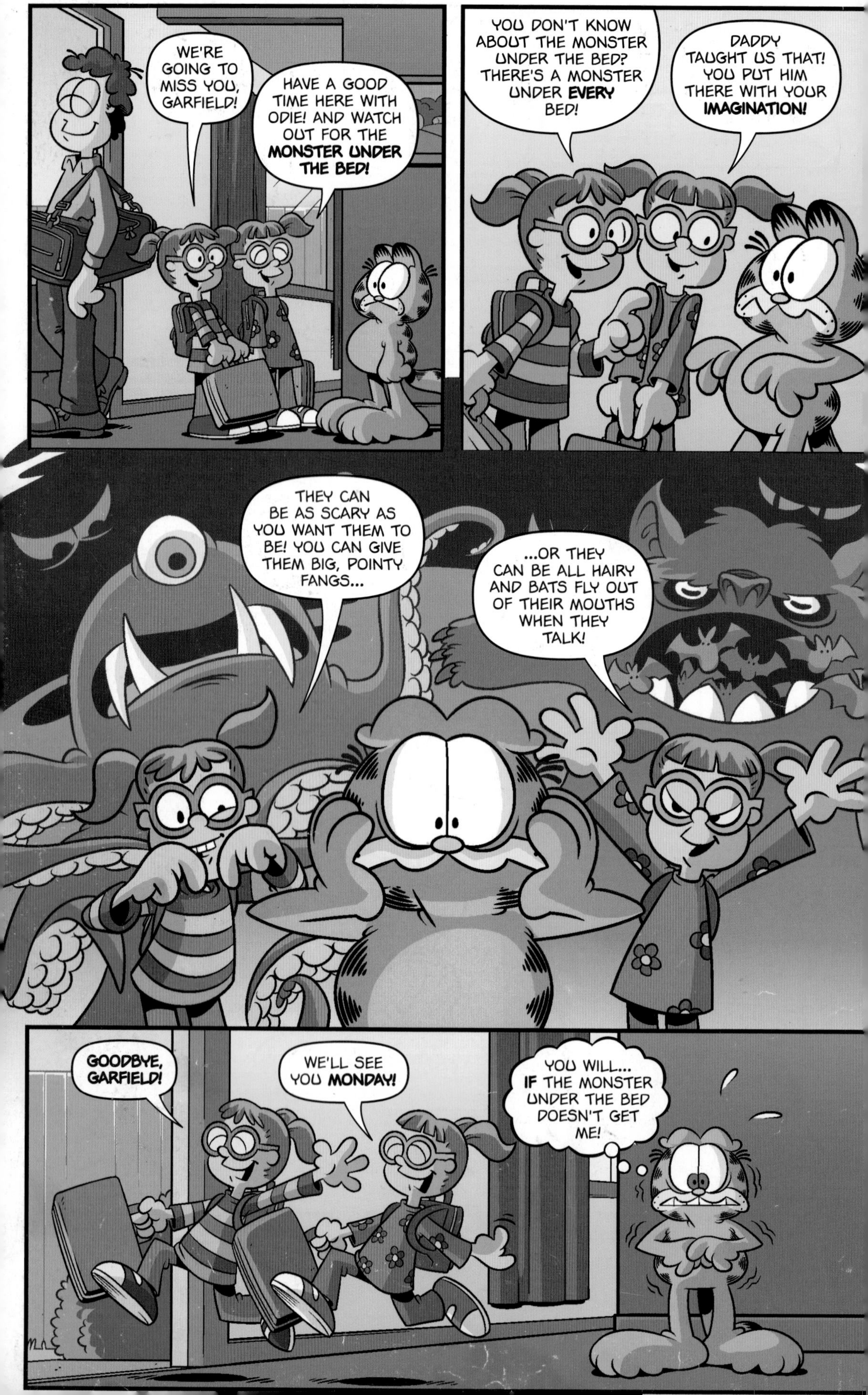
WE'RE GOING TO MISS YOU, GARFIELD!
HAVE A GOOD TIME HERE WITH ODIE! AND WATCH OUT FOR THE **MONSTER UNDER THE BED!**
YOU DON'T KNOW ABOUT THE MONSTER UNDER THE BED? THERE'S A MONSTER UNDER **EVERY** BED!
DADDY TAUGHT US THAT! YOU PUT HIM THERE WITH YOUR **IMAGINATION!**
THEY CAN BE AS SCARY AS YOU WANT THEM TO BE! YOU CAN GIVE THEM BIG, POINTY FANGS...
...OR THEY CAN BE ALL HAIRY AND BATS FLY OUT OF THEIR MOUTHS WHEN THEY TALK!
GOODBYE, GARFIELD!
WE'LL SEE YOU **MONDAY!**
YOU WILL... **IF** THE MONSTER UNDER THE BED DOESN'T GET ME!

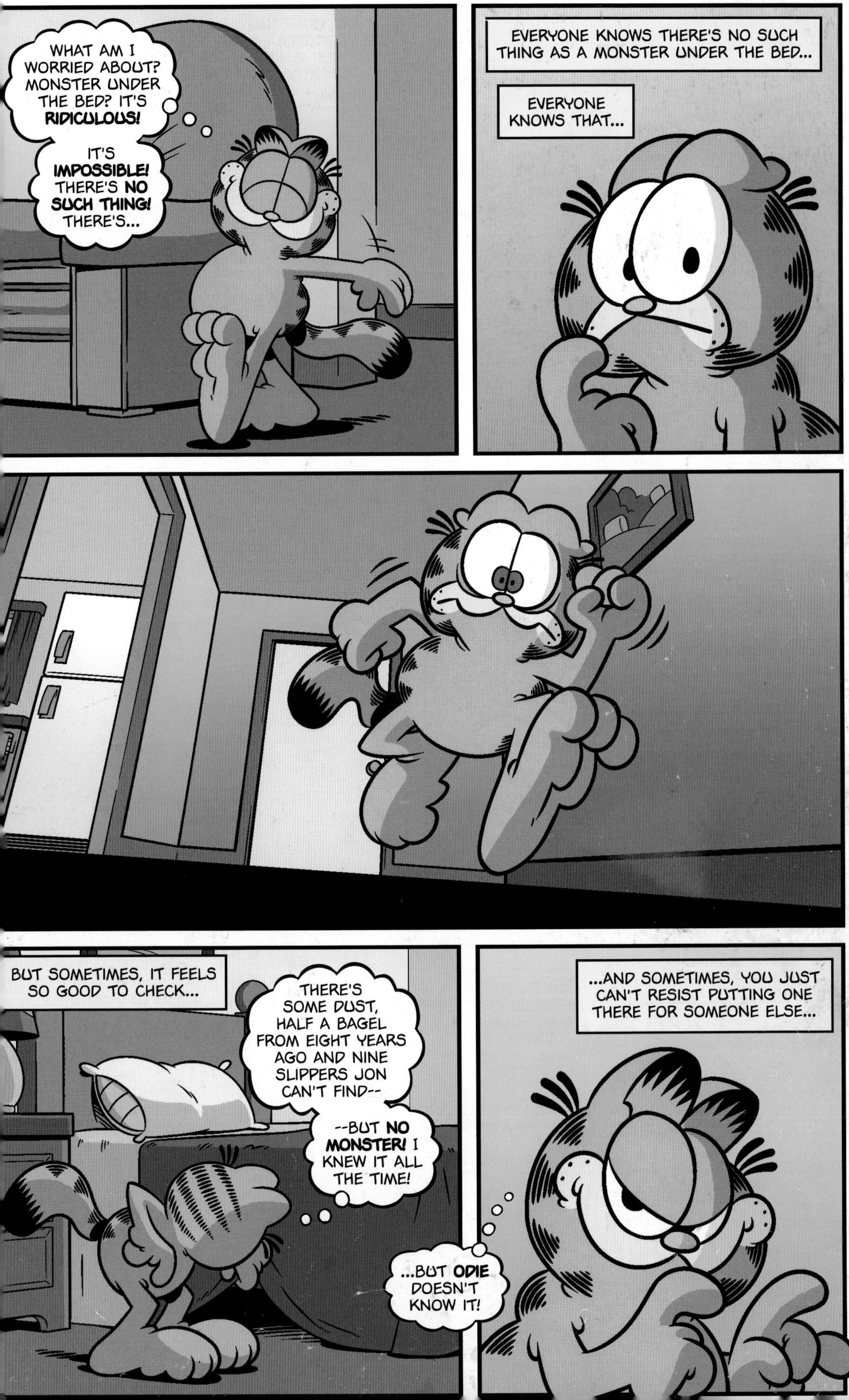
WHAT AM I WORRIED ABOUT? MONSTER UNDER THE BED? IT'S **RIDICULOUS!**
IT'S **IMPOSSIBLE!** THERE'S **NO SUCH THING!** THERE'S...
EVERYONE KNOWS THERE'S NO SUCH THING AS A MONSTER UNDER THE BED...
EVERYONE KNOWS THAT...
BUT SOMETIMES, IT FEELS SO GOOD TO CHECK...
THERE'S SOME DUST, HALF A BAGEL FROM EIGHT YEARS AGO AND NINE SLIPPERS JON CAN'T FIND--
--BUT **NO MONSTER!** I KNEW IT ALL THE TIME!
...AND SOMETIMES, YOU JUST CAN'T RESIST PUTTING ONE THERE FOR SOMEONE ELSE...
...BUT **ODIE** DOESN'T KNOW IT!

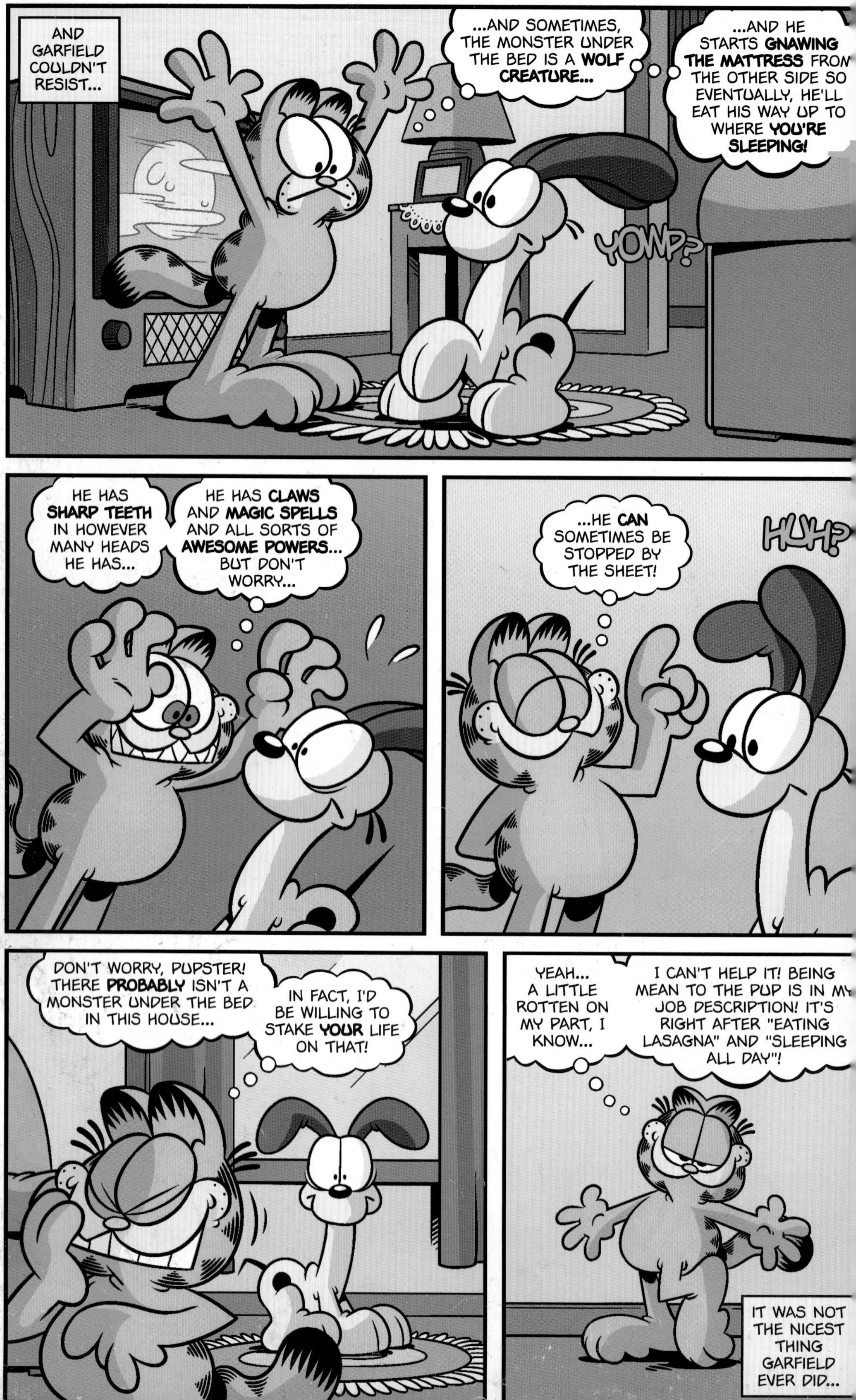
AND GARFIELD COULDN'T RESIST...
...AND SOMETIMES, THE MONSTER UNDER THE BED IS A WOLF CREATURE...
...AND HE STARTS GNAWING THE MATTRESS FROM THE OTHER SIDE SO EVENTUALLY, HE'LL EAT HIS WAY UP TO WHERE YOU'RE SLEEPING!
YOWP?
HE HAS SHARP TEETH IN HOWEVER MANY HEADS HE HAS...
HE HAS CLAWS AND MAGIC SPELLS AND ALL SORTS OF AWESOME POWERS... BUT DON'T WORRY...
...HE CAN SOMETIMES BE STOPPED BY THE SHEET!
HUH?
DON'T WORRY, PUPSTER! THERE PROBABLY ISN'T A MONSTER UNDER THE BED IN THIS HOUSE...
IN FACT, I'D BE WILLING TO STAKE YOUR LIFE ON THAT!
YEAH... A LITTLE ROTTEN ON MY PART, I KNOW...
I CAN'T HELP IT! BEING MEAN TO THE PUP IS IN MY JOB DESCRIPTION! IT'S RIGHT AFTER "EATING LASAGNA" AND "SLEEPING ALL DAY"!
IT WAS NOT THE NICEST THING GARFIELD EVER DID...

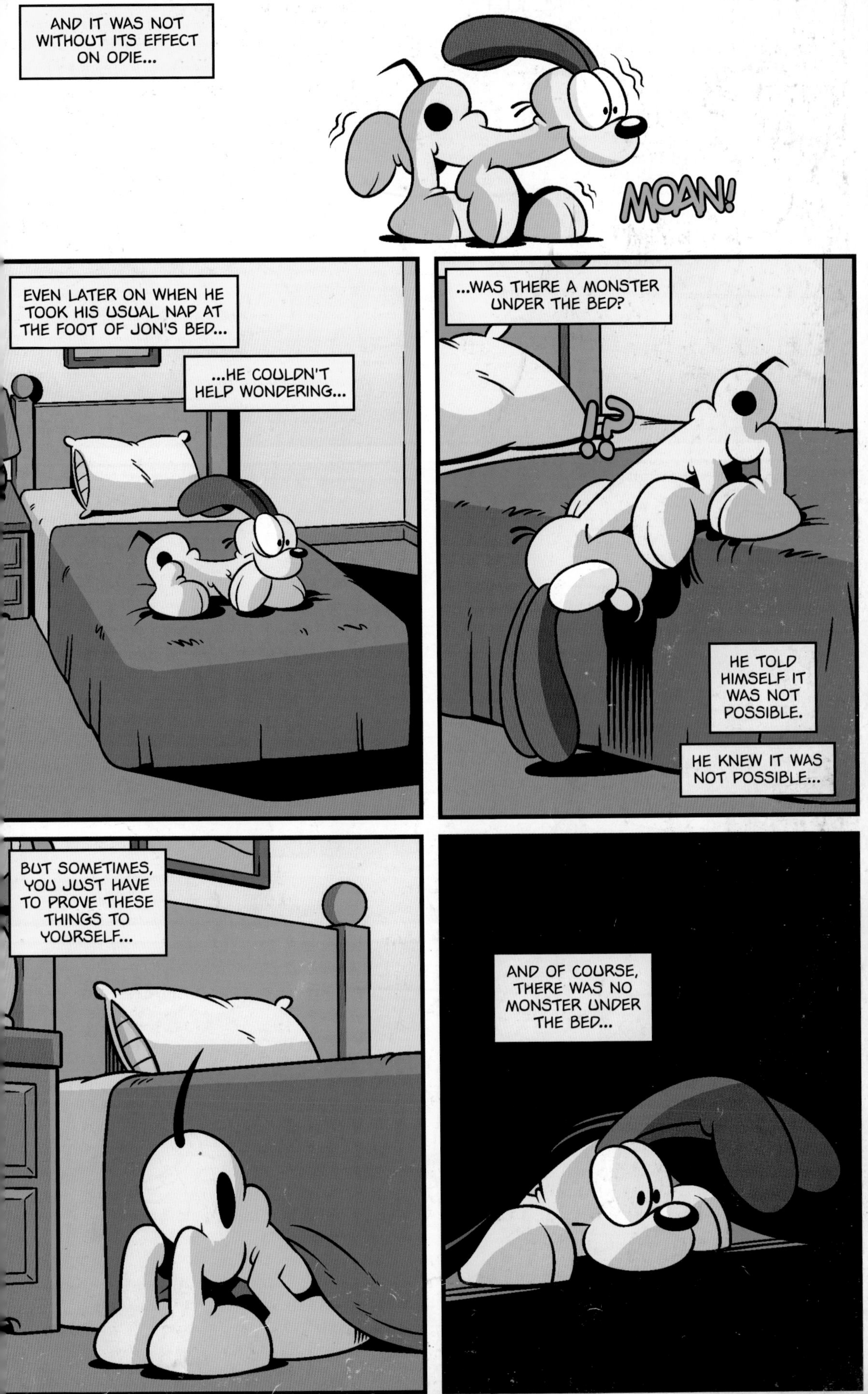
AND IT WAS NOT WITHOUT ITS EFFECT ON ODIE...
MOAN!
EVEN LATER ON WHEN HE TOOK HIS USUAL NAP AT THE FOOT OF JON'S BED...
...HE COULDN'T HELP WONDERING...
...WAS THERE A MONSTER UNDER THE BED?
!?
HE TOLD HIMSELF IT WAS NOT POSSIBLE.
HE KNEW IT WAS NOT POSSIBLE...
BUT SOMETIMES, YOU JUST HAVE TO PROVE THESE THINGS TO YOURSELF...
AND OF COURSE, THERE WAS NO MONSTER UNDER THE BED...

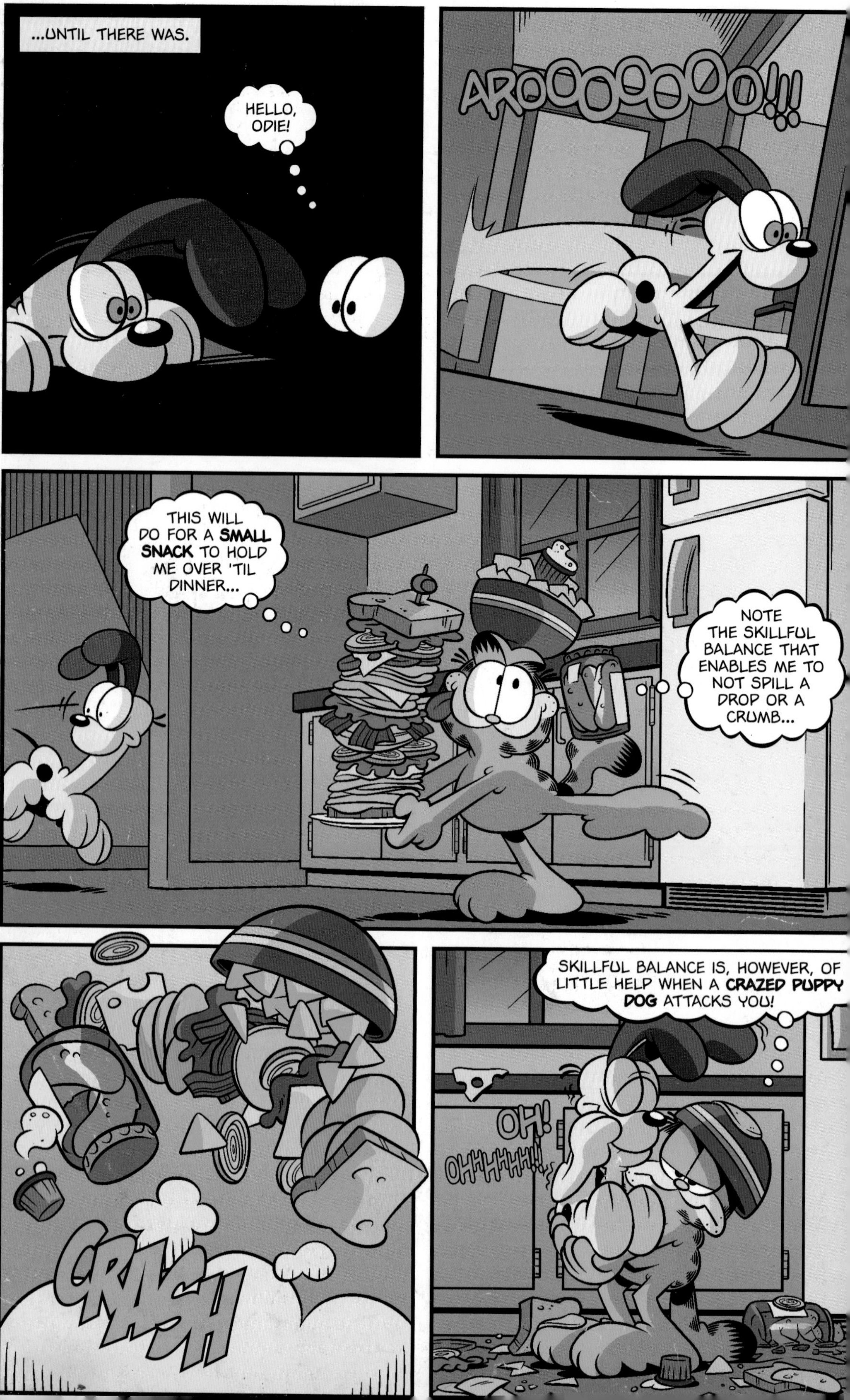

...UNTIL THERE WAS.
HELLO, ODIE!
AROOOOOOOO!!!
THIS WILL DO FOR A **SMALL SNACK** TO HOLD ME OVER 'TIL DINNER...
NOTE THE SKILLFUL BALANCE THAT ENABLES ME TO NOT SPILL A DROP OR A CRUMB...
CRASH
SKILLFUL BALANCE IS, HOWEVER, OF LITTLE HELP WHEN A **CRAZED PUPPY DOG** ATTACKS YOU!
OH!
OHHHHHH!!

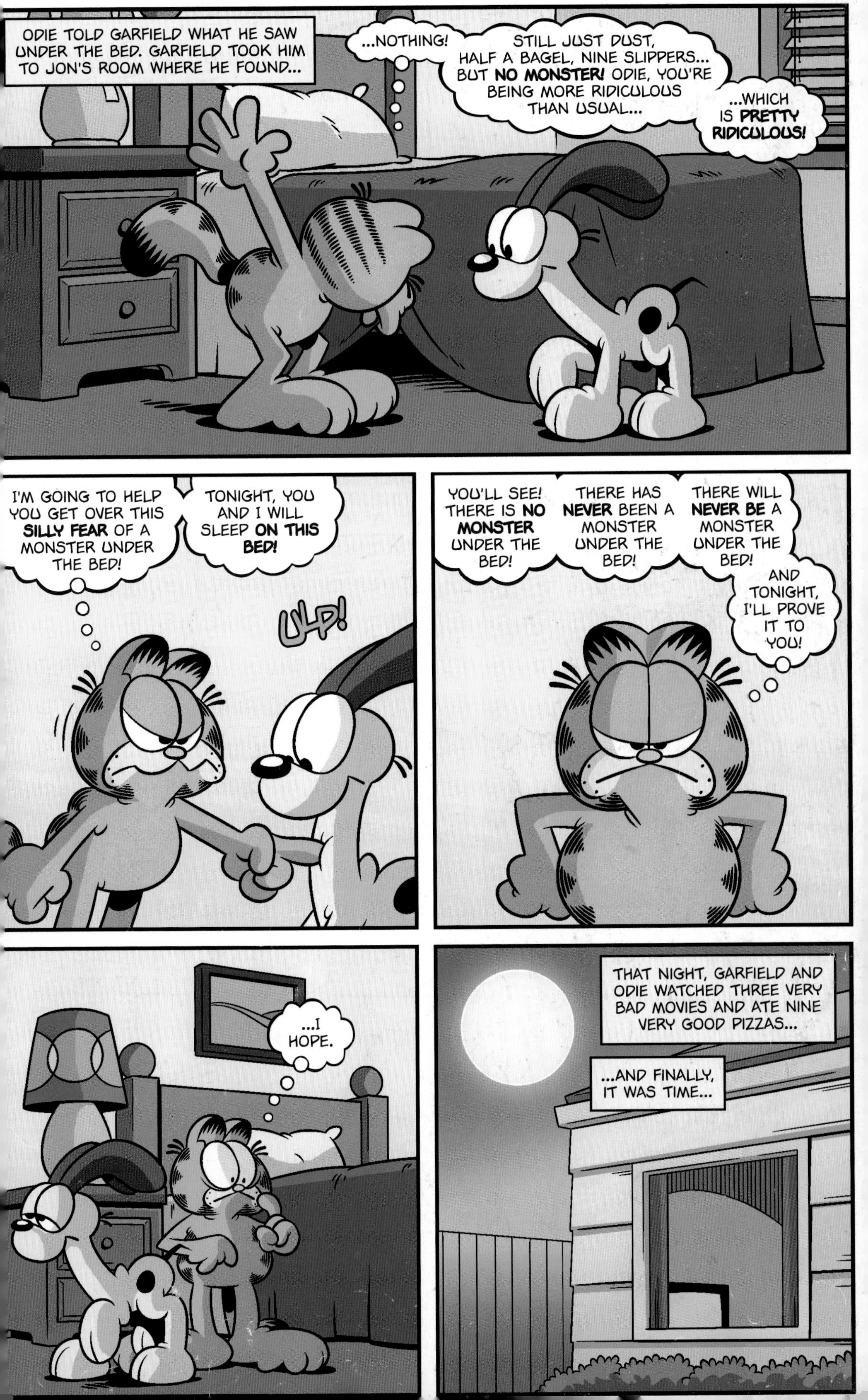

ODIE TOLD GARFIELD WHAT HE SAW UNDER THE BED. GARFIELD TOOK HIM TO JON'S ROOM WHERE HE FOUND...
...NOTHING!
STILL JUST DUST, HALF A BAGEL, NINE SLIPPERS... BUT NO MONSTER! ODIE, YOU'RE BEING MORE RIDICULOUS THAN USUAL...
...WHICH IS PRETTY RIDICULOUS!
I'M GOING TO HELP YOU GET OVER THIS SILLY FEAR OF A MONSTER UNDER THE BED!
TONIGHT, YOU AND I WILL SLEEP ON THIS BED!
ULP!
YOU'LL SEE! THERE IS NO MONSTER UNDER THE BED!
THERE HAS NEVER BEEN A MONSTER UNDER THE BED!
THERE WILL NEVER BE A MONSTER UNDER THE BED!
AND TONIGHT, I'LL PROVE IT TO YOU!
...I HOPE.
THAT NIGHT, GARFIELD AND ODIE WATCHED THREE VERY BAD MOVIES AND ATE NINE VERY GOOD PIZZAS...
...AND FINALLY, IT WAS TIME...

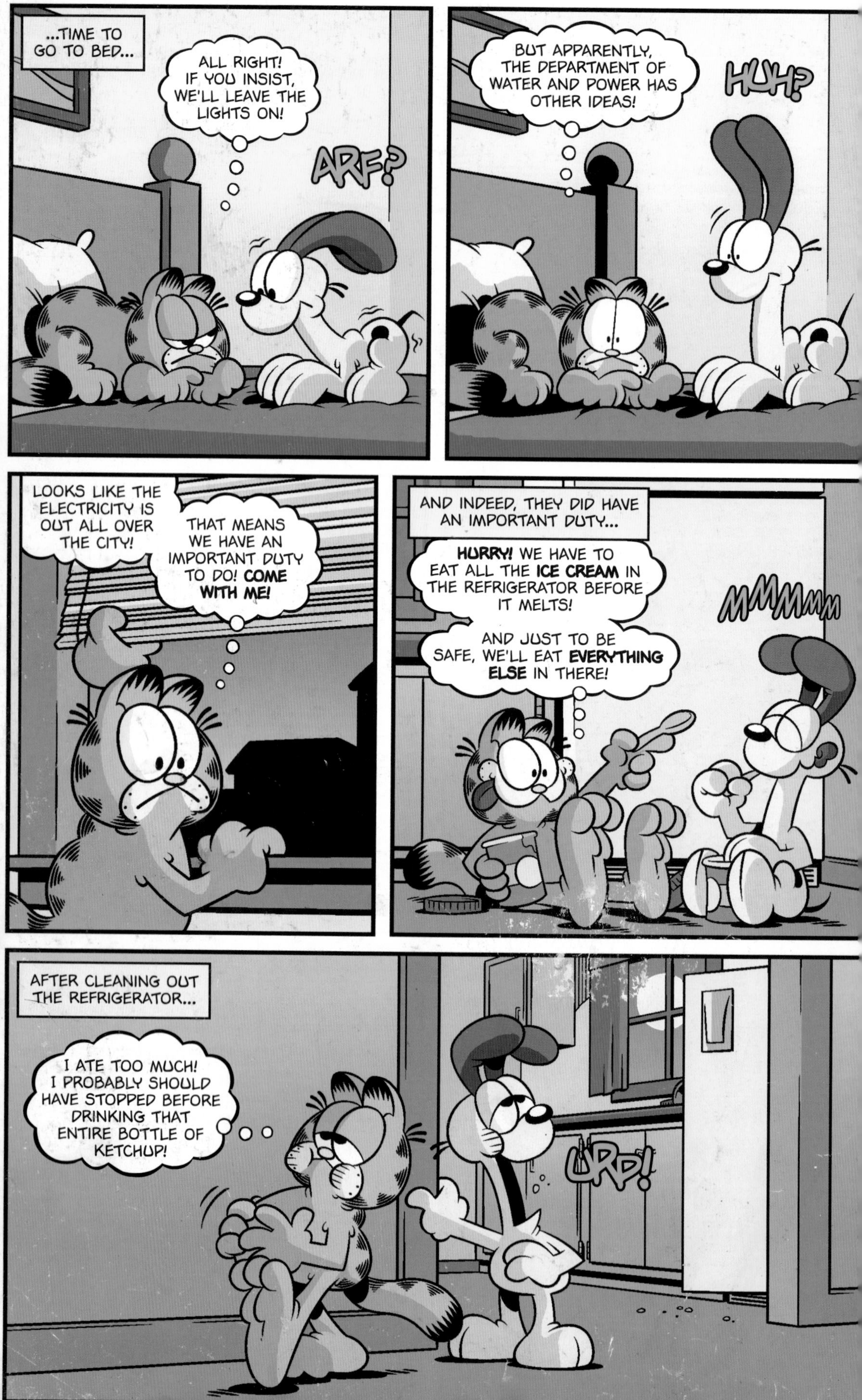
...TIME TO GO TO BED...
ALL RIGHT! IF YOU INSIST, WE'LL LEAVE THE LIGHTS ON!
ARF?
BUT APPARENTLY, THE DEPARTMENT OF WATER AND POWER HAS OTHER IDEAS!
HUH?
LOOKS LIKE THE ELECTRICITY IS OUT ALL OVER THE CITY!
THAT MEANS WE HAVE AN IMPORTANT DUTY TO DO! **COME WITH ME!**
AND INDEED, THEY DID HAVE AN IMPORTANT DUTY...
HURRY! WE HAVE TO EAT ALL THE **ICE CREAM** IN THE REFRIGERATOR BEFORE IT MELTS!
AND JUST TO BE SAFE, WE'LL EAT **EVERYTHING ELSE** IN THERE!
MMMMMM
AFTER CLEANING OUT THE REFRIGERATOR...
I ATE TOO MUCH! I PROBABLY SHOULD HAVE STOPPED BEFORE DRINKING THAT ENTIRE BOTTLE OF KETCHUP!
URP!

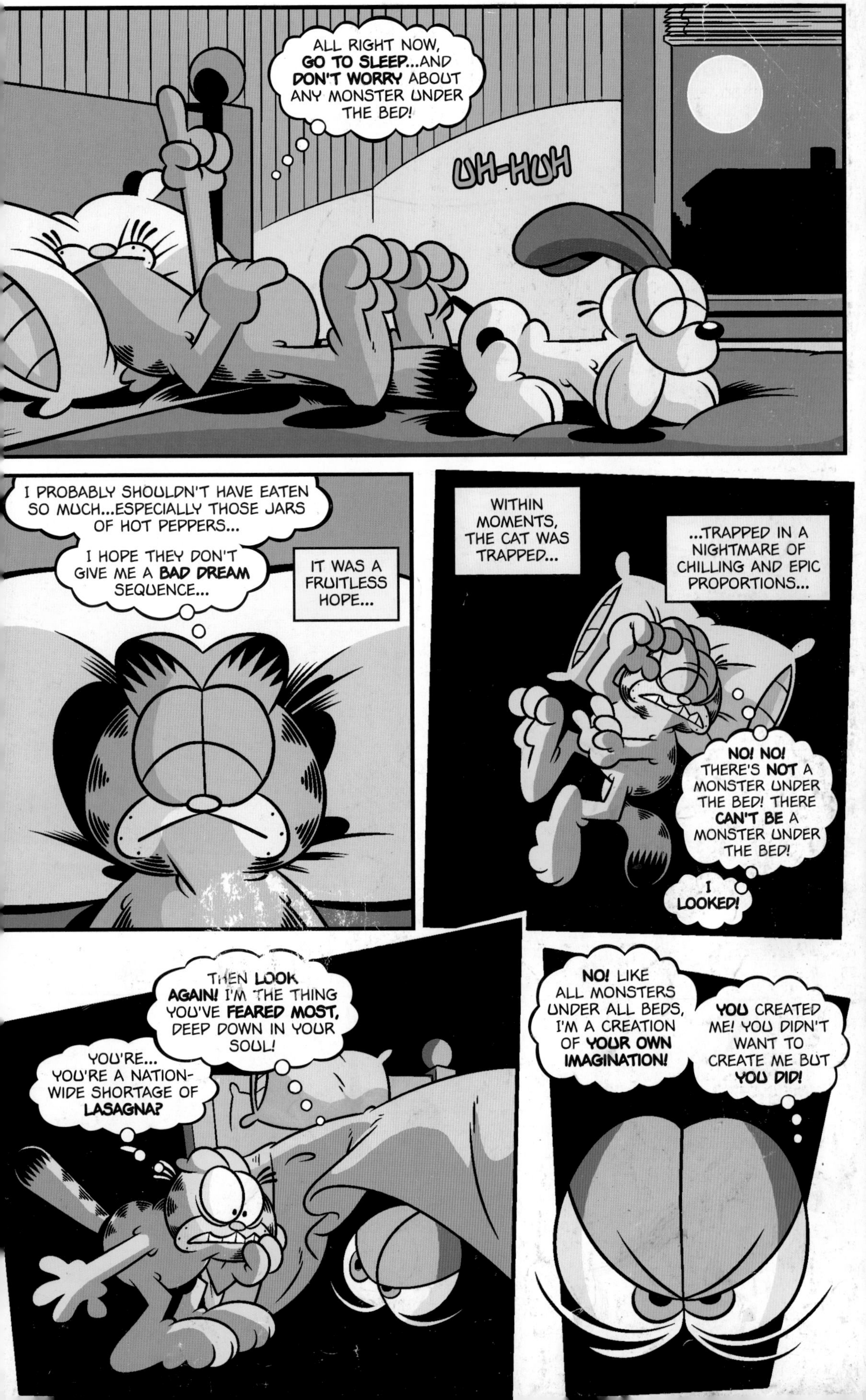

ALL RIGHT NOW, GO TO SLEEP...AND DON'T WORRY ABOUT ANY MONSTER UNDER THE BED!
UH-HUH
I PROBABLY SHOULDN'T HAVE EATEN SO MUCH...ESPECIALLY THOSE JARS OF HOT PEPPERS...
I HOPE THEY DON'T GIVE ME A BAD DREAM SEQUENCE...
IT WAS A FRUITLESS HOPE...
WITHIN MOMENTS, THE CAT WAS TRAPPED...
...TRAPPED IN A NIGHTMARE OF CHILLING AND EPIC PROPORTIONS...
NO! NO! THERE'S NOT A MONSTER UNDER THE BED! THERE CAN'T BE A MONSTER UNDER THE BED!
I LOOKED!
THEN LOOK AGAIN! I'M THE THING YOU'VE FEARED MOST, DEEP DOWN IN YOUR SOUL!
YOU'RE... YOU'RE A NATION-WIDE SHORTAGE OF LASAGNA?
NO! LIKE ALL MONSTERS UNDER ALL BEDS, I'M A CREATION OF YOUR OWN IMAGINATION!
YOU CREATED ME! YOU DIDN'T WANT TO CREATE ME BUT YOU DID!

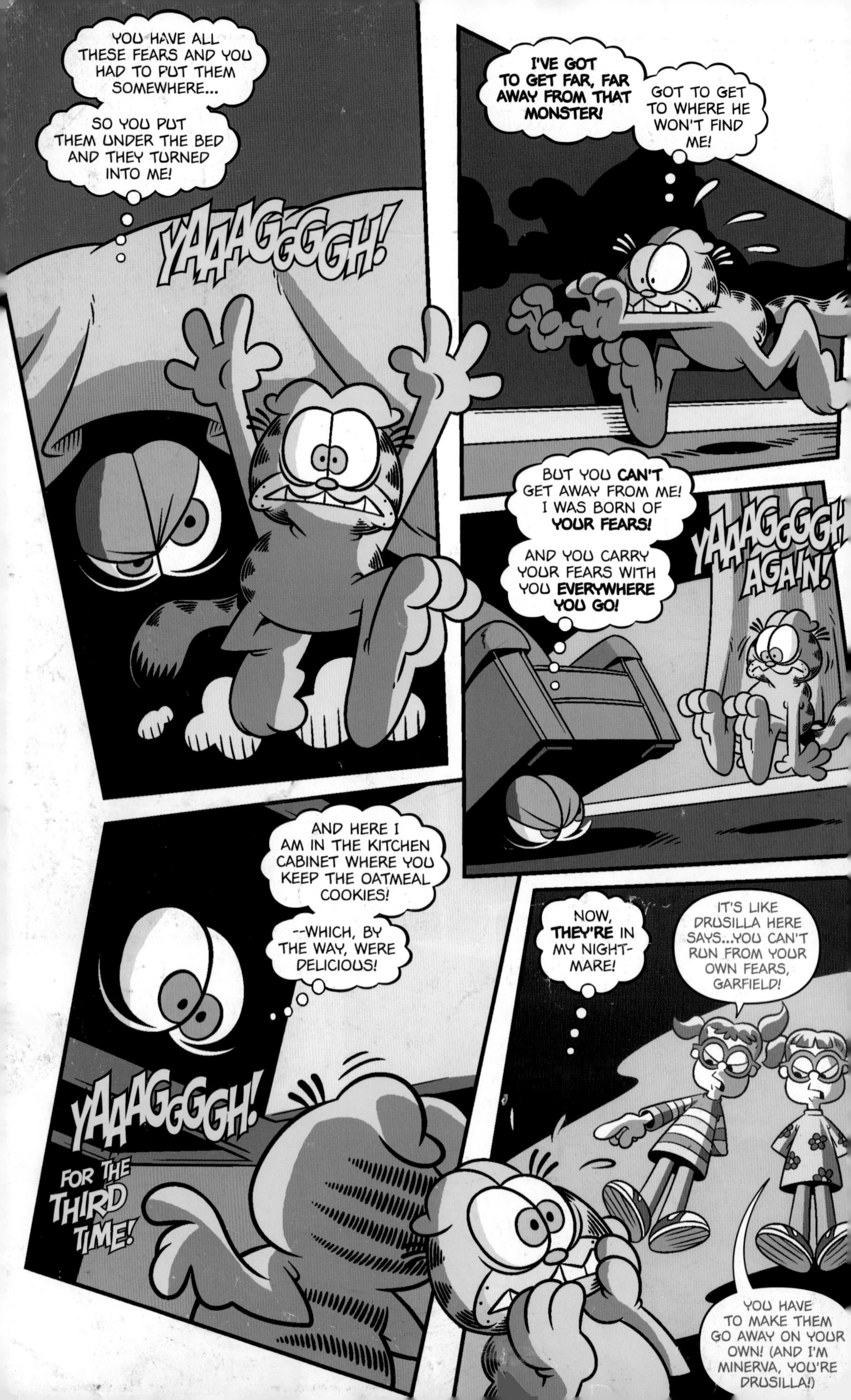
YOU HAVE ALL THESE FEARS AND YOU HAD TO PUT THEM SOMEWHERE...
SO YOU PUT THEM UNDER THE BED AND THEY TURNED INTO ME!
YAAAGGGGH!
I'VE GOT TO GET FAR, FAR AWAY FROM THAT MONSTER!
GOT TO GET TO WHERE HE WON'T FIND ME!
BUT YOU CAN'T GET AWAY FROM ME! I WAS BORN OF YOUR FEARS!
AND YOU CARRY YOUR FEARS WITH YOU EVERYWHERE YOU GO!
YAAAGGGGH AGAIN!
AND HERE I AM IN THE KITCHEN CABINET WHERE YOU KEEP THE OATMEAL COOKIES!
--WHICH, BY THE WAY, WERE DELICIOUS!
YAAAGGGGH!
FOR THE THIRD TIME!
NOW, THEY'RE IN MY NIGHT-MARE!
IT'S LIKE DRUSILLA HERE SAYS...YOU CAN'T RUN FROM YOUR OWN FEARS, GARFIELD!
YOU HAVE TO MAKE THEM GO AWAY ON YOUR OWN! (AND I'M MINERVA, YOU'RE DRUSILLA!)

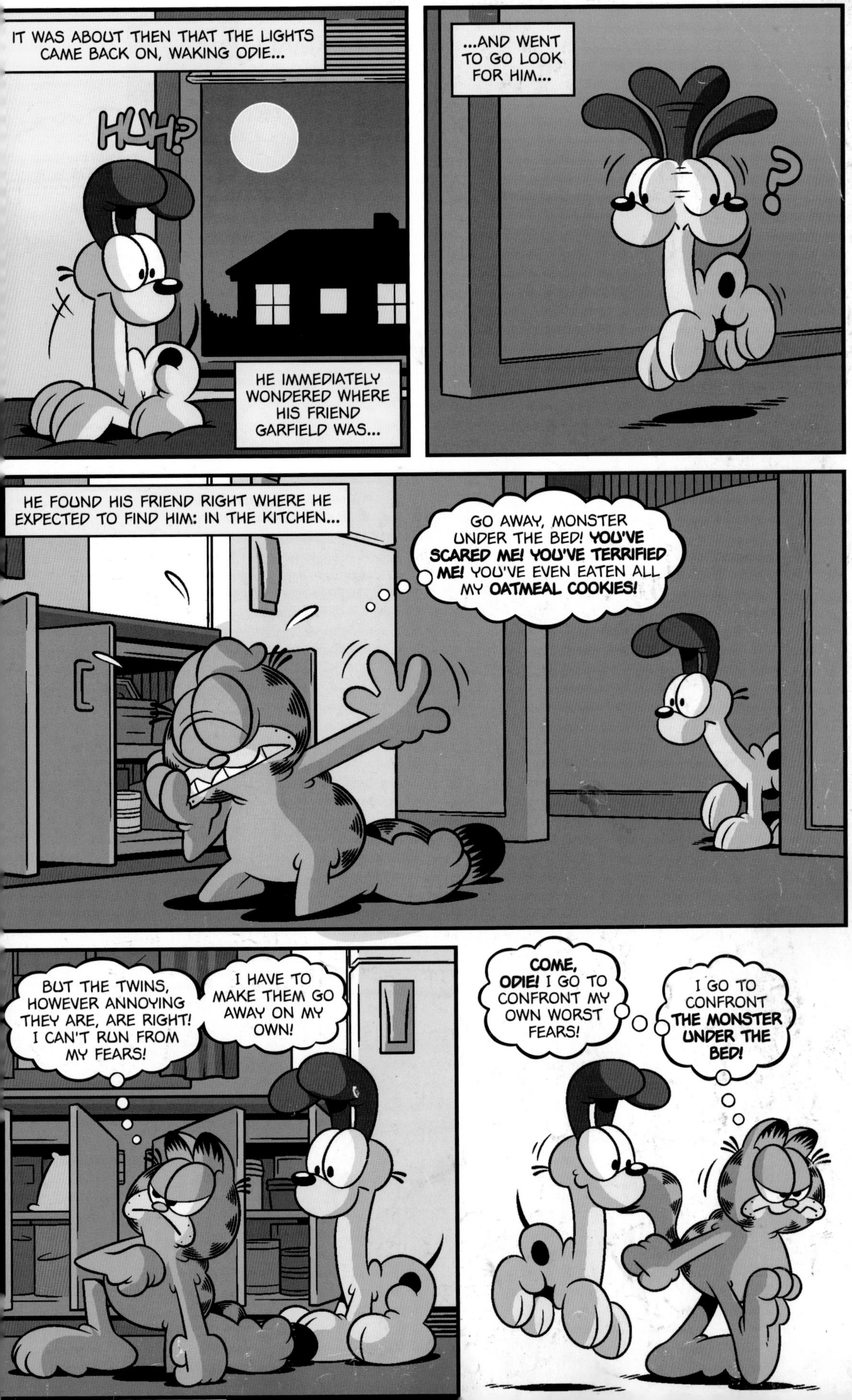
IT WAS ABOUT THEN THAT THE LIGHTS CAME BACK ON, WAKING ODIE...
HUH?
HE IMMEDIATELY WONDERED WHERE HIS FRIEND GARFIELD WAS...
...AND WENT TO GO LOOK FOR HIM...
?
HE FOUND HIS FRIEND RIGHT WHERE HE EXPECTED TO FIND HIM: IN THE KITCHEN...
GO AWAY, MONSTER UNDER THE BED! YOU'VE SCARED ME! YOU'VE TERRIFIED ME! YOU'VE EVEN EATEN ALL MY OATMEAL COOKIES!
BUT THE TWINS, HOWEVER ANNOYING THEY ARE, ARE RIGHT! I CAN'T RUN FROM MY FEARS!
I HAVE TO MAKE THEM GO AWAY ON MY OWN!
COME, ODIE! I GO TO CONFRONT MY OWN WORST FEARS!
I GO TO CONFRONT THE MONSTER UNDER THE BED!

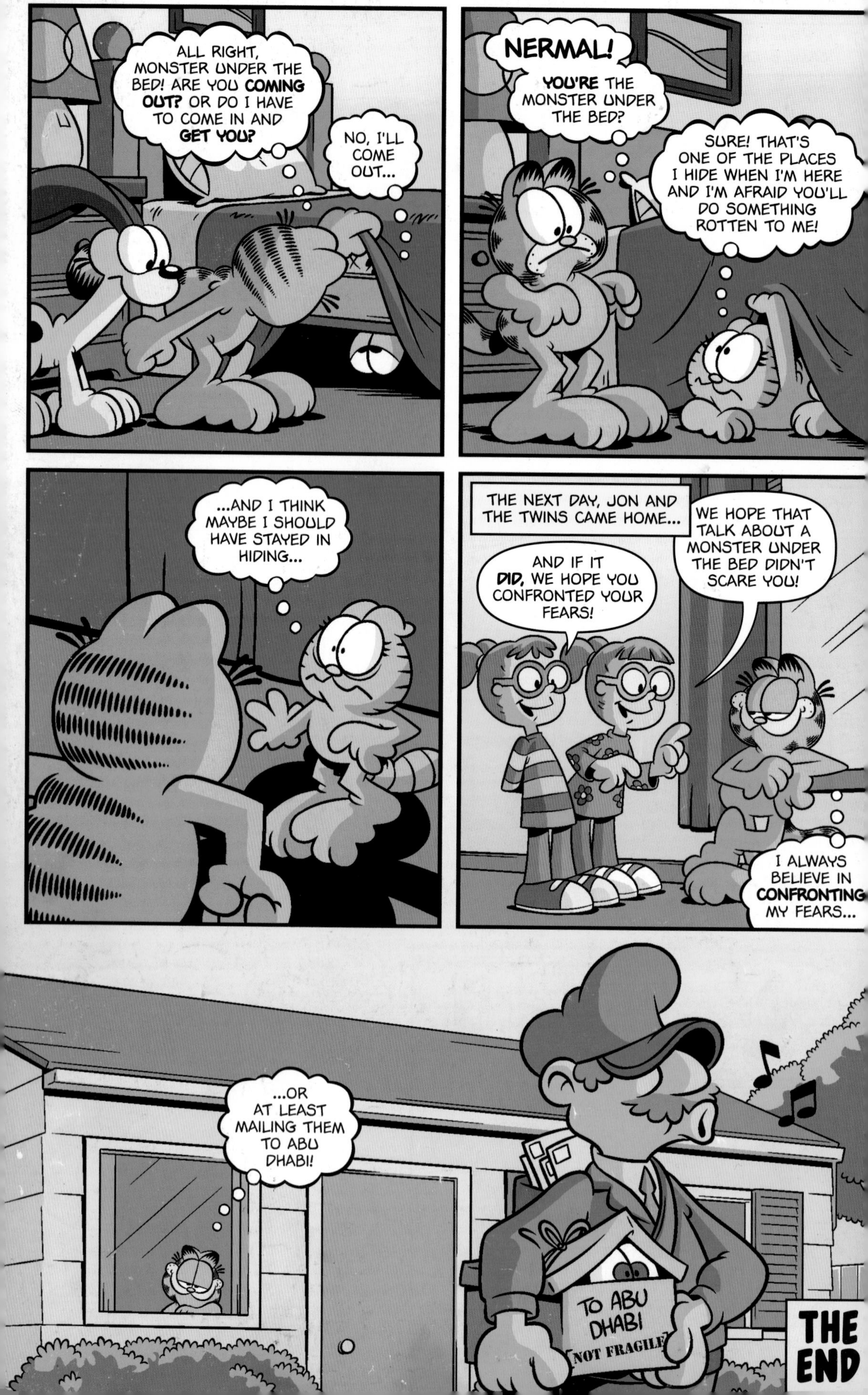
ALL RIGHT, MONSTER UNDER THE BED! ARE YOU **COMING OUT?** OR DO I HAVE TO COME IN AND **GET YOU?**
NO, I'LL COME OUT...
NERMAL!
YOU'RE THE MONSTER UNDER THE BED?
SURE! THAT'S ONE OF THE PLACES I HIDE WHEN I'M HERE AND I'M AFRAID YOU'LL DO SOMETHING ROTTEN TO ME!
...AND I THINK MAYBE I SHOULD HAVE STAYED IN HIDING...
THE NEXT DAY, JON AND THE TWINS CAME HOME...
WE HOPE THAT TALK ABOUT A MONSTER UNDER THE BED DIDN'T SCARE YOU!
AND IF IT **DID,** WE HOPE YOU CONFRONTED YOUR FEARS!
I ALWAYS BELIEVE IN **CONFRONTING** MY FEARS...
...OR AT LEAST MAILING THEM TO ABU DHABI!
TO ABU DHABI
NOT FRAGILE
THE END

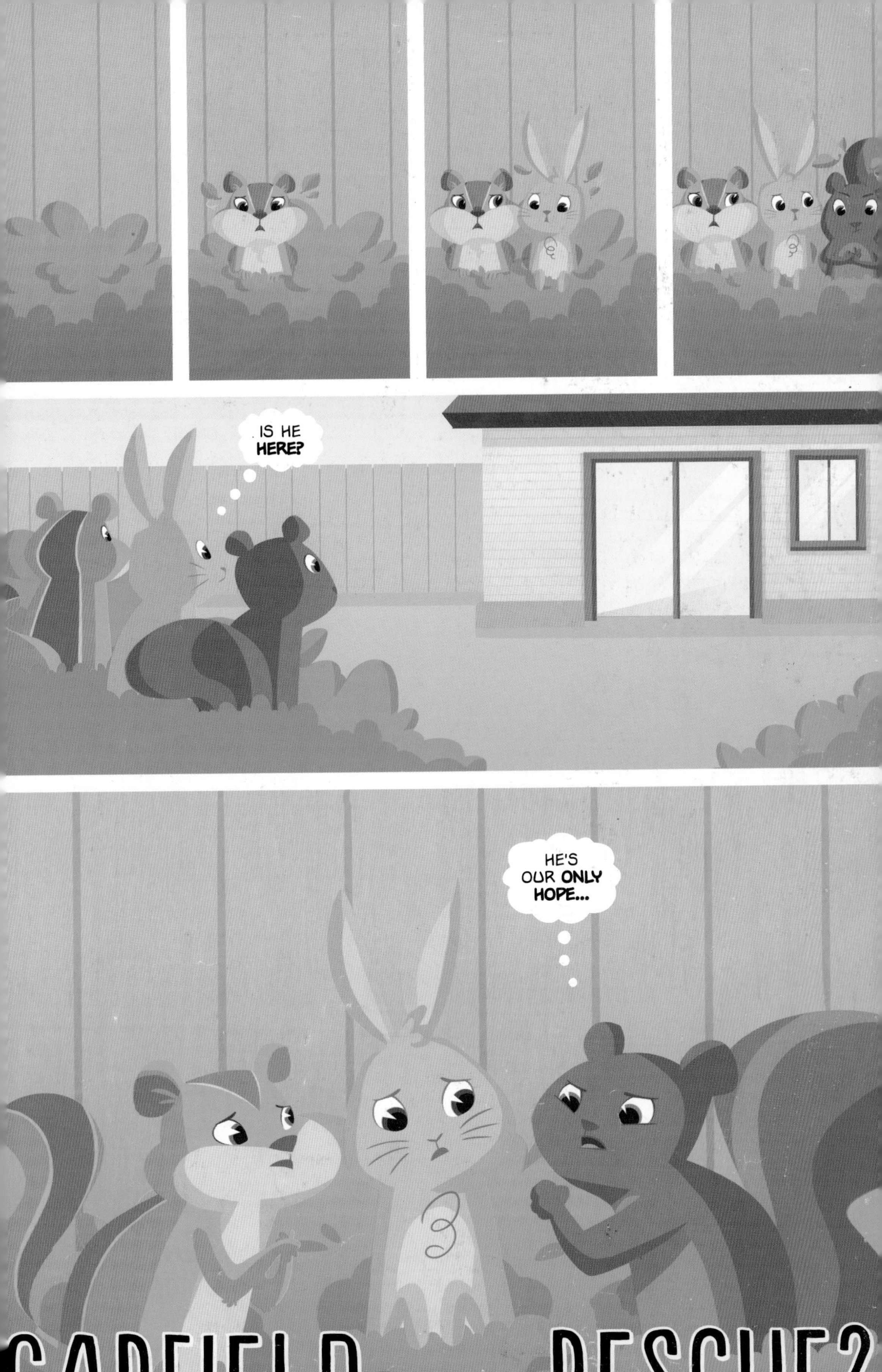
IS HE **HERE?**
HE'S OUR **ONLY HOPE...**

GARFIELD TO THE RESCUE?

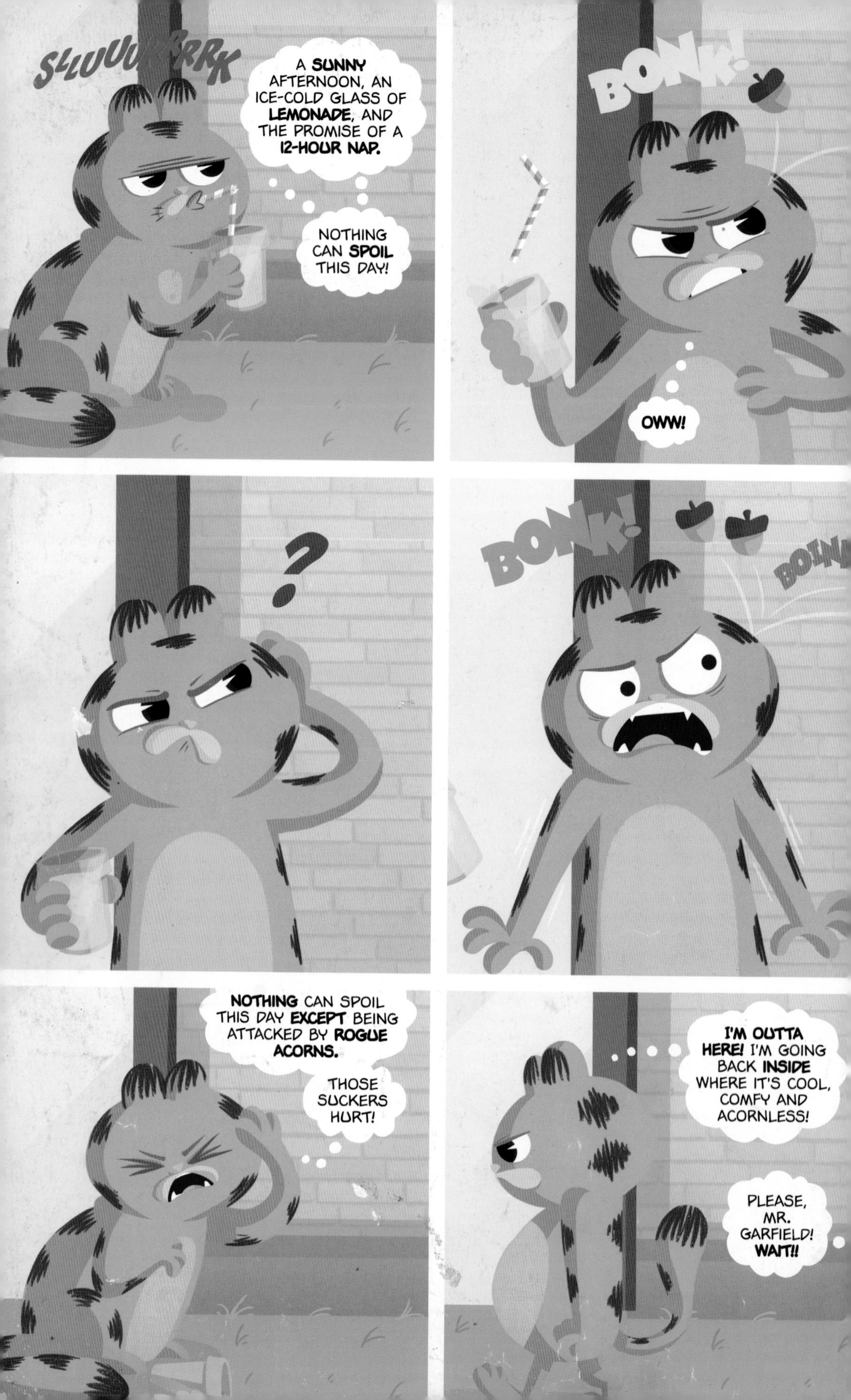
SLLUUURRRRK
A SUNNY AFTERNOON, AN ICE-COLD GLASS OF LEMONADE, AND THE PROMISE OF A 12-HOUR NAP.
NOTHING CAN SPOIL THIS DAY!
BONK!
OWW!
?
BONK!
BOING
NOTHING CAN SPOIL THIS DAY EXCEPT BEING ATTACKED BY ROGUE ACORNS.
THOSE SUCKERS HURT!
I'M OUTTA HERE! I'M GOING BACK INSIDE WHERE IT'S COOL, COMFY AND ACORNLESS!
PLEASE, MR. GARFIELD! WAIT!!

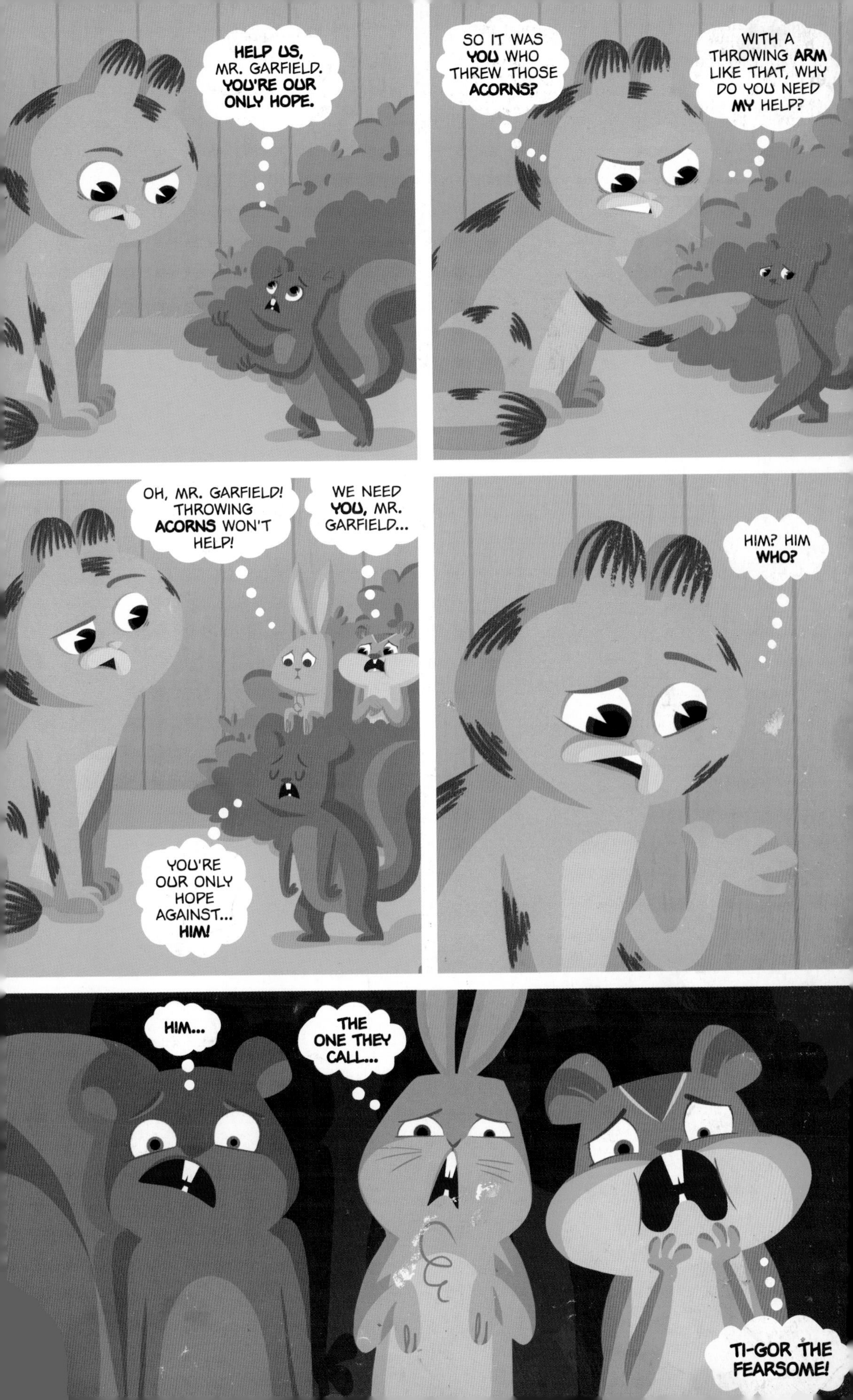
HELP US, MR. GARFIELD. YOU'RE OUR ONLY HOPE.
SO IT WAS YOU WHO THREW THOSE ACORNS?
WITH A THROWING ARM LIKE THAT, WHY DO YOU NEED MY HELP?
OH, MR. GARFIELD! THROWING ACORNS WON'T HELP!
WE NEED YOU, MR. GARFIELD...
YOU'RE OUR ONLY HOPE AGAINST... HIM!
HIM? HIM WHO?
HIM...
THE ONE THEY CALL...
TI-GOR THE FEARSOME!

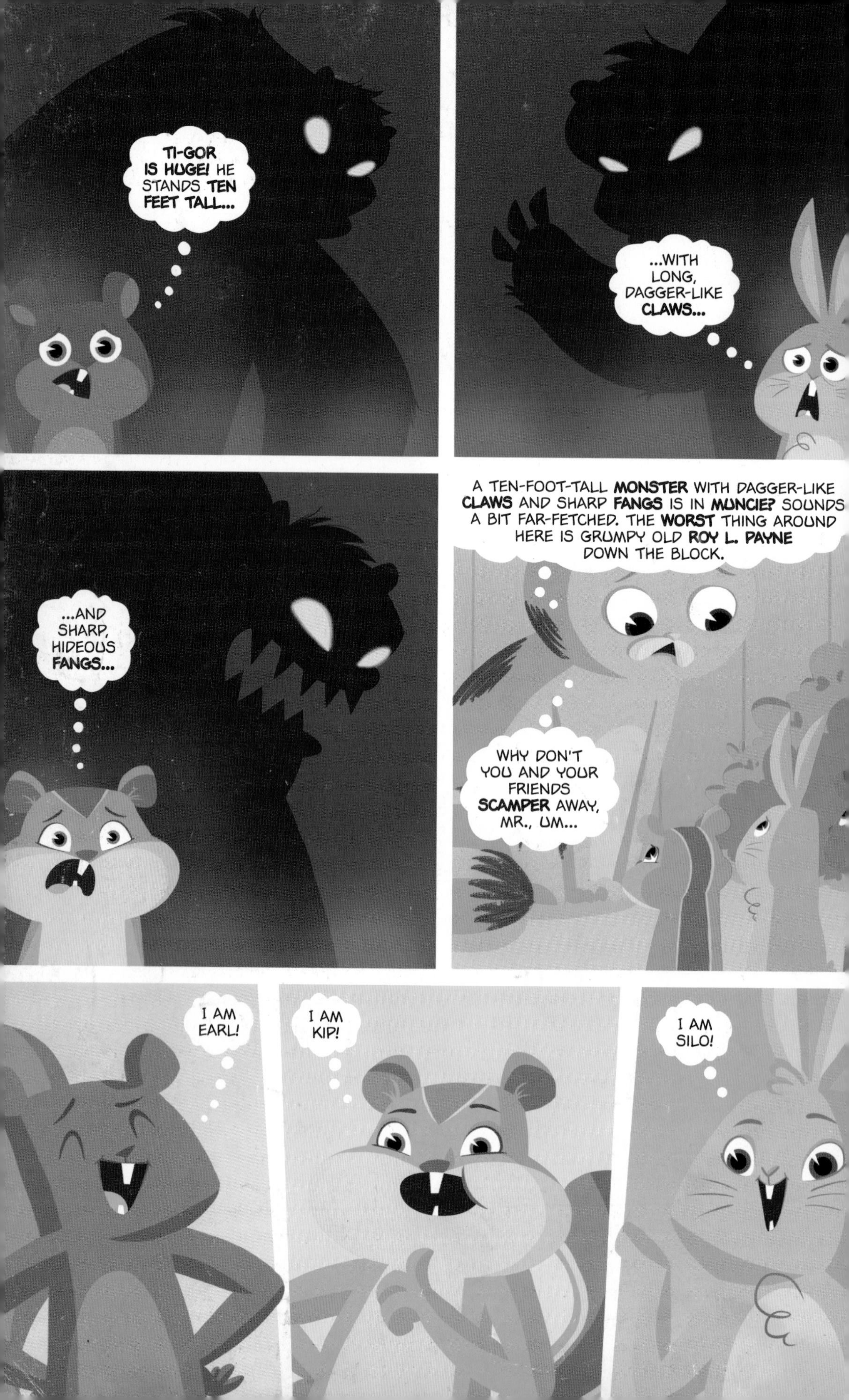
TI-GOR IS HUGE! HE STANDS TEN FEET TALL...
...WITH LONG, DAGGER-LIKE CLAWS...
...AND SHARP, HIDEOUS FANGS...
A TEN-FOOT-TALL MONSTER WITH DAGGER-LIKE CLAWS AND SHARP FANGS IS IN MUNCIE? SOUNDS A BIT FAR-FETCHED. THE WORST THING AROUND HERE IS GRUMPY OLD ROY L. PAYNE DOWN THE BLOCK.
WHY DON'T YOU AND YOUR FRIENDS SCAMPER AWAY, MR., UM...
I AM EARL!
I AM KIP!
I AM SILO!

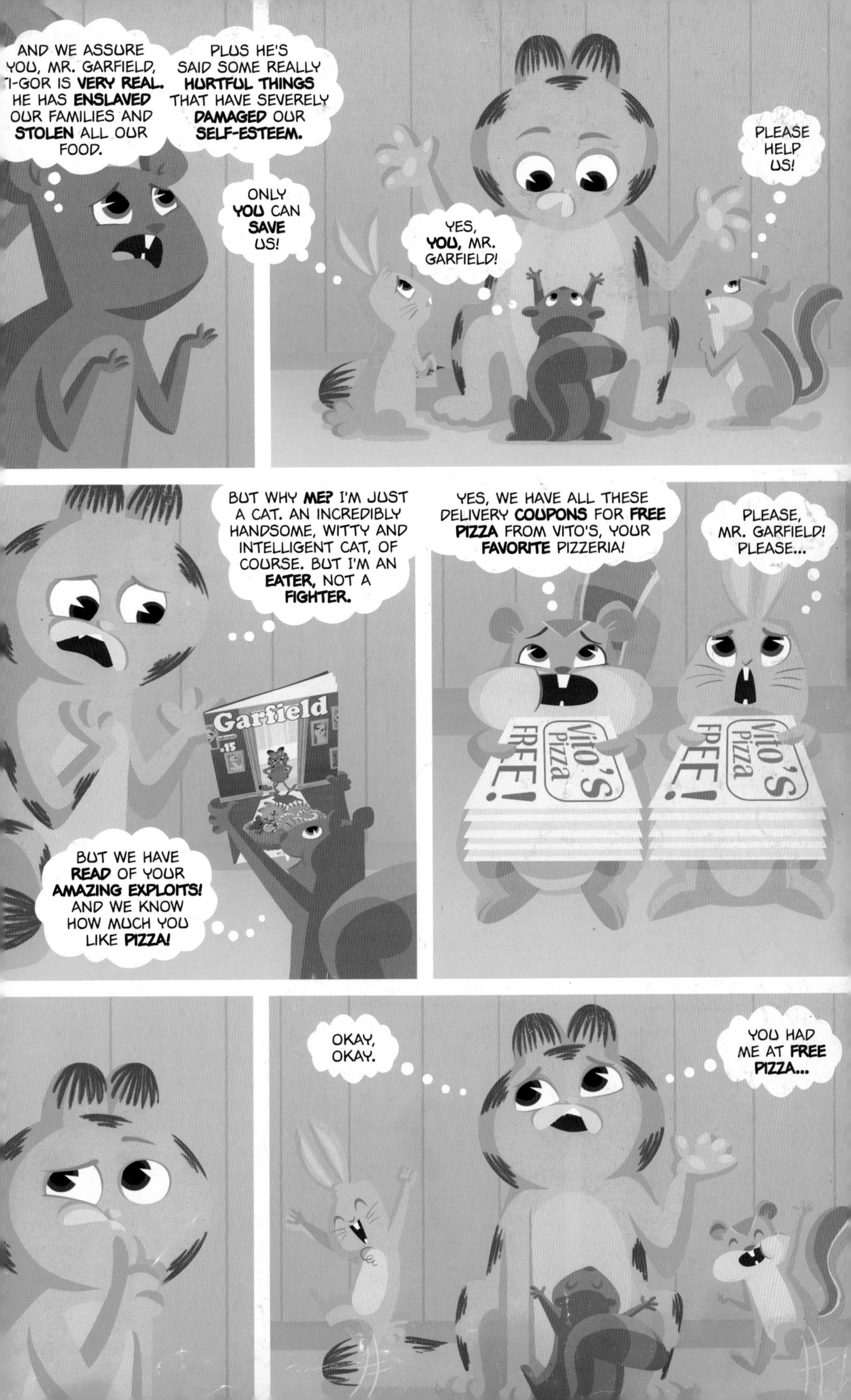
AND WE ASSURE YOU, MR. GARFIELD, TI-GOR IS **VERY REAL.** HE HAS **ENSLAVED** OUR FAMILIES AND **STOLEN** ALL OUR FOOD.
PLUS HE'S SAID SOME REALLY **HURTFUL THINGS** THAT HAVE SEVERELY **DAMAGED** OUR **SELF-ESTEEM.**
ONLY **YOU** CAN **SAVE** US!
YES, **YOU,** MR. GARFIELD!
PLEASE HELP US!
BUT WHY **ME?** I'M JUST A CAT. AN INCREDIBLY HANDSOME, WITTY AND INTELLIGENT CAT, OF COURSE. BUT I'M AN **EATER,** NOT A **FIGHTER.**
Garfield
BUT WE HAVE **READ** OF YOUR **AMAZING EXPLOITS!** AND WE KNOW HOW MUCH YOU LIKE **PIZZA!**
YES, WE HAVE ALL THESE DELIVERY **COUPONS** FOR **FREE PIZZA** FROM VITO'S, YOUR **FAVORITE** PIZZERIA!
PLEASE, MR. GARFIELD! PLEASE...
Vito's Pizza FREE!
Vito's Pizza FREE!
OKAY, OKAY.
YOU HAD ME AT **FREE PIZZA...**

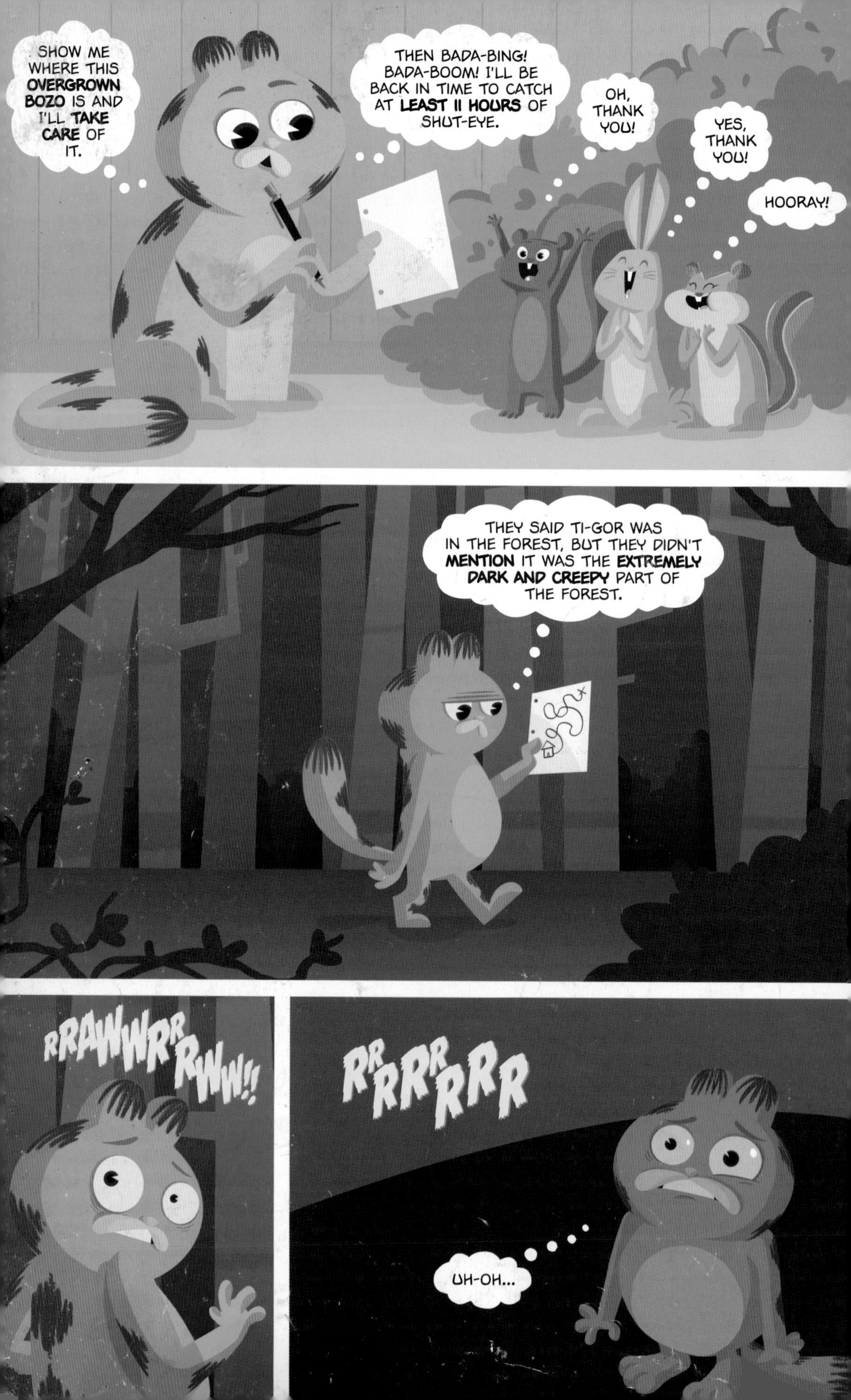
SHOW ME WHERE THIS **OVERGROWN BOZO** IS AND I'LL **TAKE CARE** OF IT.
THEN BADA-BING! BADA-BOOM! I'LL BE BACK IN TIME TO CATCH AT **LEAST 11 HOURS** OF SHUT-EYE.
OH, THANK YOU!
YES, THANK YOU!
HOORAY!
THEY SAID TI-GOR WAS IN THE FOREST, BUT THEY DIDN'T **MENTION** IT WAS THE **EXTREMELY DARK AND CREEPY** PART OF THE FOREST.
RRAWWRRRWW!!
RRRRRRR
UH-OH...

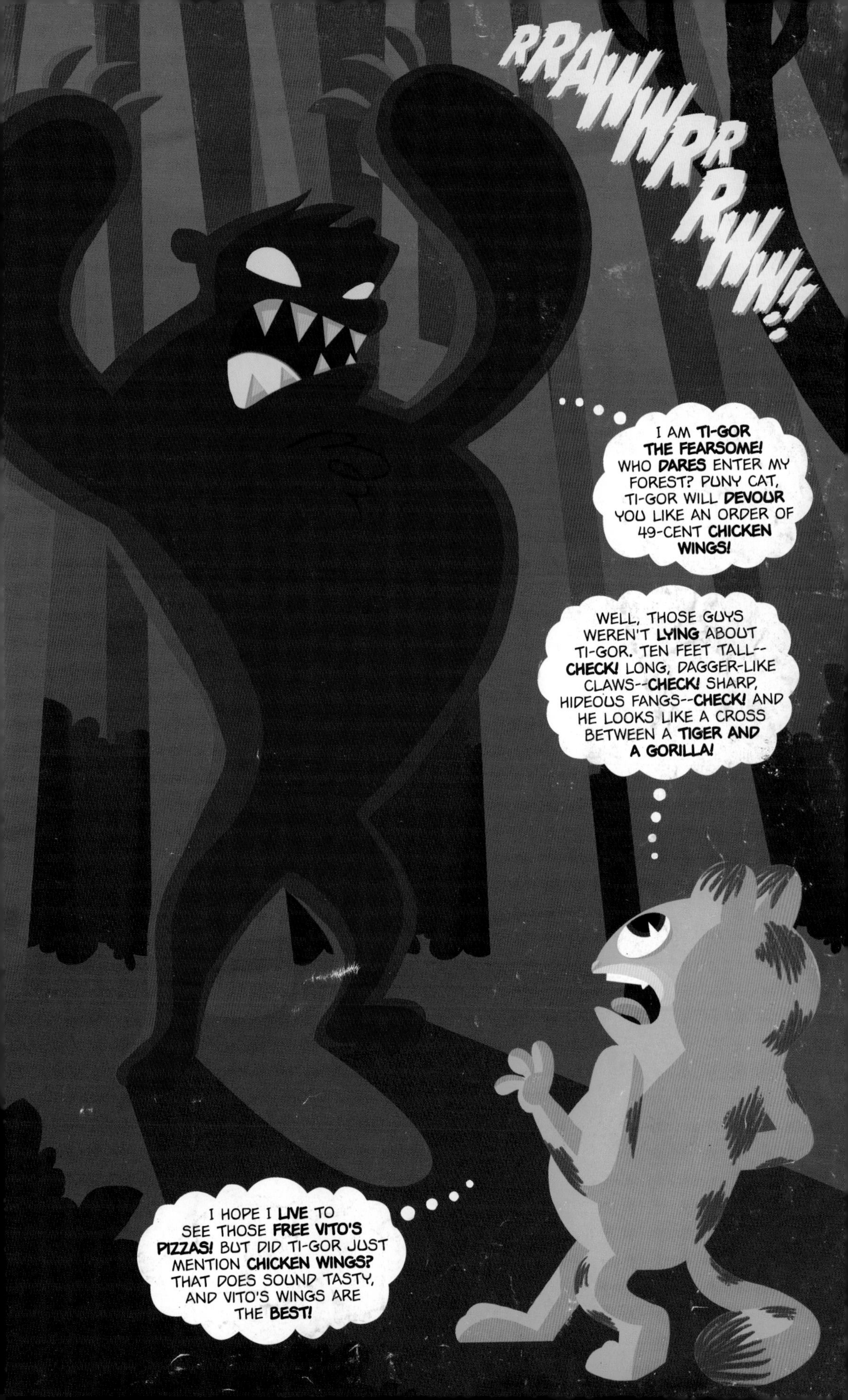
RRAWWRRRWW!!
I AM **TI-GOR THE FEARSOME!** WHO **DARES** ENTER MY FOREST? PUNY CAT, TI-GOR WILL **DEVOUR** YOU LIKE AN ORDER OF 49-CENT **CHICKEN WINGS!**
WELL, THOSE GUYS WEREN'T **LYING** ABOUT TI-GOR. TEN FEET TALL-- **CHECK!** LONG, DAGGER-LIKE CLAWS--**CHECK!** SHARP, HIDEOUS FANGS--**CHECK!** AND HE LOOKS LIKE A CROSS BETWEEN A **TIGER AND A GORILLA!**
I HOPE I **LIVE** TO SEE THOSE **FREE VITO'S PIZZAS!** BUT DID TI-GOR JUST MENTION **CHICKEN WINGS?** THAT DOES SOUND TASTY, AND VITO'S WINGS ARE THE **BEST!**

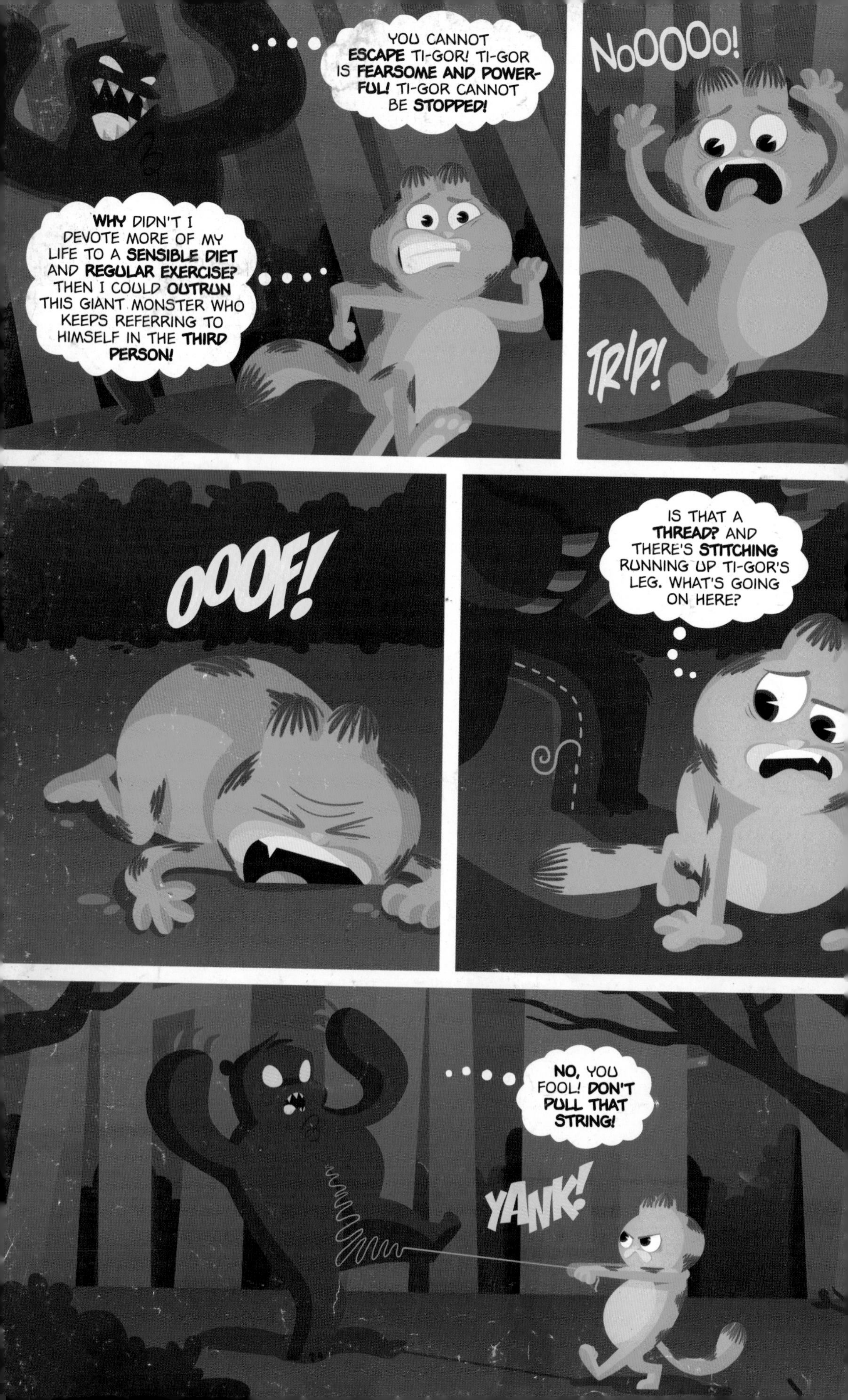
YOU CANNOT ESCAPE TI-GOR! TI-GOR IS FEARSOME AND POWER-FUL! TI-GOR CANNOT BE STOPPED!
WHY DIDN'T I DEVOTE MORE OF MY LIFE TO A SENSIBLE DIET AND REGULAR EXERCISE? THEN I COULD OUTRUN THIS GIANT MONSTER WHO KEEPS REFERRING TO HIMSELF IN THE THIRD PERSON!
NoOOOo!
TRIP!
OOOF!
IS THAT A THREAD? AND THERE'S STITCHING RUNNING UP TI-GOR'S LEG. WHAT'S GOING ON HERE?
NO, YOU FOOL! DON'T PULL THAT STRING!
YANK!

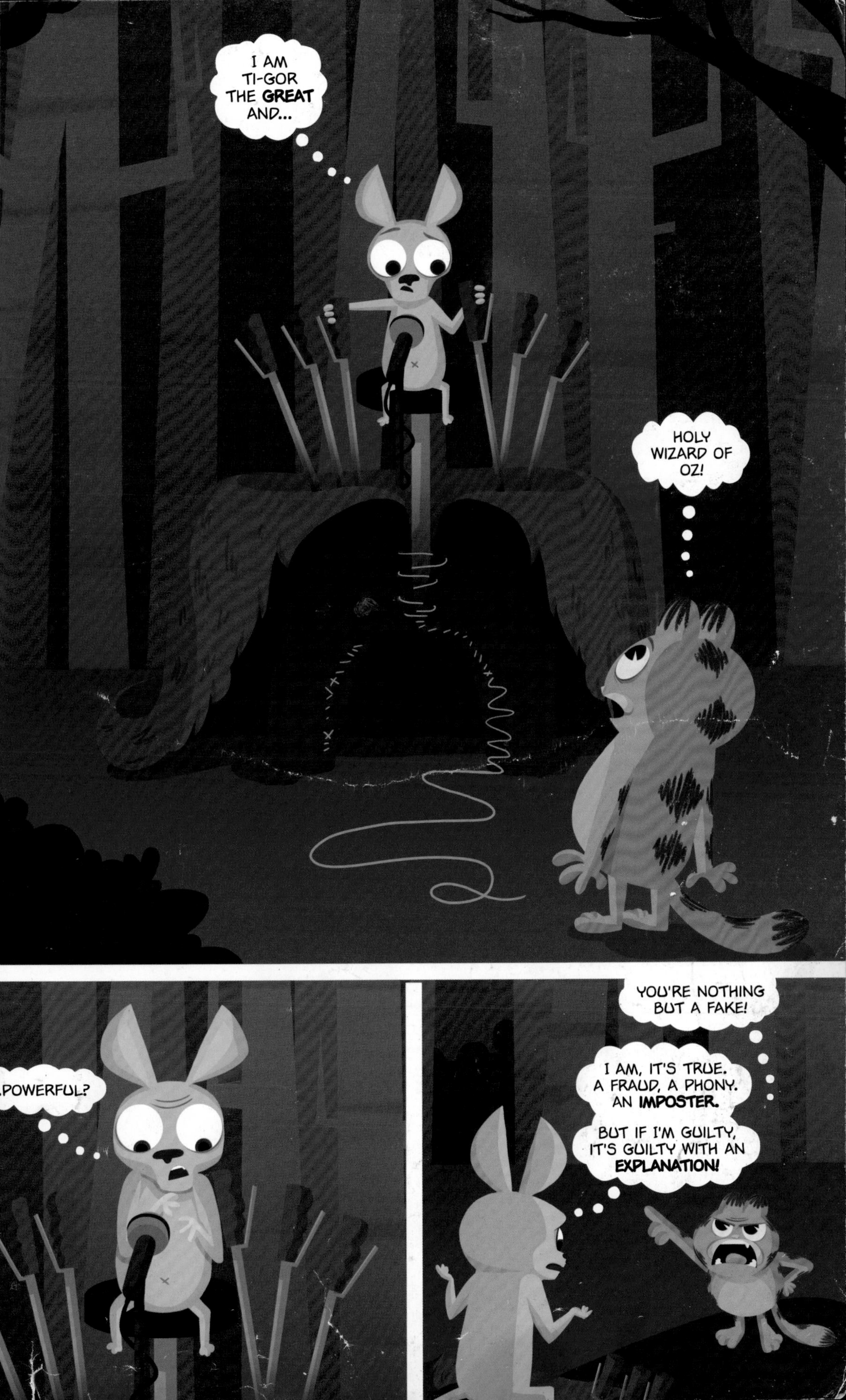
I AM TI-GOR THE GREAT AND...
HOLY WIZARD OF OZ!
...POWERFUL?
YOU'RE NOTHING BUT A FAKE!
I AM, IT'S TRUE. A FRAUD, A PHONY. AN IMPOSTER.
BUT IF I'M GUILTY, IT'S GUILTY WITH AN EXPLANATION!

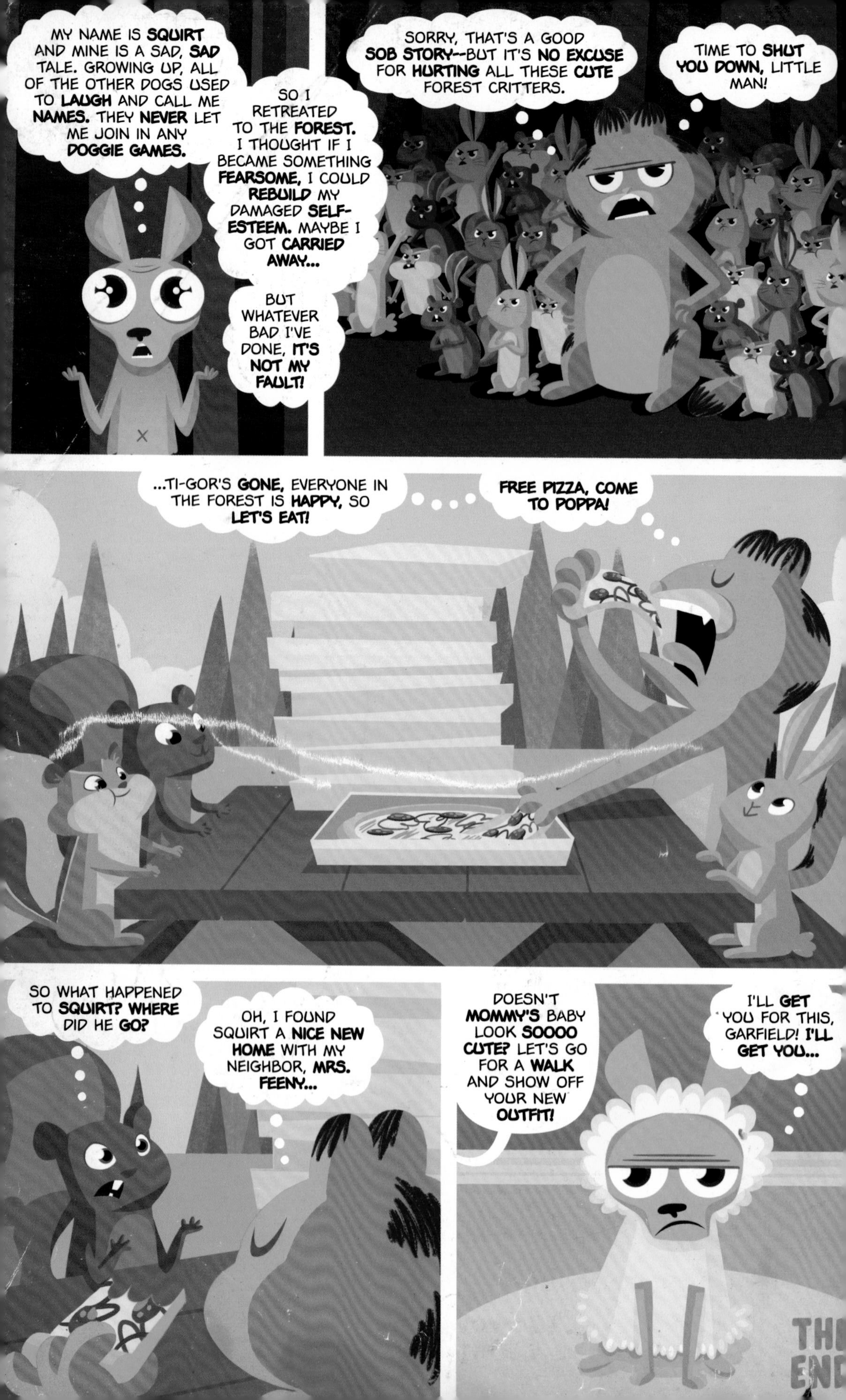
MY NAME IS SQUIRT AND MINE IS A SAD, SAD TALE. GROWING UP, ALL OF THE OTHER DOGS USED TO LAUGH AND CALL ME NAMES. THEY NEVER LET ME JOIN IN ANY DOGGIE GAMES.
SO I RETREATED TO THE FOREST. I THOUGHT IF I BECAME SOMETHING FEARSOME, I COULD REBUILD MY DAMAGED SELF-ESTEEM. MAYBE I GOT CARRIED AWAY...
BUT WHATEVER BAD I'VE DONE, IT'S NOT MY FAULT!
SORRY, THAT'S A GOOD SOB STORY--BUT IT'S NO EXCUSE FOR HURTING ALL THESE CUTE FOREST CRITTERS.
TIME TO SHUT YOU DOWN, LITTLE MAN!
...TI-GOR'S GONE, EVERYONE IN THE FOREST IS HAPPY, SO LET'S EAT!
FREE PIZZA, COME TO POPPA!
SO WHAT HAPPENED TO SQUIRT? WHERE DID HE GO?
OH, I FOUND SQUIRT A NICE NEW HOME WITH MY NEIGHBOR, MRS. FEENY...
DOESN'T MOMMY'S BABY LOOK SOOOO CUTE? LET'S GO FOR A WALK AND SHOW OFF YOUR NEW OUTFIT!
I'LL GET YOU FOR THIS, GARFIELD! I'LL GET YOU...

CHAPTER 3

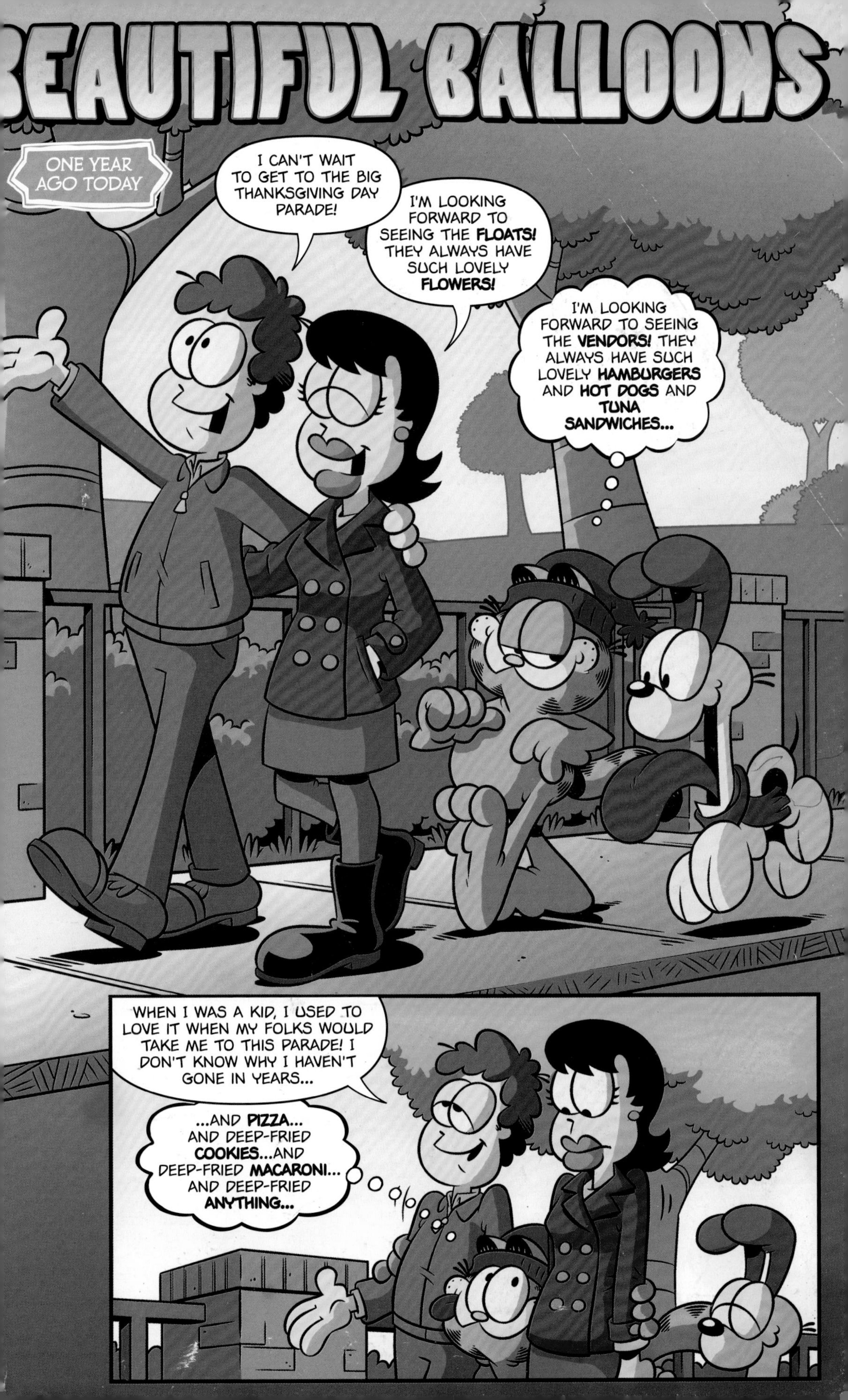
BEAUTIFUL BALLOONS
ONE YEAR AGO TODAY
I CAN'T WAIT TO GET TO THE BIG THANKSGIVING DAY PARADE!
I'M LOOKING FORWARD TO SEEING THE FLOATS! THEY ALWAYS HAVE SUCH LOVELY FLOWERS!
I'M LOOKING FORWARD TO SEEING THE VENDORS! THEY ALWAYS HAVE SUCH LOVELY HAMBURGERS AND HOT DOGS AND TUNA SANDWICHES...
WHEN I WAS A KID, I USED TO LOVE IT WHEN MY FOLKS WOULD TAKE ME TO THIS PARADE! I DON'T KNOW WHY I HAVEN'T GONE IN YEARS...
...AND PIZZA... AND DEEP-FRIED COOKIES...AND DEEP-FRIED MACARONI... AND DEEP-FRIED ANYTHING...

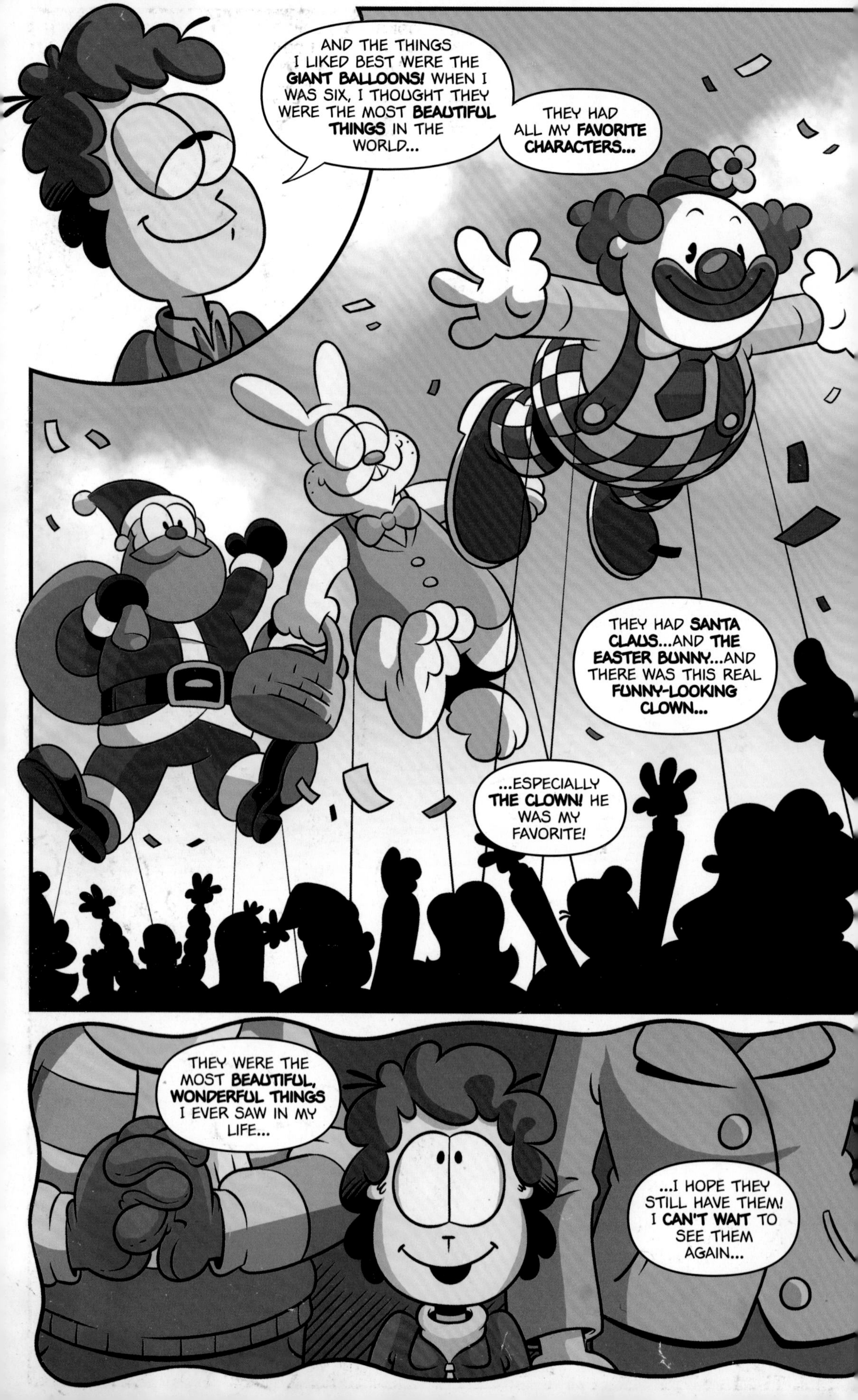
AND THE THINGS I LIKED BEST WERE THE GIANT BALLOONS! WHEN I WAS SIX, I THOUGHT THEY WERE THE MOST BEAUTIFUL THINGS IN THE WORLD...
THEY HAD ALL MY FAVORITE CHARACTERS...
THEY HAD SANTA CLAUS...AND THE EASTER BUNNY...AND THERE WAS THIS REAL FUNNY-LOOKING CLOWN...
...ESPECIALLY THE CLOWN! HE WAS MY FAVORITE!
THEY WERE THE MOST BEAUTIFUL, WONDERFUL THINGS I EVER SAW IN MY LIFE...
...I HOPE THEY STILL HAVE THEM! I CAN'T WAIT TO SEE THEM AGAIN...

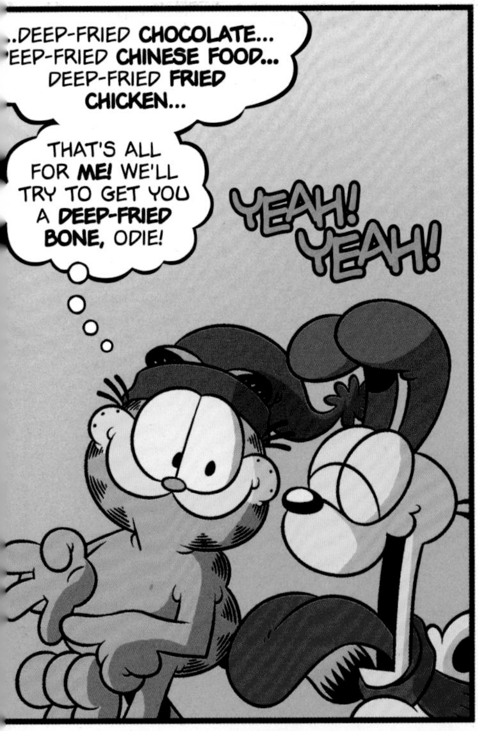
..DEEP-FRIED CHOCOLATE... EEP-FRIED CHINESE FOOD... DEEP-FRIED FRIED CHICKEN...
THAT'S ALL FOR ME! WE'LL TRY TO GET YOU A DEEP-FRIED BONE, ODIE!
YEAH! YEAH!

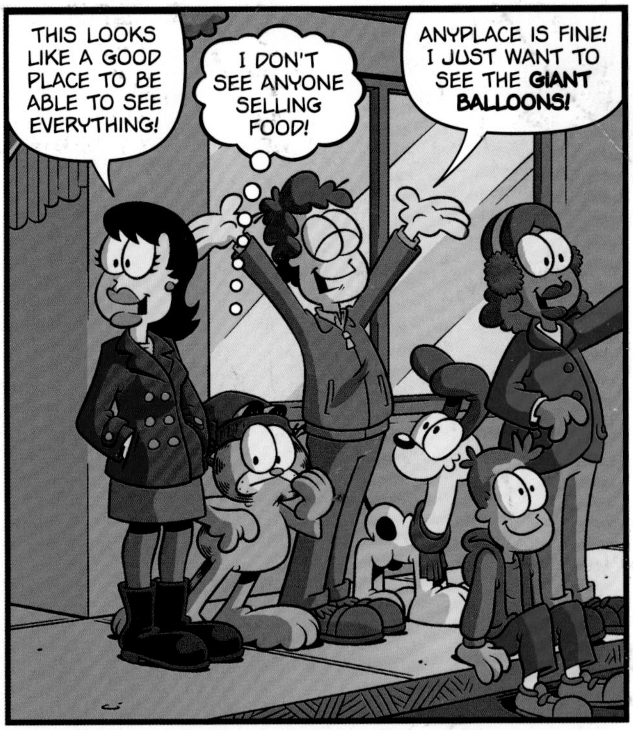
THIS LOOKS LIKE A GOOD PLACE TO BE ABLE TO SEE EVERYTHING!
I DON'T SEE ANYONE SELLING FOOD!
ANYPLACE IS FINE! I JUST WANT TO SEE THE GIANT BALLOONS!

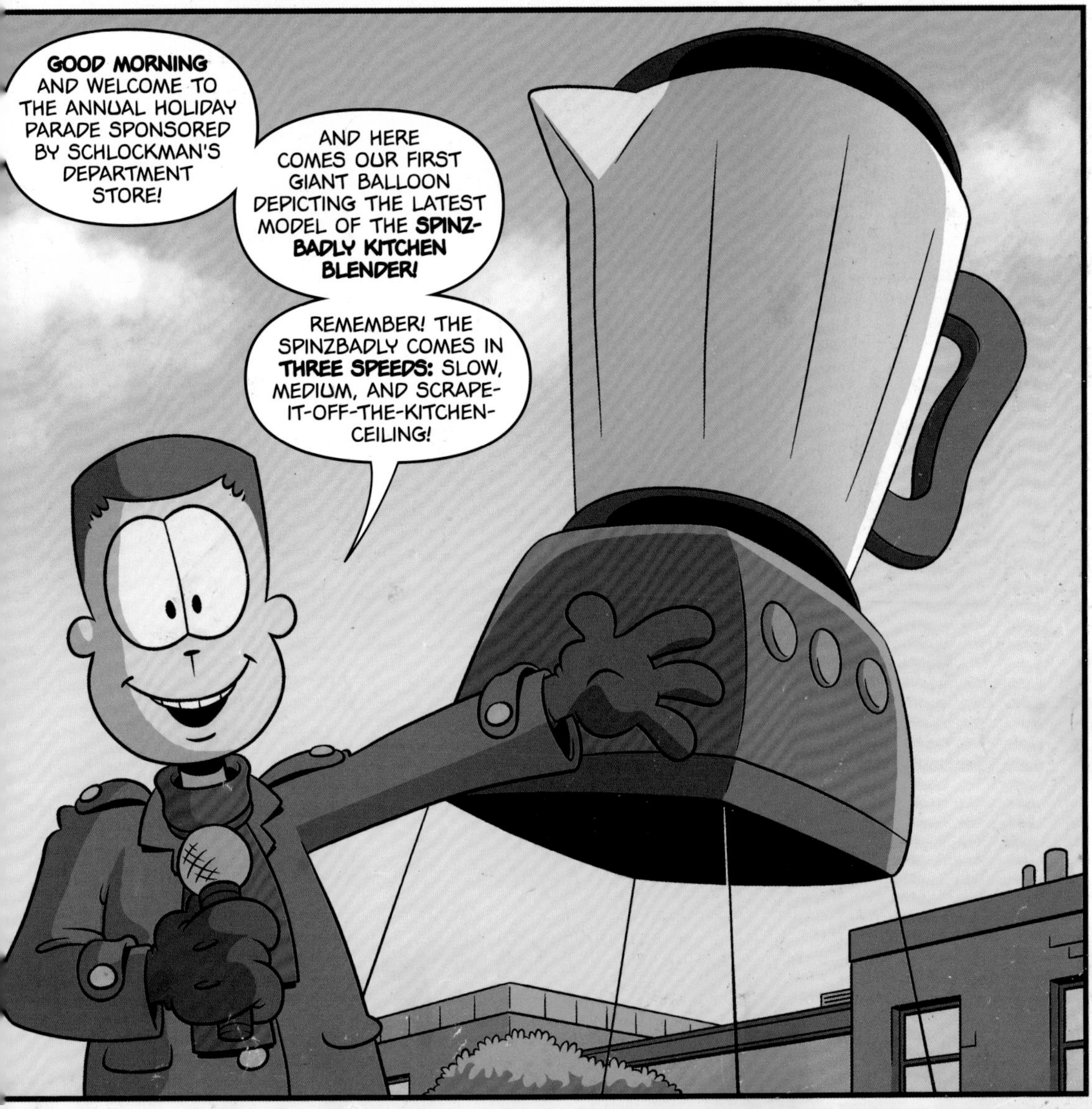
GOOD MORNING AND WELCOME TO THE ANNUAL HOLIDAY PARADE SPONSORED BY SCHLOCKMAN'S DEPARTMENT STORE!
AND HERE COMES OUR FIRST GIANT BALLOON DEPICTING THE LATEST MODEL OF THE SPINZ-BADLY KITCHEN BLENDER!
REMEMBER! THE SPINZBADLY COMES IN THREE SPEEDS: SLOW, MEDIUM, AND SCRAPE-IT-OFF-THE-KITCHEN-CEILING!

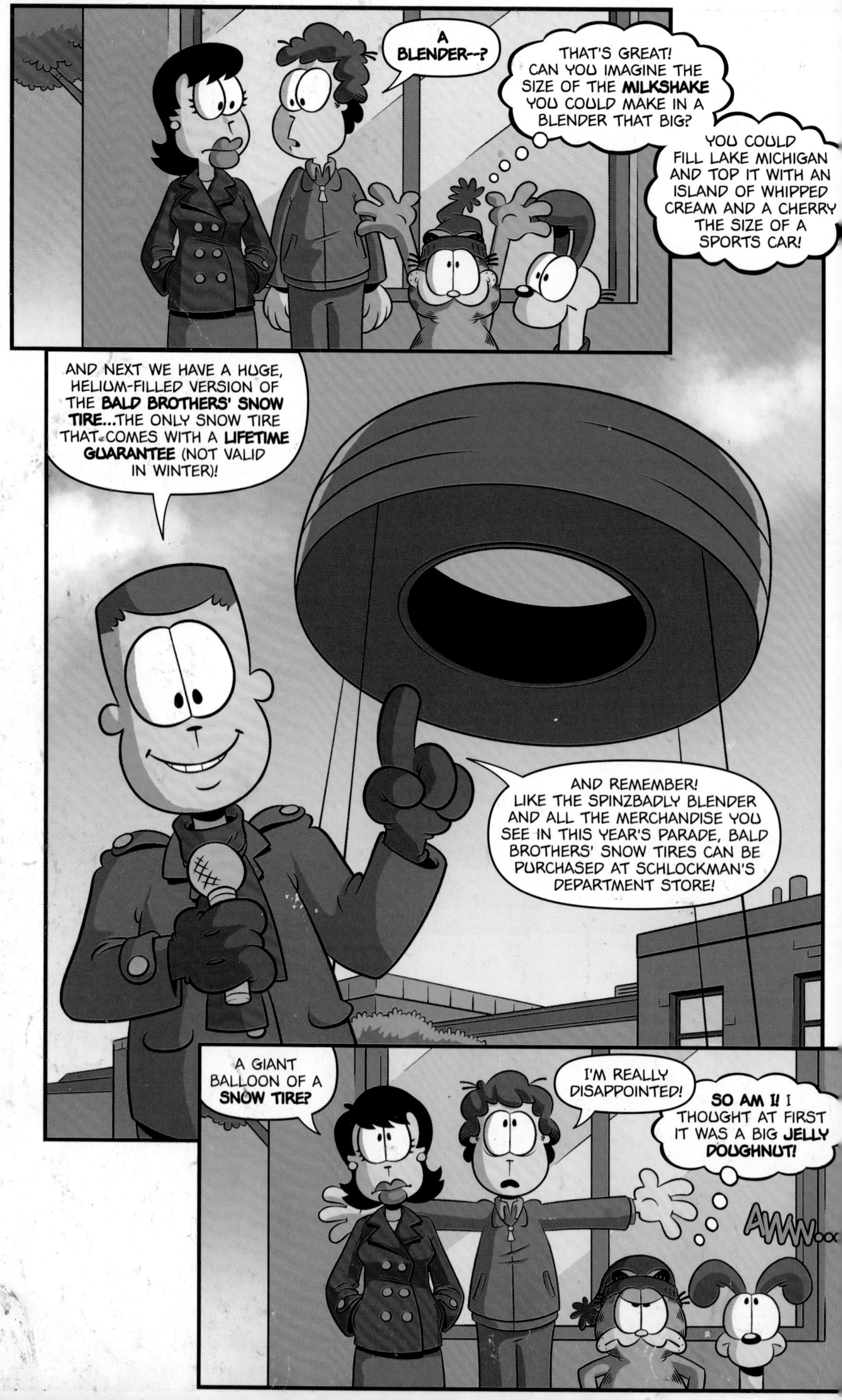

A BLENDER--?
THAT'S GREAT! CAN YOU IMAGINE THE SIZE OF THE MILKSHAKE YOU COULD MAKE IN A BLENDER THAT BIG?
YOU COULD FILL LAKE MICHIGAN AND TOP IT WITH AN ISLAND OF WHIPPED CREAM AND A CHERRY THE SIZE OF A SPORTS CAR!
AND NEXT WE HAVE A HUGE, HELIUM-FILLED VERSION OF THE BALD BROTHERS' SNOW TIRE...THE ONLY SNOW TIRE THAT COMES WITH A LIFETIME GUARANTEE (NOT VALID IN WINTER)!
AND REMEMBER! LIKE THE SPINZBADLY BLENDER AND ALL THE MERCHANDISE YOU SEE IN THIS YEAR'S PARADE, BALD BROTHERS' SNOW TIRES CAN BE PURCHASED AT SCHLOCKMAN'S DEPARTMENT STORE!
A GIANT BALLOON OF A SNOW TIRE?
I'M REALLY DISAPPOINTED!
SO AM I! I THOUGHT AT FIRST IT WAS A BIG JELLY DOUGHNUT!
AWW...

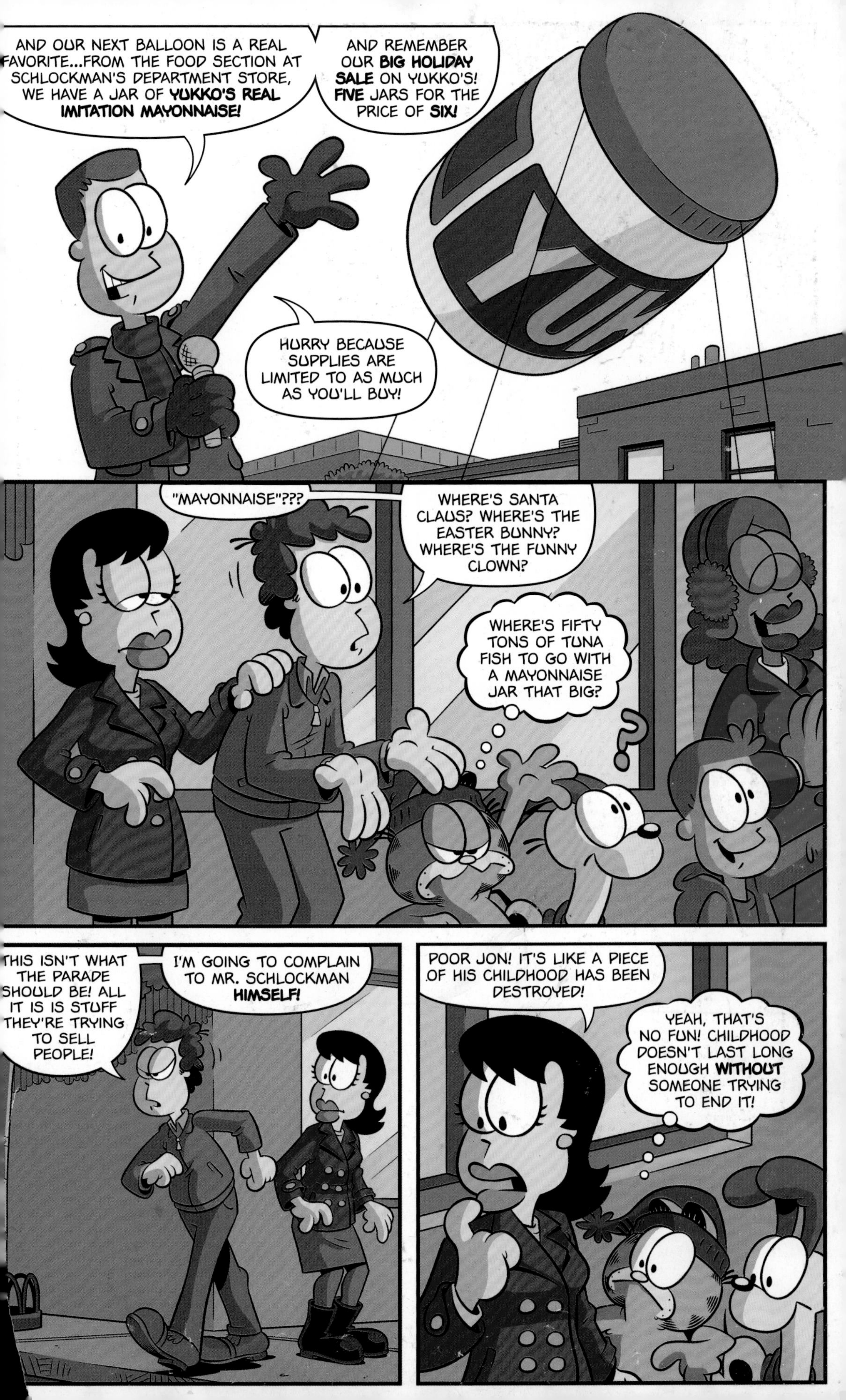

AND OUR NEXT BALLOON IS A REAL FAVORITE...FROM THE FOOD SECTION AT SCHLOCKMAN'S DEPARTMENT STORE, WE HAVE A JAR OF **YUKKO'S REAL IMITATION MAYONNAISE!**
AND REMEMBER OUR **BIG HOLIDAY SALE** ON YUKKO'S! **FIVE** JARS FOR THE PRICE OF **SIX!**
HURRY BECAUSE SUPPLIES ARE LIMITED TO AS MUCH AS YOU'LL BUY!
"MAYONNAISE"???
WHERE'S SANTA CLAUS? WHERE'S THE EASTER BUNNY? WHERE'S THE FUNNY CLOWN?
WHERE'S FIFTY TONS OF TUNA FISH TO GO WITH A MAYONNAISE JAR THAT BIG?
?
THIS ISN'T WHAT THE PARADE SHOULD BE! ALL IT IS IS STUFF THEY'RE TRYING TO SELL PEOPLE!
I'M GOING TO COMPLAIN TO MR. SCHLOCKMAN **HIMSELF!**
POOR JON! IT'S LIKE A PIECE OF HIS CHILDHOOD HAS BEEN DESTROYED!
YEAH, THAT'S NO FUN! CHILDHOOD DOESN'T LAST LONG ENOUGH **WITHOUT** SOMEONE TRYING TO END IT!

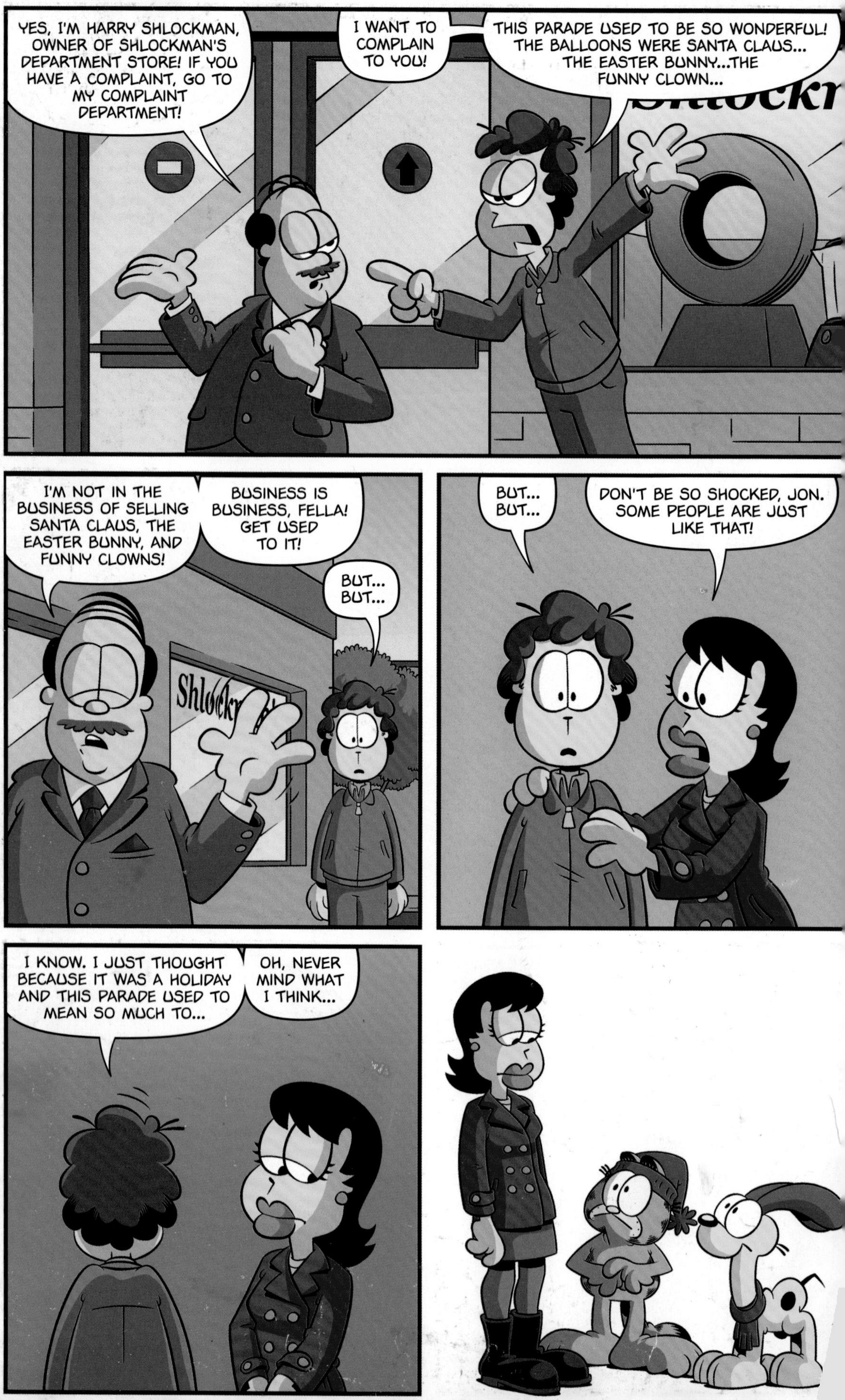
YES, I'M HARRY SHLOCKMAN, OWNER OF SHLOCKMAN'S DEPARTMENT STORE! IF YOU HAVE A COMPLAINT, GO TO MY COMPLAINT DEPARTMENT!
I WANT TO COMPLAIN TO YOU!
THIS PARADE USED TO BE SO WONDERFUL! THE BALLOONS WERE SANTA CLAUS... THE EASTER BUNNY...THE FUNNY CLOWN...
I'M NOT IN THE BUSINESS OF SELLING SANTA CLAUS, THE EASTER BUNNY, AND FUNNY CLOWNS!
BUSINESS IS BUSINESS, FELLA! GET USED TO IT!
BUT... BUT...
Shlockr
BUT... BUT...
DON'T BE SO SHOCKED, JON. SOME PEOPLE ARE JUST LIKE THAT!
I KNOW. I JUST THOUGHT BECAUSE IT WAS A HOLIDAY AND THIS PARADE USED TO MEAN SO MUCH TO...
OH, NEVER MIND WHAT I THINK...

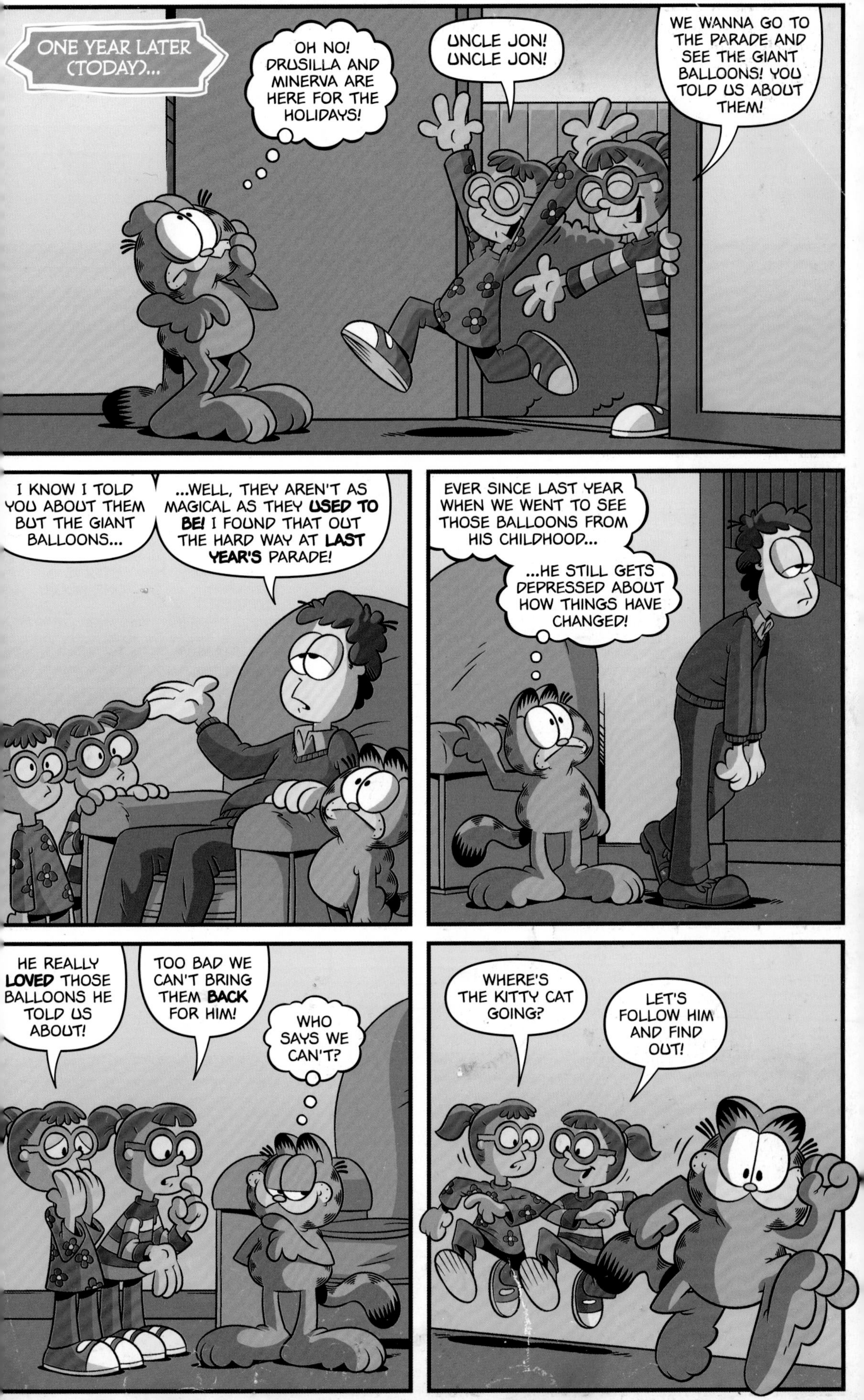

ONE YEAR LATER (TODAY)...
OH NO! DRUSILLA AND MINERVA ARE HERE FOR THE HOLIDAYS!
UNCLE JON! UNCLE JON!
WE WANNA GO TO THE PARADE AND SEE THE GIANT BALLOONS! YOU TOLD US ABOUT THEM!
I KNOW I TOLD YOU ABOUT THEM BUT THE GIANT BALLOONS...
...WELL, THEY AREN'T AS MAGICAL AS THEY **USED TO BE!** I FOUND THAT OUT THE HARD WAY AT **LAST YEAR'S** PARADE!
EVER SINCE LAST YEAR WHEN WE WENT TO SEE THOSE BALLOONS FROM HIS CHILDHOOD...
...HE STILL GETS DEPRESSED ABOUT HOW THINGS HAVE CHANGED!
HE REALLY **LOVED** THOSE BALLOONS HE TOLD US ABOUT!
TOO BAD WE CAN'T BRING THEM **BACK** FOR HIM!
WHO SAYS WE CAN'T?
WHERE'S THE KITTY CAT GOING?
LET'S FOLLOW HIM AND FIND OUT!

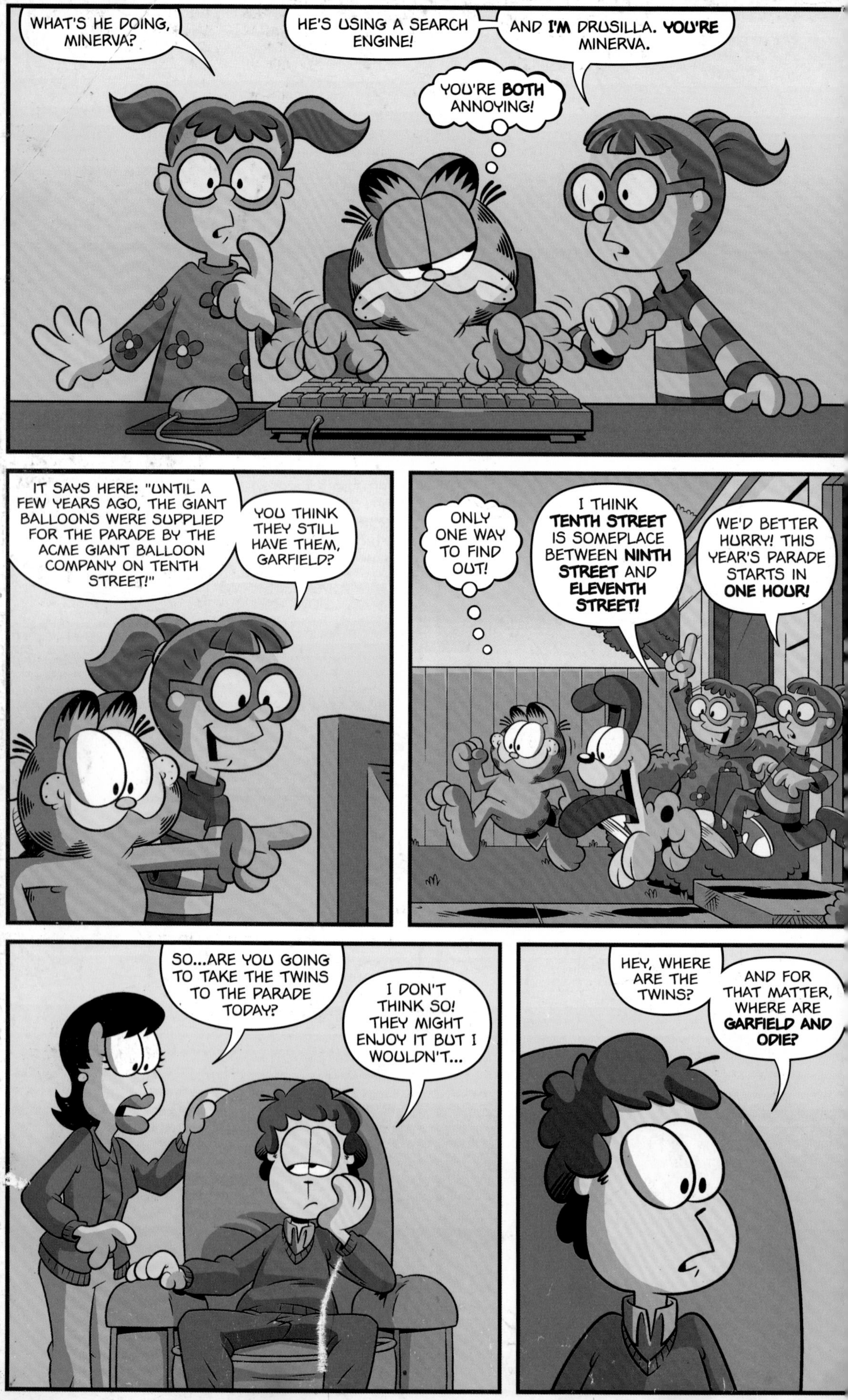
WHAT'S HE DOING, MINERVA?
HE'S USING A SEARCH ENGINE!
AND I'M DRUSILLA. YOU'RE MINERVA.
YOU'RE BOTH ANNOYING!
IT SAYS HERE: "UNTIL A FEW YEARS AGO, THE GIANT BALLOONS WERE SUPPLIED FOR THE PARADE BY THE ACME GIANT BALLOON COMPANY ON TENTH STREET!"
YOU THINK THEY STILL HAVE THEM, GARFIELD?
ONLY ONE WAY TO FIND OUT!
I THINK TENTH STREET IS SOMEPLACE BETWEEN NINTH STREET AND ELEVENTH STREET!
WE'D BETTER HURRY! THIS YEAR'S PARADE STARTS IN ONE HOUR!
SO...ARE YOU GOING TO TAKE THE TWINS TO THE PARADE TODAY?
I DON'T THINK SO! THEY MIGHT ENJOY IT BUT I WOULDN'T...
HEY, WHERE ARE THE TWINS?
AND FOR THAT MATTER, WHERE ARE GARFIELD AND ODIE?

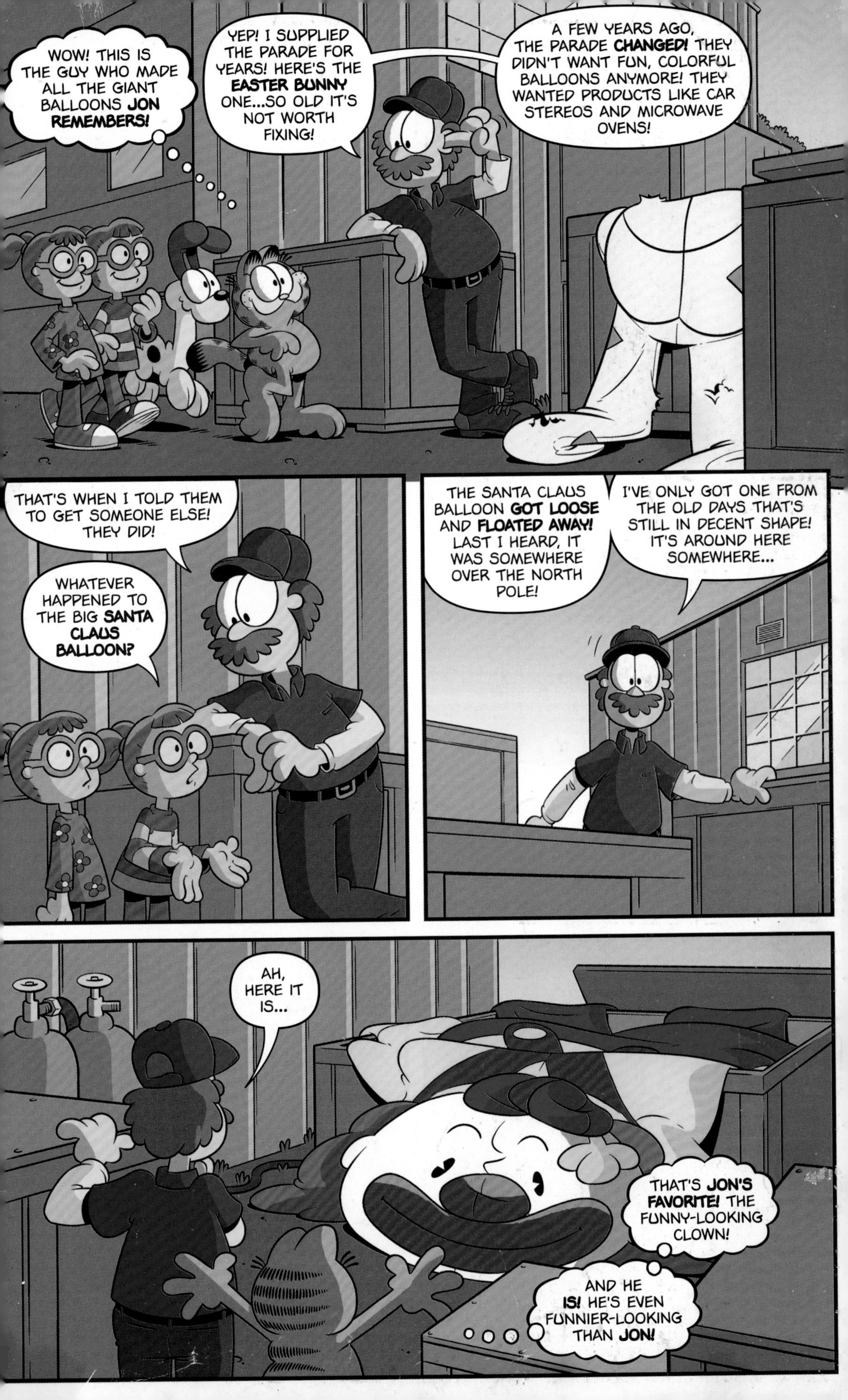
WOW! THIS IS THE GUY WHO MADE ALL THE GIANT BALLOONS JON REMEMBERS!
YEP! I SUPPLIED THE PARADE FOR YEARS! HERE'S THE EASTER BUNNY ONE...SO OLD IT'S NOT WORTH FIXING!
A FEW YEARS AGO, THE PARADE CHANGED! THEY DIDN'T WANT FUN, COLORFUL BALLOONS ANYMORE! THEY WANTED PRODUCTS LIKE CAR STEREOS AND MICROWAVE OVENS!
THAT'S WHEN I TOLD THEM TO GET SOMEONE ELSE! THEY DID!
WHATEVER HAPPENED TO THE BIG SANTA CLAUS BALLOON?
THE SANTA CLAUS BALLOON GOT LOOSE AND FLOATED AWAY! LAST I HEARD, IT WAS SOMEWHERE OVER THE NORTH POLE!
I'VE ONLY GOT ONE FROM THE OLD DAYS THAT'S STILL IN DECENT SHAPE! IT'S AROUND HERE SOMEWHERE...
AH, HERE IT IS...
THAT'S JON'S FAVORITE! THE FUNNY-LOOKING CLOWN!
AND HE IS! HE'S EVEN FUNNIER-LOOKING THAN JON!

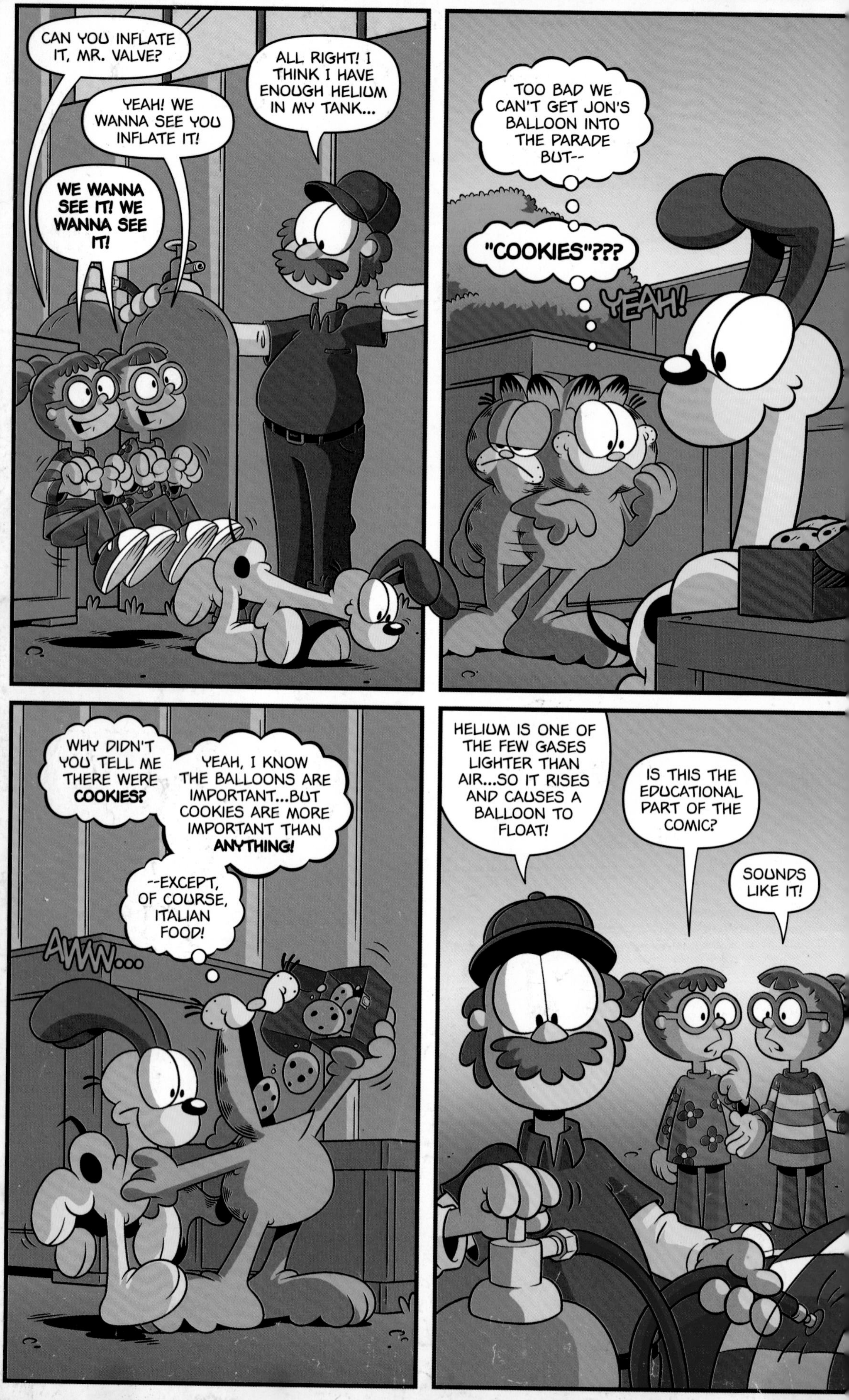
CAN YOU INFLATE IT, MR. VALVE?
YEAH! WE WANNA SEE YOU INFLATE IT!
WE WANNA SEE IT! WE WANNA SEE IT!
ALL RIGHT! I THINK I HAVE ENOUGH HELIUM IN MY TANK...
TOO BAD WE CAN'T GET JON'S BALLOON INTO THE PARADE BUT--
"COOKIES"???
YEAH!
WHY DIDN'T YOU TELL ME THERE WERE COOKIES?
YEAH, I KNOW THE BALLOONS ARE IMPORTANT...BUT COOKIES ARE MORE IMPORTANT THAN ANYTHING!
--EXCEPT, OF COURSE, ITALIAN FOOD!
AWW...
HELIUM IS ONE OF THE FEW GASES LIGHTER THAN AIR...SO IT RISES AND CAUSES A BALLOON TO FLOAT!
IS THIS THE EDUCATIONAL PART OF THE COMIC?
SOUNDS LIKE IT!

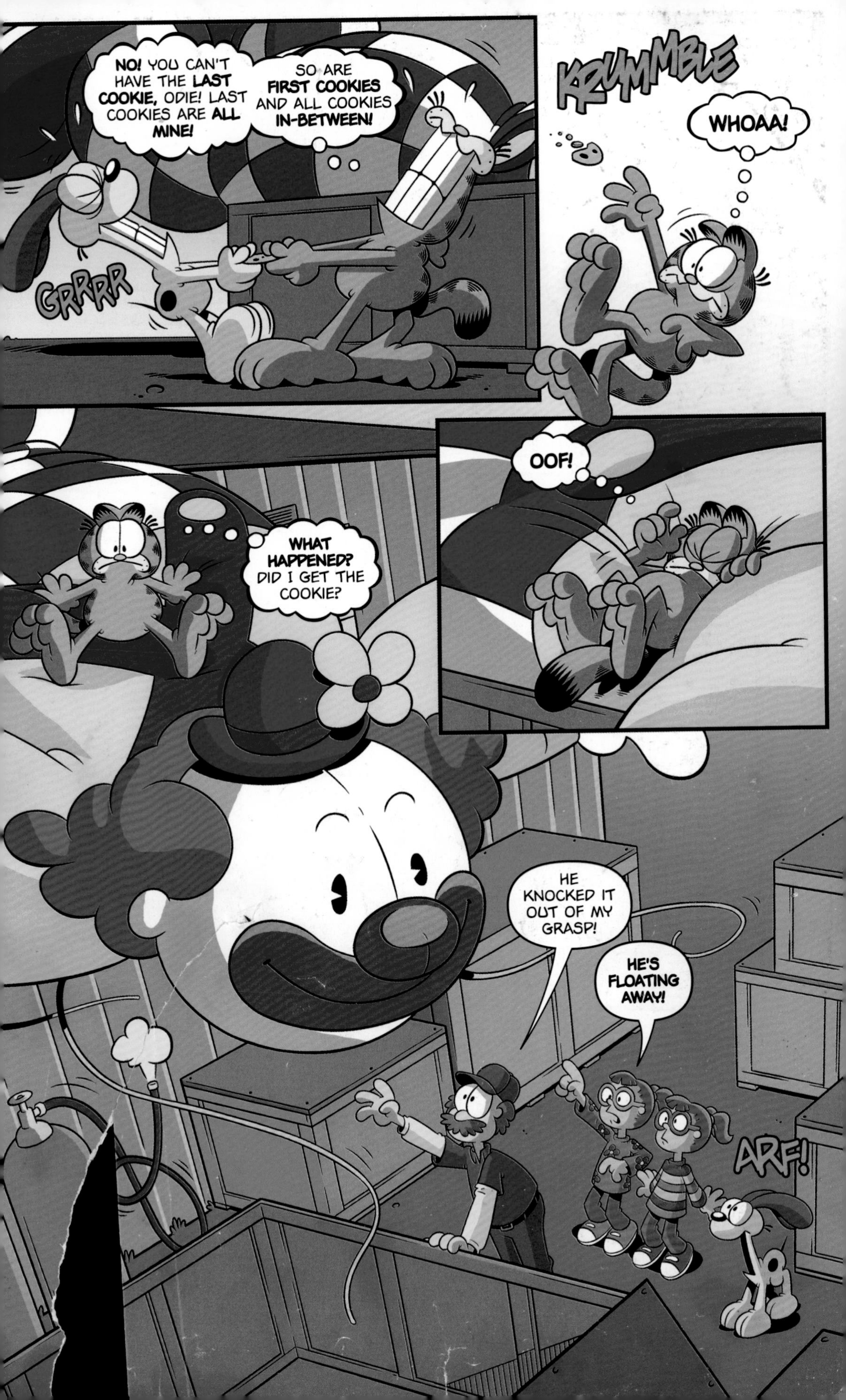
NO! YOU CAN'T HAVE THE LAST COOKIE, ODIE! LAST COOKIES ARE ALL MINE!
SO ARE FIRST COOKIES AND ALL COOKIES IN-BETWEEN!
GRRRR
KRUMMBLE
WHOAA!
OOF!
WHAT HAPPENED? DID I GET THE COOKIE?
HE KNOCKED IT OUT OF MY GRASP!
HE'S FLOATING AWAY!
ARF!

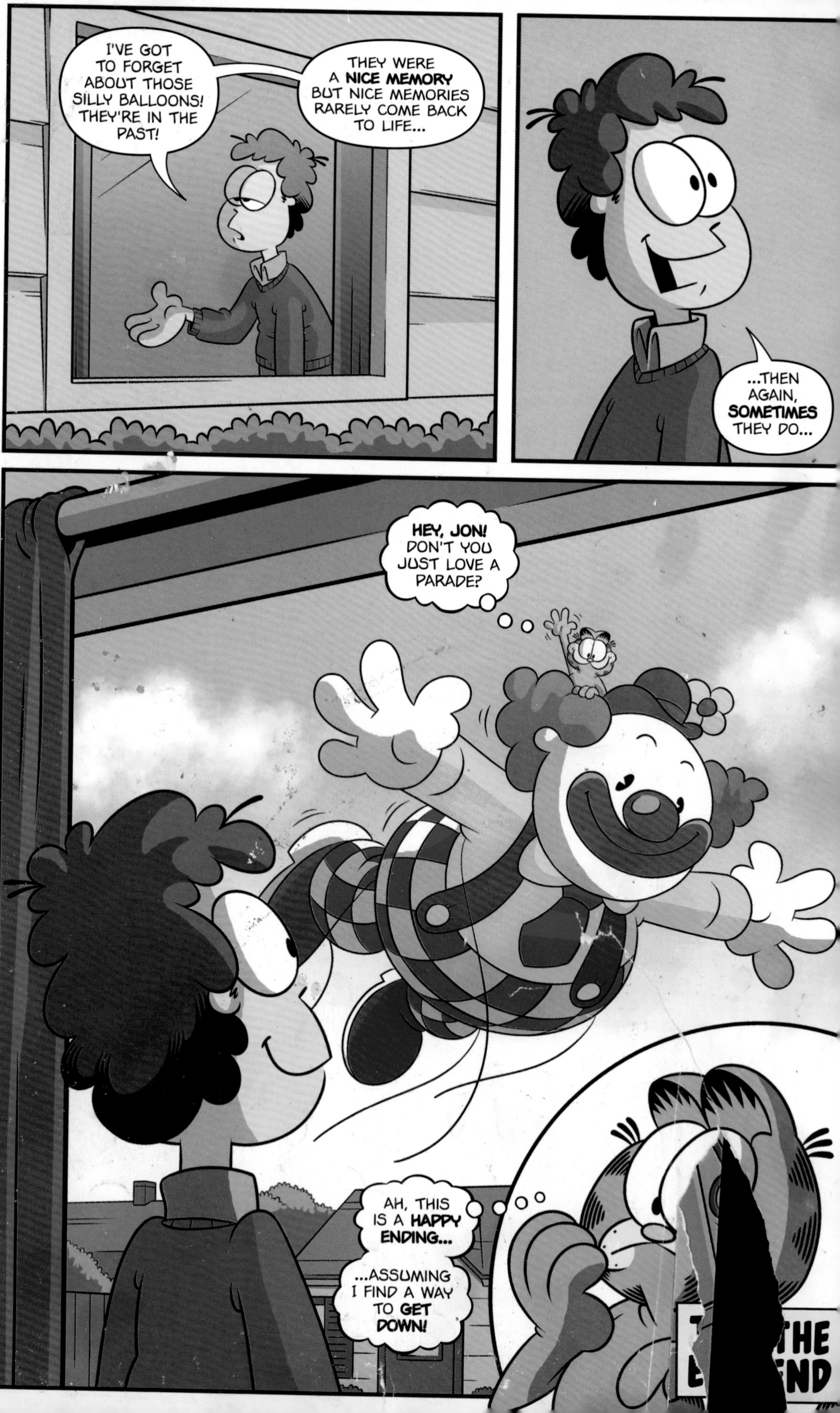

I'VE GOT TO FORGET ABOUT THOSE SILLY BALLOONS! THEY'RE IN THE PAST!
THEY WERE A **NICE MEMORY** BUT NICE MEMORIES RARELY COME BACK TO LIFE...
...THEN AGAIN, **SOMETIMES** THEY DO...
HEY, JON! DON'T YOU JUST LOVE A PARADE?
AH, THIS IS A **HAPPY ENDING...**
...ASSUMING I FIND A WAY TO **GET DOWN!**

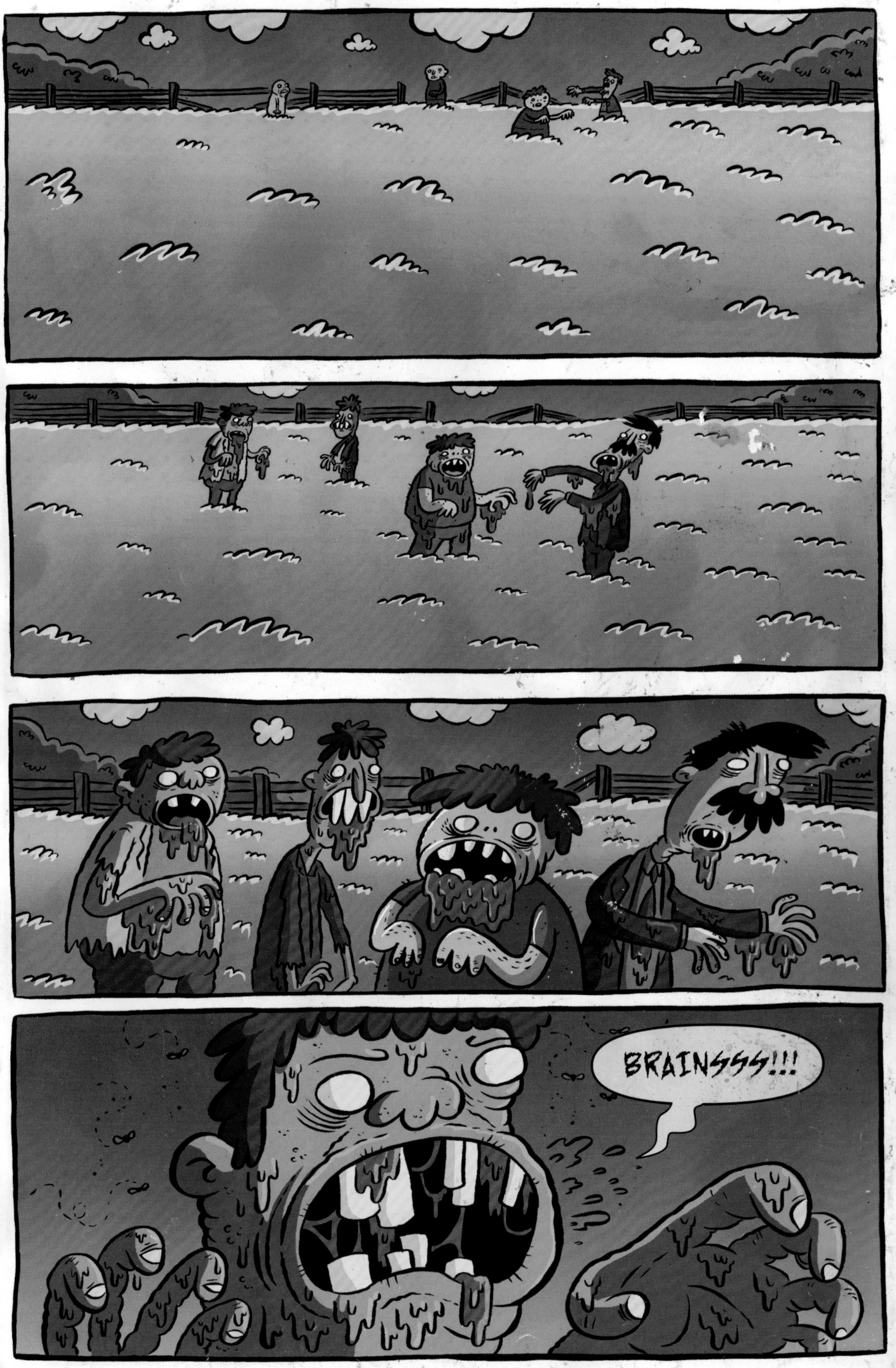
BRAINSSS!!!

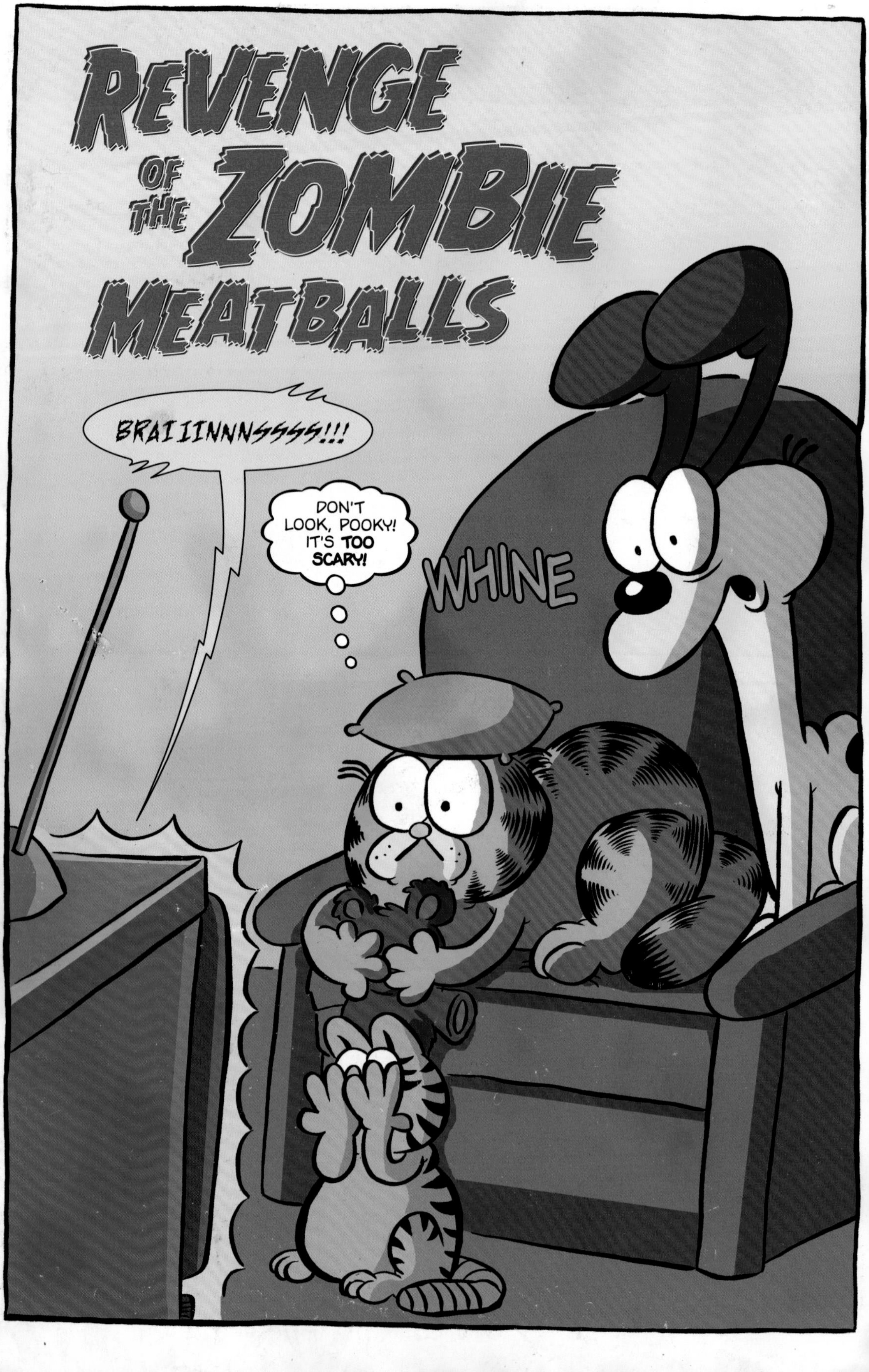
REVENGE OF THE ZOMBIE MEATBALLS
BRAIIINNNSSSS!!!
DON'T LOOK, POOKY! IT'S TOO SCARY!
WHINE

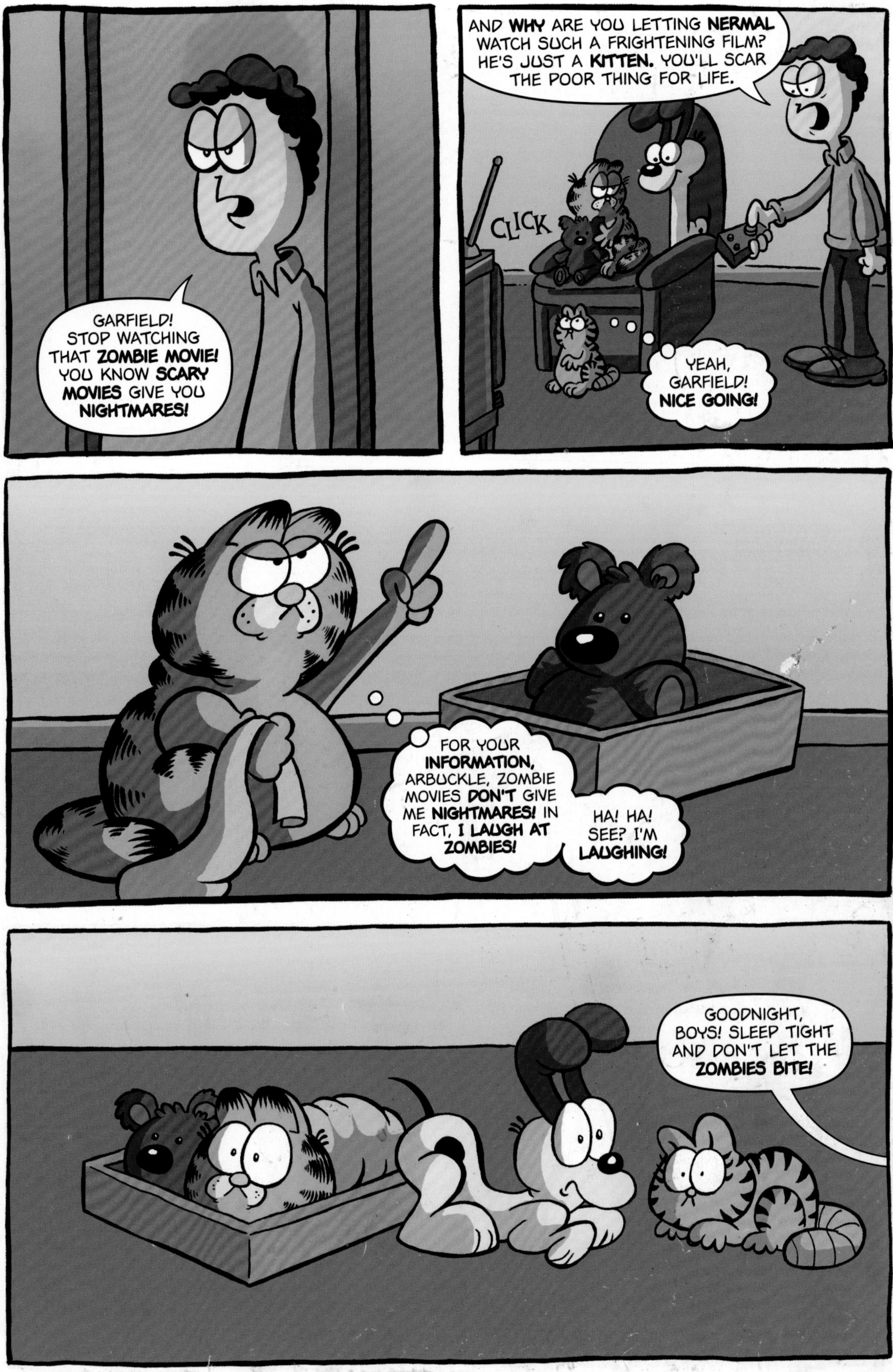
GARFIELD! STOP WATCHING THAT **ZOMBIE MOVIE!** YOU KNOW **SCARY MOVIES** GIVE YOU **NIGHTMARES!**
AND **WHY** ARE YOU LETTING **NERMAL** WATCH SUCH A FRIGHTENING FILM? HE'S JUST A **KITTEN.** YOU'LL SCAR THE POOR THING FOR LIFE.
CLICK
YEAH, GARFIELD! **NICE GOING!**
FOR YOUR **INFORMATION,** ARBUCKLE, ZOMBIE MOVIES **DON'T** GIVE ME **NIGHTMARES!** IN FACT, **I LAUGH AT ZOMBIES!**
HA! HA! SEE? I'M **LAUGHING!**
GOODNIGHT, BOYS! SLEEP TIGHT AND DON'T LET THE **ZOMBIES BITE!**

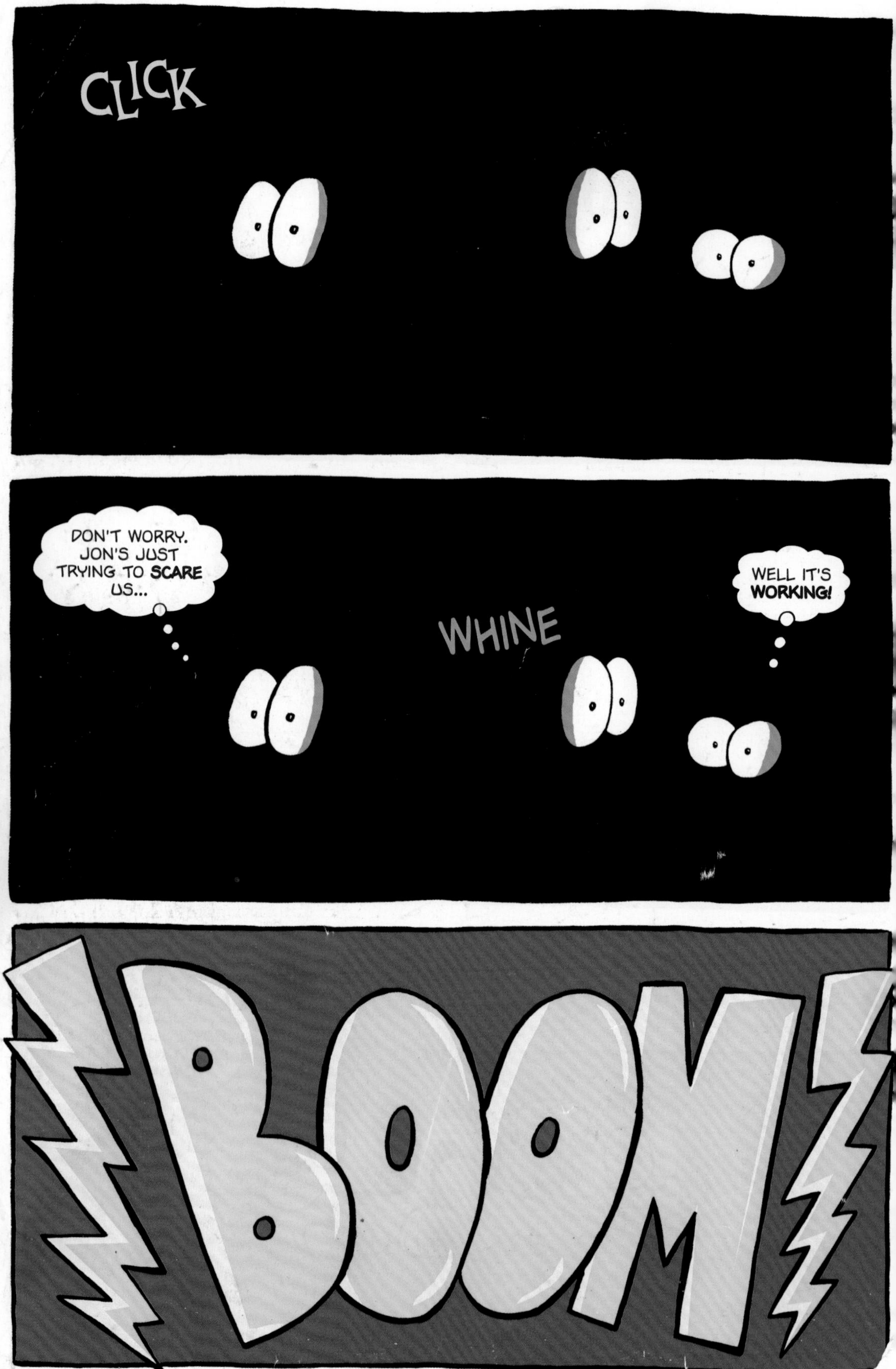
CLICK
DON'T WORRY. JON'S JUST TRYING TO SCARE US...
WHINE
WELL IT'S WORKING!
BOOM!

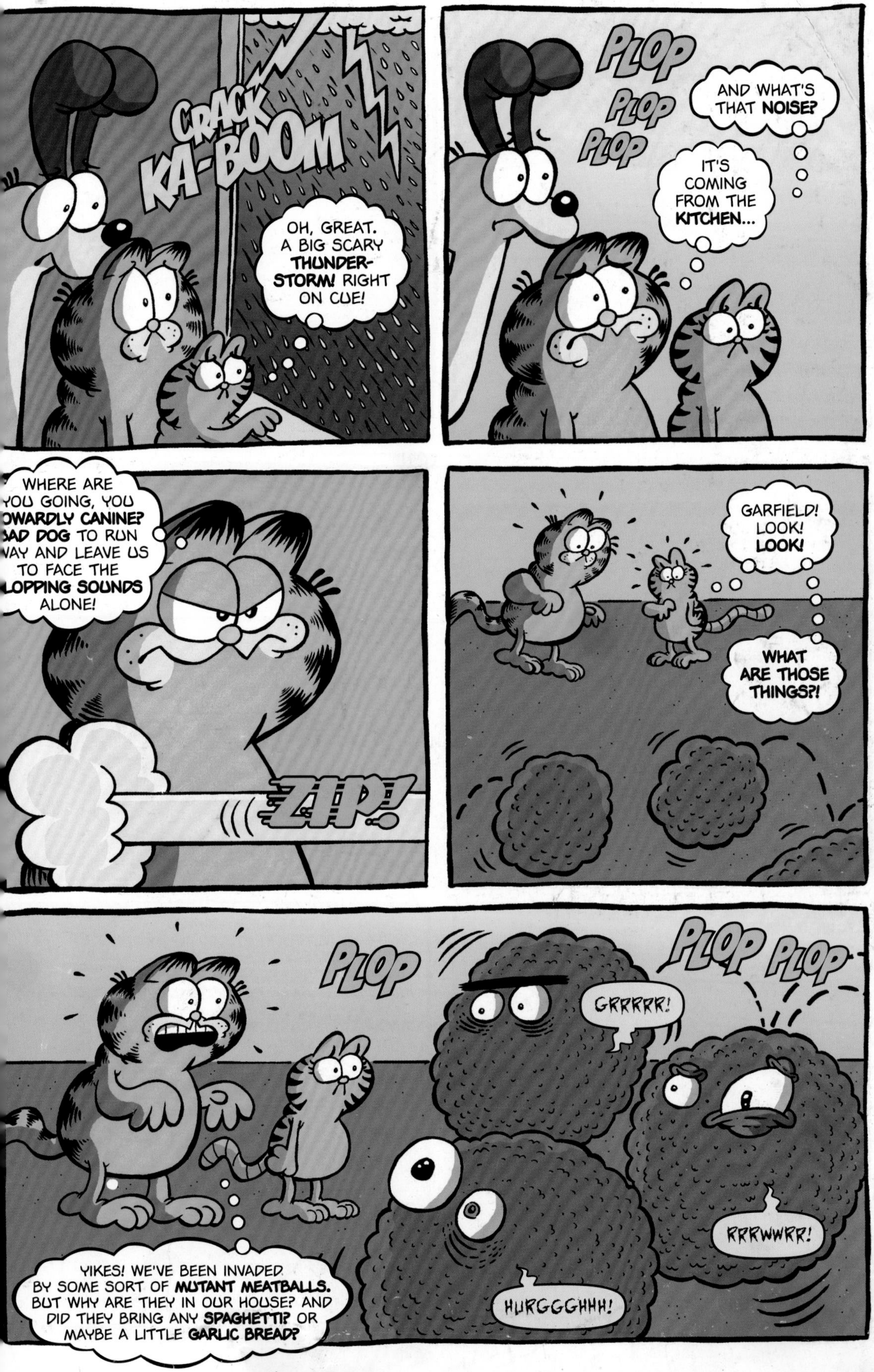
CRACK
KA-BOOM
OH, GREAT. A BIG SCARY THUNDER-STORM! RIGHT ON CUE!
PLOP PLOP PLOP
AND WHAT'S THAT NOISE?
IT'S COMING FROM THE KITCHEN...
WHERE ARE YOU GOING, YOU OWARDLY CANINE? AD DOG TO RUN WAY AND LEAVE US TO FACE THE LOPPING SOUNDS ALONE!
ZIP!
GARFIELD! LOOK! LOOK!
WHAT ARE THOSE THINGS?!
PLOP
PLOP PLOP
GRRRRR!
RRRWWRR!
HURGGGHHH!
YIKES! WE'VE BEEN INVADED BY SOME SORT OF MUTANT MEATBALLS. BUT WHY ARE THEY IN OUR HOUSE? AND DID THEY BRING ANY SPAGHETTI? OR MAYBE A LITTLE GARLIC BREAD?

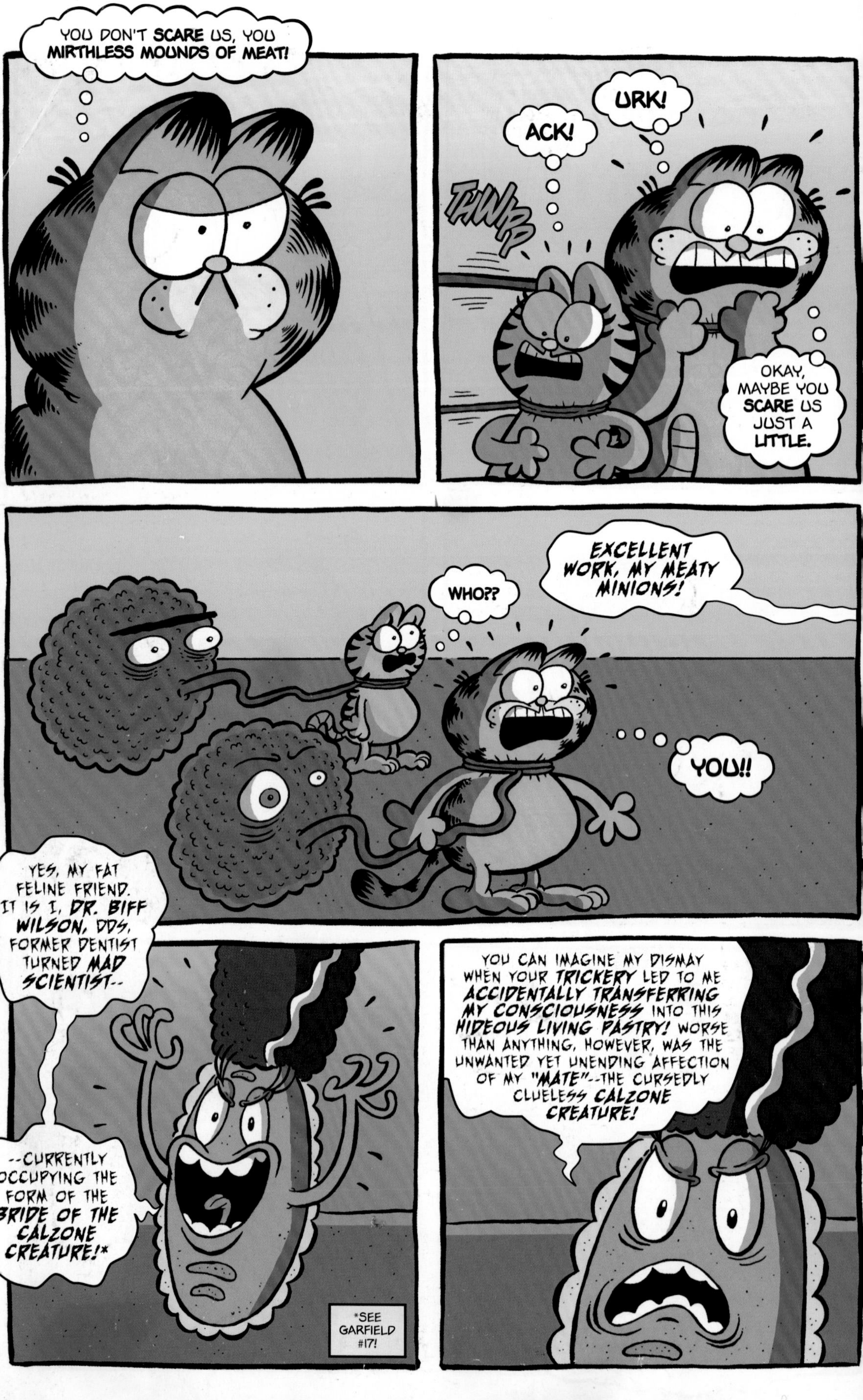
YOU DON'T SCARE US, YOU MIRTHLESS MOUNDS OF MEAT!
THWIPP
ACK!
URK!
OKAY, MAYBE YOU SCARE US JUST A LITTLE.
EXCELLENT WORK, MY MEATY MINIONS!
WHO??
YOU!!
YES, MY FAT FELINE FRIEND. IT IS I, DR. BIFF WILSON, DDS, FORMER DENTIST TURNED MAD SCIENTIST--
--CURRENTLY OCCUPYING THE FORM OF THE BRIDE OF THE CALZONE CREATURE!*
*SEE GARFIELD #17!
YOU CAN IMAGINE MY DISMAY WHEN YOUR TRICKERY LED TO ME ACCIDENTALLY TRANSFERRING MY CONSCIOUSNESS INTO THIS HIDEOUS LIVING PASTRY! WORSE THAN ANYTHING, HOWEVER, WAS THE UNWANTED YET UNENDING AFFECTION OF MY "MATE"--THE CURSEDLY CLUELESS CALZONE CREATURE!

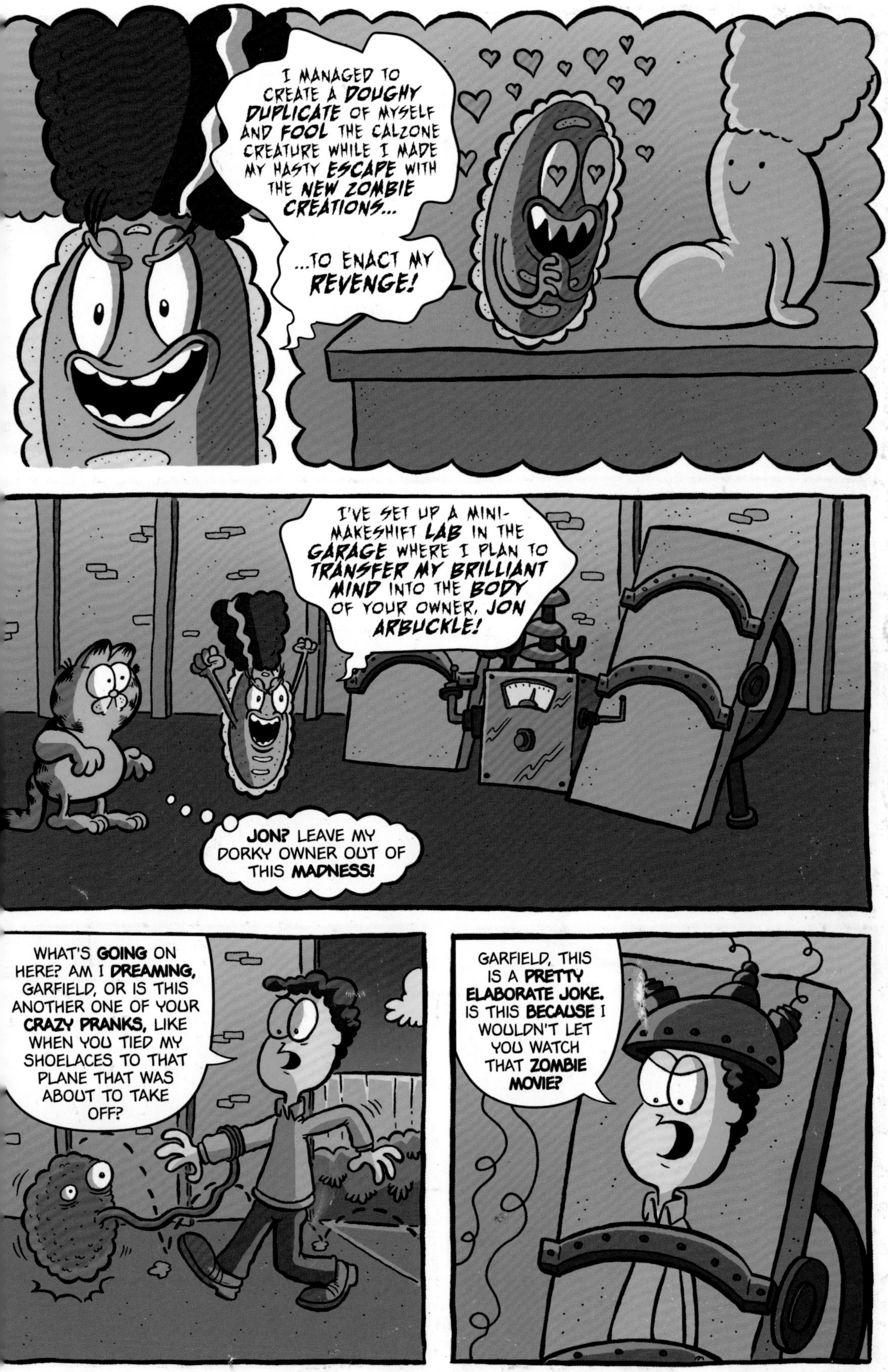
I MANAGED TO CREATE A DOUGHY DUPLICATE OF MYSELF AND FOOL THE CALZONE CREATURE WHILE I MADE MY HASTY ESCAPE WITH THE NEW ZOMBIE CREATIONS...
...TO ENACT MY REVENGE!
I'VE SET UP A MINI-MAKESHIFT LAB IN THE GARAGE WHERE I PLAN TO TRANSFER MY BRILLIANT MIND INTO THE BODY OF YOUR OWNER, JON ARBUCKLE!
JON? LEAVE MY DORKY OWNER OUT OF THIS MADNESS!
WHAT'S GOING ON HERE? AM I DREAMING, GARFIELD, OR IS THIS ANOTHER ONE OF YOUR CRAZY PRANKS, LIKE WHEN YOU TIED MY SHOELACES TO THAT PLANE THAT WAS ABOUT TO TAKE OFF?
GARFIELD, THIS IS A PRETTY ELABORATE JOKE. IS THIS BECAUSE I WOULDN'T LET YOU WATCH THAT ZOMBIE MOVIE?

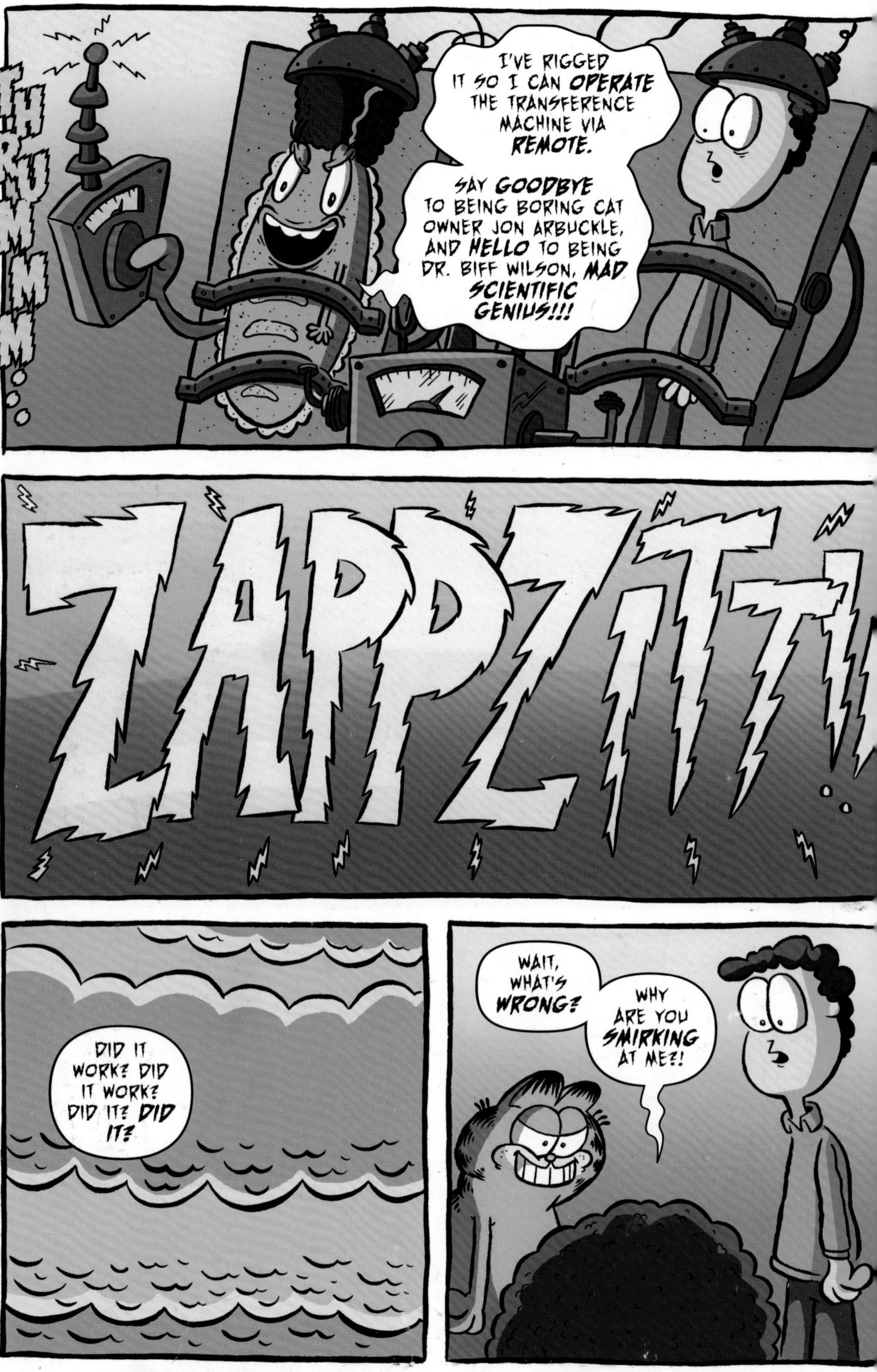
THRUMMMMM...
I'VE RIGGED IT SO I CAN OPERATE THE TRANSFERENCE MACHINE VIA REMOTE.
SAY GOODBYE TO BEING BORING CAT OWNER JON ARBUCKLE, AND HELLO TO BEING DR. BIFF WILSON, MAD SCIENTIFIC GENIUS!!!
ZAPPZITT!!
DID IT WORK? DID IT WORK? DID IT? DID IT?
WAIT, WHAT'S WRONG?
WHY ARE YOU SMIRKING AT ME?!

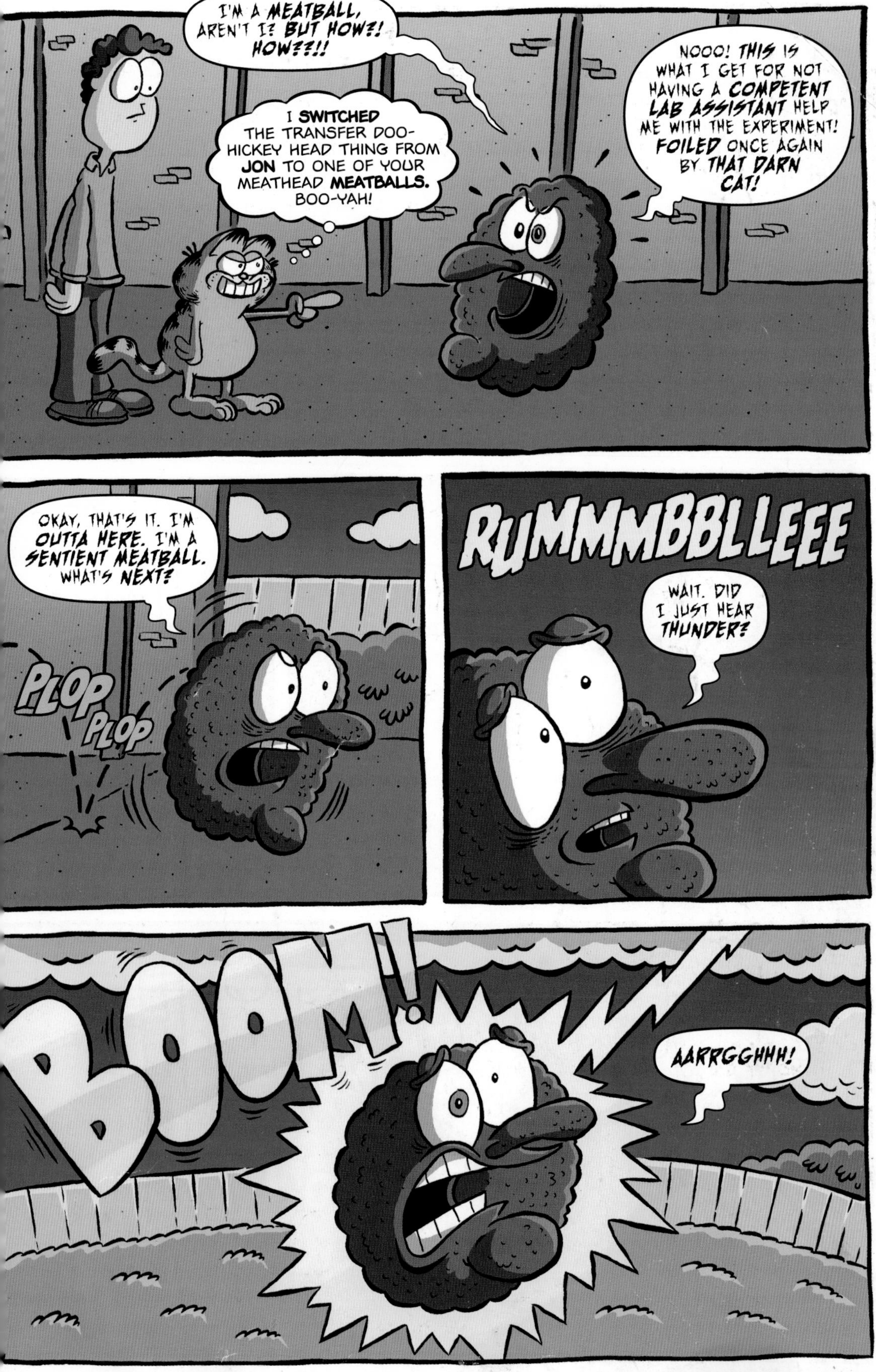

I'M A MEATBALL, AREN'T I? BUT HOW?! HOW???!!
I SWITCHED THE TRANSFER DOO-HICKEY HEAD THING FROM JON TO ONE OF YOUR MEATHEAD MEATBALLS. BOO-YAH!
NOOO! THIS IS WHAT I GET FOR NOT HAVING A COMPETENT LAB ASSISTANT HELP ME WITH THE EXPERIMENT! FOILED ONCE AGAIN BY THAT DARN CAT!
OKAY, THAT'S IT. I'M OUTTA HERE. I'M A SENTIENT MEATBALL. WHAT'S NEXT?
PLOP PLOP
RUMMMMBBLLEEE
WAIT. DID I JUST HEAR THUNDER?
BOOM!
AARRGGHHH!

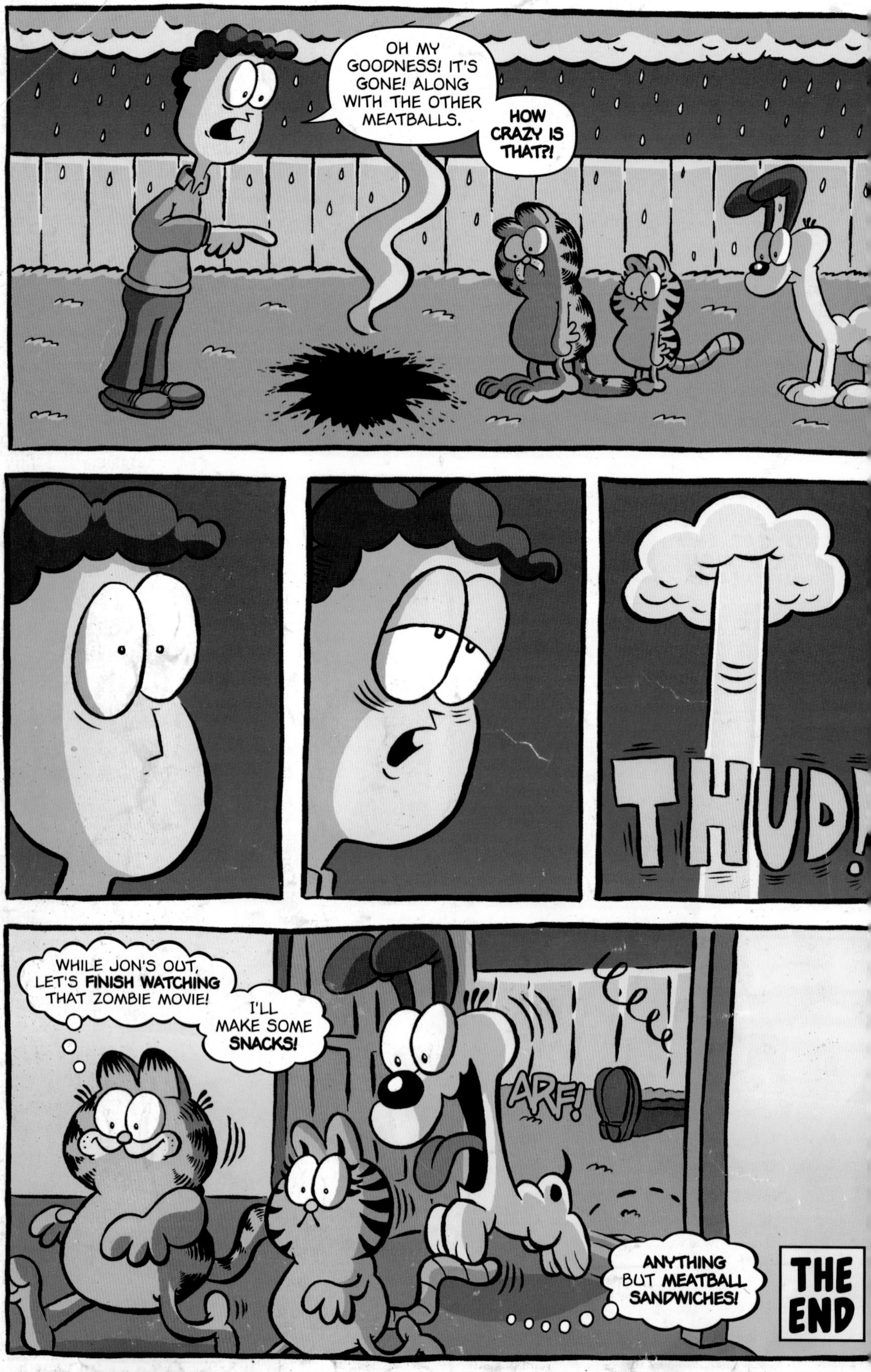

OH MY GOODNESS! IT'S GONE! ALONG WITH THE OTHER MEATBALLS.
HOW CRAZY IS THAT?!
THUD!
WHILE JON'S OUT, LET'S FINISH WATCHING THAT ZOMBIE MOVIE!
I'LL MAKE SOME SNACKS!
ARF!
ANYTHING BUT MEATBALL SANDWICHES!
THE END

CHAPTER 4

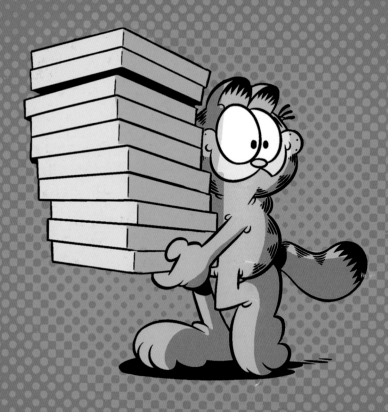

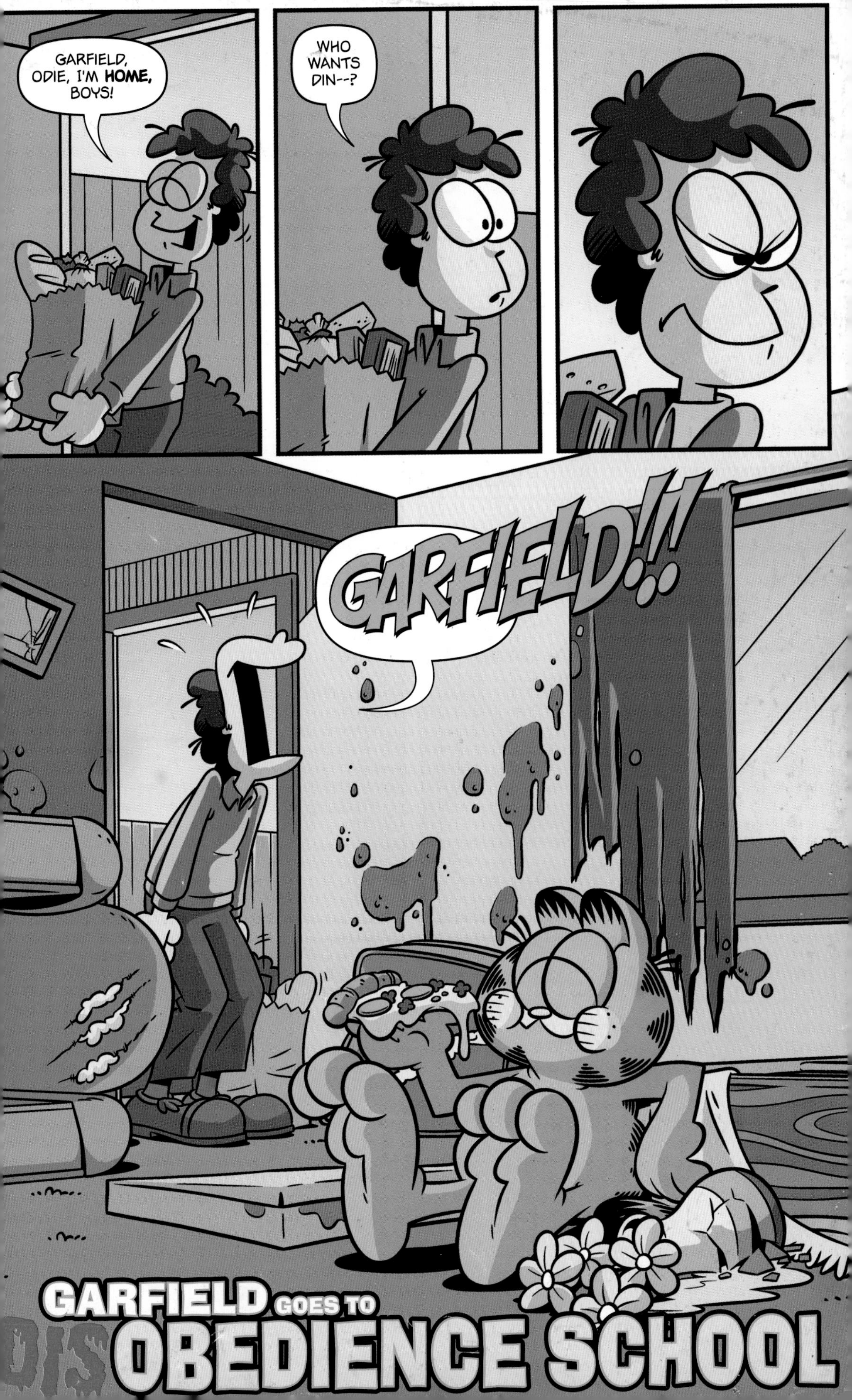

GARFIELD, ODIE, I'M **HOME,** BOYS!
WHO WANTS DIN--?
GARFIELD!!
GARFIELD GOES TO DISOBEDIENCE SCHOOL

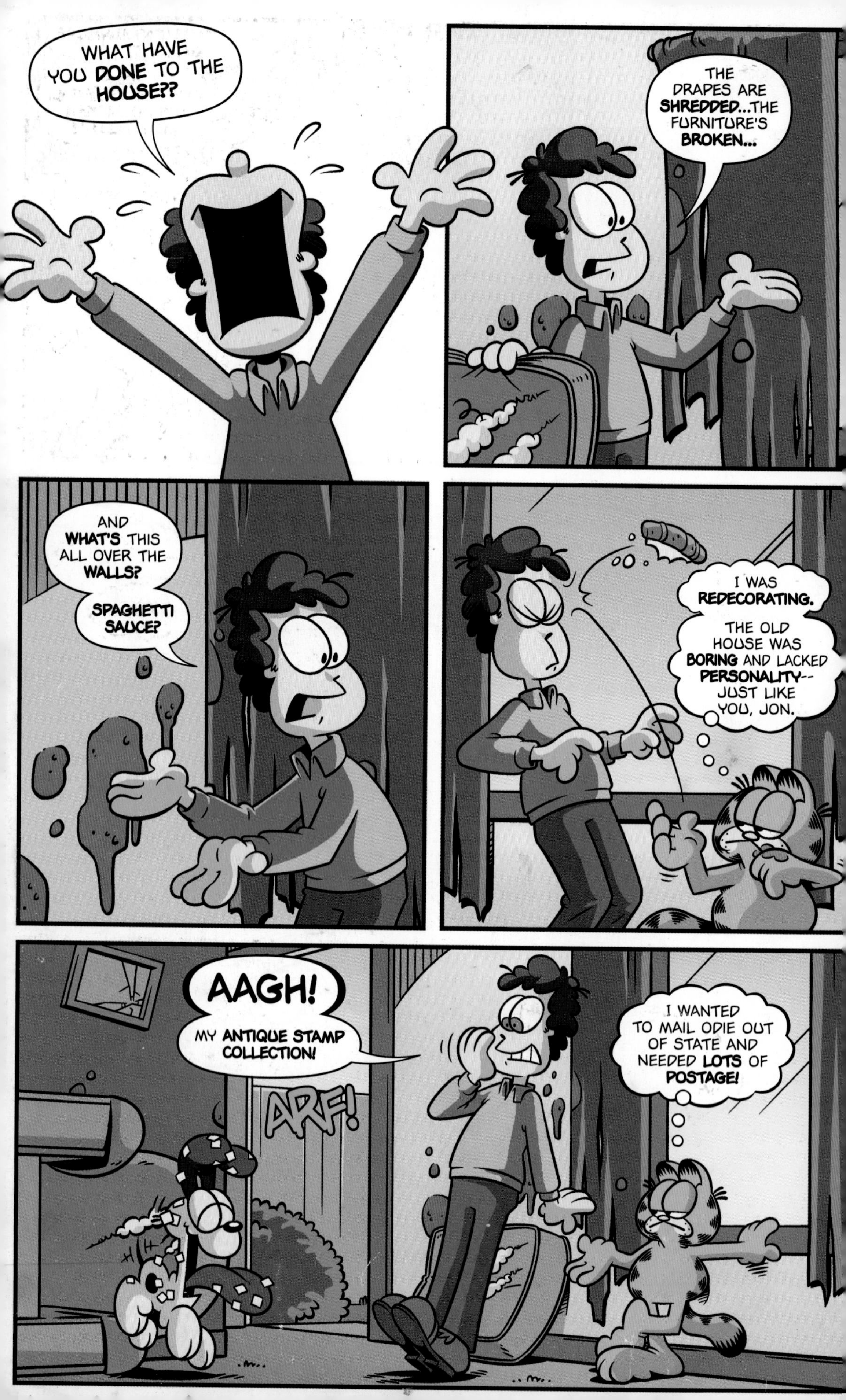

WHAT HAVE YOU DONE TO THE HOUSE??
THE DRAPES ARE SHREDDED...THE FURNITURE'S BROKEN...
AND WHAT'S THIS ALL OVER THE WALLS?
SPAGHETTI SAUCE?
I WAS REDECORATING.
THE OLD HOUSE WAS BORING AND LACKED PERSONALITY-- JUST LIKE YOU, JON.
AAGH!
MY ANTIQUE STAMP COLLECTION!
ARF!
I WANTED TO MAIL ODIE OUT OF STATE AND NEEDED LOTS OF POSTAGE!

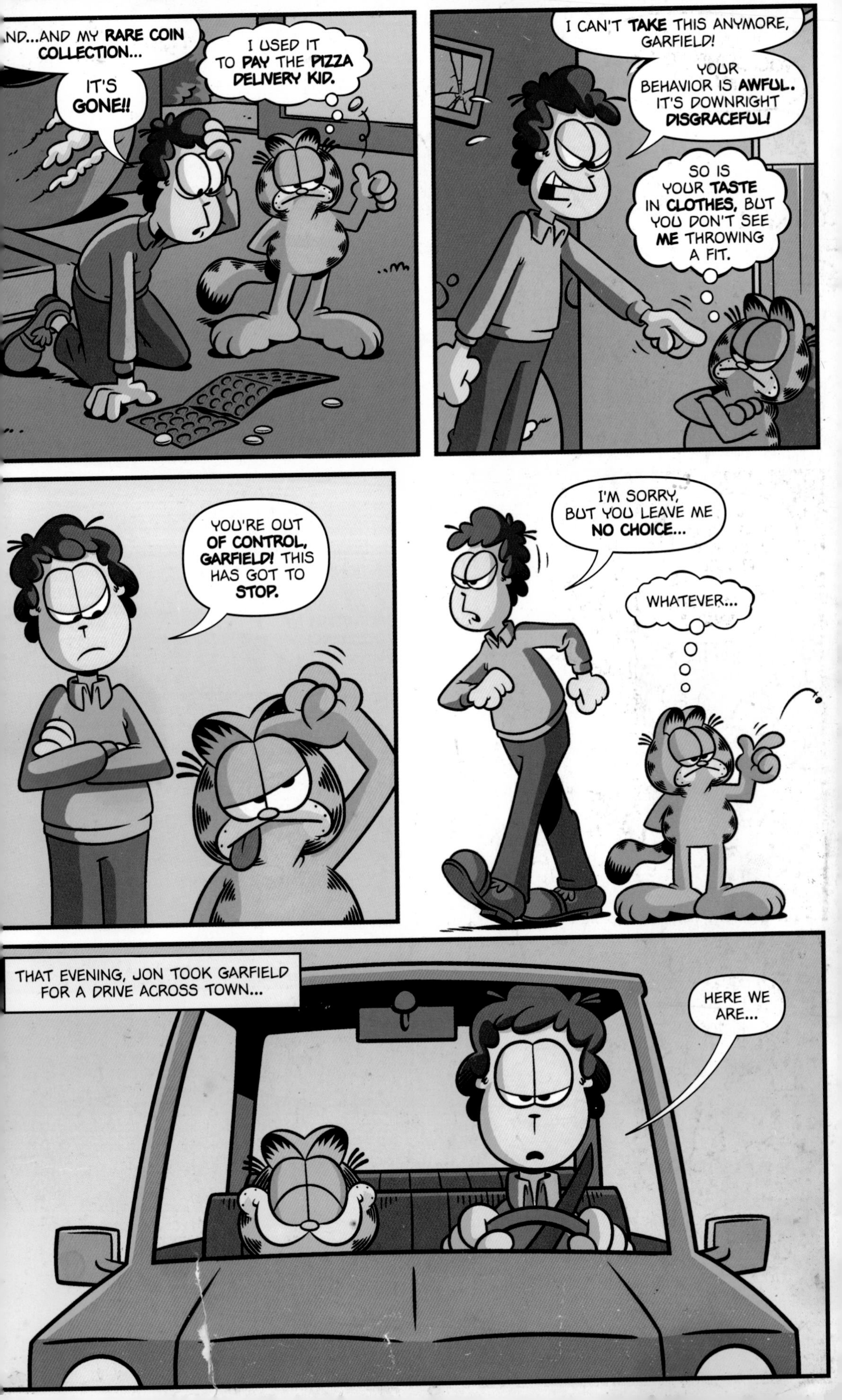
...AND...AND MY RARE COIN COLLECTION...
IT'S GONE!!
I USED IT TO PAY THE PIZZA DELIVERY KID.
I CAN'T TAKE THIS ANYMORE, GARFIELD!
YOUR BEHAVIOR IS AWFUL. IT'S DOWNRIGHT DISGRACEFUL!
SO IS YOUR TASTE IN CLOTHES, BUT YOU DON'T SEE ME THROWING A FIT.
YOU'RE OUT OF CONTROL, GARFIELD! THIS HAS GOT TO STOP.
I'M SORRY, BUT YOU LEAVE ME NO CHOICE...
WHATEVER...
THAT EVENING, JON TOOK GARFIELD FOR A DRIVE ACROSS TOWN...
HERE WE ARE...

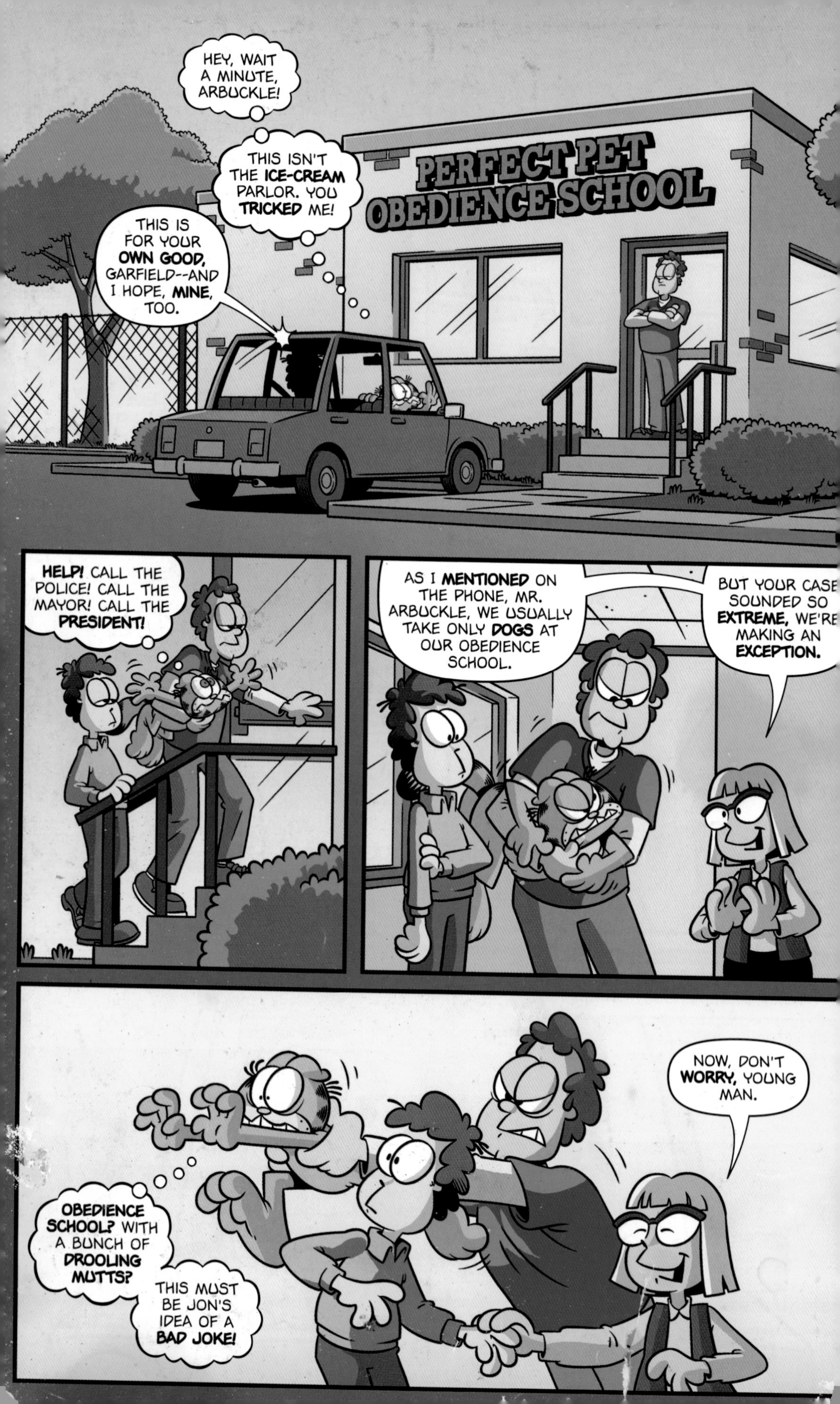

HEY, WAIT A MINUTE, ARBUCKLE!
THIS ISN'T THE ICE-CREAM PARLOR. YOU TRICKED ME!
THIS IS FOR YOUR OWN GOOD, GARFIELD--AND I HOPE, MINE, TOO.
PERFECT PET OBEDIENCE SCHOOL
HELP! CALL THE POLICE! CALL THE MAYOR! CALL THE PRESIDENT!
AS I MENTIONED ON THE PHONE, MR. ARBUCKLE, WE USUALLY TAKE ONLY DOGS AT OUR OBEDIENCE SCHOOL.
BUT YOUR CASE SOUNDED SO EXTREME, WE'RE MAKING AN EXCEPTION.
NOW, DON'T WORRY, YOUNG MAN.
OBEDIENCE SCHOOL? WITH A BUNCH OF DROOLING MUTTS?
THIS MUST BE JON'S IDEA OF A BAD JOKE!

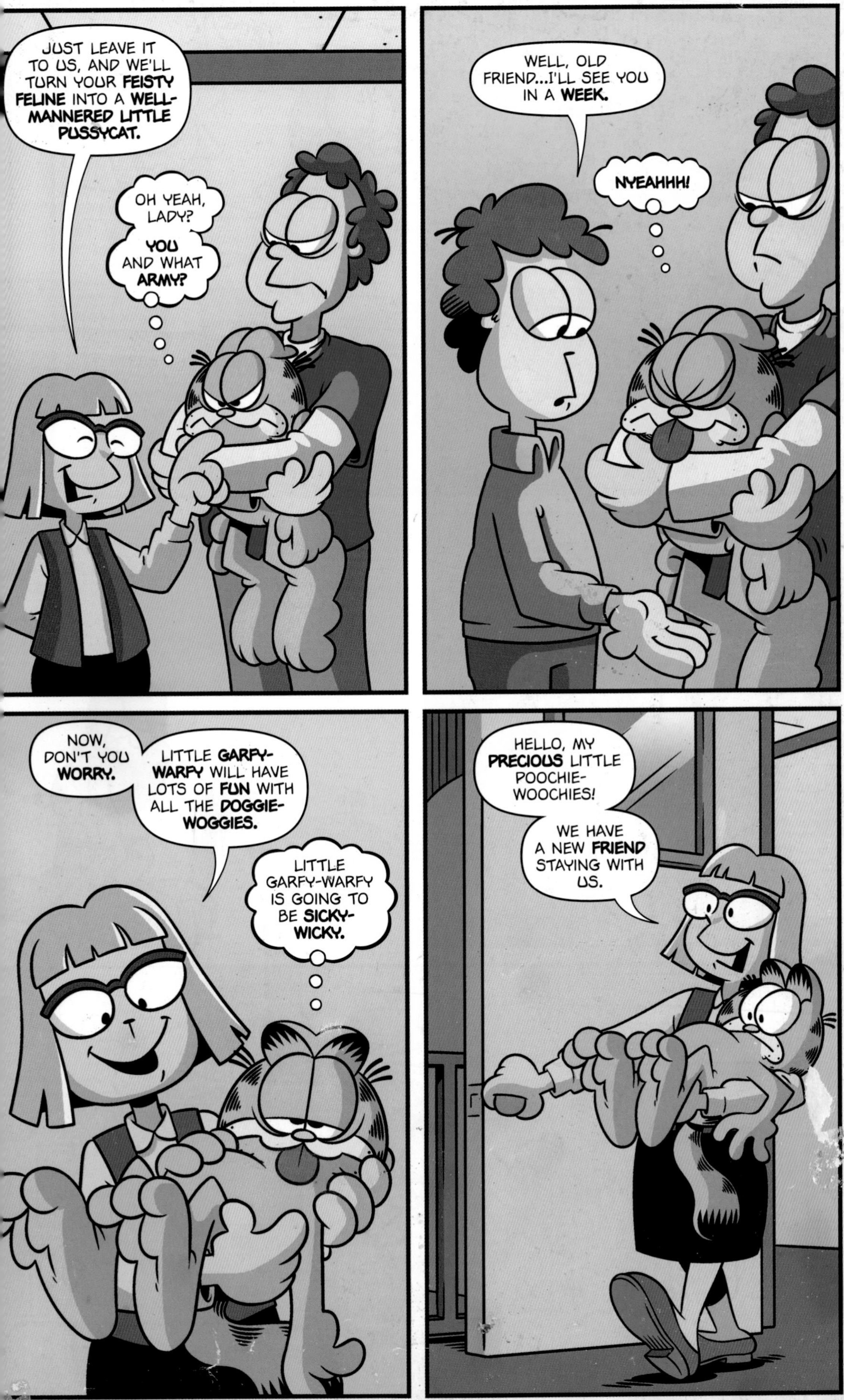
JUST LEAVE IT TO US, AND WE'LL TURN YOUR FEISTY FELINE INTO A WELL-MANNERED LITTLE PUSSYCAT.
OH YEAH, LADY?
YOU AND WHAT ARMY?
WELL, OLD FRIEND...I'LL SEE YOU IN A WEEK.
NYEAHHH!
NOW, DON'T YOU WORRY.
LITTLE GARFY-WARFY WILL HAVE LOTS OF FUN WITH ALL THE DOGGIE-WOGGIES.
LITTLE GARFY-WARFY IS GOING TO BE SICKY-WICKY.
HELLO, MY PRECIOUS LITTLE POOCHIE-WOOCHIES!
WE HAVE A NEW FRIEND STAYING WITH US.

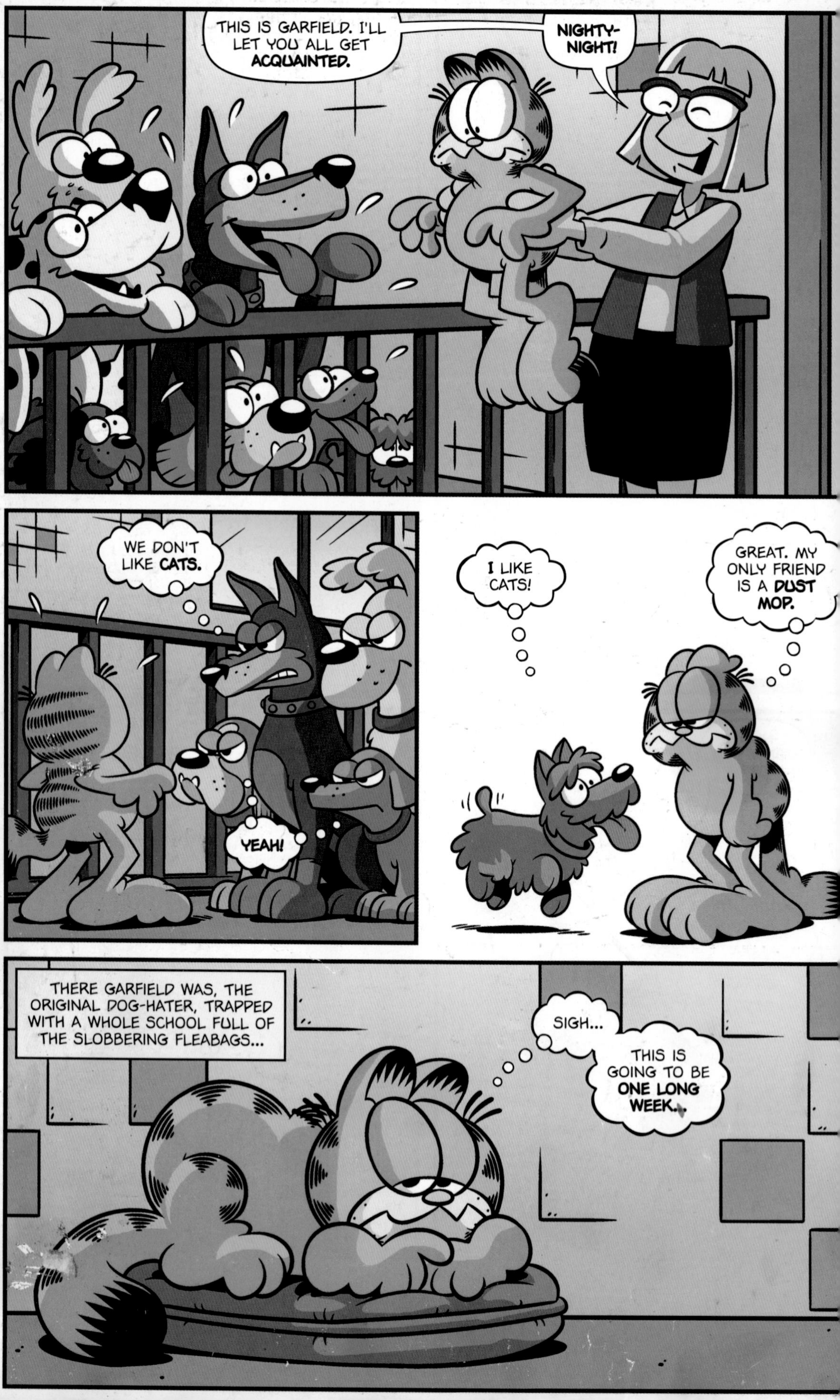
THIS IS GARFIELD. I'LL LET YOU ALL GET ACQUAINTED.
NIGHTY-NIGHT!
WE DON'T LIKE CATS.
YEAH!
I LIKE CATS!
GREAT. MY ONLY FRIEND IS A DUST MOP.
THERE GARFIELD WAS, THE ORIGINAL DOG-HATER, TRAPPED WITH A WHOLE SCHOOL FULL OF THE SLOBBERING FLEABAGS...
SIGH...
THIS IS GOING TO BE ONE LONG WEEK...

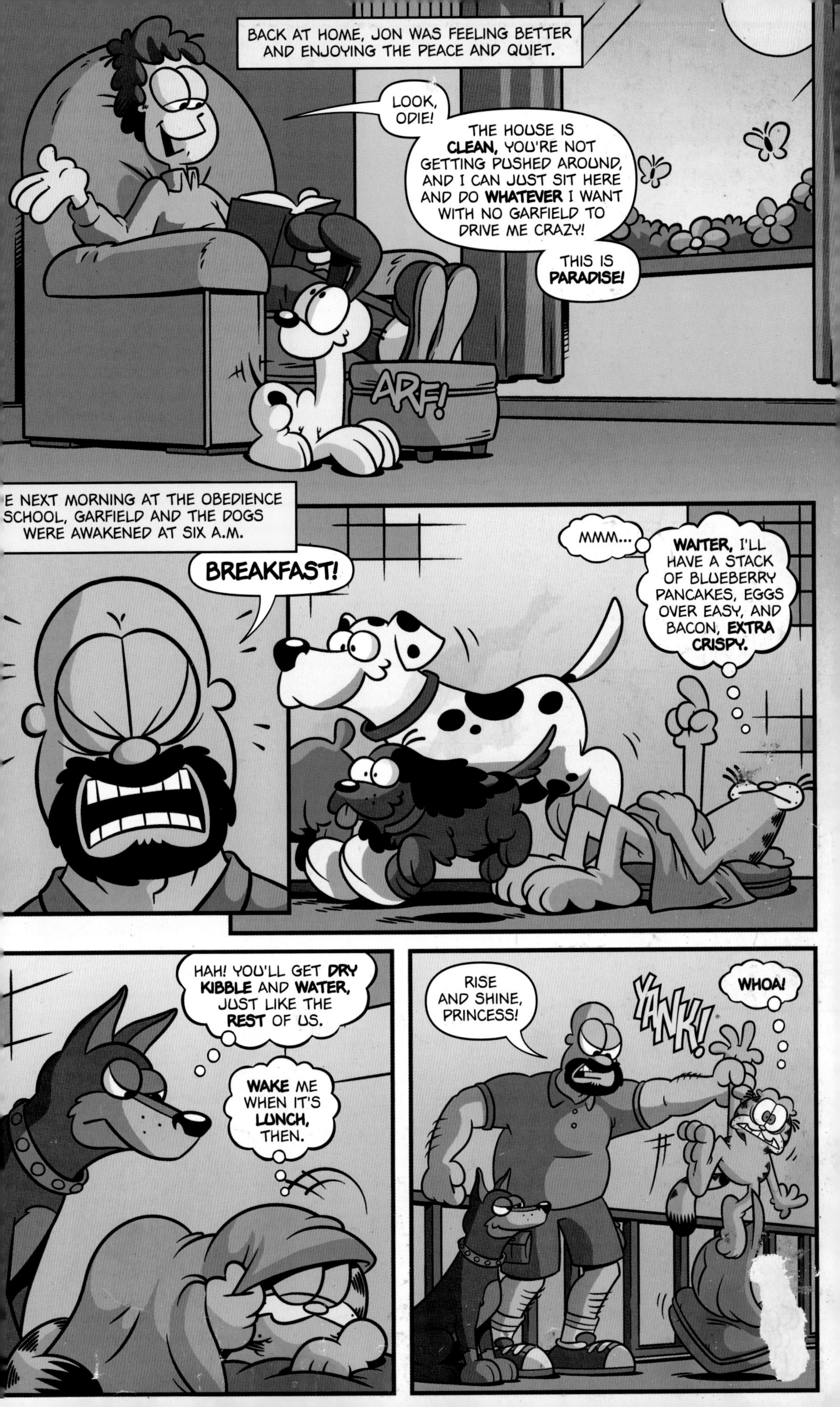
BACK AT HOME, JON WAS FEELING BETTER AND ENJOYING THE PEACE AND QUIET.
LOOK, ODIE!
THE HOUSE IS CLEAN, YOU'RE NOT GETTING PUSHED AROUND, AND I CAN JUST SIT HERE AND DO WHATEVER I WANT WITH NO GARFIELD TO DRIVE ME CRAZY!
THIS IS PARADISE!
ARF!
E NEXT MORNING AT THE OBEDIENCE SCHOOL, GARFIELD AND THE DOGS WERE AWAKENED AT SIX A.M.
BREAKFAST!
MMM...
WAITER, I'LL HAVE A STACK OF BLUEBERRY PANCAKES, EGGS OVER EASY, AND BACON, EXTRA CRISPY.
HAH! YOU'LL GET DRY KIBBLE AND WATER, JUST LIKE THE REST OF US.
WAKE ME WHEN IT'S LUNCH, THEN.
RISE AND SHINE, PRINCESS!
YANK!
WHOA!

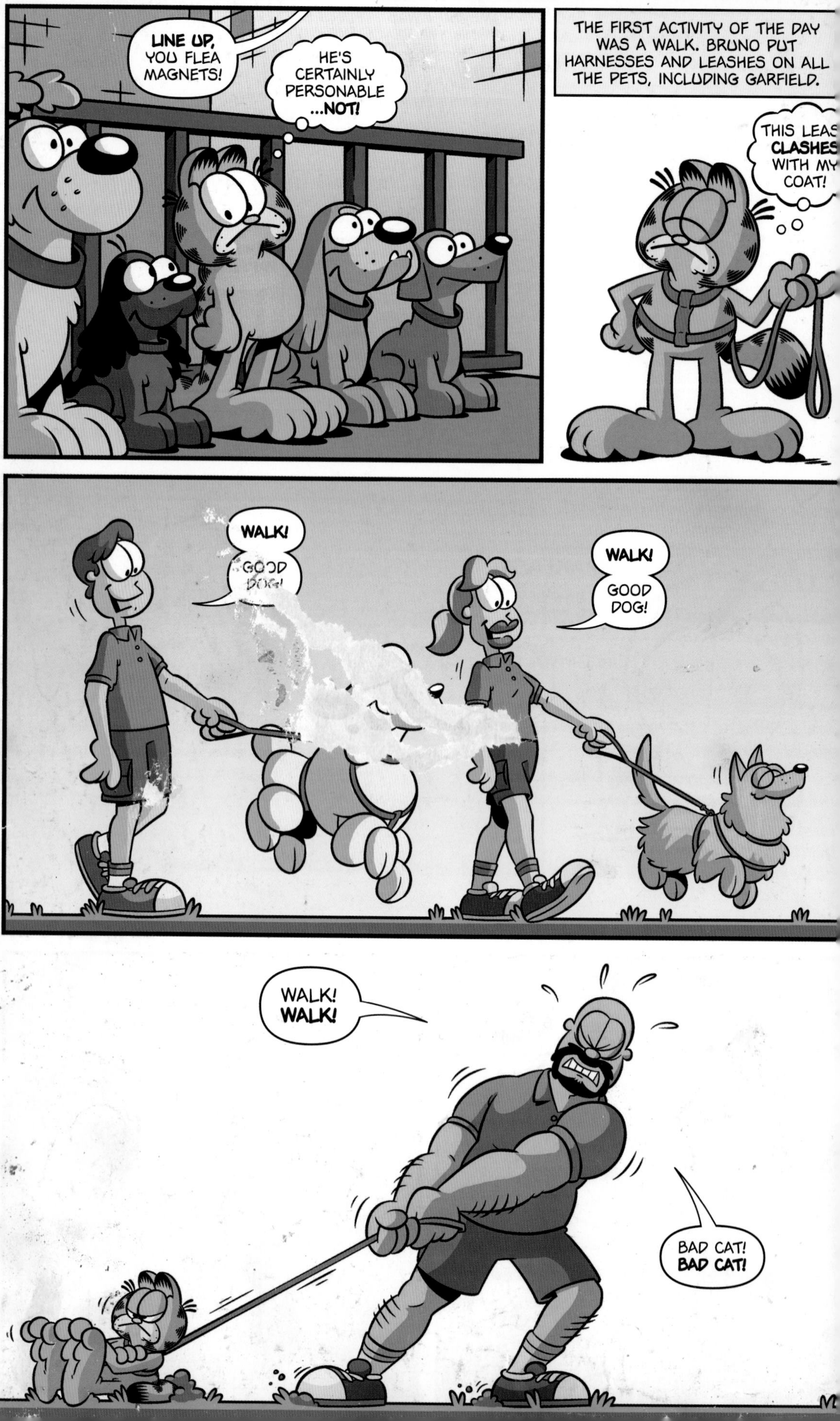
LINE UP, YOU FLEA MAGNETS!
HE'S CERTAINLY PERSONABLE ...NOT!
THE FIRST ACTIVITY OF THE DAY WAS A WALK. BRUNO PUT HARNESSES AND LEASHES ON ALL THE PETS, INCLUDING GARFIELD.
THIS LEAS CLASHES WITH MY COAT!
WALK!
GOOD DOG!
WALK!
GOOD DOG!
WALK! WALK!
BAD CAT! BAD CAT!

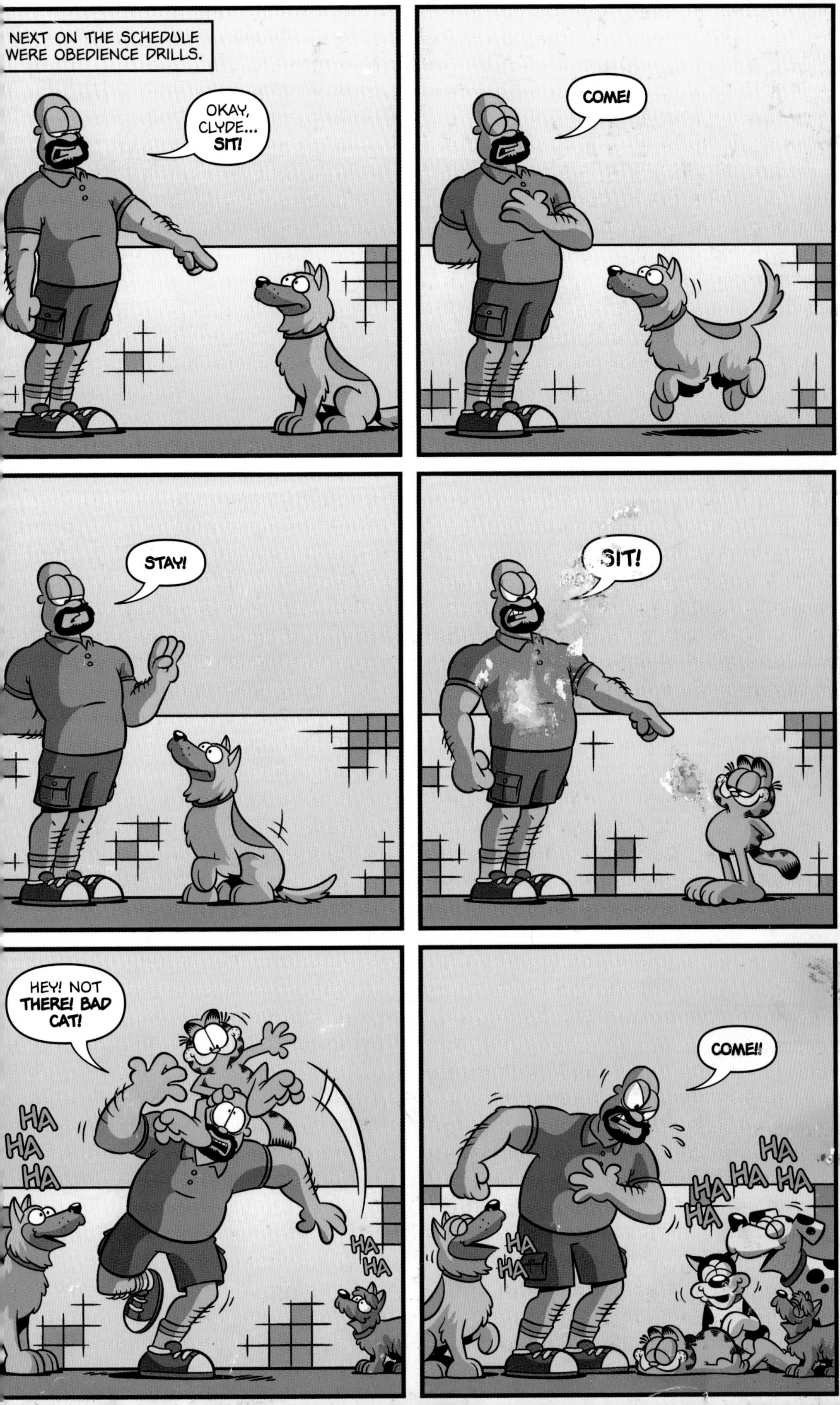
NEXT ON THE SCHEDULE WERE OBEDIENCE DRILLS.
OKAY, CLYDE... SIT!
COME!
STAY!
SIT!
HEY! NOT THERE! BAD CAT!
HA HA HA
HA HA
COME!!
HA HA
HA HA HA HA HA

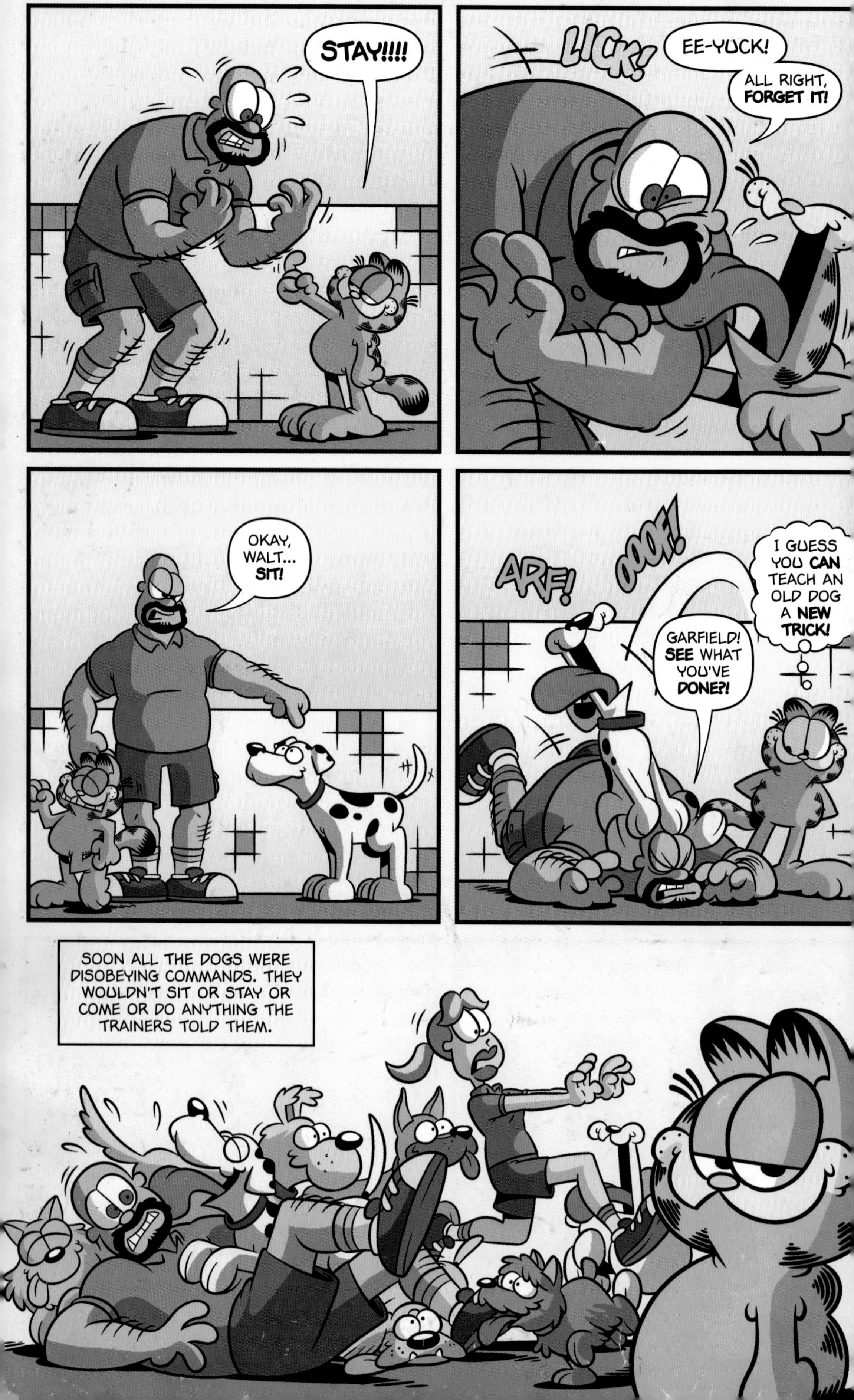

STAY!!!!
LICK!
EE-YUCK!
ALL RIGHT, FORGET IT!
OKAY, WALT... SIT!
ARF!
OOOF!
I GUESS YOU CAN TEACH AN OLD DOG A NEW TRICK!
GARFIELD! SEE WHAT YOU'VE DONE?!
SOON ALL THE DOGS WERE DISOBEYING COMMANDS. THEY WOULDN'T SIT OR STAY OR COME OR DO ANYTHING THE TRAINERS TOLD THEM.

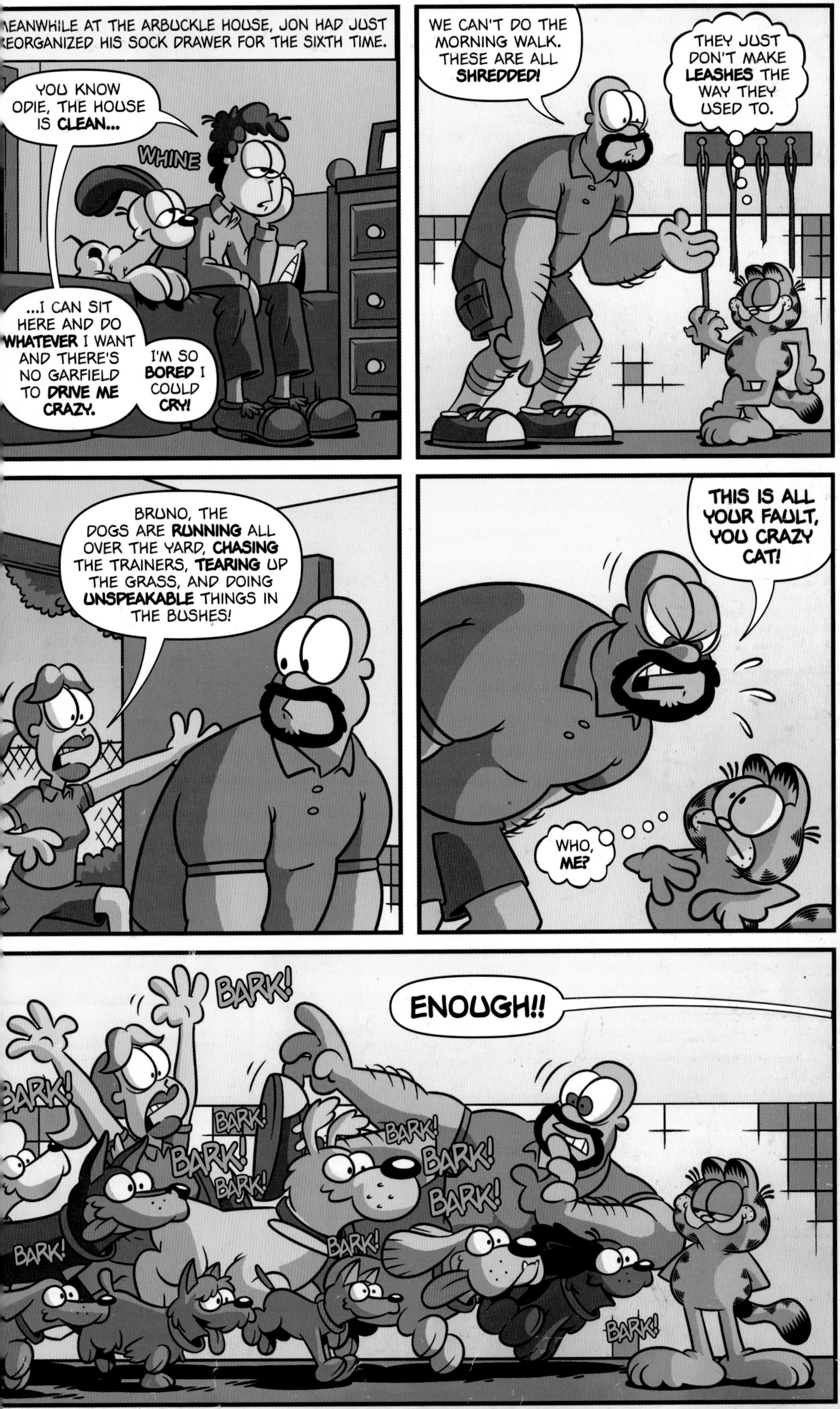

MEANWHILE AT THE ARBUCKLE HOUSE, JON HAD JUST REORGANIZED HIS SOCK DRAWER FOR THE SIXTH TIME.
YOU KNOW ODIE, THE HOUSE IS CLEAN...
WHINE
...I CAN SIT HERE AND DO WHATEVER I WANT AND THERE'S NO GARFIELD TO DRIVE ME CRAZY.
I'M SO BORED I COULD CRY!
WE CAN'T DO THE MORNING WALK. THESE ARE ALL SHREDDED!
THEY JUST DON'T MAKE LEASHES THE WAY THEY USED TO.
BRUNO, THE DOGS ARE RUNNING ALL OVER THE YARD, CHASING THE TRAINERS, TEARING UP THE GRASS, AND DOING UNSPEAKABLE THINGS IN THE BUSHES!
THIS IS ALL YOUR FAULT, YOU CRAZY CAT!
WHO, ME?
BARK!
ENOUGH!!
BARK!
BARK!
BARK!
BARK!
BARK!
BARK!
BARK!
BARK!
BARK!
BARK!

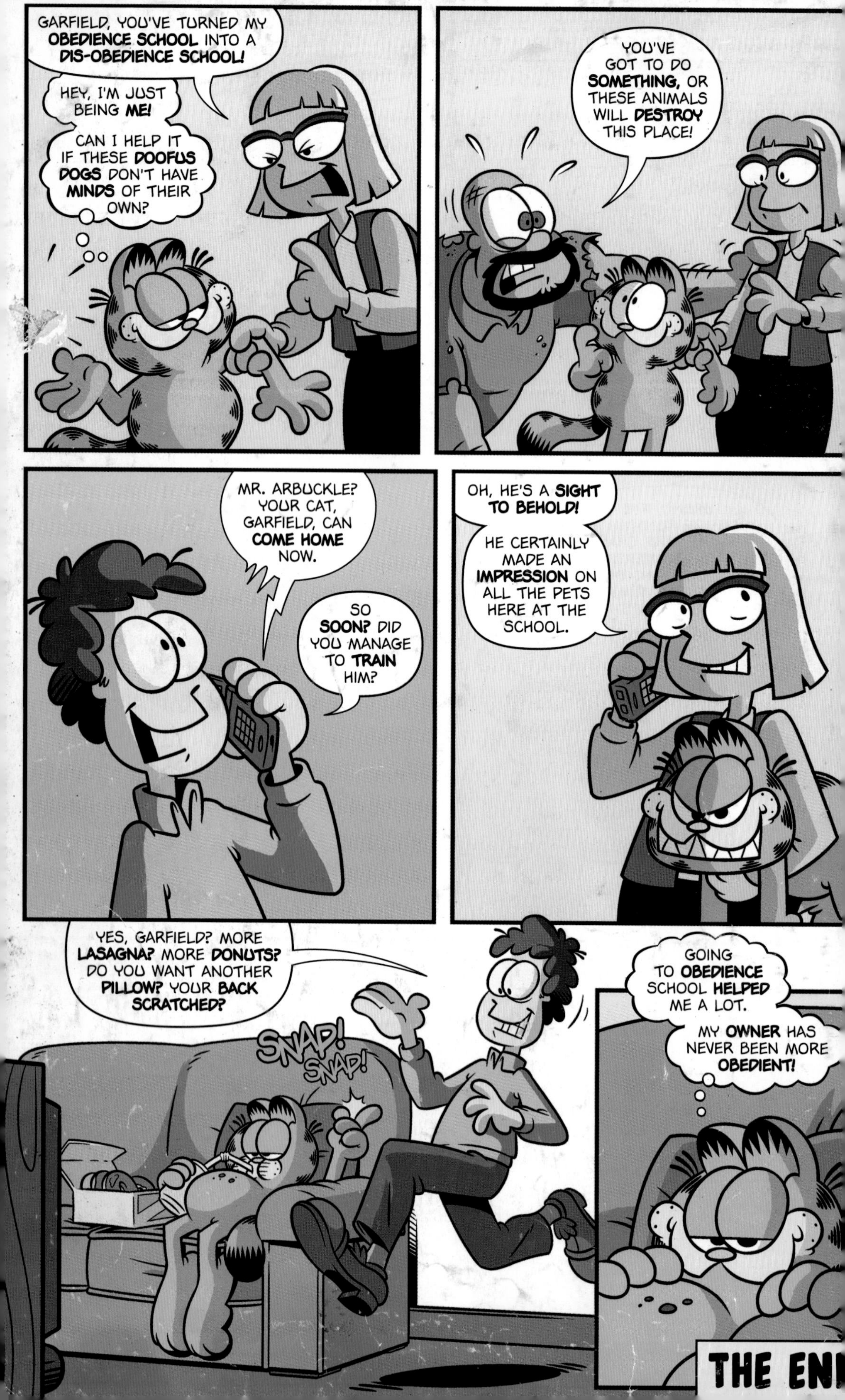
GARFIELD, YOU'VE TURNED MY OBEDIENCE SCHOOL INTO A DIS-OBEDIENCE SCHOOL!
HEY, I'M JUST BEING ME!
CAN I HELP IT IF THESE DOOFUS DOGS DON'T HAVE MINDS OF THEIR OWN?
YOU'VE GOT TO DO SOMETHING, OR THESE ANIMALS WILL DESTROY THIS PLACE!
MR. ARBUCKLE? YOUR CAT, GARFIELD, CAN COME HOME NOW.
SO SOON? DID YOU MANAGE TO TRAIN HIM?
OH, HE'S A SIGHT TO BEHOLD!
HE CERTAINLY MADE AN IMPRESSION ON ALL THE PETS HERE AT THE SCHOOL.
YES, GARFIELD? MORE LASAGNA? MORE DONUTS? DO YOU WANT ANOTHER PILLOW? YOUR BACK SCRATCHED?
SNAP! SNAP!
GOING TO OBEDIENCE SCHOOL HELPED ME A LOT.
MY OWNER HAS NEVER BEEN MORE OBEDIENT!
THE END

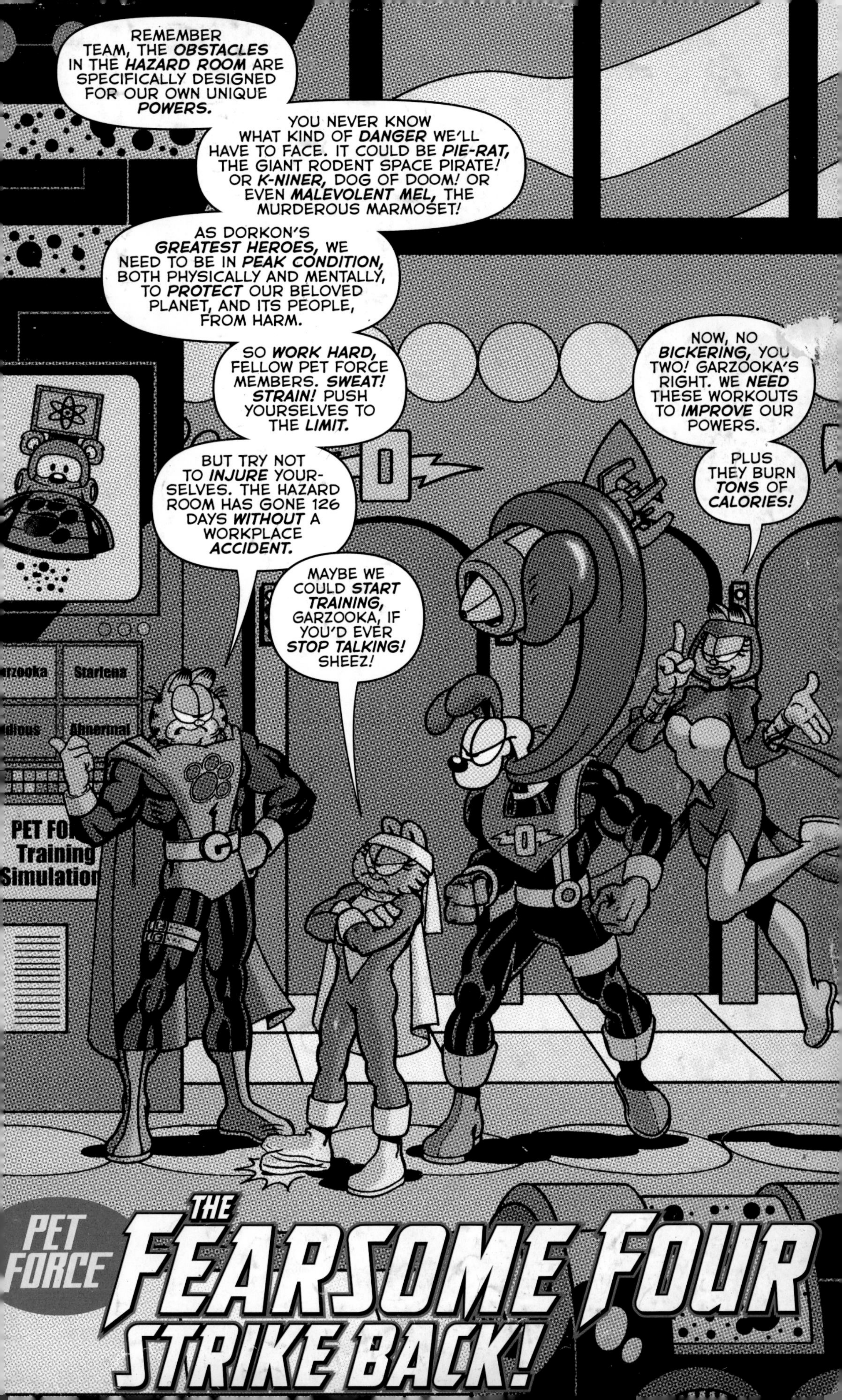
REMEMBER TEAM, THE OBSTACLES IN THE HAZARD ROOM ARE SPECIFICALLY DESIGNED FOR OUR OWN UNIQUE POWERS.
YOU NEVER KNOW WHAT KIND OF DANGER WE'LL HAVE TO FACE. IT COULD BE PIE-RAT, THE GIANT RODENT SPACE PIRATE! OR K-NINER, DOG OF DOOM! OR EVEN MALEVOLENT MEL, THE MURDEROUS MARMOSET!
AS DORKON'S GREATEST HEROES, WE NEED TO BE IN PEAK CONDITION, BOTH PHYSICALLY AND MENTALLY, TO PROTECT OUR BELOVED PLANET, AND ITS PEOPLE, FROM HARM.
SO WORK HARD, FELLOW PET FORCE MEMBERS. SWEAT! STRAIN! PUSH YOURSELVES TO THE LIMIT.
BUT TRY NOT TO INJURE YOURSELVES. THE HAZARD ROOM HAS GONE 126 DAYS WITHOUT A WORKPLACE ACCIDENT.
MAYBE WE COULD START TRAINING, GARZOOKA, IF YOU'D EVER STOP TALKING! SHEEZ!
NOW, NO BICKERING, YOU TWO! GARZOOKA'S RIGHT. WE NEED THESE WORKOUTS TO IMPROVE OUR POWERS.
PLUS THEY BURN TONS OF CALORIES!
Starlena
Abnermal
PET FOR
Training
Simulation
PET FORCE
THE FEARSOME FOUR STRIKE BACK!

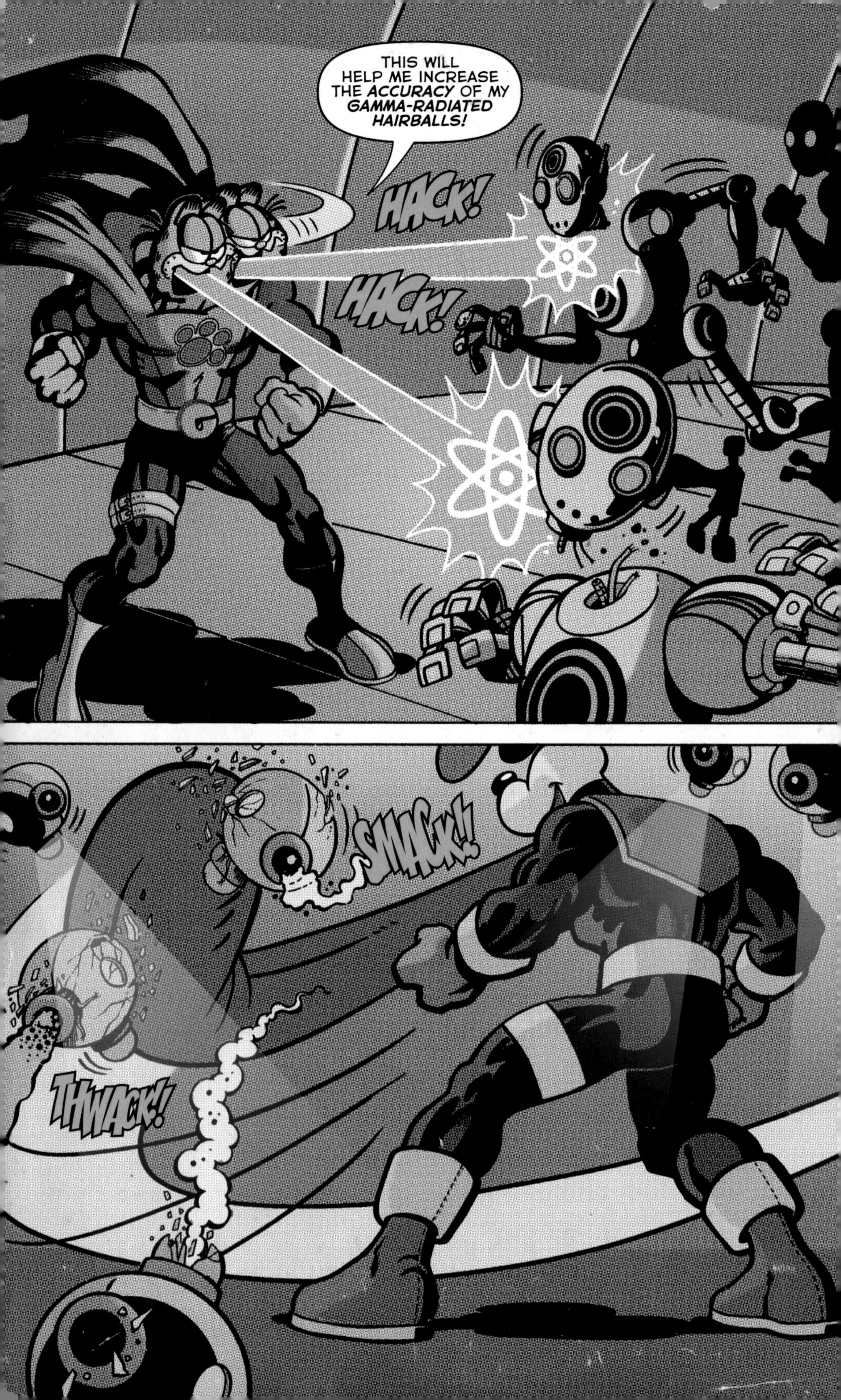

THIS WILL HELP ME INCREASE THE *ACCURACY* OF MY *GAMMA-RADIATED HAIRBALLS!*
HACK!
HACK!
SMACK!!
THWACK!!

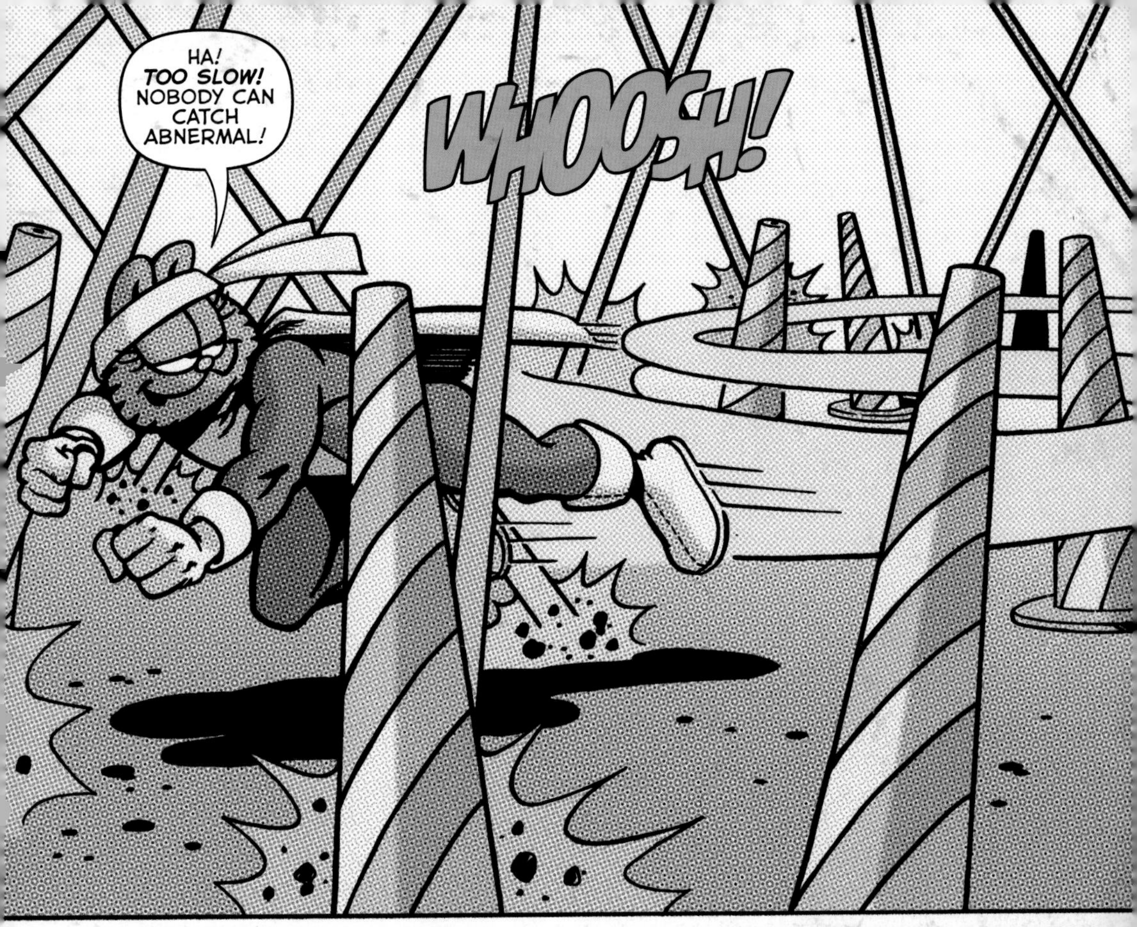
HA! TOO SLOW! NOBODY CAN CATCH ABNERMAL!
WHOOSH!

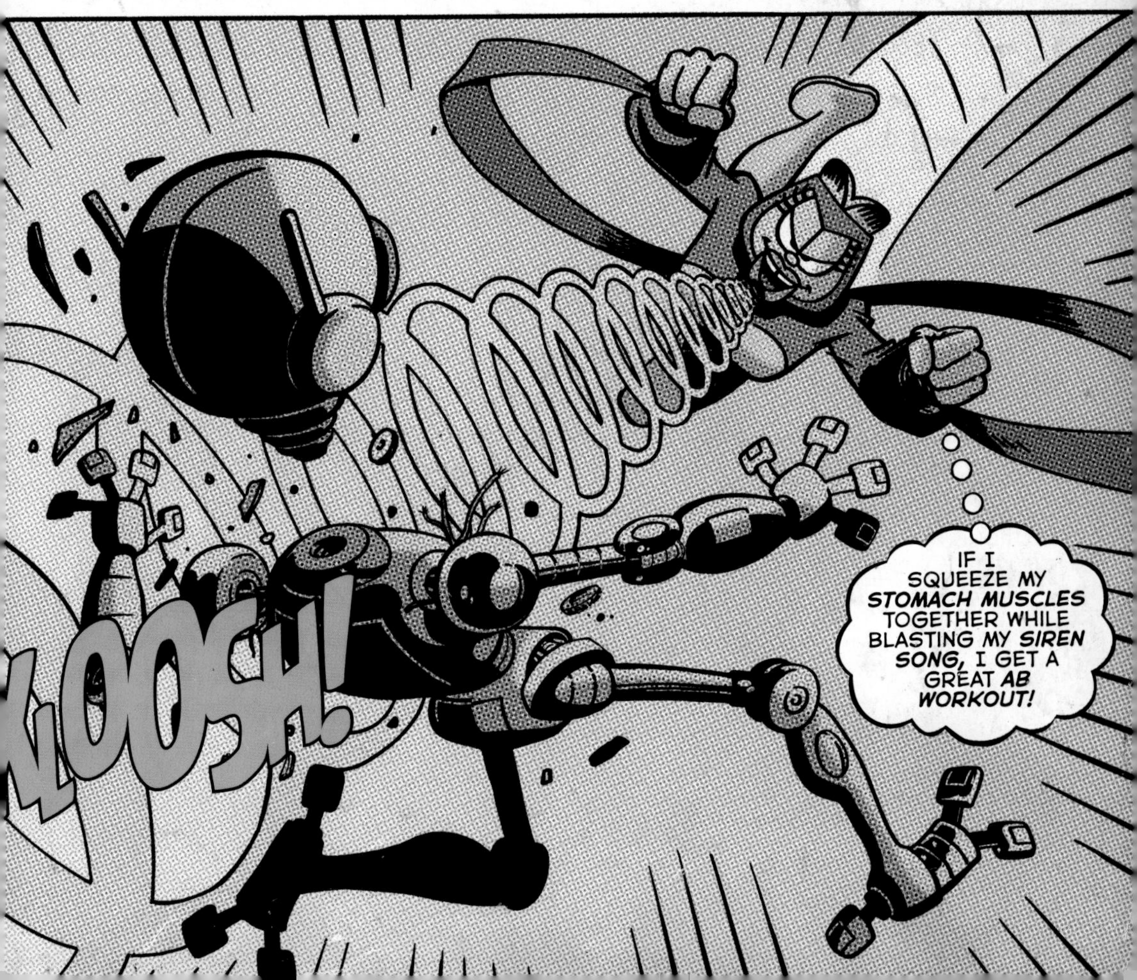
IF I SQUEEZE MY STOMACH MUSCLES TOGETHER WHILE BLASTING MY SIREN SONG, I GET A GREAT AB WORKOUT!
OOSH!

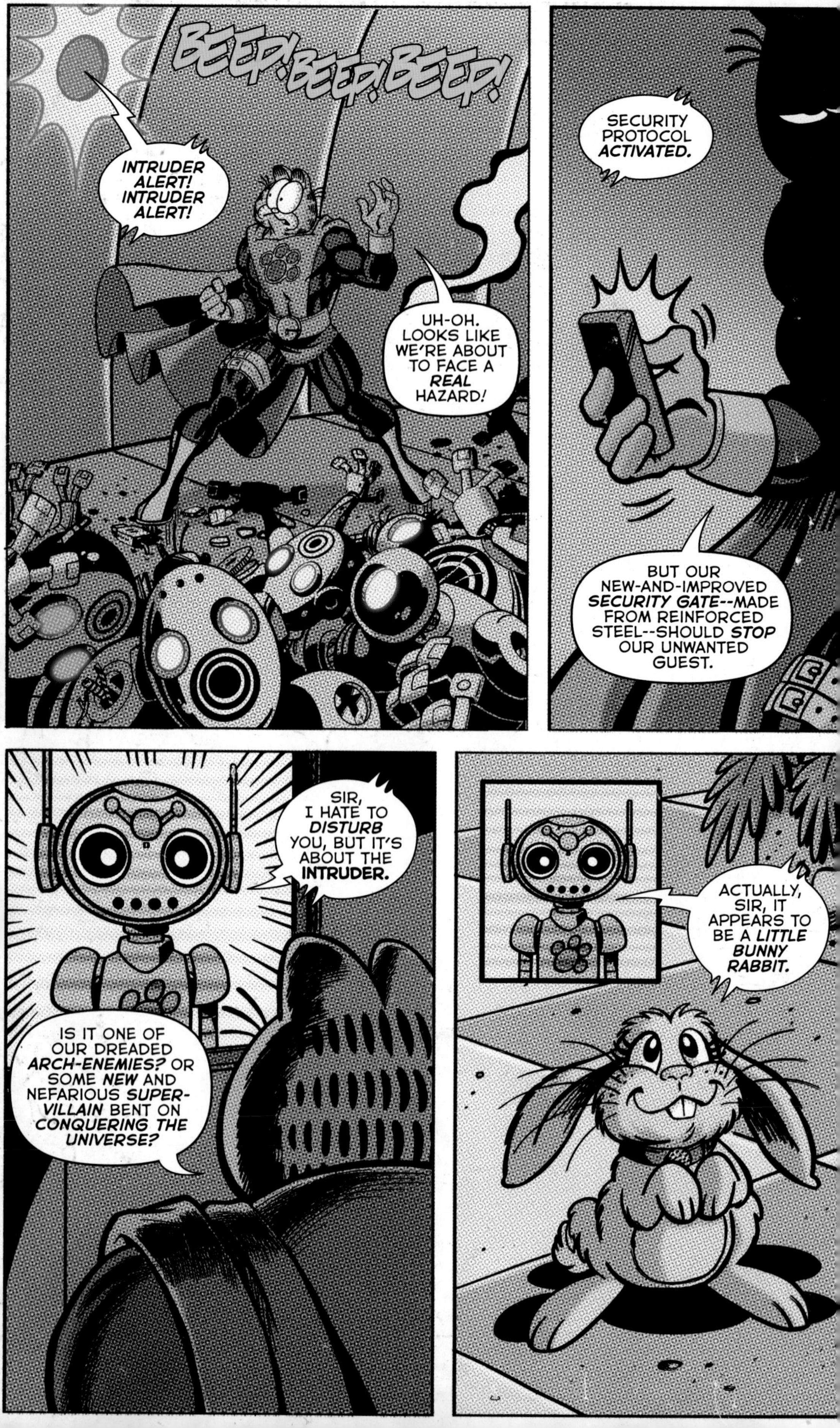

BEEP! BEEP! BEEP!
INTRUDER ALERT! INTRUDER ALERT!
UH-OH. LOOKS LIKE WE'RE ABOUT TO FACE A *REAL* HAZARD!
SECURITY PROTOCOL *ACTIVATED.*
BUT OUR NEW-AND-IMPROVED *SECURITY GATE*--MADE FROM REINFORCED STEEL--SHOULD *STOP* OUR UNWANTED GUEST.
SIR, I HATE TO *DISTURB* YOU, BUT IT'S ABOUT THE **INTRUDER.**
IS IT ONE OF OUR DREADED *ARCH-ENEMIES?* OR SOME *NEW* AND NEFARIOUS *SUPER-VILLAIN* BENT ON *CONQUERING THE UNIVERSE?*
ACTUALLY, SIR, IT APPEARS TO BE A *LITTLE BUNNY RABBIT.*

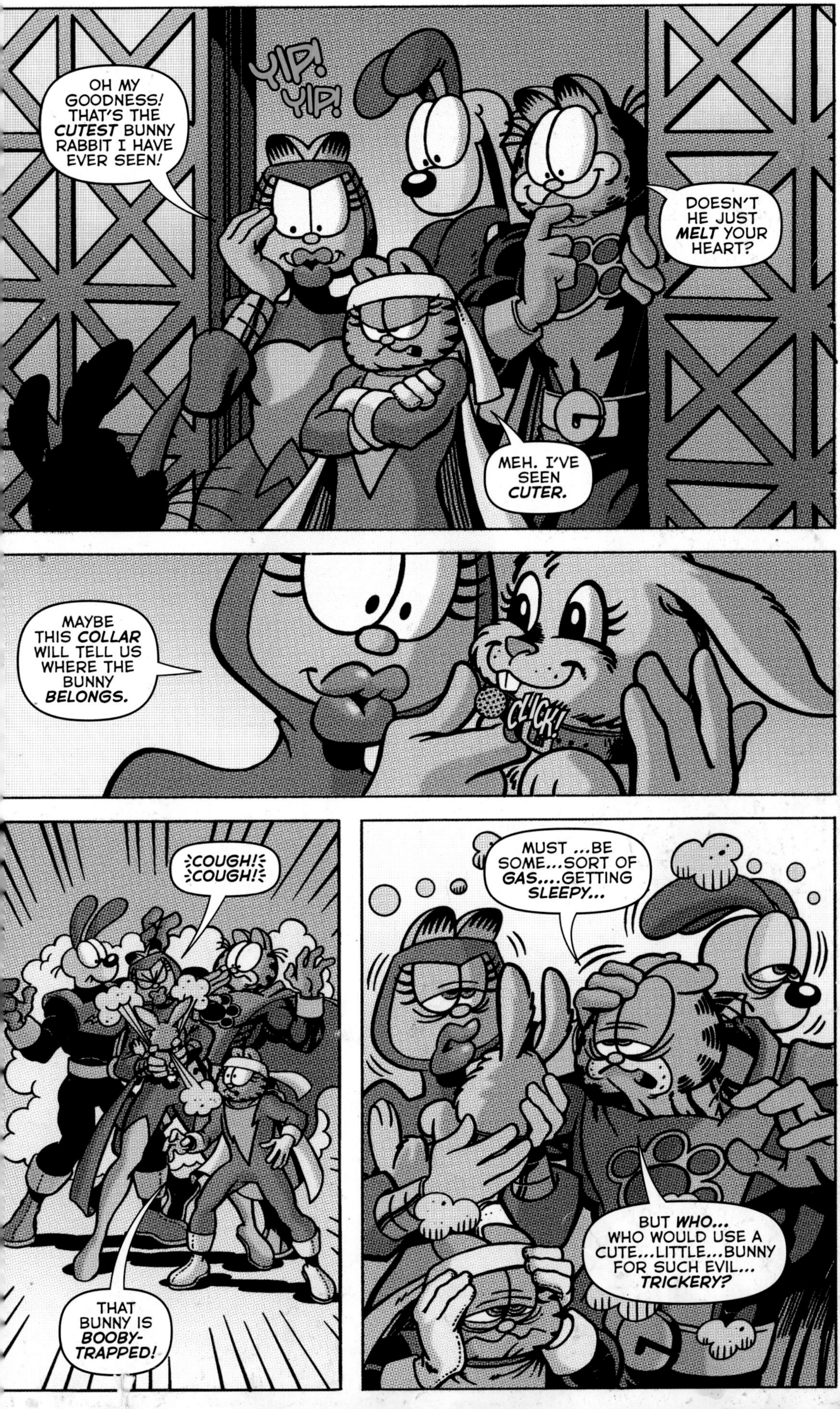
OH MY GOODNESS! THAT'S THE CUTEST BUNNY RABBIT I HAVE EVER SEEN!
YIP! YIP!
DOESN'T HE JUST MELT YOUR HEART?
MEH. I'VE SEEN CUTER.
MAYBE THIS COLLAR WILL TELL US WHERE THE BUNNY BELONGS.
CLICK!
COUGH! COUGH!
THAT BUNNY IS BOOBY-TRAPPED!
MUST ...BE SOME...SORT OF GAS....GETTING SLEEPY...
BUT WHO... WHO WOULD USE A CUTE...LITTLE...BUNNY FOR SUCH EVIL... TRICKERY?

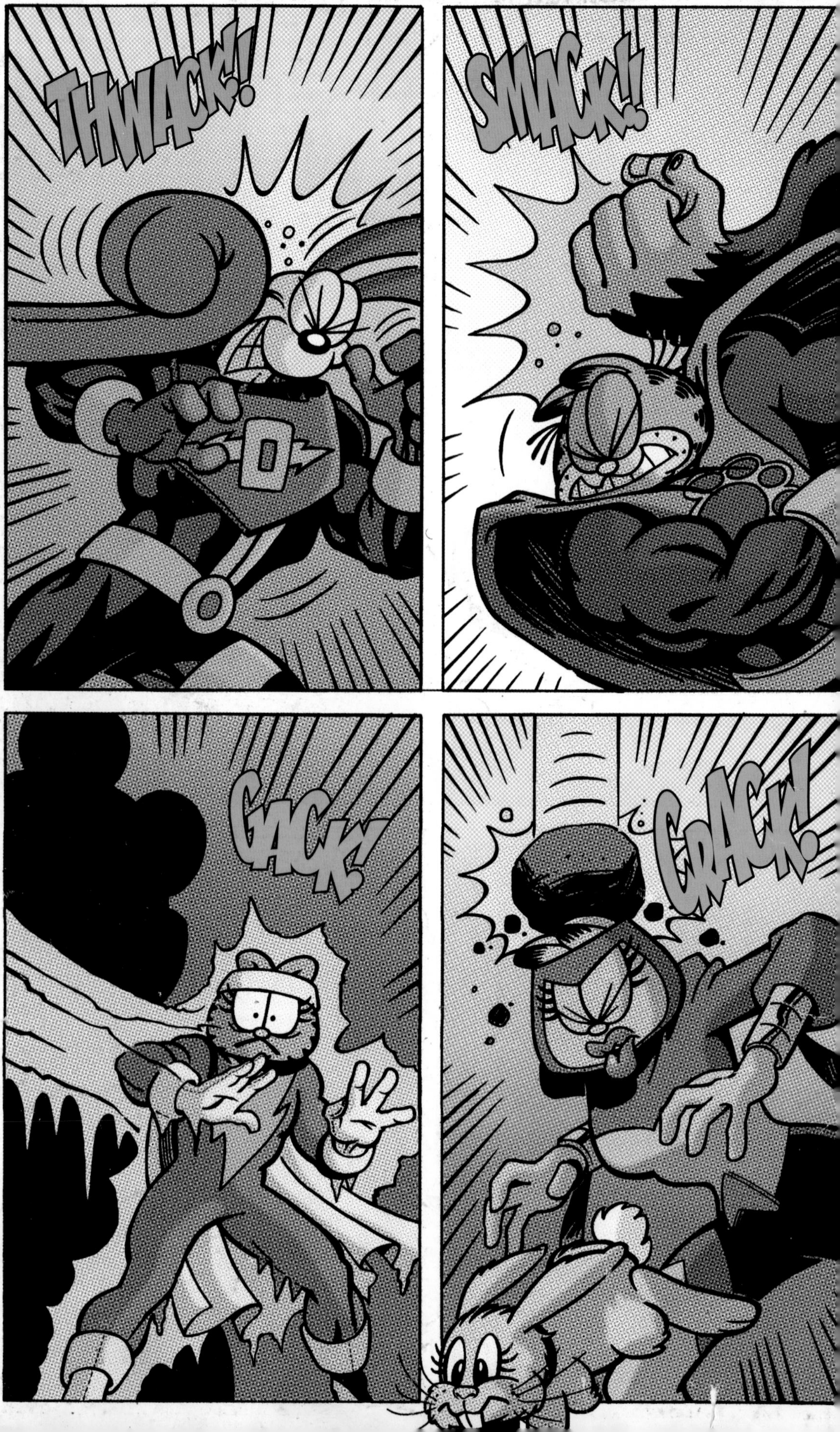
THWACK!
SMACK!!
GACK!
CRACK!

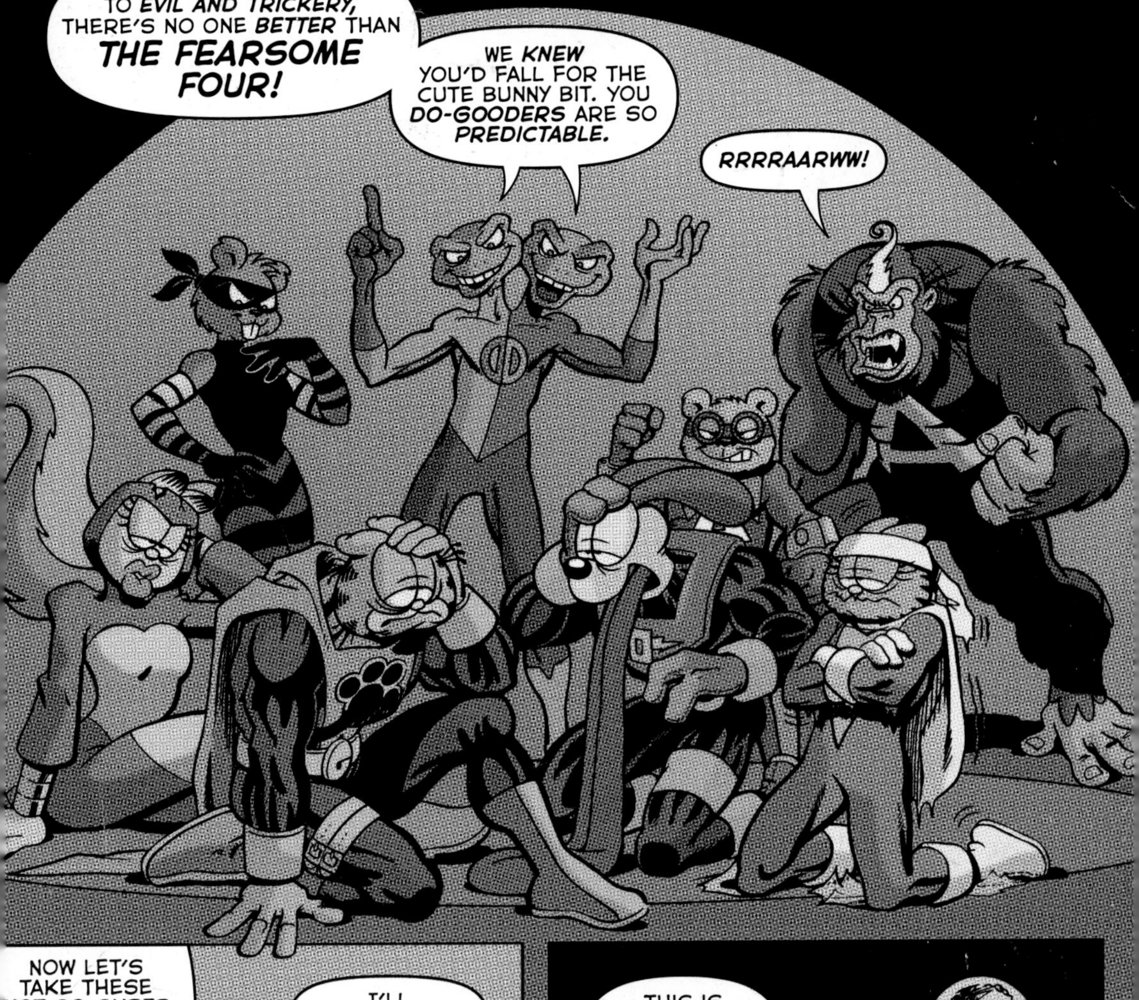
WHEN IT COMES TO EVIL AND TRICKERY, THERE'S NO ONE BETTER THAN THE FEARSOME FOUR!
WE KNEW YOU'D FALL FOR THE CUTE BUNNY BIT. YOU DO-GOODERS ARE SO PREDICTABLE.
RRRRAARWW!

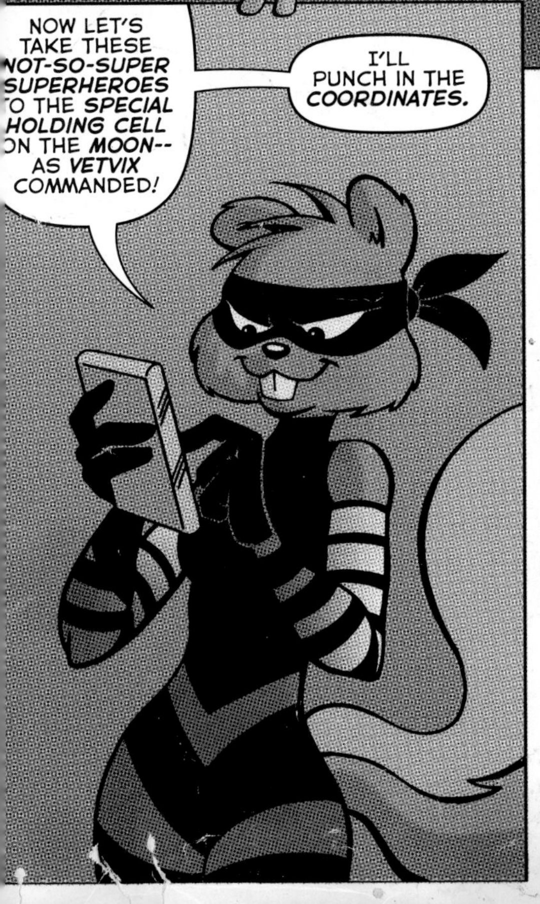
NOW LET'S TAKE THESE NOT-SO-SUPER SUPERHEROES TO THE SPECIAL HOLDING CELL ON THE MOON-- AS VETVIX COMMANDED!
I'LL PUNCH IN THE COORDINATES.

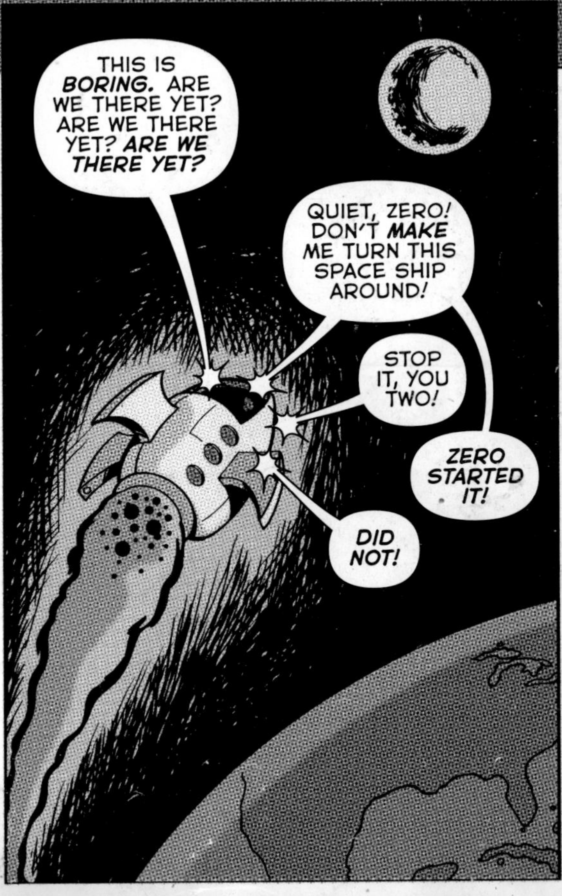
THIS IS BORING. ARE WE THERE YET? ARE WE THERE YET? ARE WE THERE YET?
QUIET, ZERO! DON'T MAKE ME TURN THIS SPACE SHIP AROUND!
STOP IT, YOU TWO!
ZERO STARTED IT!
DID NOT!

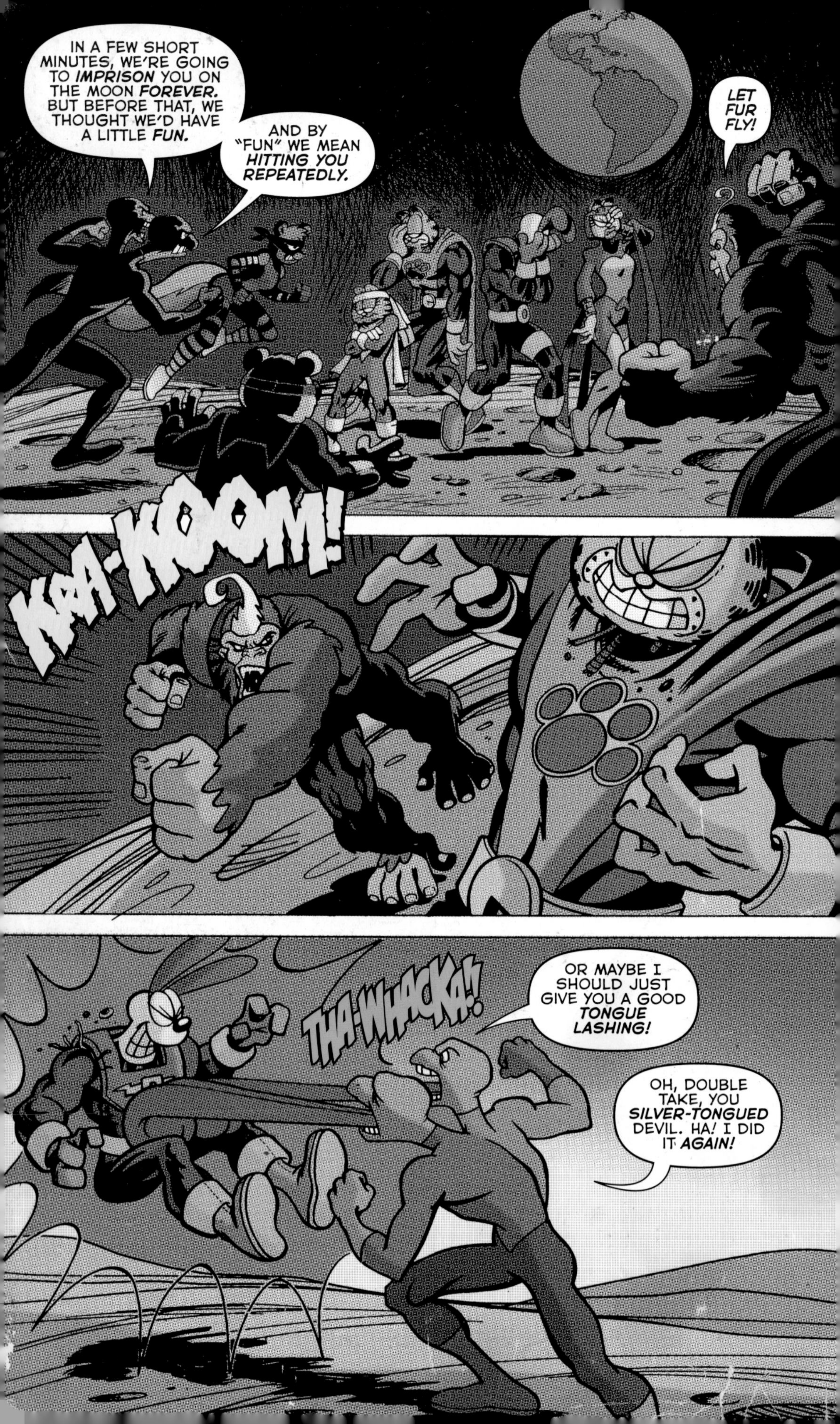
IN A FEW SHORT MINUTES, WE'RE GOING TO *IMPRISON* YOU ON THE MOON *FOREVER.* BUT BEFORE THAT, WE THOUGHT WE'D HAVE A LITTLE *FUN.*
AND BY "FUN" WE MEAN *HITTING YOU REPEATEDLY.*
LET FUR FLY!
KRA-KOOM!
THA-WHACKA!!
OR MAYBE I SHOULD JUST GIVE YOU A GOOD *TONGUE LASHING!*
OH, DOUBLE TAKE, YOU *SILVER-TONGUED* DEVIL. HA! I DID IT *AGAIN!*

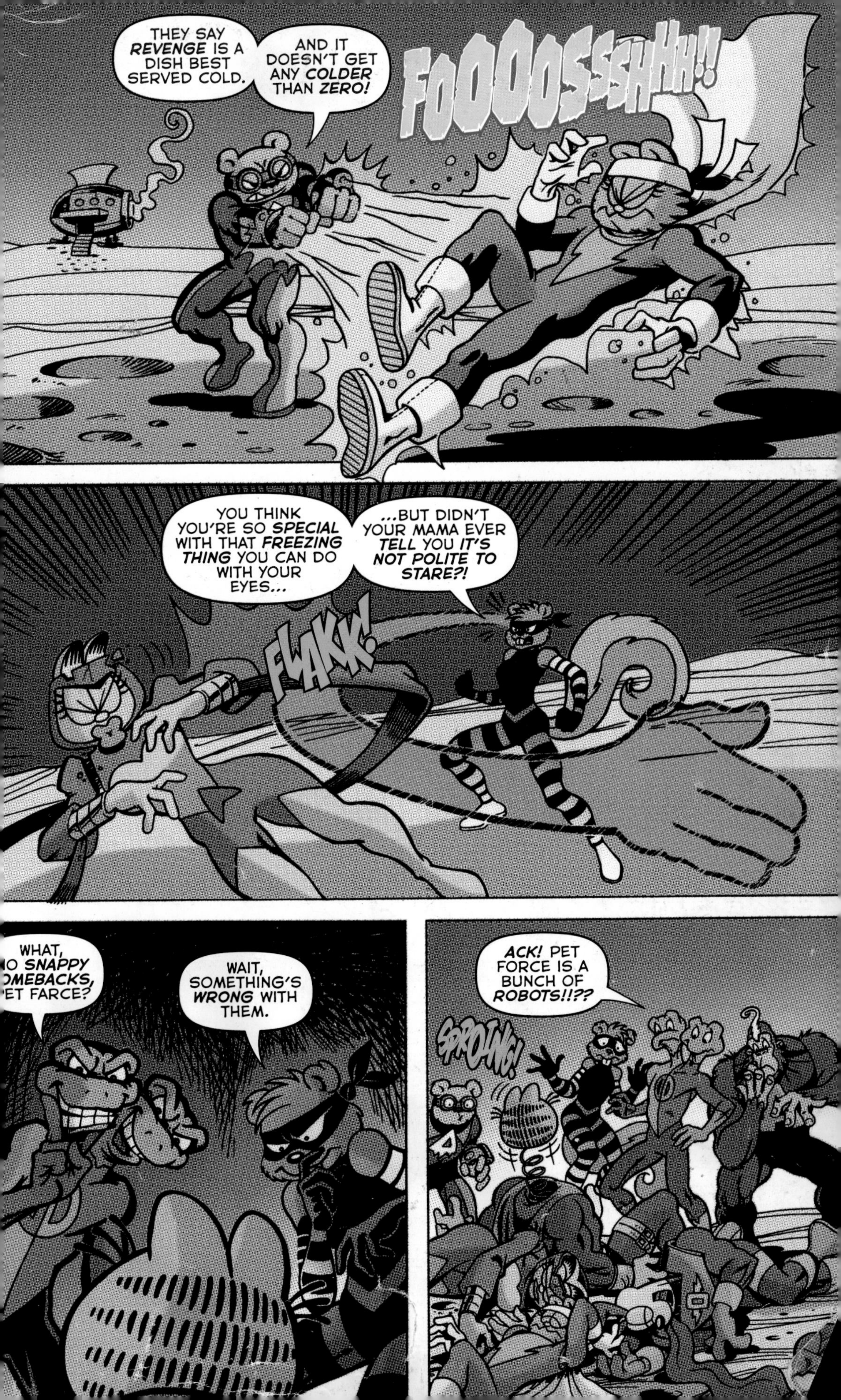
THEY SAY REVENGE IS A DISH BEST SERVED COLD.
AND IT DOESN'T GET ANY COLDER THAN ZERO!
FOOOOOSSSHHH!!
YOU THINK YOU'RE SO SPECIAL WITH THAT FREEZING THING YOU CAN DO WITH YOUR EYES...
...BUT DIDN'T YOUR MAMA EVER TELL YOU IT'S NOT POLITE TO STARE?!
FLAKK!
WHAT, O SNAPPY OMEBACKS, ET FARCE?
WAIT, SOMETHING'S WRONG WITH THEM.
ACK! PET FORCE IS A BUNCH OF ROBOTS!!??
SPROING!

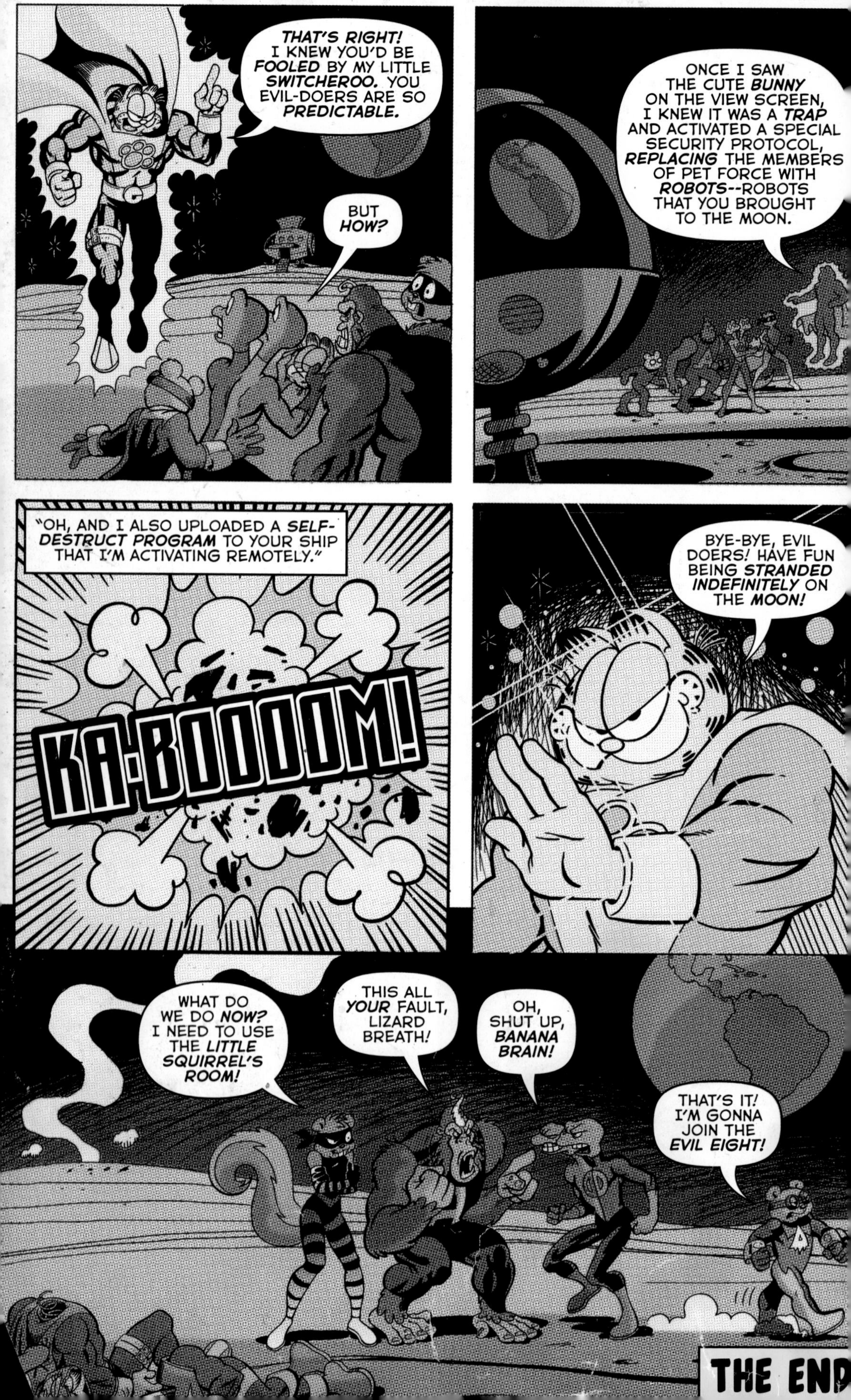
THAT'S RIGHT! I KNEW YOU'D BE FOOLED BY MY LITTLE SWITCHEROO. YOU EVIL-DOERS ARE SO PREDICTABLE.
BUT HOW?
ONCE I SAW THE CUTE BUNNY ON THE VIEW SCREEN, I KNEW IT WAS A TRAP AND ACTIVATED A SPECIAL SECURITY PROTOCOL, REPLACING THE MEMBERS OF PET FORCE WITH ROBOTS--ROBOTS THAT YOU BROUGHT TO THE MOON.
"OH, AND I ALSO UPLOADED A SELF-DESTRUCT PROGRAM TO YOUR SHIP THAT I'M ACTIVATING REMOTELY."
KA-BOOOOM!
BYE-BYE, EVIL DOERS! HAVE FUN BEING STRANDED INDEFINITELY ON THE MOON!
WHAT DO WE DO NOW? I NEED TO USE THE LITTLE SQUIRREL'S ROOM!
THIS ALL YOUR FAULT, LIZARD BREATH!
OH, SHUT UP, BANANA BRAIN!
THAT'S IT! I'M GONNA JOIN THE EVIL EIGHT!
THE END

COVER GALLERY

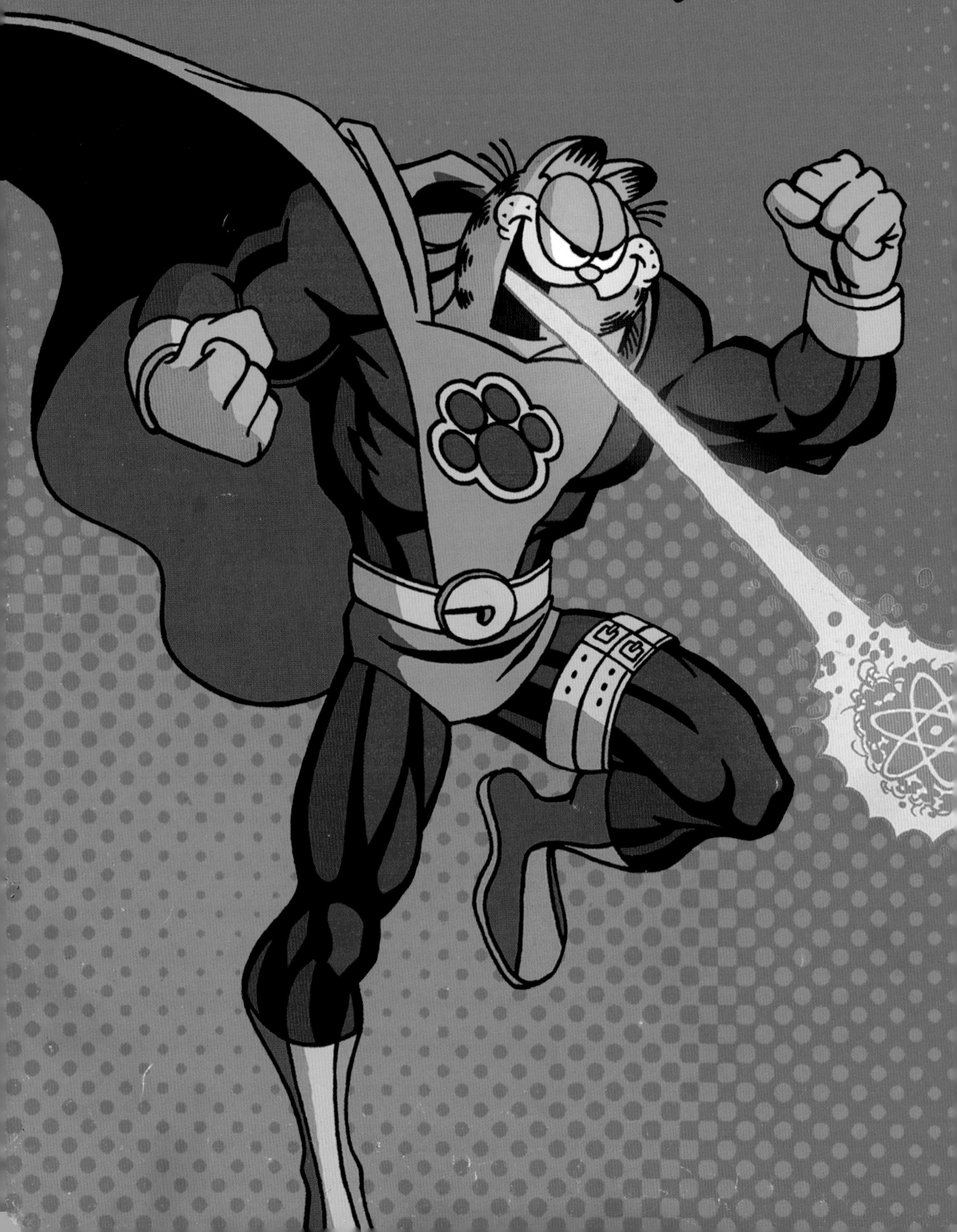

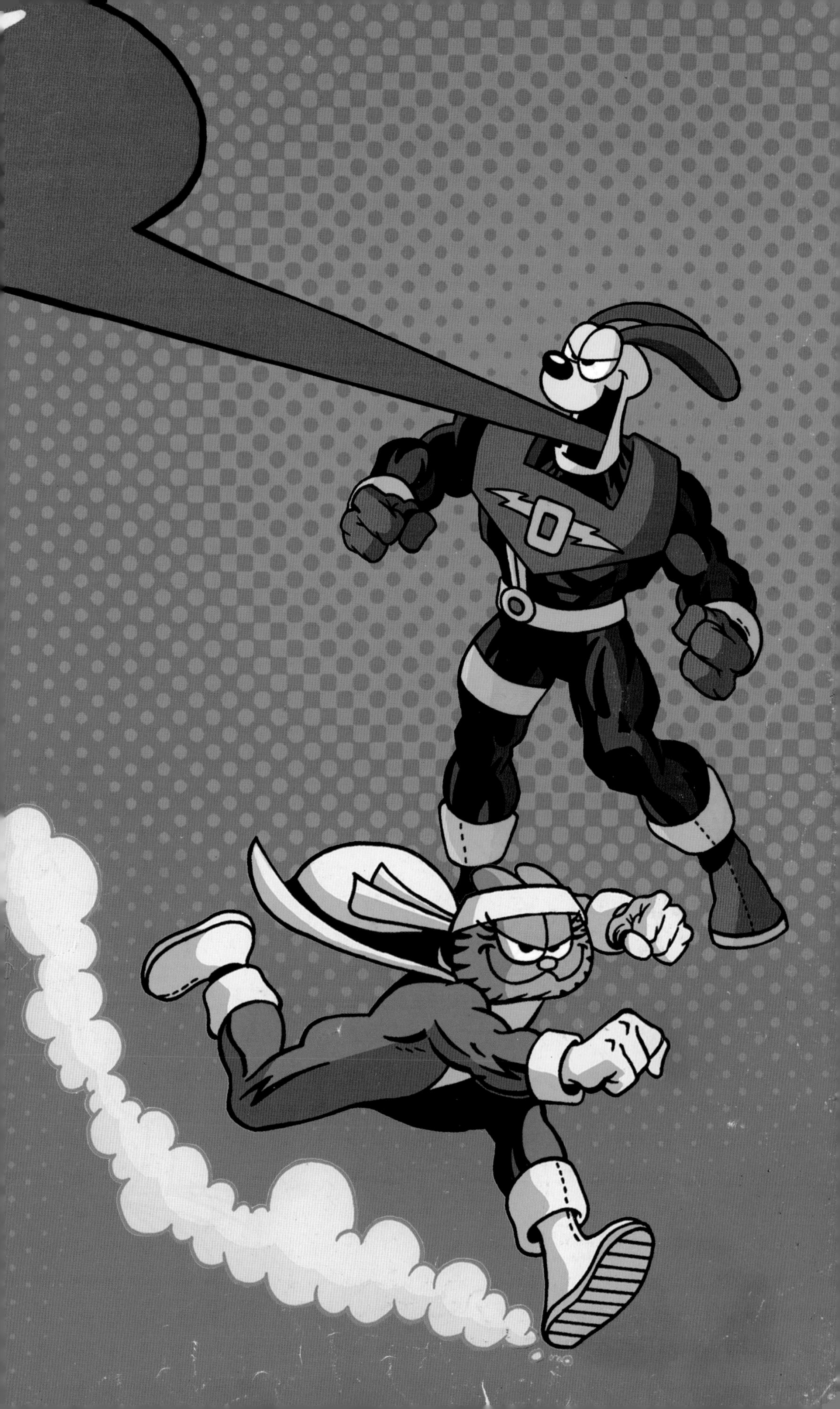

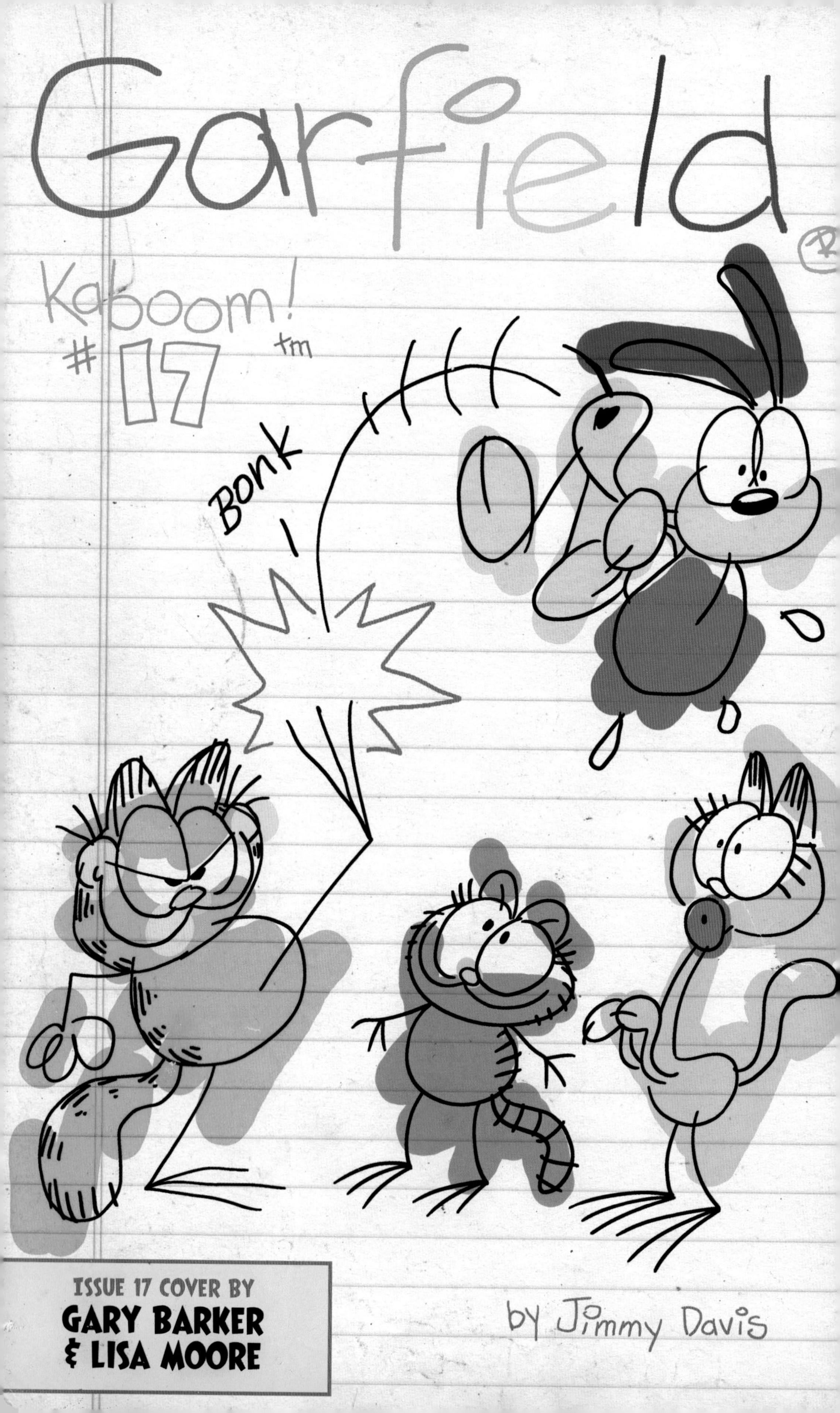
Garfield®
Kaboom!
#17 tm
BONK
by Jimmy Davis

ISSUE 17 COVER BY
GARY BARKER
& LISA MOORE

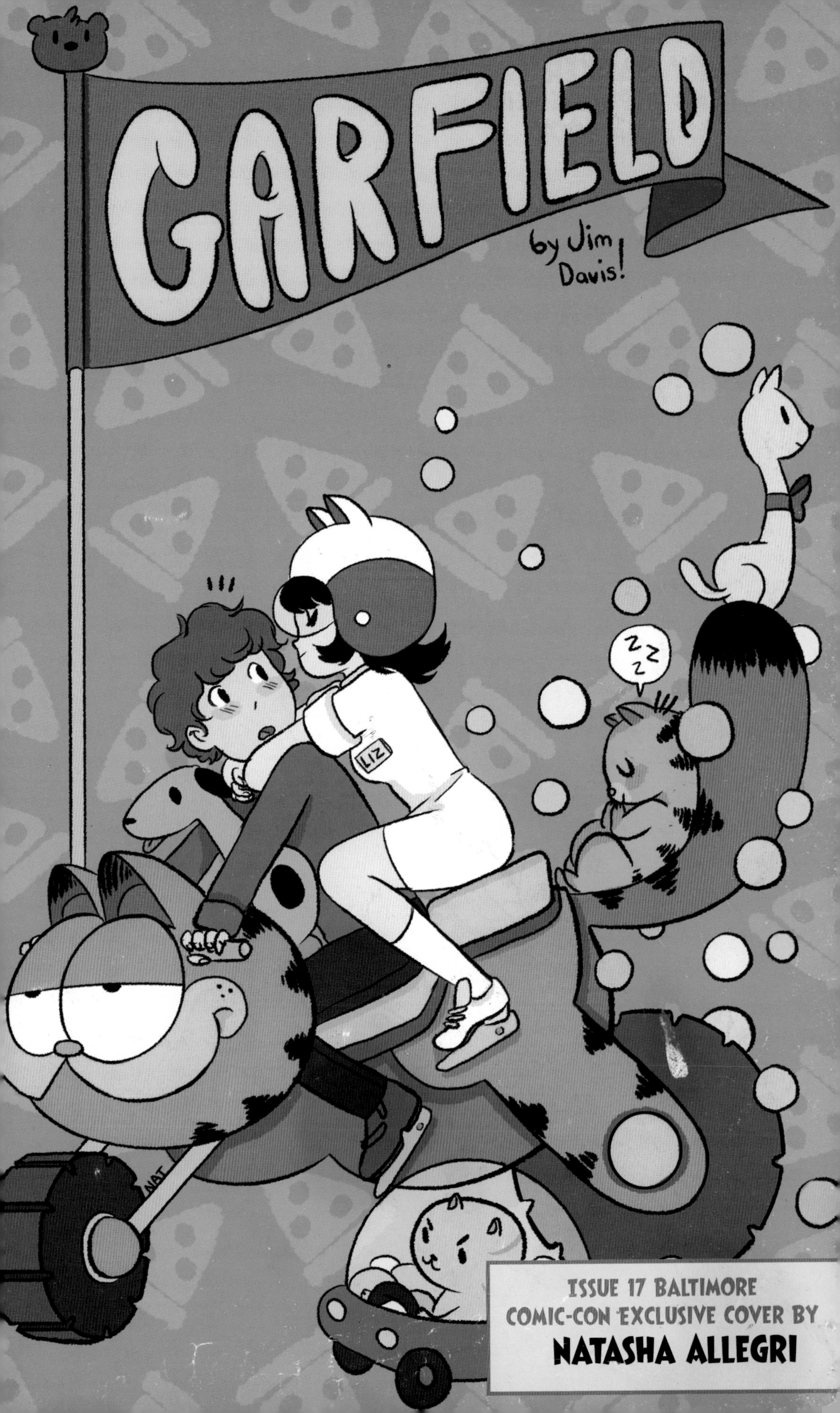
GARFIELD
by Jim Davis!
LIZ
Z Z Z
NAT
ISSUE 17 BALTIMORE
COMIC-CON EXCLUSIVE COVER BY
NATASHA ALLEGRI

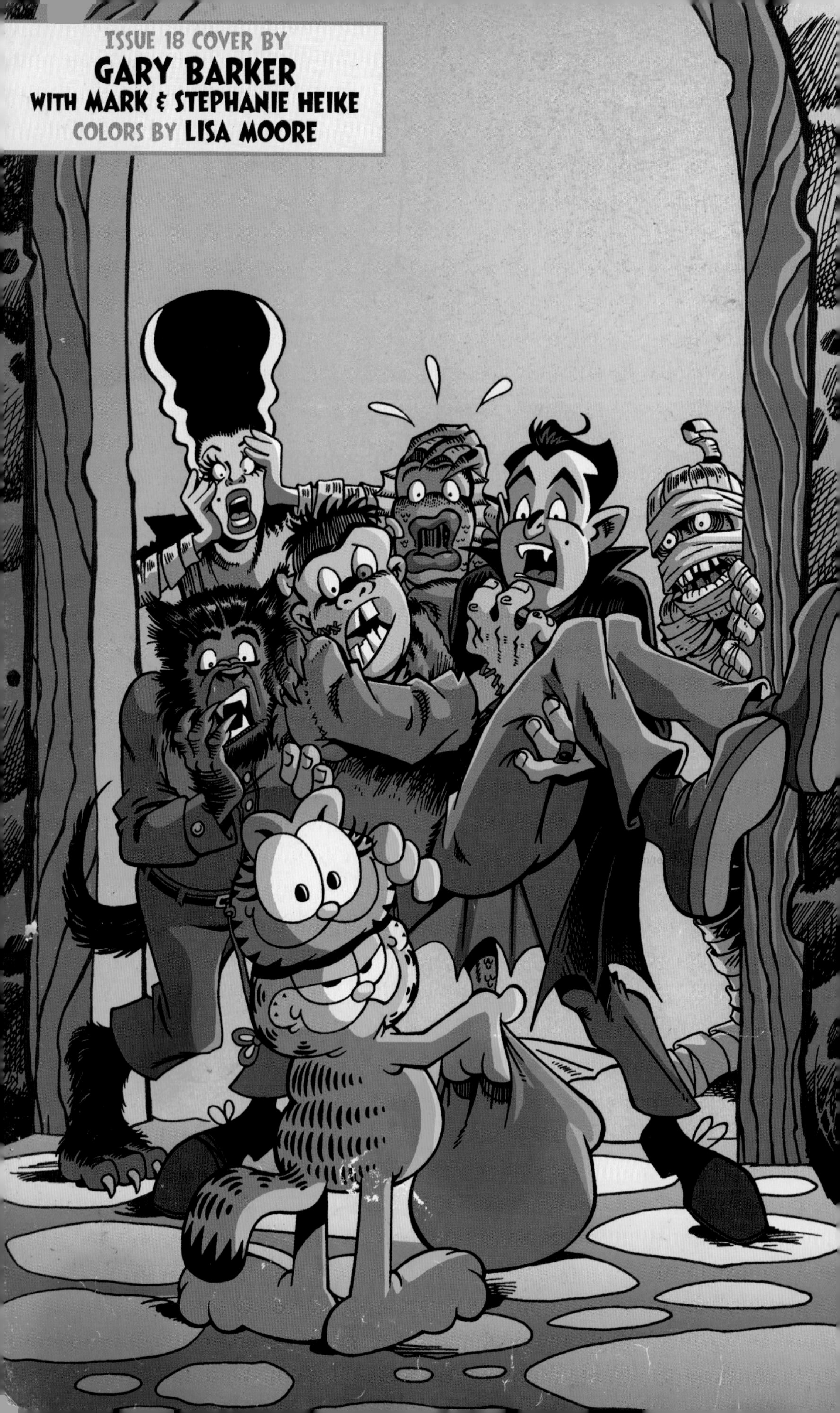

ISSUE 18 COVER BY
GARY BARKER
WITH MARK & STEPHANIE HEIKE
COLORS BY LISA MOORE

ISSUE 19 COVER BY
GARY BARKER
WITH MARK & STEPHANIE HEIKE
COLORS BY **LISA MOORE**

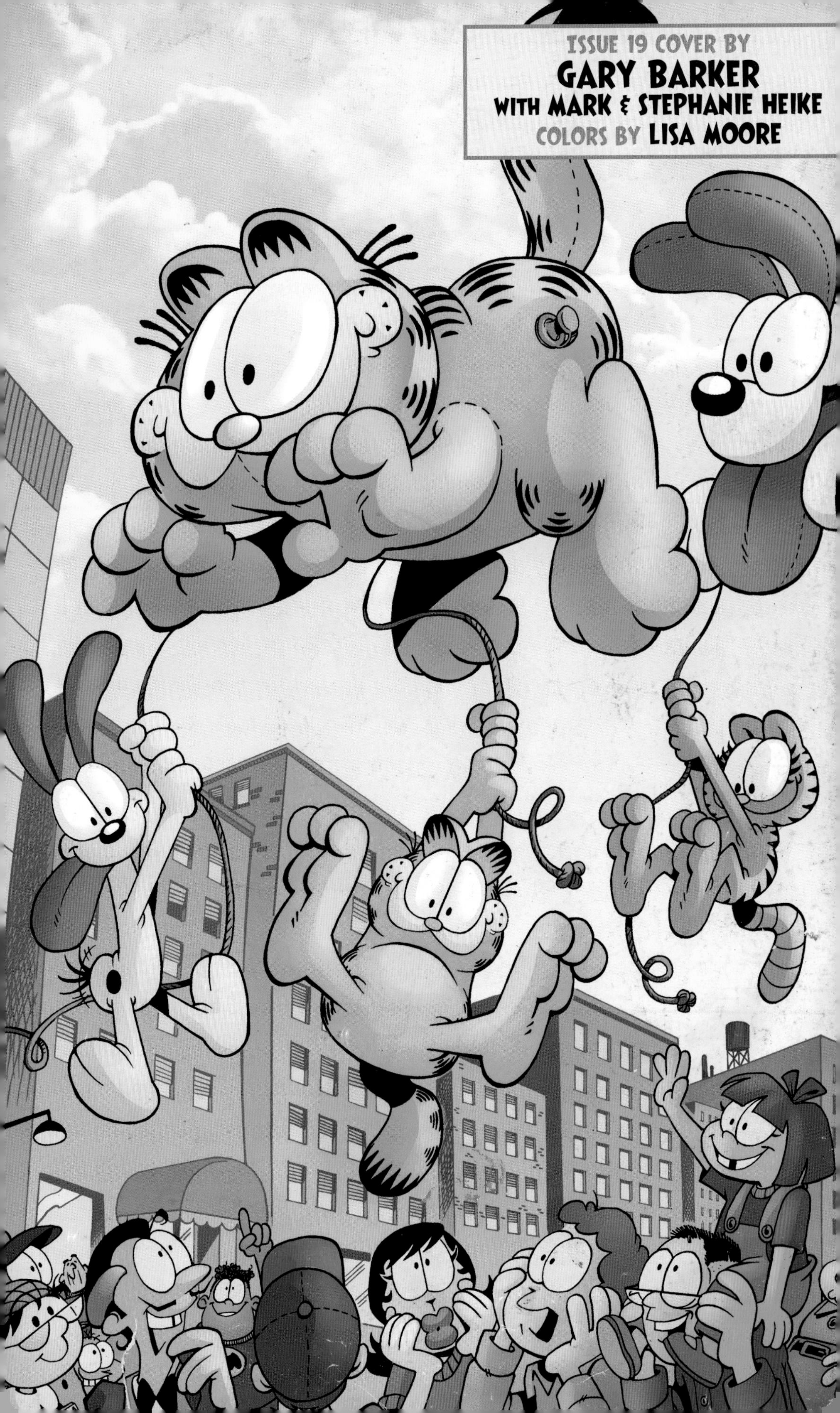

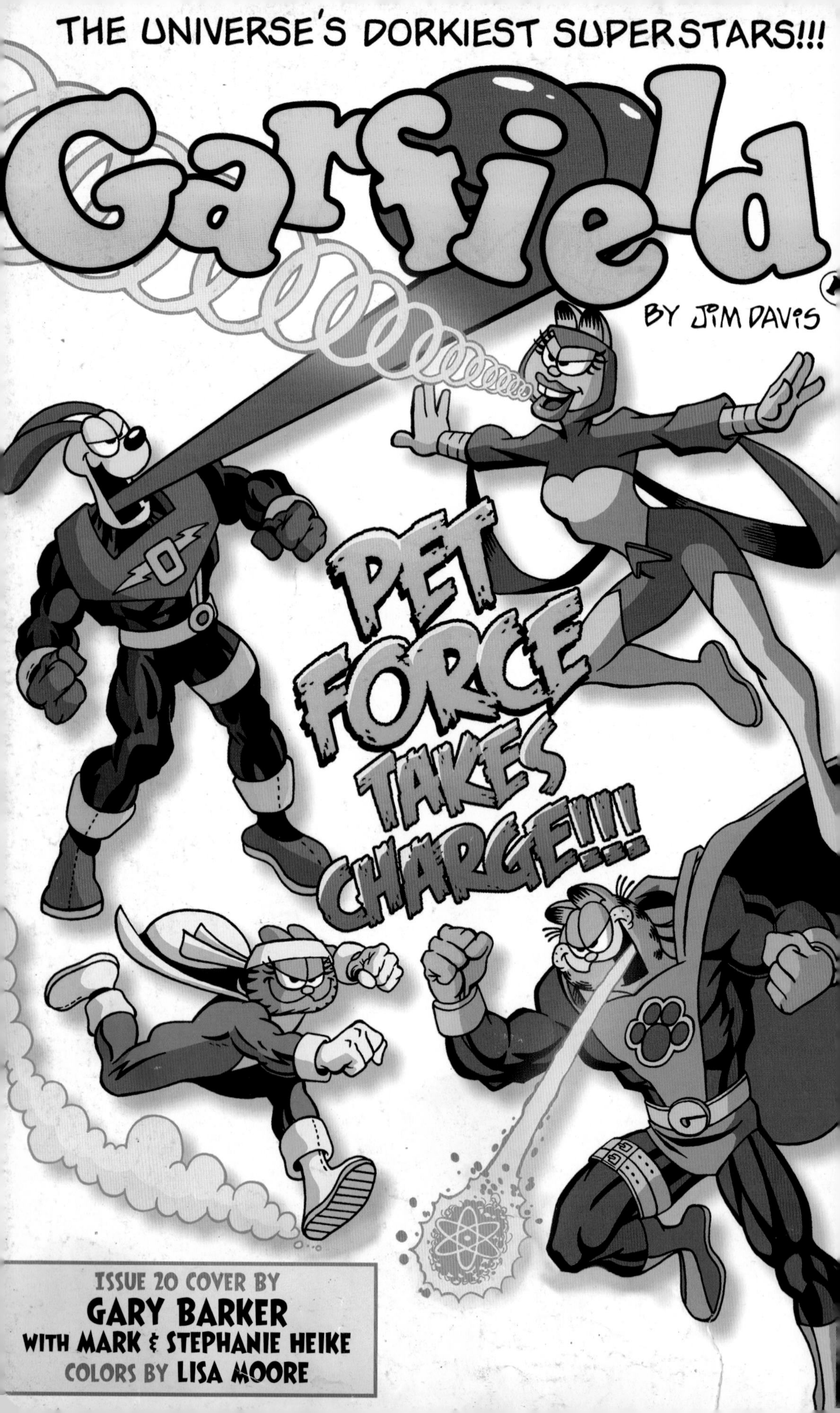
THE UNIVERSE'S DORKIEST SUPERSTARS!!!
Garfield
BY JIM DAVIS
PET FORCE TAKES CHARGE!!!!
ISSUE 20 COVER BY
GARY BARKER
WITH MARK & STEPHANIE HEIKE
COLORS BY LISA MOORE

Garfield Sunday Classics

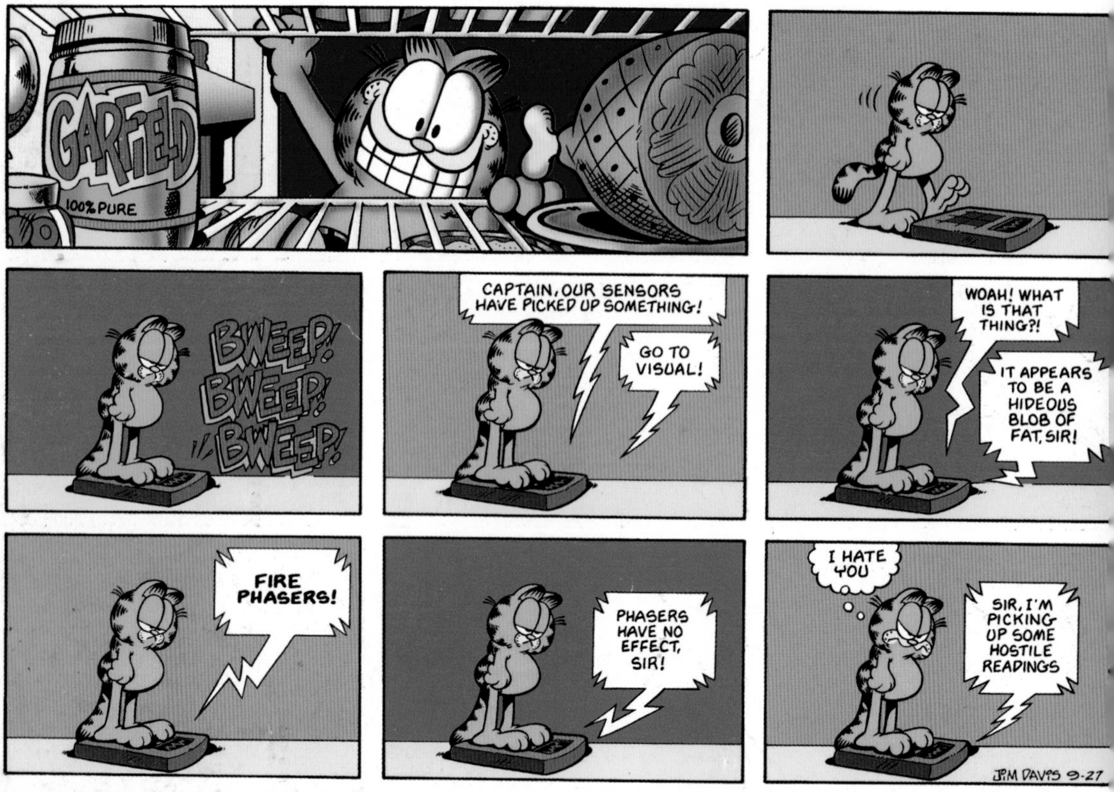
GARFIELD
100% PURE
BWEEP! BWEEP! BWEEP!
CAPTAIN, OUR SENSORS HAVE PICKED UP SOMETHING!
GO TO VISUAL!
WOAH! WHAT IS THAT THING?!
IT APPEARS TO BE A HIDEOUS BLOB OF FAT, SIR!
FIRE PHASERS!
PHASERS HAVE NO EFFECT, SIR!
I HATE YOU
SIR, I'M PICKING UP SOME HOSTILE READINGS
JIM DAVIS 9-27

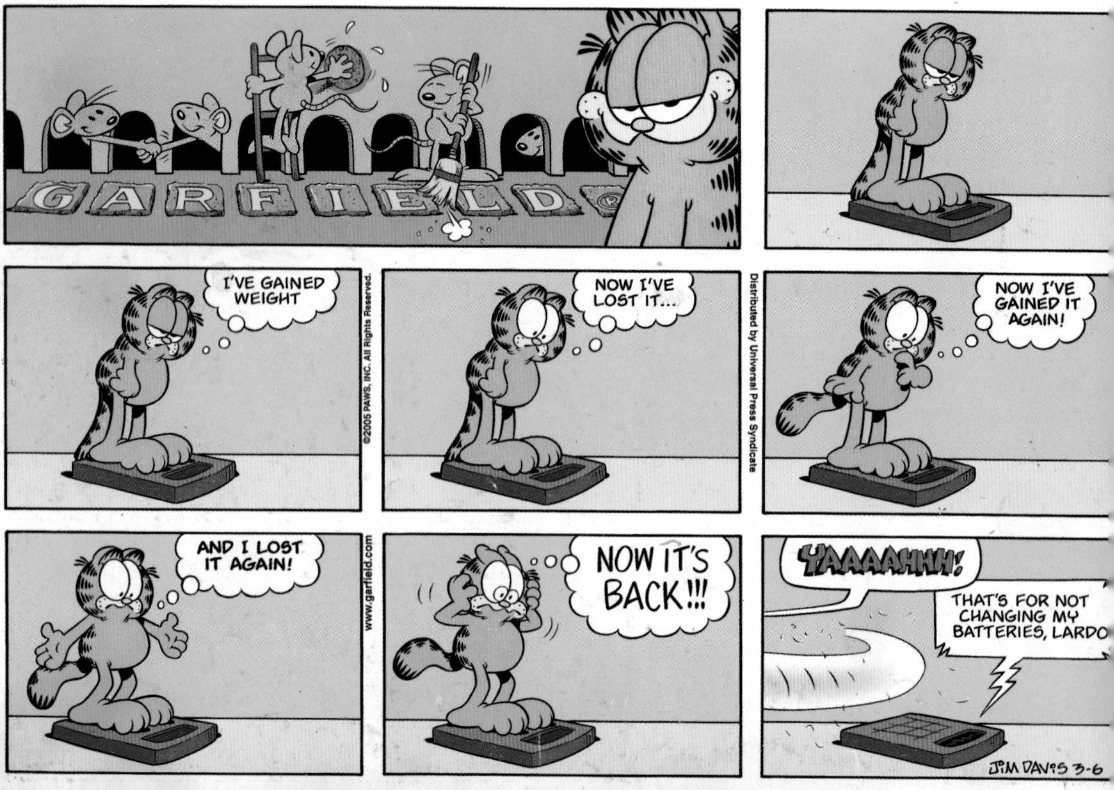
GARFIELD®
I'VE GAINED WEIGHT
©2005 PAWS, INC. All Rights Reserved.
NOW I'VE LOST IT...
Distributed by Universal Press Syndicate
NOW I'VE GAINED IT AGAIN!
AND I LOST IT AGAIN!
www.garfield.com
NOW IT'S BACK!!!
YAAAAHHH!
THAT'S FOR NOT CHANGING MY BATTERIES, LARDO
JIM DAVIS 3-6

Garfield Sunday Classics

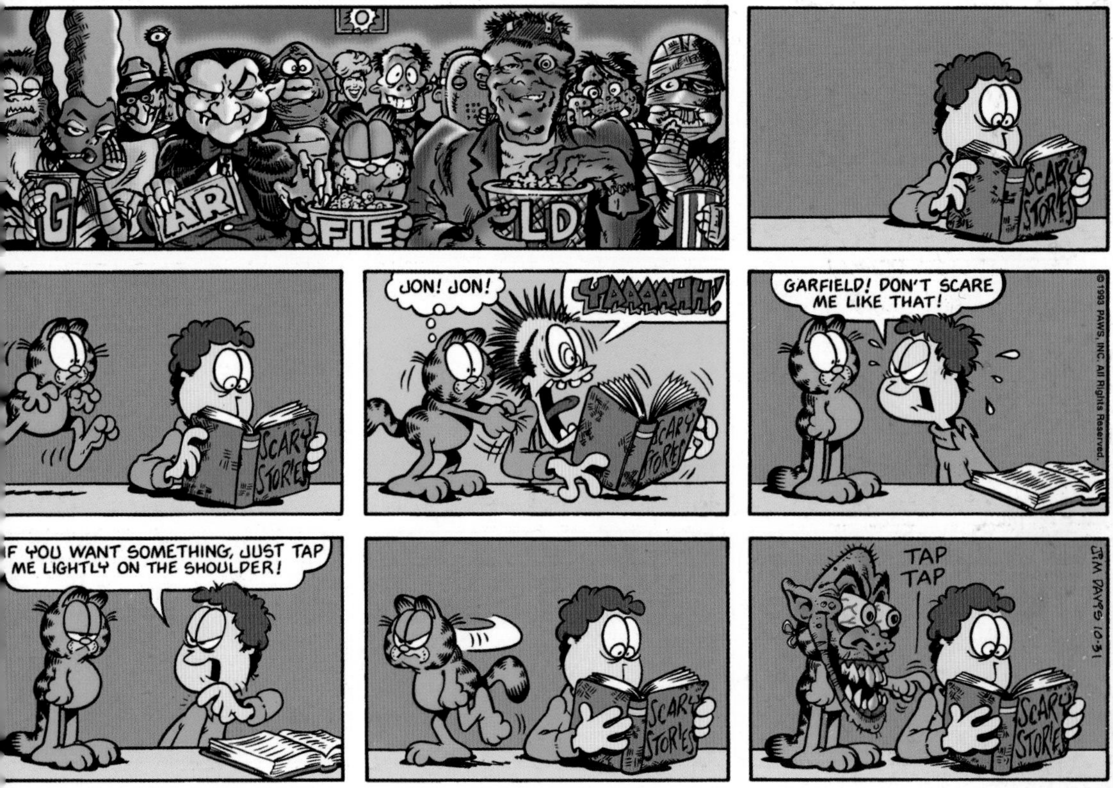

GAR
FIE
LD
SCARY STORIES
JON! JON!
YAAAAHH!
GARFIELD! DON'T SCARE ME LIKE THAT!
© 1993 PAWS, INC. All Rights Reserved.
IF YOU WANT SOMETHING, JUST TAP ME LIGHTLY ON THE SHOULDER!
TAP TAP
JIM DAVIS 10-31

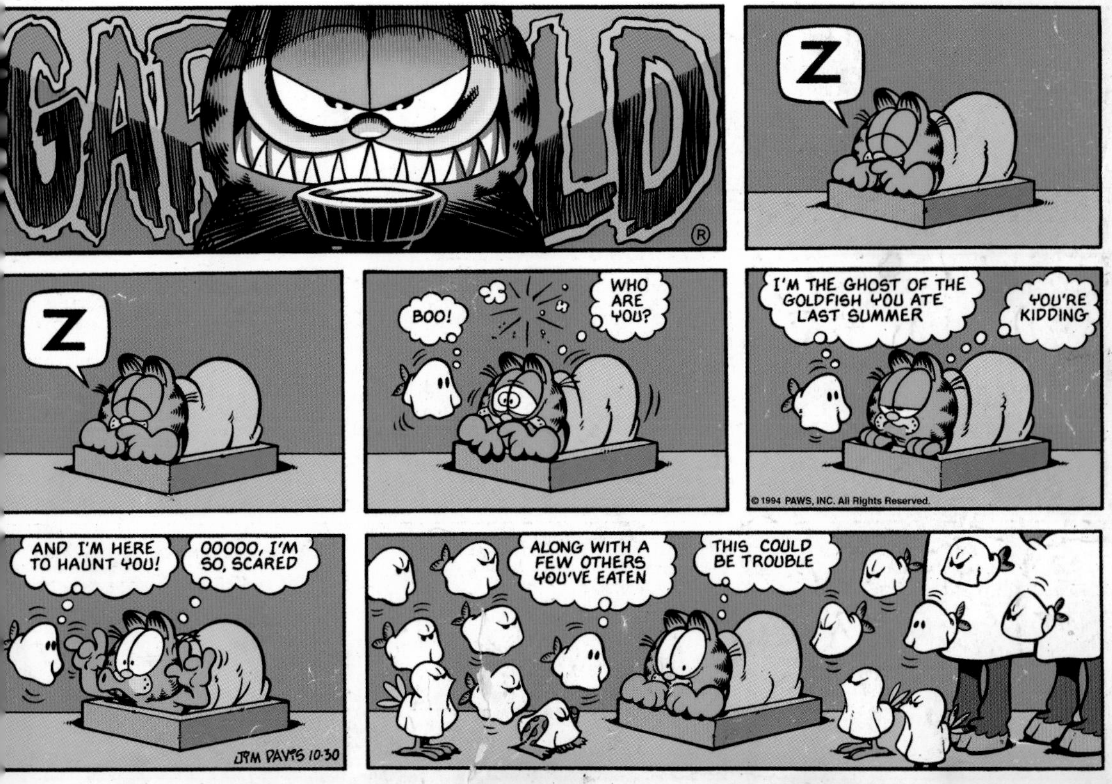

GARFIELD
Z
Z
BOO!
WHO ARE YOU?
I'M THE GHOST OF THE GOLDFISH YOU ATE LAST SUMMER
YOU'RE KIDDING
© 1994 PAWS, INC. All Rights Reserved.
AND I'M HERE TO HAUNT YOU!
OOOOO, I'M SO, SCARED
ALONG WITH A FEW OTHERS YOU'VE EATEN
THIS COULD BE TROUBLE
JIM DAVIS 10-30

Garfield Sunday Classics

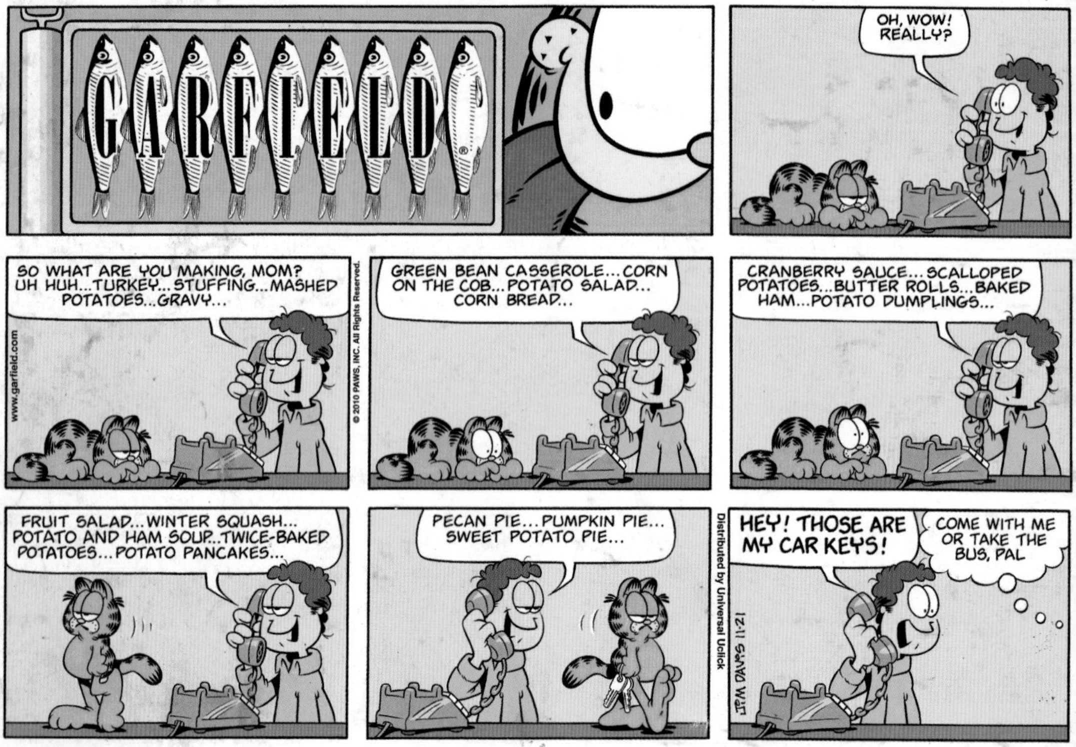
GARFIELD®
OH, WOW! REALLY?
SO WHAT ARE YOU MAKING, MOM? UH HUH...TURKEY...STUFFING...MASHED POTATOES...GRAVY...
www.garfield.com
© 2010 PAWS, INC. All Rights Reserved.
GREEN BEAN CASSEROLE...CORN ON THE COB...POTATO SALAD... CORN BREAD...
CRANBERRY SAUCE...SCALLOPED POTATOES...BUTTER ROLLS...BAKED HAM...POTATO DUMPLINGS...
FRUIT SALAD...WINTER SQUASH... POTATO AND HAM SOUP...TWICE-BAKED POTATOES...POTATO PANCAKES...
PECAN PIE...PUMPKIN PIE... SWEET POTATO PIE...
Distributed by Universal Uclick
JIM DAVIS 11-21
HEY! THOSE ARE MY CAR KEYS!
COME WITH ME OR TAKE THE BUS, PAL

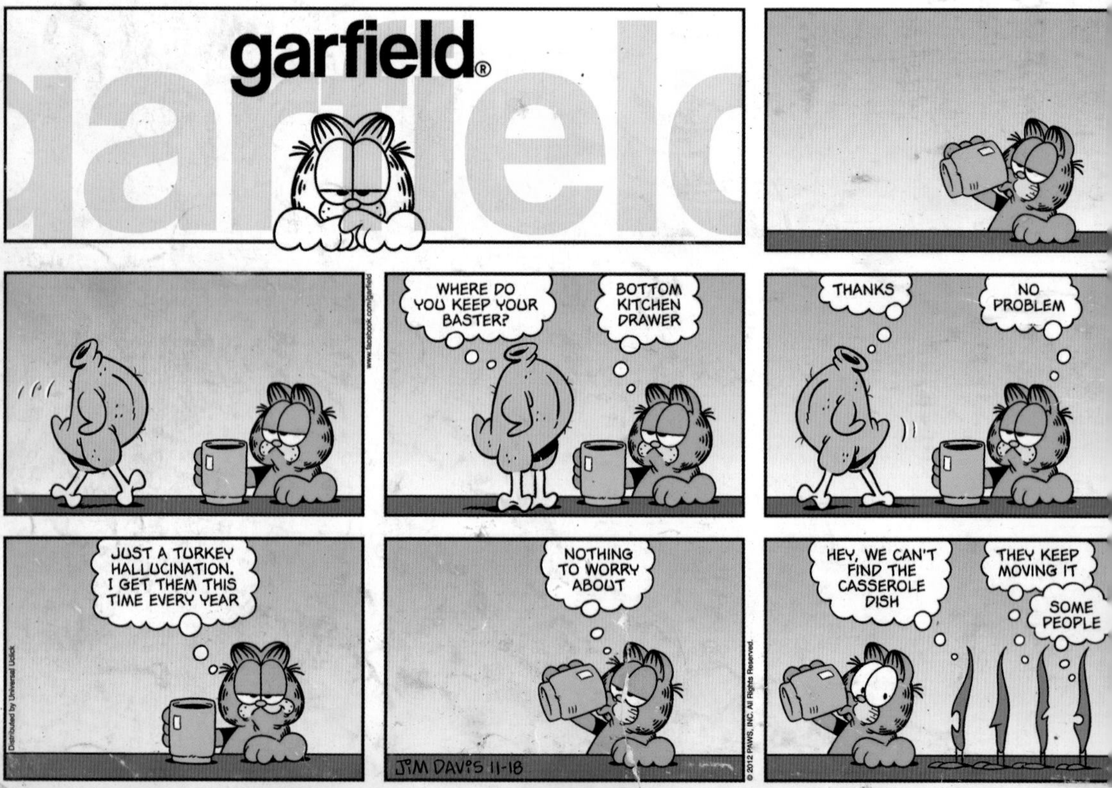
garfield®
www.facebook.com/garfield
WHERE DO YOU KEEP YOUR BASTER?
BOTTOM KITCHEN DRAWER
THANKS
NO PROBLEM
Distributed by Universal Uclick
JUST A TURKEY HALLUCINATION. I GET THEM THIS TIME EVERY YEAR
NOTHING TO WORRY ABOUT
JIM DAVIS 11-18
© 2012 PAWS, INC. All Rights Reserved.
HEY, WE CAN'T FIND THE CASSEROLE DISH
THEY KEEP MOVING IT
SOME PEOPLE

Garfield Sunday Classics

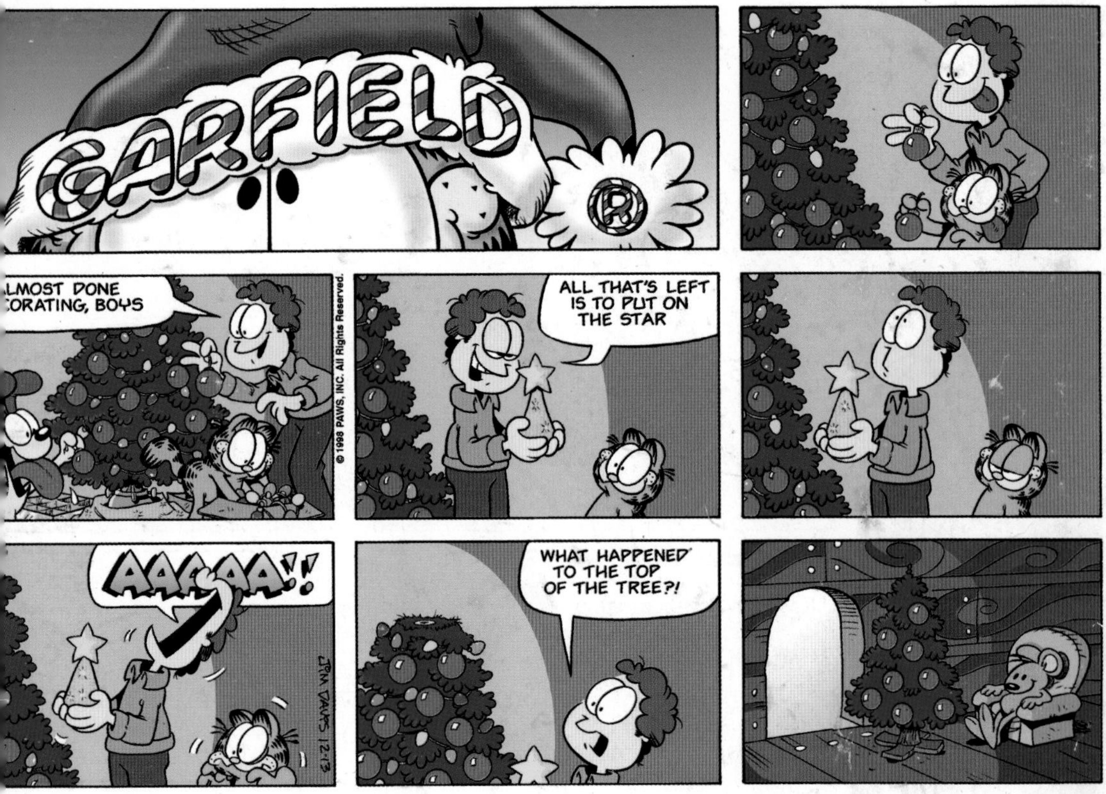
GARFIELD
LMOST DONE
ORATING, BOYS
ALL THAT'S LEFT IS TO PUT ON THE STAR
AAAAA!!
WHAT HAPPENED TO THE TOP OF THE TREE?!
© 1998 PAWS, INC. All Rights Reserved.
JIM DAVIS 12-13

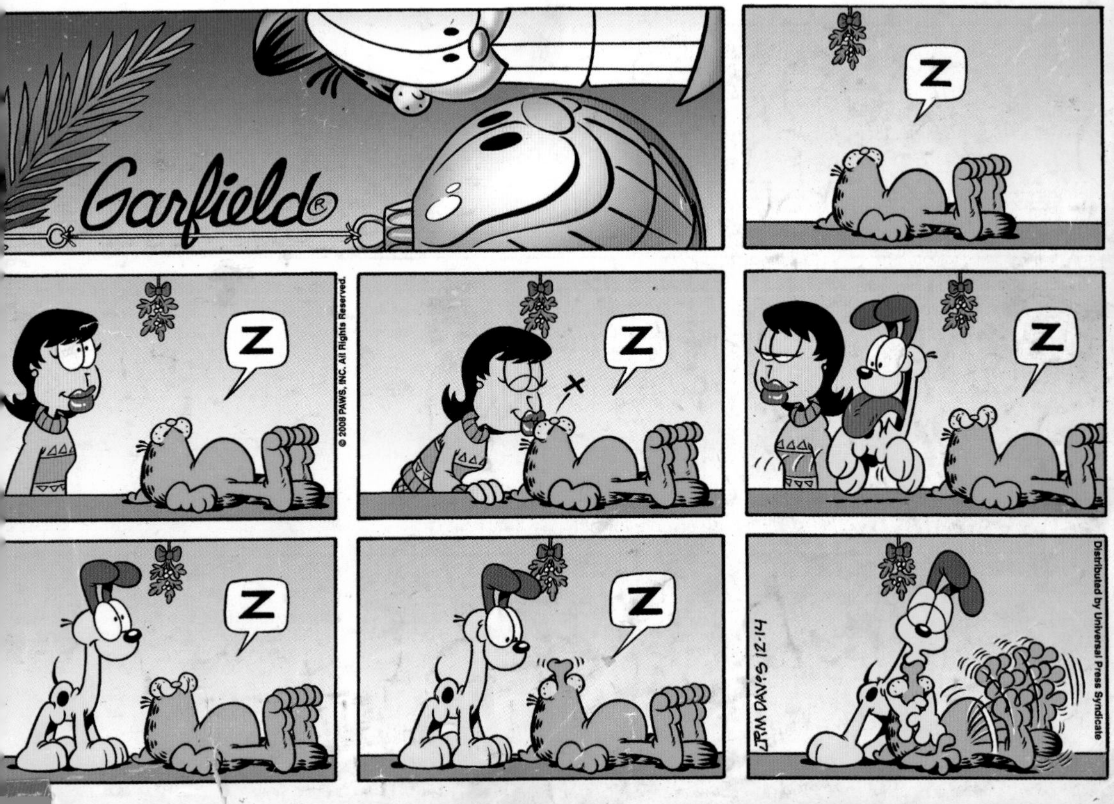
Garfield
Z
Z
Z
Z
Z
Z
© 2008 PAWS, INC. All Rights Reserved.
JIM DAVIS 12-14
Distributed by Universal Press Syndicate